GAME OF ROYALS

A skillful blend of medieval fantasy-type setting, court intrigue, and science fiction elements. As always, Taylor's gift for small human details makes her imaginary world real. —Eric Heideman, editor, *Tales of the Unanticipated*

L.A. Taylor has published a series of mysteries, a science fiction novel, and a charming fantasy, *Cat's Paw*. Now, in [this novel], she gives us a quirky, complex, interesting tale that combines court intrigue with mysteries both scientific and criminal, and a thoroughly satisfying story of an orphan rising from obscurity and oppression. While definitely science fiction, it offers the pleasures of several other kinds of fiction–historical romance, fantasy, and mystery–as well as the greater pleasure of watching an intelligent, sensible author play with, undercut, and reverse genre cliches. A neat book, fun to read. I recommend it. –Eleanor Arnason, author of *Ring of Swords, A Woman of the Iron People* (winner of the James Tiptree, Jr., and Mythopoeic Fantasy Awards), *Daughter of the Bear King, To the Resurrection Station*, and *The Sword Smith*

Once again, L. A. Taylor has put a strong woman in a dangerous situation that requires all her wits. I love the subtly-revealed details of everyday life—and the way the author deals with things the characters don't fully understand without leaving the reader behind. Taylor gives us well-realized individuals; for example, Fenne, who is part villain, part impetuous girl, part vamp. Both the men and the women in this story defy stereotyping. —Laurel Winter, Rhysling and Asimov's Readers' Poll Awards for best poem, author of the novel *Growing Wings,* World Fantasy Award winner for best novella, "Sky Eyes."

Also by L. A. Taylor

Cat's Paw
Footnote to Murder
Blossom of Erda
A Murder Waiting to Happen

GAME OF ROYALS

L. A. TAYLOR

FTL PUBLICATIONS
MINNEAPOLIS, MINNESOTA

Copyright © 1999 by Allau Press

FTL Publications
P O Box 22693
Minneapolis, MN 55422
www.ftlpublications.com
mail@ftlpublications.com

Paperback version issued by FTL Publications
in association with Allau Press

Previously published as The Fathergod Experiment

Printed in the United States of America

ISBN 978-1-936881-38-3

Edited by Lyda Morehouse

Memorial Edition
L. A. Taylor 1939-1996

Always someone who knew what she wanted, L. A. Taylor had already chosen a writing career by the time she was in first grade. "Staring at the usual exhortation to Spot ('Run! Run! Run! Run, Spot, run!'), I was vouchsafed a blinding insight: people make this stuff up! I can do that!" At the age of 11, she sent her first story to *Analog*, and got back the first of many rejection letters. She wasn't exactly discouraged, but real life got in the way for a while, and it was almost thirty years before she went back to writing science fiction.

In the meantime, she went to college and majored in math, then worked at a variety of jobs, each having as little to do with her degree as possible. For a while, she was a medical research technician. Then she worked for the Pittsburgh School Board keeping track of the kids in federal programs and tried being a potter and then a jeweler in the late '60s and early '70s. Along the way, she married an engineer, Allen, and had two children, Eleanor and Catherine. Since it was hard to take care of a baby with her hands covered with clay or solder flux, she went back to writing, which she did from the basement of her home in Minneapolis, Minnesota, with her cat Smitty for company.

Although science fiction was her first love, she began writing mainstream poetry and won the Minnesota Voices Award in 1981. She published several mystery novels, too, before returning to science fiction and fantasy. Since then, she has published the science fiction novel *Blossom of Erda*, the fantasy *Cat's Paw*, and a number of short stories. *Game of Royals/The Fathergod Experiment*, written in 1993-1994, was not yet published at the time of her death from cancer, but she considered it one of her best. It is published in her memory.

Partial Cast of Characters

The Hasten Family

Nevan Hasten, Dych of Summerlea — Head of the Hasten family, one of the most powerful in Kinland

Olen Hasten, Iarl of Meadowlands — Nevan Hasten's son, Fenne's father — later Dych of Summerlea

Fenne Hasten — Daughter of Olen Hasten and granddaughter of Nevan Hasten — As the story begins, she is married to Rovvo Standfast, but later she is married to Kav Treadwell

Ruppet Hasten — Oldest son of Olen Hasten

Delle Makeright — Wife of Olen Hasten and Fenne's mother

Cals Hasten — Younger son of Olen Hasten

Säen Hasten — Fenne's cousin

Other Nobility

Edwe Speaksoft, Iarl of Oakforest — Nobleman allied to the Hastens

Merrow Strengthen, Dych of Lealands — Friend of Greencrags

Tessen Strengthen — Merrow Strengthen's son

Tern Gudgeon — Lord Chief Justice of Kinland

Rovvo Standfast, Iarl of Greencrags — A young nobleman

Kav Treadwell, Iarl of Northlands — Nobleman and favorite of King Guyr

Jen Makeready — Nobleman and advisor to King Guyr

Some Others

Evin Clock — A pharmacist

Onma Stump — Dressmaker who resides in Miense

Senvar Elm — Warden of the royal prison

Chapter One

Lilz brought her horse to a stop just below the crest of the hill to get her bearings. Below her, the faint broad line of the limestone-graveled trail she had followed for the past two hours seemed to glow in the starlight, descending gently for another hundred sashlengths before it disappeared into thick shadow. A glance at the sky told her: the trail had turned southwest. In the distance a single yellow light twinkled. She sat watching it for a moment or two. The motion was only a trick of her eyes, she was sure.

"That must be House-Among-Oaks, Matanda."

The horse took a step or two in place at the sound of Lilz's voice.

"At last, yes," she sighed.

Between Lilz and the light lay a rustling valley dark with trees, a dark relieved only by an occasional dull glint where a leaf caught the starlight as it moved in the breeze. An hour ride, at least. She'd need her lantern in the forest. Lilz glanced again at the stars.

This time she was certain that one moved slowly, brightening and dimming, among its brothers. A galloping star! Had it seen her? Lip caught under her teeth, she watched the star disappear over the horizon. No help for that now.

She twitched the reins and the bay gelding moved down the trail. Despite the anxiety that dried her mouth, Lilz let him choose his own speed; here, the gravel had sunk into the earth. As they neared the wood she dismounted and reached for a bull's-eye lantern hooked to her saddlepack. Lucifers dipped in wax were in an outer pocket. She got one out and struck it, talking to steady the horse as the match flared over the lantern's fat candle.

I've been on the road too long, she thought, aiming the half-focused yellow beam at the packed dirt. Waiting this long to use the lantern was idiocy. As if the king's spies weren't everywhere, even whirling across the sky above her head—if rumor could be trusted, already chittering to the palace about this horse and rider on the track to House-Among-Oaks. What would King Guyr make of that? Would he know who the rider was, that she was on her way to see her mistress, Fenne Hasten?

Lilz walked along the forest path holding reins and lantern until she spotted a thick log close beside the trail. She used the log to remount, talking softly to remind Matanda that lunging shadows bore no threat. As she rode on she listened for the telltale hum of a whizzer, speeding back to the New Palace with pictures and sound recorded for the king to view at his leisure, or arriving to investigate whatever the galloping star might have reported. All she heard was ordinary insects, whispering leaves, the creak of her saddle and the jingle of the bridle, the clop of hooves, Matanda's occasional soft snort, a calling owl. She cursed each sound as it filled her ears.

A large toad, red-eyed in the lamplight, jumped onto the trail. Matanda's even stride wavered. "Steady, steady," Lilz soothed. The toad hopped toward the stream Lilz could hear off to her right. Matanda did a little side-step as he passed the spot, catching her nervousness.

But not yet her weariness, thank heaven! Her eyes burned. She closed them and let the horse pick his way along the dank path. If toads were the boldest game the Iarl of Oakforest stocked in his wood she was in scant danger. What if someone should come from the other direction? She was tall and thin. Straight in the saddle, she might pass for a man in her heavy cloak, a cloak far too warm for this late summer night. Only her long hair, pulled into a braid, would give her away, and that was hidden under the cloak. Even her face was too angular to betray her sex.

Lilz squinted to inspect the trail. Other hoofprints, yes, but blurred by rain, old. She let her eyes close again.

Lord Jen Makeready is dead. What's the hurry, Lilz? Just to tell Fenne, waiting for news at House-Among-Oaks? Because he took so long to die? Because you're late to attend?

"Who'd have thought it, Matanda?" she murmured. With a sniff of surprise, She caught herself before she said more. Confiding in horses was a bad, bad habit. No sense in giving the king any more entrance to her thoughts than he otherwise had.

The stars had wheeled past the peak of the night when House-Among-Oaks loomed over her. Only one window in its whole bulk was lit, high above her head. Lilz crossed a short wooden bridge over the stream and came into the cobbled courtyard. Here, not a single light showed. She made for the stable, to the left as she'd been told. Stopping beside the keeper's door, she knocked without dismounting.

The courtyard was still as she waited. Not so much as the cluck of a chicken. You'd think Fenne could notice I've arrived.

Lilz frowned. Not fair. Fenne would have gone to bed long ago. Lilz had forgotten for the moment how late the hour was. Still no sound from the stable keeper's room. Lilz tapped again.

"Coming, I'm coming." The woman's voice was clogged with sleep; Lilz examined the starlit courtyard, prepared to wait several minutes.

The keeper's door swung inward. "Yes, sir, what is it, sir?" A pale oval tilted toward her, on which Lilz could detect none of the apprehension she heard in the question.

"Ho, keeper. I've a horse needs bedding."

"Yes, miss," with relief. "Right away."

Lilz slid to the ground on the near side of the horse and flipped open the clasp of her saddlepack. "Sorry to call you out of your bed to so much work, mistress," she said.

"Can't be helped, milady."

The pack slipped into Lilz's hands as the keeper led Matanda away, talking to him soothingly although the gelding was scarcely so spirited a mount as to need soothing for anything short of a fire.

What about that toad?

A spy? Some said horses were more sensitive to spies than were people. Fear trickled down her back.

Don't think about it. Lilz slung the pack from one shoulder and strode across the courtyard to knock on the residence door. Instantly, the door opened, spilling light across the gray cobbles. Fenne grabbed her wrist and pulled her in. "Lilz, thank heaven! I thought you'd forgotten to come! Is he—?"

"Shh!" Lilz leaned the door shut and glanced up the dim stairs and along the dark hall. "My mistress, please! You must be more circumspect. Another room?"

"Oh. Oh, of course." Fenne turned to go up the steps, looking over her shoulder for Lilz to follow with the same coquettish air she used on men, though she meant nothing by it.... What a beauty she's grown into, Lilz thought. Fenne's blonde hair shone in the light of the lamp she held high, hair that hadn't darkened at puberty as so many women's did. Thick pale lashes surrounding dark brown eyes gave her a look of inviolable innocence, very useful. She was small and light-footed and quick with a smile, not at all like her bond-servant. Lilz knew very well what she herself looked like: no great beauty! Eyes of no particular color, ordinary brown hair. No wonder Fenne liked having her nearby.

"Here?" Fenne entered a small room on the outer side of the house. A lamp was already lit; the wide window was the one Lilz had seen from across the valley. Some half-embroidered linen lay on a table in the lamplight. "I've waited up every night." Fenne waved at the cloth. "I was just about to go to bed when I heard you cross the bridge."

"I think we'd best close the shutters," Lilz suggested. Fenne hurried across the room and leaned out to pull the shutters closed. "Lock them."

Fenne pushed the bolts into the stone windowsill and returned to Lilz, who had dropped her pack beside the closed door and stood assessing the room as she stripped off her riding gloves. She didn't like it. Obviously they were in the oldest part of the house. Deep red draperies hung against the stone outer wall for winter warmth— dangerous with that window open for who knew how long, to let who knew what fly in. The furniture was sparse, but as usual in aristocratic houses ornately carved. Too good a hiding place. Some of the beams above her head braced the ceiling without meeting it along the whole of their length. Bad, bad. She wished the lamps and the lantern cast fewer shadows. But the room was Fenne's choice.

"Well?" Fenne tugged at the already snug sash of her nightrobe. "We've heard nothing about him."

Lilz wet her lips. "The man's dead."

"Oh, I thought I'd never hear those words!" Fenne sighed extravagantly and dropped into a chair. "Sit down, Lilz, sit down. Does anyone suspect?"

Lilz sank onto the one other chair, her eyes on the space under the door. "No one has given any sign of suspecting."

"Not even old Gudgeon?"

"The Lord Chief Justice?" Her eyebrows rose. "No, my mistress."

"Ah. Is he buried?"

"Tomorrow."

"Then after that, I'll be safe."

"One hopes."

"One hopes! What do you mean, one hopes? They can't dig him up again, can they?" Fenne bounced forward in her seat, her small fists on her knees. "Lilz, tell me no one will care!"

"He has family," Lilz pointed out.

"Oh, family! What family? Have they the ear of the king, as mine does?"

"Not long ago, they did."

"Lilz, don't scare me. What finally killed him?" Fenne's eyes narrowed. "You weren't with him, were you?"

"No, of course not." An unexpectedly clever question; Lilz was afraid she knew where a yes might have led. "I've never been in the Old Palace in my life."

"You sent the food into the prison with Mistress Stump, then, as we agreed? You didn't put my name on it, did you?"

"No, my mistress. I've done just as before you came here."

"It wasn't—oh, sky above, he didn't die right after one of your tarts?"

"Not my tarts, my mistress," Lilz took care to point out. "And no, the timing wasn't that obvious. We agreed to use only enough poison to sicken him and to let that weakness kill him, don't you remember? He died under the physician's eye, as we expected."

"Then surely no one can make any case against us." Fenne switched subjects, to desultory questions about Lilz's long ride and a few more interested queries about life in Miense, the capital. She had stood to leave when a small object rose from one of the draperies and zoomed at the shuttered window. "Whizzer!" Fenne gasped.

Lilz moved. In three strides she was across the room and had grabbed the whizzer. Hot! Her hand opened. The whizzer hummed for the door. She grabbed a broom that had been left near the door, batted it to the stone floor, and crushed the spy under the heel of her worn riding boot. The heel smoked when she lifted her foot, but the whizzer was split open, its artificial guts smoking too. She swallowed, nauseated by the stench of burnt leather. "There may be more."

"No." Fenne was standing against the inner wall, clutching the collar of her robe to her throat. White showed all around her dark irises. "No, you must have brought it with you." She nudged the saddlepack with her toe. "Why would Guyr send whizzers to me?"

"The king's spies are everywhere, my mistress. You know that." Lilz stuffed her cloak into the space under the door and returned to the outer wall. "We'd better check as best we can." She began moving the warmth-curtain carefully, running her gaze down each of the folds, alert to motion at the fringe of her vision.

She felt Fenne watch her a moment before going to the other end of the wall to inspect the other half of the warmth-curtain. The two women worked in silence toward the window. When they reached it, Fenne said, "It's you the king suspects, my bond-servant Lilz."

Lilz stared down into the innocent brown eyes. Time, past time, to declare herself. "I am your servant by no choice of my own, my mistress." She watched Fenne's face take on the calculating mask she'd first noticed when the girl was just over two years old. "I will serve you as I have from the day of your birth," she added. "But I will not die for you."

"Die!" Fenne giggled. "Who's talking about dying? Not you, Lilz, not when I'm sure to marry my Kav so soon! I'll need you more than ever now, won't I?"

Probably, Lilz thought, smiling despite herself. Fenne's merry grin was one of her most formidable weapons, as Lilz had every reason to know. "I imagine so. Let's check the rest of the room."

Fenne helped her upend the smaller chair to look under the seat, then took a lamp and scrunched down to look under the larger chair and the single table. "Nothing here."

Lilz looked up at the ceiling beams. Even standing on a chair she wouldn't be able to feel the upper surface. Didn't want to, truth be told. Like as not bring down three centuries' dust. We'll just have to trust to fate, she thought. She slung her cloak over her arm and picked up her lantern and pack. "Is there a place for me to sleep, my mistress?" she asked. "I've ridden a long way today, and I'm tired."

"Aster has a pallet for you in the servants' attic, first room to the right. You'll find a flask and some food beside it, I think, unless she's given up. We expected you three days ago."

"If I'd left three days sooner, I could have brought no news, my mistress. News seemed likely to come any moment, so on his Grace your grandfather's advice I waited."

"Yes, of course. I'm glad you did." Fenne prodded at the broken whizzer with the tip of one silk slipper. "Is this thing cool enough to touch? Take it away with you."

Holding the whizzer—which weighed barely more than a crow's quill—in the lightest grasp possible, Lilz carried it down to the little bridge and dropped it into the stream below. As she re-entered the courtyard she noticed a lamp still lit in the stable, so she joined the keeper to finish rubbing Matanda down and wrap his legs after the long ride, while he munched at a pan of oats mixed with mash.

"I've wiped saddle and bridle," the woman said, "but not polished them."

"They'll keep for morning." Yawning, Lilz went back to the darkened house to find the servants' attic.

Far Away, A Birth

Lilz remembered the day of Fenne's birth all too well.

Well under eighteen years had passed since Fenne was born, three days' ride northeast of House-Among-Oaks in a manor house called Summerlea, which sprawled amid its meadows like a succession of afterthoughts: exactly what it was. Somewhere in the core of Summerlea were a few small stave-built rooms centuries old, but along the face presented to the drive were larger, more ornate rooms with plastered walls and gessoed ceilings, some of them decorated in vermilion and blue and gold leaf, or with damasked walls, as was suitable for a noble residence.

The manor was the ancestral seat of one of the five dychdoms of Kinland. Nevan Hasten, sixteenth Dych of Summerlea— Fenne's grandfather—had an entire afterthought to himself at the west end of the house, staffed by a snobbish bunch none of the servants of the rest of the house could abide. When Lilz had first come to the manor, late in the summer before Fenne was born, the house had been full of extended Hasten family, all of them sirs or milords or miladies of one sort or another. For a month after she arrived Lilz had had trouble keeping them all straight, with the exception of Lord Säen, whose five-year-old rear end she often longed to bend over her knee and give an over-earned swat or two. Even new to service, Lilz had known better than to do that!

Her mother had recently died. Orphaned, not yet nineteen years old, without prospects, Lilz had gladly seized the unexpected chance to mortgage her future to the Hastens: well-born herself to a family shorn of power, she was well aware that the Dychs of Summerlea had been trusted seconds to the monarchs of Kinland—at that time the king was Oerl, father of the present king, Guyr—as long as they'd had the dychal surname Hasten, a good many generations. Consequently the opportunity had seemed a gift of fate beyond hope. Of Court intrigue Lilz had known next to nothing at the time, or she might have hesitated longer before trading her name for the promise of an easy old age.

Like all aristocrats, Fenne's mother elected to give birth at home, attended by a midwife: superstition held that a son born away from the manor would lose his inheritance. That a blizzard was threatening just at the critical time made no difference to this decision. Milady was accustomed to having her way. Her way was to follow custom. Nor, despite Lilz's tentative suggestion, did Lady Delle trouble to have the midwife called to attend her in case labor should begin while the storm impeded travel, although she was a full week past her time when the first snowflakes fell. Both the dych and his son, the Iarl of Meadowlands—Fenne's father—were at Court in Miense for the winter. The servants were left with no one to appeal to for help in changing Lady Delle's mind.

Late that evening, with the windows of Summerlea blank with snow, Lady Delle felt the first strong contraction.

Then—only then—a stable lad was sent to fetch the midwife back in a sled. Panic arose when the sled stuck at the end of the drive, but the lad and the gardener and a couple of footmen pulled the sled out and the lad went on, leaving everyone wondering whether the midwife would ever arrive or the lad return.

Lilz was stationed in the kitchen to keep some small blankets warm and water half on the boil. At first someone came every five minutes to ask after the midwife, but as the night wore on these interruptions became infrequent. The kitchenmaid who had kept Lilz company went to bed. Even Lady Delle was reported to be dozing off and on. But in the small hours she began to cry out with each pain, high thin noises that penetrated even to the kitchen and struck fear into Lilz's heart. She could do nothing but sit with her fists clenched and her eyes shut and wish the midwife would come.

At last the sled drew up behind the house. Lilz met the midwife at the main servants' door in early-morning darkness, holding a heated blanket for her to wrap her arms in before going to the woman in labor.

"How goes it?" the midwife asked.

"Not well. She's been straining for half an hour, but nothing's happened. Her other two came far more quickly, her body-maid says. She thinks the baby may have to be turned."

"What luck! It would have to be me." The midwife walked into the kitchen and shrugged out of her winter cloak. "I see the kettle's on. Do I have time for a quick swallow of tea?"

Lilz turned up her palms as Lady Delle screamed.

"Ach, listen to her! I'd better go straight up. Be a dear, and bring me a hot drink, would you? It's cold enough to make stone of a new lover's heart out there, say nothing of the snow."

"She did pick her time." Lilz cast a smile over her shoulder as she went to the hall door. "Pearl?"

An elderly hallmaid drowsed in a chair just outside the kitchen door. Lilz shook her awake. "Pearl, the midwife's here. Could you show her upstairs?"

The kettle was already starting to sing. Making the tea was a matter of under three minutes, but as Lilz mounted the stairs carrying the cup with an extra saucer over the top to keep in the heat, she heard a shriek that stopped her breath. She hurried to her mistress's room, put the tea down on the first level surface and rushed to the bed. The midwife was sweating even in this cool room. Lady Delle's body-maid stood beside her, holding her hands, with tears dripping off her chin.

"Blow in her face, blow in her face," the midwife ordered. Pearl gasped and pressed her hands to her cheeks and Coral only wiped her own tears with her shoulders, so Lilz moved to the head of the bed and blew into the laboring woman's face.

"Yes, good, thank fate! It's working. Keep it up," the midwife said. "We can't have her pushing, don't let her push—"

Forever came and went in a steady trickle of blood and came and went again while Lilz blew herself dizzy. "I've got both feet," the midwife announced breathlessly. "Let's hope—"

Two minutes later she moaned with relief. "Here we go—it's a girl. Oh, but so blue—where are those hot blankets?" She was holding the child over her arm to empty her lungs, smacking her back to start her breathing. The baby sputtered and began to wail. Everyone sighed aloud as she turned bright red.

"Do you need more help?" Lilz asked.

"I'm all right now." Coral settled the new baby on the warm blanket between milady's legs, so the placenta could be drained into her the moment it arrived. "I'll stay. You and Pearl can go get some sleep" — she glanced at the midwife — "Unless you think you still need them?"

"No, here's the afterbirth already. We're in good shape, thanks." The midwife reached for pinchers to clamp off the cord.

"Lilz," Lady Delle said weakly. "Come to me, once I've rested."

"Yes, milady."

"She's lucky she's not resting forever," Pearl muttered, as she and Lilz left the room. "That woman has less wit than a sparrow and morals to match."

"Hush!" Lilz looked about for a whizzer.

"Oh, I dusted yesterday afternoon," Pearl said.

"Even so—"

Pearl gave her a strange glance. "These are the Hastens," she said. "You don't think the king would spy on them?"

Lilz recalled that Pearl belonged to the house and shut her lips over the suggestion that the Hastens might enlist the king's help to spy on their servants. She went back to the kitchen to wash her hands and made a cup of tea for herself. The cook came into the kitchen as she drained the last of it, still so sleepy he only yawned at the news of his mistress's new daughter.

Almost two days passed before Lilz was called to Lady Delle's bedside. Milady had her newborn nestled beside her under the fine quilts. As usual she wore one of her lacy, embroidered bedgowns, but she looked pale, her face unpainted and bloodless. "You showed good sense day before yesterday, Lilz," she said.

"Thank you, milady. "

"You didn't panic, I'm told, though the others did. I should have listened to you — what if the midwife hadn't come at all?"

Lilz mumbled something about managing somehow.

"You know better than that! You're young and bright, Lilz, and you speak well. Clearly you were raised in a good house. I'm sure you can teach my daughter all the necessary refinements, so I'm going to make you her bond-servant." Lady Delle looked down at the sleeping baby with a wry little smile and touched the blonde fuzz on her scalp. "She's a Hasten — she'll need someone with good sense to serve her."

Lilz schooled her surprise out of her face. The Lady Delle was not precisely noted for her own good sense, either among her servants or in her own society.

Her mistress squinted at her. "What do you know about babies?"

"Very little, milady. I'm the youngest of my family."

"Time you learned, then. We have the nursemaid to help you, but I expect you to serve my daughter, starting now."

"Yes, milady."

"Well, girl, what are you standing there for? Go shift your things into the nursery suite."

The dych himself gave Fenne her name. Despite the rough birth, she was a beautiful newborn, round of head and placid of face. Within six months her hair had grown in white-blonde and her eyes turned deep brown — signs that on at least one occasion her mother had kept to her marriage bed, just as the similar coloring of the stable-keeper's son showed that on at least one occasion her father had left it.

One blonde daughter after one dark-haired and one redheaded son. For some reason this amused Fenne's grandfather the dych. She quickly became the old man's favorite, to the disgruntlement of her brothers and some of the nearer cousins. Before Fenne could talk in whole sentences she had gran'papa wrapped twice around each of her small fingers. Not long after, Lilz first noticed that blank expression, the eyes slightly narrowed, that meant that Fenne had been denied something she was about to get.

Chapter Two

Waking, Lilz blinked at the faint shapes of strange roof boards over her head. Oh, yes.

As she stretched, yesterday's long ride tugged at her legs and back. A spot on the palm of her right hand itched. So did the tip of her fourth finger. She licked at them: blistered.

The room under the tiles of House-Among-Oaks was gray with the first light of a new day. From her pallet Lilz could just make out the plump shape of one of the house-servants in a bed near her feet. The familiar soft snore of Fenne's body-maid, Aster, came from the cot beside her. Lilz glanced to her right, where a glass flask of some clear liquid—water? White wine?— caught the faint light. Beside it lay something wrapped in oiled paper, probably bread and cold meat. Her stomach growled, but in view of the past few months and the news she had brought, it was difficult to eat anything that might have come from her mistress.

Still tired, Lilz rubbed her eyes and wondered whether she dared risk a headache by going back to sleep until the other servants got up—surely not for a while yet. How long?

She listened for birdsong, but while did she hear a few tentative cheeps under the eaves her ear was caught by a different musical sound. Somewhere in the house someone was chanting the morning invocation to God the Mother. The voice was male. That decided her: asleep or not, she would stay on her pallet.

Well, that someone would sing a psalm here made sense, didn't it? One of the most ill-kept secrets—from their servants, at any rate—of the Hasten clan was that they adhered to the old religion banished from the kingdom by King Guyr's great-grandfather. Anyone who wanted to keep his freedom these days professed, in public at least, to worship the god King Lehrr the Prophet had made of the Engenderer, once only spouse to the Mother of All, now the Fathergod. Lilz herself had been raised to do so without question or dissembling, although for years she had prayed only in moments of sheer terror.

So. Fenne had come to hide at House-Among-Oaks with a group of fellow worshippers. No wonder a whizzer had been stationed in that room! Probably the house was jumping with them. Just plain good luck that this one had flown at the moment it had, or they might never have seen it. Lilz shuddered. What if she hadn't thought to ask Fenne to lock the shutters?

She let her thoughts drift over what she knew of the people at House-Among-Oaks. She couldn't recall any sign that Edwe Speaksoft,

Iarl of Oakforest, bowed to the Mothergod. No whispers at Court, at least not among servants... What would lead a Speaksoft to make his invocation aloud? The Hastens had nearly as much power as the king, but Speaksofts were small influence. Flighty as some of them were, no Hasten would chant audibly with strangers in the house. Not even Fenne.

In any case, the song had stopped. A little later, Lilz heard a bed creak on the other side of the wall behind her head as someone sat up, a long, loud yawn that set her yawning herself, another creak as the person got out of bed, the scratch of a match and the pop of a lamp taking fire. Either the cook or the houseman....

She woke again in red sunlight. The servant who had been asleep in the bed was gone. Aster was just pulling on her clothes, to be ready when Fenne called. Lilz wished her good morning.

"Good morning." Aster looked a bit startled, but she smiled. "How was your journey?"

"Smooth." Lilz sat up. "I had a good horse—the bay gelding."

"What's the news?"

Lilz grimaced. "Success."

Aster sighed. "I guess it doesn't pay to get in some people's way. Or service." She straightened the placket of her shirt to fasten the buttons. "You didn't eat."

"Would you?"

"It's been my breakfast for the last three days!" Aster grinned. "She didn't get near it. I got it from the kitchen and brought it up myself."

"Ah, thanks. I'm famished." Lilz reached for the packet, careful to notice whether the folds of the paper were the same as when first made. Sliced bread and cold ham, as she'd hoped. When Aster turned to the tiny mirror hung over a rickety dressing stand Lilz looked more closely at the food. She saw no peculiar discoloration of the meat or any fine dust on the bread or in the creases of the paper, so she put the two slices of bread outside the ham and bit into the whole stack at once.

"I guess you're hungry!" Aster finished combing her hair and twisted it into a quick knot at the nape of her neck. "Wedding in about three months, then. What will that mean for us, Lilz?" Groping for hairpins on the shelf beneath the mirror, she looked at Lilz in the reflection.

"Keep her clothes neat and clean, don't let her run out of rose water, get her bath the right temperature, don't miss any stray hairs when you do her coiffure, keep your mouth shut to outsiders including milord Kav, and give no advice of any sort. That should leave you safe enough."

"And you?"

"Father only knows." The water jug was tempting, but even Fenne might have thought to creep upstairs in the dark and dissolve one of her white powders in that. The bottom of the jug did look clean; still, Lilz decided to bear her thirst until she could get water for herself.

Aster pushed in the last of her hairpins and came close enough to whisper into her ear, "Lilz, they sing in this house."

"I heard."

"What protects them?"

Lilz shrugged.

"The house-servants say they've sometimes found whizzers."

"If you see one, don't touch it. They get hot when you grab them." Lilz displayed her hand, with the two tiny, angry-looking blisters. "I broke one last night."

"Broke one! What did you do with it?"

"Dropped it into the brook outside the back gate."

Aster took a deep breath and let it out very slowly. "Now the king will surely know where she is."

Lilz opened her saddlepack for a clean set of underwear and started to dress. "King Guyr knew where Fenne was going before she ever got here." Pulling on the shirt she had worn the day before, she smiled at Aster's slack-jawed shock. "After all, you can bet milord Kav knows exactly where Fenne is! What Kav knows, the king will know sooner or later, more likely sooner."

"But why would the king let her come here?"

"He has his amusements." Lazy he might be, but Guyr was no imbecile. Better to let the Hastens think they had Fenne hidden safely away than to take the chance that they might really find a secure place.

"But what about—her project?"

What about Fenne's project? Lilz took a clean pair of Hasten-blue trousers out of the pack and sat on the edge of the house-servant's bed to put them on.

What Fenne didn't know was that her project should not have succeeded. Lilz had followed each of her mistress's orders but one: she had never once in the whole six months of Sir Jen Makeready's ordeal actually put any of the strange powders Fenne had obtained into the delicacies sent into the prison to tempt the man's palate. Not that she hadn't sometimes wondered whether the more humane course might not be to put a full lethal dose into something. Lilz sucked in her lips, remembering the poor man's increasingly desperate letters to Kav Treadwell, intercepted on Fenne's orders and given to Lilz to keep.

But Lilz had not been able to bring herself to murder. The man had died of something else. Perhaps the dark and the damp of his cell, the isolation, had withered his spirit until it could no longer support his flesh. Or perhaps he had contracted a perfectly ordinary disease and the king's physician had...misdiagnosed. Or perhaps someone else had had a project, other pastries or sweet cream puddings or roast fowl had been offered to a man sick of the prison's cold oat porridge. Any or all of them spiced with death. Certainly a plethora of candidates for that hypothesis could be postulated!

"I don't know," she said.

"I've got to go." Aster tugged her shirt straight and stepped into her shoes. "She'll have fits if I'm late." She hurried out of the room, leaving Lilz to mull the question over while she combed her hair.

Fenne was not likely to call before she had taken her morning bath, broken fast and dressed, so Lilz went down to the kitchen and introduced herself to the cook. She got a big mug of raspberry tea and two scrambled eggs in return for some hints on pleasing the iarl's finicky houseguest, learned when and where the servants took meals, and went out to the stable to check on Matanda.

Fresh, sweet hay had been forked into his stall. His bay coat gleamed. He greeted Lilz with a soft whicker and went on eating as she ran her hand over his short-clipped mane to see that no one had introduced a whizzer. The lad had just ridden out with a string of horses to exercise and the keeper was busy in another stall. Lilz examined what was left of Matanda's black tail after cropping and bent to see that nothing had been hidden in any of his shoes. Bad enough to have a spy with her. Worse to have a lame horse. While she thought of it, she went out the back gate and looked into the stream to see if the broken whizzer of the night before was still there. She couldn't quite be certain, but she thought she saw a glint of metal under the weeds of the streambed.

All her life, Lilz had known about whizzers, small flying mechanical spies that reported to the king whatever a subject he was curious about might be doing. She looked down at her hands on the rough rail of the bridge. The rail of the bridge she understood: a tree had grown somewhere, someone had felled it, someone's adz had shaped it into this timber, someone had cut the timber to length and pegged it in place. The whizzers were different, almost as if they were part of a different world, a world that might include many things like the whizzers, or like the galloping stars that circled the globe...where did they come from?

Her curiosity would tell her no more now than it had any of the other times it had flared. The current flipped a tendril of weed aside. She clearly saw the crushed whizzer lodged among small stones under the shallow water. At least they couldn't heal themselves, something she had wondered about as she waited for sleep last night.

Lilz stood gazing at the whizzer, aware again of the itching blisters. A small metallic fleck. No sign that the water found it any stranger than a stone. Perhaps it couldn't even heat itself? Had she broken it that far?

With a glance at the back of the house, Lilz crossed the rest of the bridge and climbed down beside the stream. Hidden by the bridge's deep shadow she rolled up her pantslegs and sleeves and quickly retrieved the whizzer.

Back on the bank, she examined the object while she waited for her skin to dry. A little larger than a blackbeetle, and about the same shape before she had stamped on it, the casing held a tiny crystalline plate, no larger than the nail of her little finger and far thinner, that reflected even tinier squares of rainbow as she tilted it back and forth. Packed as tightly as the layers of mica and looking much the same were a few more small plates, also marked with squares of rainbow. Maybe they were what held its records. Would the information still be there?

As she turned the object, part of it fell into her palm: a tiny flat metal pill marked on one side with a squared-off x. Strange. She had never seen anything like it before in her life. What its purpose could be, she could not imagine.

Her arms and legs had dried. The whizzer was as cool as ever. Lilz slipped it into a pocket and rolled down her sleeves and pantslegs and put on her shoes to go back into the house.

Aster met her on the back staircase. "She's calling for you, Lilz. She wants to hear the whole story."

"Over breakfast?" Lilz sighed. "Sky above! I suppose I'll have to go tell it, then." She followed Aster up the bare stone steps and into the luxury of the bedroom wing.

A Marriage Is Arranged

The day all the trouble began, Lilz remembered, had been cool and sunny.

Lilz was basting together a muslin pattern for a gown for her mistress, who having passed her thirteenth birthday five months before was to be presented at Court in Miense on the first day of fall. Lilz had borrowed the cook's bench in the kitchen garden behind Summerlea for the good light.

The sun warmed her shoulders pleasantly. Bees hummed in a bed of clove pinks in bloom against the sunny limestone wall that divided this haven from the family gardens. A shifting breeze brought their scent to her now and then; she could hear the beat of a wire whisk through the open kitchen window as the cook constructed dessert for that evening's dinner. Smiling as she stitched, Lilz relished the peace of being alone with her thoughts to herself for a time, although somewhere in the house one of the cousins was singing an endless something in a nasal monotone—rather more loudly than she considered necessary, and in not quite the same key as he was fingering his guitar.

The peace didn't last long. Fenne came into the garden from the family side of the wall wearing a deep frown, which gave way to a smile when she saw Lilz. "Did you look at the dressmaker's samples, Lilz?" she said as greeting.

"I glanced at them, yes."

"What did you think of that silk velvet, the one the color of old brandy?" Fenne perched beside her on the bench and tucked her feet under her. In the house the solo suddenly stopped. Two male voices, one adolescent and one adult, were raised in argument. "About time," Fenne said. "Säen can no more tell the difference between singing and caterwauling than he can fly. What did you think of the velvet?"

"Very pretty."

"It would be lovely with my coloring, don't you think?"

Fenne's hair was no longer the white of early childhood. Now, at age thirteen, it had become a pale gold, just exactly curly enough for beauty. She kept it—or rather, Lilz, acting as body-maid in those days, kept it—brushed to a shine. Lilz glanced at the girl to see the deep brown eyes narrowed against the sun. "Yes, I think the color might set you off nicely."

"That amber and pearl necklace grandpapa gave me would look good with it, don't you think?"

The necklace was two colors of amber, the smaller beads almost as light as Fenne's hair and the larger ones a little darker than the sample of velvet, nearly as dark as the girl's eyes; the strands were twisted together with one of small pearls interspersed with gold beads. "Yes, that might look nice," Lilz said, intent on matching the curves of the muslin bodice.

"Father's so stupid! He says I can't have it."

Oh-oh, Lilz thought.

"Mother, too. She says it's beyond my years."

"I'd think that would depend on the style," Lilz remarked, as a preliminary to backing off.

"Well, but to display that necklace properly I'd need a low bodice, wouldn't I?" Fenne sighed. "I guess I'll just have to go to grandpapa."

Lilz stopped sewing to give her a warning glance. "Your parents would not be pleased at that, young lady."

Fenne twitched a shoulder and made a small pout. "I'll just tell them you agree it would look stunning. Mother's always saying how sensible you are."

Sky above, Lilz thought. When will I learn to hold my tongue with this child? She put her head down as if trying to see her stitches better. "Perhaps next year," she said.

Fenne went still. Lilz braced herself for a storm, but before it could break the dych's houseman came around the end of the garden wall as Fenne just had. "Miss Lilz," he said. "His Grace would like to speak with you as soon as he may."

"With me?"

"Oh, Quern, you stupid oaf, you've got it all wrong. Grandpapa must have meant me." Fenne jumped to her feet. "I'll ask him about the brown velvet."

Quern bowed with the blandest of faces. "A thousand pardons, milady, but his Grace told me particularly that it was Miss Lilz he wished to see, and that he wished to see her alone."

"See Lilz alone?"

Quern showed what he was made of: his expression didn't change in the slightest. "That was his Grace's request, milady."

Lilz folded her sewing together. "Thank you, Quern, I'll put this away and meet you at the inner servant's door as quickly as I can."

"Why can't I come?" Fenne demanded.

"That is his Grace's wish, milady." Quern had a faraway look; Lilz ran into the house with the sewing before Fenne could turn her protest to her. As the door shut behind her she heard Fenne say, "But I must speak with grandpapa right away, Quern, it's so important."

Lilz dashed up the stairs to the room she shared with Coral and dropped Fenne's half-basted gown pattern on the bed, her thoughts echoing Fenne's shocked, "Me alone?" Dear heaven! Why would the dych want to see her? He'd already claimed his bed-right, not two days after she'd come into service. She'd made less response than he'd have had from one of the statues that lined the long drive and he'd left her alone the fourteen years since.... But the old lecher's wife had died last spring. A couple of the younger maids had been complaining that his calls were becoming far too frequent. Feeling a little sick, Lilz pushed a few strands of hair into place, patted down her everyday shirt and pants, and swallowed hard. She would not primp further.

By the time she got to the bottom of the stairs her face was under control, and by the time she had slipped through the door under them and walked through the zigzagging hallways to the dych's part of the house she had decided that whatever the old man wanted, it wasn't likely to be that. Lilz had met men who preferred long-limbed women, who cared more that they were warm and direct in love than that their breasts were small. The dych was not one of them.

She passed through what had once been an outside door and turned right, to take the narrow corridor that led to the inner servants' entrance. Quern was waiting, hands in his pockets, leaning against the doorjamb. As she neared he levered himself upright and grinned at her.

"What is it, Quern, do you know?"

"No idea." His eyebrows darted up and down twice. "But he's in the library with the iarl, so I think your virtue's safe."

"Prettier women are available," Lilz said. "I wasn't worried."

"No?" Quern's grin turned into a leer. "You've got more pink in your cheeks than you did in the garden, my dear Lilz."

"Only distaste at your impertinence, my dear Quern."

Quern led her through the kitchen into the front hall and from there to what the dych called the library. The two or three times she'd entered the small room before this, she'd seen nothing to read but the Summerlea ledgers and diaries stacked in all the corners, but Lilz didn't doubt that at some time in the past century or two someone had carried a real book through the room, surely an occasion worthy of being commemorated in a name.

Nothing had changed. The dych was sitting behind his desk with his heels on the edge, scarcely what one would expect of a man with hair as white as that on his head; while his son, Fenne's father, stood at the glazed doors to the garden with his hands clasped behind his back, looking out across the meadows. Both men were dressed casually, the dych in blue trousers and pullover and the iarl wearing a short-sleeved shirt. For some reason, the door was shut against the beautiful day. Lilz glanced past the iarl just in time to see the head gardener walk up to the ha-ha between lawn and meadow and jump over the edge. He disappeared as neatly as if the earth had swallowed him.

"Sit down, Lilz." The dych swung his heels from his desk and sat up, crossing his legs. Lilz felt apprehension begin to flutter in her belly.

She took a seat, trying to read from the old man's face what was about to be visited upon her.

"Fenne pleases me."

She almost sighed relief. "I am glad to hear so, your Grace."

"You've taught her a good many useful arts—she sits a horse with ease in trousers or in gown, fingers a guitar with a good ear, sings well and according to Jonquil the poet can construct a tolerable rhyme—although that may be nothing but flattery; the man's a notorious suck-up."

"He's not that bad," the iarl said to the meadow.

The dych didn't so much as glance at his son. "And I'm told the sweet girl knows the figures of a dozen dances."

"I've done my best, your Grace."

"With no help from her mother, I'm sure." The iarl's hands tightened at that, but he didn't turn from the door.

"Lady Delle has many other responsibilities," Lilz said. "I assure you, she lacks no concern for her daughter."

"I knew the day I bought you from your future I'd driven a good bargain." The dych teetered on the back legs of his chair. "It's turned out even better than I thought, with you bondservant to Fenne."

The iarl struck the door jamb with the heel of his hand and crossed the room to sit opposite Lilz, scowling.

Once again, his father paid no attention. "I'm told you have good judgment, Lilz." His Grace opened a desk drawer and pulled out a small red leather book, which Lilz, her heart pounding, recognized as a spy-report dossier. Had the king had an interest in her? Impossible!

"And that you are an intelligent woman." The dych raised an eyebrow. "I'd expect you to know of young Rovvo Standfast?"

Ah! Standfast's dossier—far more likely. "The Iarl of Greencrags, yes."

"Have you observed the boy? While wintering at Court, perhaps?"

"Only from a distance, your Grace."

Fourteen years with open ears had taught Lilz a great deal: while she was still sometimes taken aback by palace intrigue, her surprise was not nearly as frequent as it once had been. This time, she saw instantly where the dych's questions were heading.

The Hastens were the oldest and strongest faction at the Court of King Guyr. But while their influence and hereditary position had continued over the reigns of six monarchs, three of them long reigns indeed, even at Court the Hastens were in a sense outsiders: suspected of worshipping the Mothergod, the female god by whose divine disposition the monarchs of Kinland themselves had once claimed their right to govern.

The present king's great-grandfather had abolished the old religion. He'd elevated an ancient legend into a new male god—a god no less inclined to give him the right to reign, to no one's surprise, although even this god had the good sense not to dispute the right of the Peers of the Blood to elect any king within the line of descent.

Why Lehrr the Prophet had risked this act was unclear. He had never otherwise shown any theological inclination. Yet in proclaiming the Fathergod he would not be swayed, although in so doing he had alienated bordering nations to the point of a war with Galtriva, to the west, from which his troops had returned victorious but which had flared from time to time ever since. Worse, despite the victory, which he had claimed as a sign of divine intervention, King Lehrr had brought upon himself the distrust and secret rebellion of powerful nobles in his own land—among them, reputedly, the Dych of Summerlea and all his heirs and relations.

Lilz had long since decided the suspicion their peers had of the Hasten clan was based on truth. At Summerlea she had— rarely, it was true—heard soft pre-dawn chants, no part of the Fathergod's worship, that raised the hair on her arms. Once in a while the whole family disappeared, to reappear silent and sober, without excuse or explanation. She had even met an occasional unannounced stranger creeping along the back halls— elderly women for the most part—and after noting that the absences of the family coincided with the visits of these strangers had concluded that they were priestesses of the Mothergod.

Had Lilz decided to tell the king about those old women, someone would surely have died or gone to jail. To cling to the old religion was to court execution, if only by rotting away while imprisoned in the Old Palace. But the Hastens were entrenched in every aspect of government; no king of Kinland could maintain his reign without their help. Certainly not Guyr, whose interest in politics came in two forms only: theory, and love of machination. The death might well have been her own. So Lilz had kept silent.

The Standfasts bore no such taint—nor did they have the vast Hasten influence. More importantly, the young Iarl of Greencrags was the only child of one of King Guyr's father's most trusted advisors. A young man upon whom a moderate amount of wealth and—to judge by the gossip she had heard— not a shred of tact, charm, or good manners had been bestowed. Although long-since orphaned, with time he would surely become head of his own still-important faction at Court. Possibly he would then prove bolder than his predecessors had been. From his own position of unquestioned adherence to the law, Rovvo Standfast could, if ambitious and clever, mount an effective challenge to the Dych of Summerlea's power. Marrying Fenne off to him would obviate any such threat.

Summerlea chuckled. "Your face is a study, Lilz. See, Olen? She's quicker than you."

"I understood the reasons." Fenne's father leaned forward, one fist clasped in the other hand. "Tell me, Lilz, what do you honestly think of the boy?"

"He is not the most handsome young man I've ever seen, milord," she said cautiously. "But he's not ugly."

"Loutish," the old dych said. "Sullen, arrogant kid with a face full of pimples and a shape like a pumpkin." He chuckled. "A pumpkin who talks like a bumpkin. How's that for a rhyme?"

"Perhaps he is merely somewhat roughly reared?" Lilz suggested.

His Grace laughed loudly. "What else could you expect? His mother was as crazy as a cellar spider and his father lived and died a lusty fellow—I shared a few hunts with him myself. I'm sure the lad was passed from servant to servant from the moment he was weaned with not a soul giving a thought to his future."

"He can read and write?" the iarl asked anxiously.

"Oh, read, yes, I'm sure he can read. Well, Lilz?"

Lilz couldn't stop a small smile. "The young man may not please my mistress, your Grace."

"Hah!" The dych chuckled. "Greencrags couldn't please a randy kitchenmaid. But it's not a matter of pleasing, bondservant Lilz. King Guyr himself made the suggestion." Oh, yes? Lilz thought. With whose prompting? She barely missed raising an eyebrow. "He thinks they'd be a handsome couple."

Fenne and Greencrags could look like cat and toad together and Guyr would think them a handsome pair if their coupling might insure his peace. Besides, he'd have the pleasure of organizing a noble wedding, something this particular king preferred to the routine of government. "Reign, yes; govern, never," he was reputed to have said to his current favorite. The comment had been passed among the nobility and their servants as one of the better jests of the season.

The dych let his eyelids fall slightly, much the way his granddaughter had when bringing up the topic of her dress. Lilz felt her suspicion confirmed: the marriage was Nevan Hasten's idea. "King Guyr proposes to announce the wedding to the peerage when Fenne's presented," the old man said.

"I am sure Greencrags will be delighted."

"And so will Fenne. You'll see to that."

Lilz swallowed. So that was why she was here. "I will do my best, your Grace, but in Fenne's case, it would be unwise to depend entirely upon my ingenuity."

The iarl sighed and stretched. He looked disgusted. "I suppose this means I'll have to buy the brat that damned brown velvet."

Yes, Lilz thought. The young Iarl of Greencrags would be beyond delight; he'd be ecstatic: he couldn't hope to obtain such a prize as Fenne by his own non-existent charm. Fenne, on the other hand, could be depended upon to raise such a fuss as King Guyr had never seen in his life. "May I speak plainly, your Grace?" she asked.

"Speak."

"I am bound to say that you have spoiled your granddaughter somewhat, your Grace. She's thirteen years old, and I'm sorry to say more than ordinarily willful and thoughtless. She could work great mischief if she takes it into her head."

"You mean if she doesn't like the boy."

"Yes."

"Oh, well, right after the wedding he's to be sent to Chrems for a good university finishing, anyway. She won't be bothered with him for at least three years." The dych's eyelids drooped. "Meanwhile everyone will treat her as an adult and she can have the time of her life at Court—put it to her that way."

"And when Greencrags returns?"

"Fenne's a darling, but she's not very bright. She won't give him a thought before then unless someone reminds her." The dych leered. "By then, he'll be almost nineteen—at least he should be past the worst pimples. He may even have lost some of that babyfat. Who knows? Maybe they'll teach him some manners at Chrems, along with his math and political science. Or if not, I'm sure he's equipped to beat some sense into her."

Both Lilz and Fenne's father sucked in their breath.

"In bed, of course." The dych laughed. "She'll be ready for it by then. What's this about brown velvet?"

Chapter Three

Aster opened the door to Fenne's bed chamber and Lilz walked in.

Her mistress was sitting up in bed, a light silk shawl over her shoulders against the cool morning, her hair already combed into a bright spill of curls. A traytable across her knees held half a fried egg smeared over a plate. She'd tossed the plate's heat lid to the foot of the bed despite the fragile lace comforter-cover, which someone else would now have to clean so unobtrusively that Fenne couldn't notice that it had been taken away and returned. Sunlight from the open window fell across the pale pink fabric, emphasizing the damp spots and a yellow fleck of egg.

"Piece of toast, Lilz?" she offered, when Aster had been dismissed. "The butter's made it too soggy for me."

"No, thank you, my mistress."

"Sweet butter, though." Fenne picked up her cup and sipped. Her eyes narrowed. "Oakforest's cook blends a good tea. I wonder if he's attached to the house or to the iarl?"

"It's not nice to steal your host's good servants, my mistress." Lilz sat in the chair Fenne had pointed at, shaking her head at a mute offer of the cold remains of the egg.

"No, I s'pose not. Mother would give it a try, though."

Probably. The woman had, if possible, even less forethought than did her daughter. "I think you'd best keep Oakforest on your side, my mistress," Lilz cautioned. "At least until everything's settled."

"Yes, he does have the king's ear once in a while. I'd forgotten. It's a good thing I've got you to remember all this stuff for me." Fenne sighed. "Why is life so complicated, Lilz?"

Because that's the way you make it, Lilz thought, but she only smiled and shook her head.

"Have you heard anything about the commission?"

"Nothing, my mistress."

Fenne made a face.

"But I remind you, my mistress, they have the support of King Guyr—if he's ever denied Kav Treadwell anything, I can't remember what it was." Lilz watched: Fenne smiled slightly but the tension didn't leave her forehead. "I think the path will be clear, now that Sir Jen is out of the way," she continued.

"His vile mouth shut, you mean." The frown cleared. Fenne attacked a bunch of red grapes, plucking them off the stem and sucking each into her mouth with a small pop, as she'd done to every grape she'd eaten for the past fifteen years. "Wagging tongues make short lives." Seeds crunched between her teeth. "Sir Jen should have known that if anyone does."

True. Lilz kept quiet.

"Tell me how he died."

"You remember, I wasn't there." Lilz stopped until Fenne had nodded. "So what I have is only the report of others."

The others, in this case, had been three representatives of the king and three of the Lord Chief Justice; five of them Hasten minions of one stripe or another. Nevan Hasten, Dych of Summerlea, had picked them all, though Lilz doubted whether that fact was on record anywhere.

"Have? You have a report?"

"Yes, my mistress. His Grace your grandfather sent it to your rooms yesterday morning with instructions to transmit it to you, but you seemed so tired last night I thought it better to wait. It's upstairs in my saddle-pack."

Pop! went a grape. "I hope you read it."

"Yes."

"Is it icky?" Fenne asked. Lilz nodded.

"Then just give me the gist."

Lilz watched Fenne eating grapes for a moment. The report had sickened her. Brilliant as he had been, Sir Jen Makeready had had his flaws. No one would deny that. A vain, rather overbearing man, nakedly ambitious, he had been inclined to underestimate the minds and hearts of those around him. But he had also been witty, cheerful, and generous and loyal to a fault. Lilz—from afar, of course, and silently, as required by her station in life—had enjoyed his deadpan drolleries and the dancing, understated wit sometimes reflected in the manuscript poems that went the rounds of the peerage.

She remembered seeing Sir Jen for the first time, at a small distance: a tall man, a full sashlength or more in height, with a long, oval face embellished with a short, exquisitely trimmed dark beard. He had a rounded forehead and deepset brown eyes, at that moment lively with amusement; a pleasant voice and a warming chuckle. A well-made man, Sir Jen moved with the lithe grace of the physically fit. His clothes were cut to the epitome of fashion, as Lilz would soon learn they always were.

He'd walked across the room, talking to someone beside him, taking no notice of the women standing just inside the door. Fenne, beside her, had sucked in her breath. A few minutes later Sir Kav, as he'd been then, had come in: as the boy greeted the other two men Lilz had been amused by the parallel—Sir Jen, a man her own age, so obviously the mentor of Kav, who wasn't much older than Fenne; herself secretly steering the girl through the forms Fenne had not had the wit or patience to learn. Lilz had good reason to think that not long after, Sir Jen had not only noticed Fenne but had done some instructing of his own, in a field Lilz was not competent to teach. That might explain the malicious poems of last winter, so unusually impolitic of Sir Jen.

"The report describes him as emaciated," Lilz said now, watching Fenne. "His belly was bloated. On his chest, the flesh had sunk between his ribs except for a small area around each nipple extending upward to the armpit. One of the examiners reports that he could touch his thumb to his middle finger around Sir Jens's upper arm. So it seems the food sent into the prison for him was not as nourishing as one might have thought."

Fenne gave her a wide-eyed glance and blinked.

Lilz pressed on, grimly enjoying her small opportunity to avenge herself. "Open sores were found on his body, where his bones had worn away his skin after he became too weak to move. He was naked, lying in filth. The prison warden said that had become usual over the past few weeks. Huge red welts marked his back around the sores."

Fenne had just plucked a grape. She put her hand down without eating it. "Lilz, just the gist, please?"

"This is the gist, my mistress. The report described each of the sores, its location, the amount of pus pressed out of it—"

"Lilz, please?"

"One of the examiners—your cousin Lord Säen, whose singing used to annoy you so—found that he could pull tufts of hair from Sir Jens's beard with a tweak of two fingers—"

"Lilz!"

"He's sure to tell you himself, as you must know, my mistress," Lilz said demurely. "I thought you should be prepared."

"Thank you." Fenne's voice was faint. "I think I can manage Säen by myself."

"As to Sir Jen, his belly and thighs were covered with small yellow pustules, I think they said—"

"Lilz! Enough!" Fenne looked down at her fingers, where the crushed grape dripped juice onto her shawl. "Now see what you've made me do. All I wanted to know was how he died."

Lilz waited five seconds. "Alone."

Fenne pressed her lips thin. A cloud passed across the sun, dimming the room.

"Alone, cold, in the dark."

Light returned in a wave, reflected from the coverlet into Fenne's scowling face. After a moment she raised her head and glared at Lilz. "You're the one who put the poison in his food!"

"My mistress, you brought the powders to me," Lilz said calmly. "At first, you recall, you told me they were to prevent the infections common to prison life, because Kav Treadwell—"

"He's Iarl of Northlands, now, Lilz, don't you forget!"

"Because Lord Northlands wished to have Sir Jen released as soon as it was decided whether your first marriage could be ruled invalid. Later, of course, you told me—"

"Go away." Fenne swallowed. "Just get out."

Lilz got up and went to the door.

"Lilz! Don't you dare say a word about any of this to Kav or anyone else, or you'll regret it, I swear!"

"I am not a fool, Lady Greencrags."

"Send Aster!"

Lilz closed the door behind her. She managed eight or ten steps down the hall before her knees began to give way. Not a fool? She leaned against the brocaded wall and covered her face with her hands. Not a fool? A thousand kinds of fool, letting some whizzer hiding in Fenne's pretty bedclothes take all that in, letting Fenne glimpse her loathing, letting herself become enmeshed in this mess in the first place! She should have taken up the cloistered life, weak as her belief was, and soiled the honesty of her tongue with daily hymns of praise to a Fathergod she'd half decided was the invention of a crazy man. At least it would have been a harmless lie.

Someone touched her shoulder. "Miss?"

Lilz looked up. The Iarl of Oakforest himself had approached unheard over the thick carpet and now stood blinking at her with puzzlement and concern. Sky above! She wiped her tears away with the heels of her hands and made a quick bow.

"Do I know you?" the iarl asked.

"No, milord. I'm Lilz, bond-servant to Lady Greencrags, arrived last night when the house was asleep."

"Ah." He smiled. "Lady Greencrags told me you might be coming. Why so distressed? Do you bring such disastrous news?"

Lilz hesitated. What was Oakforest's interest? Did he have some stake other than the usual hope of future power and money? Could he be sheltering Fenne out of true friendship with one Hasten or another? Or was he just another convenience to the Hastens, bought with the threat of being accused of worshipping the Mothergod, as Sir Jen had been accused, and terrified because there was substance to the threat?

She decided to let him make what he would of the news. "Just that Sir Jen Makeready died early yesterday morning, milord."

Oakforest stood rubbing an index finger under his lower lip for several seconds. "I see." He gave her a sharp glance. "Well, we must all just hope for the best, then."

He turned and walked away. Lilz stared after him. What on earth had he meant by that?

A Wedding Planned By a King

Lilz was almost as nervous as Fenne.

Three of this year's girls had already been presented, in increasing order of rank. The body-maids who had been standing with them had rushed upstairs to share the moment from the servants' gallery, leaving only three of the palace staff and a minor vikent waiting in the antechamber with the last two girls and their maids. The vikent was wearing a ceremonial red vest. He was surely entitled to be seated among the audience in the hall lit by hundreds of candles, but although his duties had ended with getting the young ladies lined up in the right order he seemed inclined to linger in this dim little room. Lilz had coolly stared him down a moment ago. He was now trying to look as if he were not inspecting Fenne, though he was apparently unable to stop.

Her mistress stood a step away, fussing with the ruffled cuffs of the brandy-colored gown. The amber necklace glowed above the edge of the velvet, but not on Fenne's bare skin. Lilz had devised a compromise: the velvet bodice was cut low to suit Fenne, but had been filled in with a pale chiffon to give the illusion of daring without quite achieving it. A narrow velvet collar framed the necklace from above, and chiffon ruffles inside the velvet ones at Fenne's elbows gave unity to the design. When Lilz had presented the idea Lady Delle had been pleased, all that was necessary to gain the iarl's approval. The dressmaker conceived of herself as a co-conspirator and was much puffed up.

Fenne, predictably, had sulked for a week. But although the Hastens were now in residence in town, the Dych in one of his many roles at Court had been called to the palace to supervise preparations for the coming ceremony. With three against her and grandpapa away, Fenne had been forced to give in.

Lilz had taken the precaution of misplacing the scissors from her sewing kit and had recruited Coral to hide the finished dress in the iarlena's closet, in case the chiffon should develop an inclination to disappear. One last tantrum this afternoon had been brought to an instantaneous halt by Lady Delle's pointing out that if the velvet dress were ruined Fenne would have to wear the pale green silk made for her last winter, which was a little short, a bit snug, definitely designed for a child, and had an embarrassing stain on the back of the skirt.

The girl ahead of Fenne—one of the Ridehard daughters— stepped forward to a blare of trumpets. "Oh, Lilz, I'm next!" Fenne whispered. "What am I supposed to do, again?"

Lilz bit off a sigh. "Wait until the crier says your name. Walk along the white carpet. Bow to King Guyr. One of the redvests will come to offer his arm. Take it. Go with him. He'll show you a seat. Sit in it."

"Oh, Lilz!" Fenne's teeth caught at her lip. "How am I going to remember all that?"

From the crowded hall on the other side of the open portal a man's voice shouted, "Fenne Hasten, daughter of Olen Hasten, Iarl of Meadowlands, and of the Lady Delle Makeright."

"I think I'm going to faint."

"No such thing. Act your age." The trumpets sounded. "Get in there! Now!"

Fenne walked smoothly into the hall, her head modestly lowered. She had entered with a faint smile that told Lilz she was scanning the audience from under those thick pale eyelashes. About as likely to faint as a turtle! Lilz sprinted into the narrow corridor beside the anteroom and up the steep staircase to the servants' gallery to take her place with other bond-servants and body-maids. She wriggled into a tiny space beside Coral and leaned forward to peer through the lattice that hid them from the important people in the hall.

"She's so pretty," Coral whispered. "You did such a nice job with her hair."

"Thank you."

"Who thought of curling the ribbons?"

"Me."

Fenne reached the end of the white carpet and made a low bow to King Guyr. One of the redvests started forward, but the king motioned him back. Fenne glanced behind her as if looking for someone.

"Fenne Hasten, come to me." As always, King Guyr's ceremonial voice was magnified far beyond anything normal, a gift of the Father of All during the rites of coronation, like his crown and the red jewel that glittered on his chest. Fenne slowly mounted the seven steps toward the throne while Lilz's heart thumped. The idiot child forgot to kiss the king's ring.

Guyr stood and took her hand. His lips moved, but Lilz heard no words. Fenne nodded and turned to face the audience.

"My dear subjects," the king boomed. "I have the great pleasure—no, joy—of announcing the coming marriage of this delightful sprite to one of my own heart treasures, Rovvo Standfast, Iarl of Greencrags."

A murmur, partly surprise and partly didn't-I-tell-you, went through the crowd.

"Greencrags, come forward."

Pumpkin was unfair, Lilz thought. The boy was a little pudgy, yes, and his clothes had an unfortunate rustic cut, but he was hardly round. He seemed dazed and scared as he approached the dais, although he was fully fifteen years old. An expression of profound distaste crossed Fenne's face.

Smile, Lilz thought. Oh, please, smile! Her shoulder blades pulled together as she glimpsed the Dych of Summerlea seated at the head of that grand assembly, wearing the crimson robe of the King's Marshal.

Only six weeks ago he'd ordered her to make sure Fenne would be delighted! She closed her eyes. When she opened them, Greencrags had climbed the seven steps and the king had taken his hand. Fenne, praise heaven, had assumed one of her more dazzling grins.

"We will fete their union on the last day of autumn," Guyr said. "All with the right to stand now in this hall are invited."

At that, all with the right to stand, stood. Under cover of the general rustle, the king turned his head and spoke to the redvest who had started to escort Fenne to her place—Lady Fenne, Lilz thought with a start: she'd just been presented—the king spoke to the redvest, who now completed his task while Greencrags fell over his feet getting back to his seat on his own. "Poor Fenne," Coral murmured.

To be given in marriage by the king was to be instantly wealthy, surely something the Dych of Summerlea had considered when deciding to manipulate Guyr into having the idea. A distinct note of envy colored the congratulations offered by the other half-dozen presentees during the dancing after the ceremony, despite the unprepossessing Greencrags. That young man stood against the wall watching the dancers, looking alternately dumbfounded and eager. No one stopped to speak to him.

The festivities were sure to continue into early morning, but by midnight all of the girls presented that evening were sent home with their body-maids in attendance.

"Lilz, I danced with Prince Jath," Fenne chanted, with elegant swoops and twirls along the sidewalk. Three of the armed retainers sent with them scuttled to keep up with their master's daughter, the one clutching the lantern a little behind the others. Fenne danced so far ahead Lilz had to call to her to wait and, with the one man who had stayed behind, run after her. When Lilz caught up Fenne was off again, twirling her way home —up the steps of Hasten House, along the main hall and up to her rooms on the second floor.

"I danced with Prince Jath," she sang, barely standing still for Lilz to unbutton the back of the velvet dress. "Oh, isn't he handsome?" She held her hands out and stared at them. "Can you believe it, Lilz? Prince Jath touched these hands! Mine!" She lowered her arms to let Lilz slip the dress off her shoulders. "I'll never wash them again."

"Then he's not likely to want to dance with you two months from now," Lilz remarked tartly. "Do remember, you are betrothed to the Iarl of Greencrags! The king himself announced the wedding date not four hours ago." The caution went unheard. "Fenne!"

That got her attention. "Lady Fenne, Lilz."

"If you are to be a lady, you must behave like one, my mistress. Do remember that what King Guyr arranges we must all obey. It's folly to talk as you just have where you might be heard by outsiders."

Fenne looked at her round-eyed, stiff fingers pressed to her mouth. "Whizzers?" she whispered.

Lilz nearly laughed. "Not likely, not here." She frowned as Fenne stepped into another little twirl. "But please remember, we are in Miense, not Summerlea. The street is surely not immune. "

"He has such pretty eyes!" Fenne said breathlessly. "Blue, Lilz, like the sky, but with little silver flecks in them. When he smiles — "

"Fenne, do be still! What makes you think those four men have no ears or mouths?"

"What four men?"

"The ones who escorted you home."

"Oh, them!" Fenne laughed. "They don't count. They're only servants!"

Lilz lay awake for hours. How to knock some sense into that child's head? The last day of autumn was a scant two months off. Lilz was still staring at the invisible ceiling when Coral slipped into the room and fell into the bed, so weary she didn't bother to undress. Some animal or bird skittered over the roof tiles as Coral's breathing slowed. The window had already become a pale rectangle in the dark wall.

At breakfast next noon it was still Prince Jath, Prince Jath, Prince Jath, until even Lady Delle snapped at her daughter and flounced out of the room.

"Well," Fenne exclaimed. "What wormed into her?"

Lilz stepped away from the wall and poured the last of the tea into the cup Fenne held out. "My mistress, I'm sure she expected you to be more excited about your wedding. "

"Oh, the wedding." Fenne wrinkled her nose. "Well, but that's just a form, grandpapa says. Mother must have a headache. She probably drank too much last night." A craftiness crept into Fenne's smile. "Maybe she'd like the prince for herself."

"My mistress, whether you've been presented or not, I think such speculations are quite out of place."

Fenne shrugged. "She's probably pissed because she's too old."

"That, Lady Fenne, will be enough." The iarl strolled into the breakfast room. "You are to behave yourself." Meadowlands frowned at his daughter. "We're in Miense, at Court, and you have just been presented to the king. That means you are obliged to conduct yourself as an adult." He picked up the teapot and looked into it. "What's the matter with these people? This thing's empty. See to it, will you, Lilz?" He set the pot down.

"What do you mean, conduct myself as an adult?" Fenne thrust out her chest as Lilz rang for the maid. "I am—"

"In name only, young lady. An adult would never make such a comment about her mother as you just did."

Lilz, without being bidden, faded through the open door to intercept the maid: the last thing the Hastens needed now was more gossip.

She stopped outside to listen as the iarl stood over Fenne to outline the behavior now expected of her, the longest speech she had ever heard him make.

He had barely finished before a messenger arrived from the palace bearing the first of the gifts, a necklace of glowing rubies set in gold with a pendant of more rubies and a scattering of pearls and diamonds that lay upon Fenne's breastbone as if she had been born solely to wear such jewels.

"I like my amber better." Fenne pressed the necklace against her chest and leaned forward to look into the mirror. "This is sort of flashy, don't you think?"

Gaudy is the word, Lilz thought. "It's exquisite," she said firmly. "The messenger's waiting. You are to sit down this minute and write your thanks to the king for his magnificent, generous and unexpected gift, and you will show the note to me before you seal it."

"Am I going to have to wear this thing at the wedding?"

"I don't doubt it."

"Ecch. It looks like blood."

Lilz handed Fenne paper and pen. She made her rewrite the note twice. Given more time, she'd have had her try again, but the messenger was cooling his heels in the hall; the dych would never forgive her keeping the king waiting, and given Fenne's age and inexperience perhaps her phrasing would be excused. How will I live through the next two months? Lilz wondered as she handed the note, sealed sloppily with Fenne's initials impressed in wax, to the messenger — and added a few coins of her own, Fenne having none to supply and not the wit to think of it if she had. The messenger tipped his crimson cap with open relief and left at a trot.

As usual when festivity was in sight, Guyr spared nothing.

Mistress Stump, the costumer to the Court, appeared that afternoon to measure Fenne for her trousseau. She had the design for Fenne's wedding dress in hand, sketched by the king himself. Typical of Guyr, Lilz thought, to assume command of the theatrics.

She watched, amused, as Mistress Stump chatted away, whisking the tape from waist to arm to backbone, and it slowly dawned upon Fenne that this extravagant item of clothing was to be made to her own measure. Blue silk of the Hasten shade, it would be, the full skirt split in front to reveal a pleated underskirt in a deep rose to compliment the ruby necklace, big sleeves slashed to show more deep rose, a square decolletage "to show off your ladyship's lovely fair skin," and a short train whose box pleats started at the waist and were lined with more rose-pink. Each of these pleats would be edged with pearls stitched into a lacework of gold, as would the split in the front of the skirt and each of the slashes of the sleeves....King Guyr, Lilz thought, whether by arrangement or not was following Nevan Hasten's plan of action:

keep Fenne's mind on the wedding and don't give her time to think about the groom.

That weekend, the servants emptied a bright room on the north side of the house. Beginning on Moonday an artist arrived at two each afternoon for a week and a half: Fenne, at Guyr's behest, was to sit for her portrait.

The room soon stank of linseed oil and turpentine. Fenne complained of the smell and might even have refused to continue, but the artist was a reasonably good-looking middle-aged man with a line of patter that kept her in good humor—a pleasure reflected in the finished likeness. Lilz, who had sat to the side as chaperone, privately thought the man's clever tongue as important to his success as his artistic talent. Later, the man copied his work twice over "in small," once for the dych and once so that Standfast could carry a memento of his wife with him to Chrems.

Closer to the wedding day gifts from the other nobles began to arrive. Even Lady Delle seemed taken aback. Fenne, still four months shy of her fourteenth birthday, owned exquisite porcelain crusted in gold, enough gilt silverware to give a dinner for forty from soupspoons through fish forks to the grandest demitasse spoons Lilz had ever seen, tureens of silver and porcelain and gold, linens and coverlets enough to entertain an army of peers had she any tables or beds to spread them on, four white horses to draw her wedding carriage from the townhouse to what was still called the New Palace although it had been built by King Lehrr nearly a hundred and forty years before, and innumerable other items of which everyone lost track. Except, that is, for the sapphire-studded book with the gold cover sent by Queen Prenta: a collection of daily prayers to the Fathergod, a bit of spite not lost even on Fenne.

None of this counted the avalanche of gifts from the palace. Young Greencrags now resided on an estate called Sweetdawn, twice the size of the distant one on which he had been raised and only three days' journey from Miense. A mere baron had been displaced to make room. How many falcons and hounds had been added to Greencrags's hunt was anyone's guess. The royal costumer had been unleashed on him, too, providing a wardrobe twice as large as the sum of all the garments he'd worn since infancy—almost enough to match what had been added to Fenne's.

And Jonquil the poet had created a masque.

The masques played at weddings were the sole remnant of the worship of the Mothergod anyone would presume to present in public. Even King Lehrr had not dared tamper with them: without a proper masque, how was a marriage to be blessed with children? Guyr's father, Oerl, had once tried to ban the wedding masques and been faced with a near-revolution. Guyr wouldn't dream of such a thing. Not when they provided such opportunity for intricate, rivalrous costume, lavish song, cavorting players, dancing for everyone, glitter, glitter, glitter!

This masque differed only in being more splendid than any other ever presented. A pity Rovvo Standfast could not dance. Prince Jath took his place in the figures, beaming on Fenne and being beamed upon in return, while the young iarl stood against the wall watching his new wife with an expression of such sadness and envy that Lilz, in the gallery with the rest of the family servants, wanted to take him into her arms and tell him everything would be all right.

The players had left after a second round of jest and the dancing was about to start again when one of the palace staff came to the gallery to ask for Lilz: Lady Greencrags wished some assistance with her attire. The man led her through a maze of hallways she'd never traveled before, to meet Fenne at a side door to the ceremonial hall.

"Oh, Lilz, I've got to pee so bad!" Fenne was all but jittering in place. "But I don't know what to do with this train!"

"Fenne, I'm sorry—Do you know where the toilets are?"

"Just down here, Mother says." Fenne started confidently to her right. "She could've helped me herself," she groused, "But she was just started dancing and she didn't want to spoil the figure, and it's going to go on for ages—" With a small, apologetic smile, Fenne shrugged. "I didn't want to ask—I mean, I don't know anybody here but Mother."

They arrived at a door. Fenne stood aside. Lilz opened it. Inside, a stench of urine, feces, vomit and thick perfume awaited. Lilz almost retched. She held the train while Fenne relieved herself.

"Do you need to go, Lilz? It's only for peers, but I'll stand guard," Fenne offered.

"Thanks, yes."

Done, they returned to the Hall. Fenne slipped back into the celebration. A blast of music and laughter was snuffed by the closing door, leaving only a dull, distant noise, like the coal left behind when a candle flame is blown out. Shaking her head at her fancifulness, Lilz looked about for the palace servant. He'd disappeared. She started back to the gallery on her own.

All these doors were just alike. The cold corridors, once she had left the crimson carpet outside the ceremonial hall behind, were identical echoing stone with identical flickering lamps making small islands of light in the gloom. Coming, she'd been thinking of what Fenne might need and had assumed that the palace servant would be on hand to guide her back, so Lilz had paid little attention to their route. Now that she needed one, of course, there wasn't a servant to be seen of the hundreds who worked in the palace. Lilz soon took a wrong turn.

She knew it was wrong when she stepped through a half-open door into the middle of a hall whose carpeted floor—not red, as the one near the Hall had been, but blue—stretched far to left and right. A few steps to her right someone was walking away from her.

Lilz drew a breath to call to him and stopped. Something was odd about that man. His clothes...his clothes...she'd never seen trousers cut so close to the body, or a shirt so plain. And he moved...oddly. Not with the forthright march of a peer, but not with the gliding servility of one of her own rank, either. A tradesman, perhaps? But here? At this hour? And something was not quite right for that, either; he carried his shoulders like no other man Lilz had ever seen—or woman, for that matter.

Whoever he was, he could hardly tax her with being lost.

"Sir?" she called. "Milord?"

The man turned. His eyes widened.

"Milord, I beg of you, I've taken a wrong turn and don't know how to go back to the servant's gallery over the Hall—"

The man neither came forward, looking either genial or displeased, to give her directions—which was what she had expected—nor stood where he was to castigate her, the only other possibility that would ever have occurred to her. He turned away and ran.

While Lilz watched open-mouthed the stranger fetched up against a door, rapped on it in a peculiar rhythm, and flung himself through when it opened.

I'm only lost, Lilz thought, but he's up to no good. She went to the door and was about to open it when she heard someone talking inside, a fast, anxious sentence answered by an equally anxious question in another voice. Both spoke a language she had never heard.

Deciding to improve her courage with discretion, Lilz retreated to the stone-floored corridor she had just left. To confuse any chase, she pulled the door shut behind her. Her hand tingled. She let go with a snap like the spark that jumps from a just-touched object in winter and ran back the way she had come, shaking her hand. Once through another door, she stopped to catch her breath and rub her tingling fingers. Yes. She'd been turned completely around, gone left when she should have gone right. Having a rough idea of the palace layout she found her way back to familiar ground and then to the servants' gallery.

Coral was giggling in a corner with one of Greencrag's men while the other two watched the festivities. Lilz sat down a distance from them and leaned her head against one of the bars of the lattice. She could think of no one to ask about the men who spoke so strangely so deep inside the palace. Guyr's business. Yes, they had to be there with the king's knowledge. Perhaps just having seen them would cause her trouble. Did the king have spies even in the palace?

Ignoring the muffled gasps from the corner, she watched the dancers below. Fenne's bright head whirled precisely through the patterns; the music pumped one's blood; after a time a young baron came into the gallery with two huge bottles of bubbly wine for the servants to share, a gift from Greencrags. Lilz put the thought of the strangers away. Why waste herself on a mystery when it was her mistress's wedding day?

The dancers stopped so some singers could continue the masque. Greencrag's body-man, a man of her own age named Stone, poured Lilz another glass of wine. He had a charming smile.

Gala as the night had been, it ended in the usual domestic chores: at the king's behest Lady Greencrags was hustled straight home before the festivities had even begun to wane, so that she wouldn't have to think too much about her plump and pimpled husband, who left for Chrems the next morning without having had two minutes alone with his bride.

Chapter Four

My dearest, my sweetheart, my love, my own Kav—
Lilz rode out yesterday to tell me Sir Jen Makeready is dead. I am
sure you are as shocked as I am—I had no idea he was even ill. I wish
I could be with you to comfort you. He did say dreadful things about
me and about Mother, but he was your friend for such a long time and
you are so sweet and forgiving that I know you can't help but grieve.

"Bitch," Lilz murmured. Matanda twitched an ear as if a fly had
settled on it, but the easy rhythm of his hooves didn't alter. Lilz glanced
at the sun filtering through the leaves of the oak trees over her head
and sighed before going back to the letter.

Oakforest is treating me well, though of course nothing can fill the
emptiness I feel without you at my side. I can't wait for the commission
to finish that stupid investigation so we can be together again. I hope
Greencrags hasn't changed his mind about not contesting? (Do you
think he might really be impotent? Wouldn't that be funny?)

Lilz scanned the rest of the letter—chiefly descriptions of what
Fenne hoped to do with Kav when they were together again—with
her eyebrows raised. Had Greencrags been treated to a tenth of
that interest, he'd have had to have been made of water to fail to
consummate the marriage, as Fenne had charged. Not that Fenne
had given the lad a winter fly's hope.

Lilz nodded at the big round signature that ended the letter. Fenne
had written precisely what her bond-servant would have predicted.
Only a small uncertainty about whether her mistress might have
taken it into her head to denounce her to milord Kav had decided
Lilz to open the thing.

But Fenne hadn't.

After all, why should she? Lilz asked herself. Most of Fenne's life
I've been closer to her than her own mother. With someone as self-
centered as Fenne it may never occur to her to wonder what I think
of what she's become. Or of her grandfather.

In the Dych of Summerlea, Lilz sometimes thought she had met
the principle of evil. What atrocities she had committed in another life
to deserve to live under his rule in this one, she could not imagine.
The simple knowledge that she must have done something for which
she was now being punished shamed her so deeply that she felt her
cheeks heat, alone as she was.

She folded the letter and put it back into the inside pocket of her travelling cloak. Please heaven, Kav Treadwell wouldn't notice it had been opened. Let Fenne complain, and Nevan Hasten would have her head. Lilz the bond-servant would disappear, and who would even notice she was gone? Look at Makeready. Eight months ago he had been all but king in everything but blood and title. Today he was to disappear into an unmarked grave filled with quicklime, if he hadn't already.

"I get so angry, Matanda," she sighed. "I hate being such a coward and so helpless." The horse plodded on, while Lilz bit her lower lip and looked about for small animals like the toad of the night before. She saw none.

The crowns of the oaks stripped heat from the sunlight, leaving only dancing gold and shadow through which an occasional insect flitted. Lilz relaxed in the saddle, in no hurry to reach Miense. Overhead, birds called; once she rounded a bend in the path and sent a deer crashing into the underbrush before she had quite seen it. She played with the image of escape, of living under the trees like the deer, but her good sense kept intruding with visions of snow, hunger, a loneliness even greater than what she sometimes felt in the company of her fellow servants. After a while she gave it up and focused on what she must do next.

Mistress Stump.

The costumer would need reassurance. A reason for hurry. Lilz hoped the woman hadn't yet heard of Makeready's death: handing over the report, eyelids half-lowered, the Dych of Summerlea had enjoined her to tell no one but Fenne and Oakforest. Lilz had understood. The Hastens wanted the man rotted away before any uproar. In a month or so, the quicklime could be explained as an effort to prevent the spread of whatever contagion Makeready could reasonably be rumored to have died of, the burial within the Old Palace as mere convenience.

So, with luck, Lilz could break the news to the costumer and put a quick stop to any hysteria. She clenched her teeth. Mistress Stump and Fenne made a perfect pair: neither had an ounce of forethought nor a dram of imagination. I want, I see a way, I act. Tomorrow be damned.

Lilz knew her mistress well. She was sure Fenne had never once stopped to think what the life of a man in prison might be like, quite apart from whether he was being slowly poisoned. Fenne had thought of Sir Jen, when she thought of him, as he looked the day before he was locked up in the bleak stone mountain of the Old Palace. In Fenne's mind Makeready had been tall, proud, handsome, healthy, and clever to the very end. That man, the insults he had made to her reputation, his opposition to dissolving her marriage to Greencrags and to her marrying his own link to power, was the man Fenne was acting against. The pitiful shriveled creature of her grandfather's report must have come as a complete surprise.

Therefore Fenne had put the results of her own mischief out of her mind and recreated Sir Jen as she'd known him last, all by the time Lilz had been called to take the letter to Kav, not two hours later. To Mistress Stump's credit, the costumer would not be able to do that—at least, not nearly as quickly.

Little Mistress Stump, tripping back and forth in her fashionable gowns from pharmacist to Fenne, from Hasten House to the Old Palace. She'd known perfectly well that the noxious powders she'd brought into the townhouse in Miense were intended to leave in the food she took to the warden for Makeready's supposed pleasure. So far as Mistress Stump knew, they had.

If I were Nevan Hasten, Lilz thought, I'd get rid of Mistress Stump. And if I were Mistress Stump, I'd view Fenne as the source of a lifetime's income.

That Mistress Stump had not yet tried blackmail, Lilz thought she understood. She just hadn't thought of it yet. For all her faults, the woman was essentially a pleasant middle-aged widow with a strong urge to please and an instinct for currying favor. The notion of blackmail would occur to her the day news of the way Sir Jen had been buried came out. Lilz toyed with the idea of planting the suggestion in the woman's mind: surely Fenne deserved to pay somehow for Sir Jen's agony!

That Mistress Stump was still alive was more of a puzzle. The dych must have some purpose in mind for her.... Perhaps to use as a sacrificial goat should rumors of poisoning arise? The widow Stump was a handsome woman. Her profession, among other things, made her a familiar figure at the New Palace. Credible that Sir Jen had dallied with her, spurned her for another—Fenne, perhaps?—and that she had her revenge to take. Yes. That would be the way the rumor would go.

In that case, should the costumer try blackmail, she was as good as dead. Lilz sighed. Lucky Greencrags, so soon to be rid of Fenne! Poor Kav Treadwell, with all his honors and riches, so soon to take her as a bride.

At the edge of Oakforest the trail climbed a low hill and turned due east. A rolling landscape of sparsely-inhabited meadowland lay before her, the hills enlarging with distance to an undulating blue horizon. Just the other side of those farthest hills lay Miense, its exact location marked by a smudge of smoke in the still sky. Lilz tapped her heels against Matanda's sides to urge him into his loping walk, a gait he could keep up for hours. She recalled passing a small, neat-looking hostel just at sunset on her way out; with luck it would be a good place to reseal Fenne's letter. At this pace she might reach it by early afternoon.

After a time the trail joined a minor road. The sun was hotter here, but the road easier going. Matanda snorted and picked up his heels. Passing through grassland spangled with asters and goldenrod, Lilz could now see wheat fields far ahead. Tiny peasants sickled the grain and left it in shocks she could just make out if she squinted. Maybe one of the workers would have a waterskin and be willing to give her a sip.

A sweet dry grassy scent filled the air; as horse and rider passed they flushed first a pheasant and then some partridges from the brush beside the road. Lilz was startled by a vague memory of her father and oldest brother coming back from a hunt, the dogs muddy to their bellies and a bundle of pheasants tied by their feet thrown over her father's shoulder. She saw him striding cheerfully down a broad hall with warm pale gray walls, a big, handsome, dark-haired man with a rolling laugh. In the old house, that would be. Back before her father had displeased King Oerl in some way no one had ever explained to Lilz and had been banished, with his family, from the Court. She couldn't have been more than seven years old.

To travel like this, just like this, forever...

Lulled by the steady clip-clip-clip-clip of Matanda's hooves, Lilz envisioned what her life might be if she had grown up in that house with the gray main hall, instead of the tiny, crowded cottage she remembered best. But then she'd be traveling with half a dozen retainers, cooped up in a carriage with a couple of vapid maids stupefied by the impossibility of gossiping in front of her. As far from her present journey as a woman could get...

An hour later she shook herself out of another daydream. The hostel lay at the foot of the hill she had just topped. Lilz touched her heels to Matanda to signal a trot. Five minutes later she turned in at the open gate. The sun had passed its height. A large grassy field surrounded the inn, with no signs posted to say it could not be used, although she saw no other horses. She buckled a restraint from foreleg to rear to keep Matanda from wandering and exchanged his bridle for a halter so he could graze in comfort while she got a meal for herself. The hour was late, the sunny aleroom empty of customers. The innkeeper sat at a table near the back of the room, eating. He looked up from his plate as she entered.

"Ho, goodman," she said. "Can I still get lunch, this late?"

"Certainly, miss." The man set his knife and fork crisscrossed on his plate, glanced at her and straightened them to lie side by side. She pretended not to notice. "Today it's fresh tomatoes, fried potatoes and fried green beans with garlic. Will you have that with a mug of ale?"

"Indeed I will. A large one, please." She dug some coppers out of her pocket to pay for the lunch. The man went to the window into the kitchen and called to the cook. Lilz looked at his plate. He'd been eating the day's lunch himself before making that automatic little gesture that said here, too, was someone who remembered God the

Mother. Common enough among the lower classes, but it implied a certain security. This man was not afraid of spies.

Lilz sat at a small table in a corner and examined the room. The walls and ceiling had recently been whitewashed. The windows were undraped for the summer, their frames painted white. The furniture was plain, tables and chairs without carving or cushions. After the aleroom closed for the day they'd be moved, upended, to mop the red tile floor—from the look of the place, every day. A man who crossed knife and fork over a half-eaten meal to preserve its vital essence would be alert to whizzers. As safe a place as she would ever find.

The innkeeper came to her table and set down the mug of ale. "Is that all, miss?" he asked.

"If you have it, I'll need use of a candle."

He glanced at the sun-struck windows.

"Or other means of heat. To seal a letter."

"Ah." The man went back to the service window and returned with a lit candle, shielding the flame with one hand as he walked. "Are you traveling far?" he asked.

"Only to Miense."

"A pleasant day to ride."

"It is." She kept her face blank, although her tone was friendly, hoping he'd give up the conversation. He already looked puzzled, perhaps by her upperclass accent. Somebody with a rich, fat woman's voice called from the service window. As the innkeeper fetched her lunch, another late-comer entered the hostel and claimed his attention.

Lilz had split Fenne's seal with the sharp knife now sheathed at her waist. Some of the wax still adhered to each side of the paper. While the newcomer completed his transaction she balanced a coin on her fork to warm it in the candle flame and set it on the table. Matching the parts of the broken seal, she placed the folded letter over the coin with the seal uppermost and pressed lightly. The heat of the coin would soften the wax just enough that the pieces would stick together, leaving Fenne's crest intact and the seal apparently untouched. The ruse would never have passed Sir Jen, who would surely have noticed the join, but Kav Treadwell was a very different order of business. He might not even have noticed if she'd left the seal broken.

And if a whizzer had recorded what she had just done?

She couldn't see a whizzer, so no whizzer could see her face. As to whether one had seen her hands, she would have to trust to luck. She put the letter and the cooled coin into her cloak and picked up her knife and fork.

Even cold, the green beans were delicious.

Prince Jath

Lilz seldom found any sympathy for the behavior of nobility, much less for royalty, but when it came to Queen Prenta she had no such difficulty. Like Lilz, the Queen was tall, awkward, angular and not a beauty; like Lilz, she spoke seldom and kept as close to the fringes of activity as she could with any semblance of propriety; like Lilz, she had grown up a stranger to this court; like Lilz, she had an air of mixed self-sufficiency and loneliness about her.

What she had brought to her marriage to Guyr was a womb with a pedigree that strengthened her children's claim to this throne. She had gained precious little besides those children: Jath, the crown prince; Oerl, his younger brother; and Kreshni, a dreamy-eyed girl of whom it was rumored that her mind was not quite right. Given Guyr for a father, Lilz could well believe it. In any case, Queen Prenta treated her children with a fierce protectiveness Lilz thought she understood.

Prenta was the daughter of the king of Travaltia, whose mother had been the paternal great aunt of King Oerl. Judicious inbreeding was the norm for royalty. Even Fenne knew that: she'd once remarked that it was a good thing she wasn't a princess, or she'd probably be stuck marrying Säen, and end up looking like her husband's sister.

Even Lord Säen, in Lilz's never-stated opinion, would be far preferable to Guyr. What it was like to have for husband a man whose fondness for hearty young men was so widely gossiped about, Lilz could well imagine. It didn't matter that the king's demands seemed limited to fawning public attendance, or that his gifts seemed limited to estates and titles and odd jobs about the government. Given his wife's lack of personal charm, other rumor was unavoidable. Especially when the king's private secretary was known to keep a young man for "company in carriage," as the usual euphemism had it.

On the second day after her wedding, Fenne entered the breakfast room and announced that she would be attending at Court that afternoon.

Lady Delle turned from the sideboard still holding the spoonful of creamed barley she had been about to put on her plate. "Today?" She sounded flustered. Lilz, standing behind Fenne, had the impression the iarlena had not considered that her daughter might decide to leave childhood behind quite so soon.

"It's Thornday, isn't it?"

"Yes, but ..." Lady Delle finished serving herself from the breakfast buffet and seated herself. "Fenne, dear, I'm afraid you'll find it all quite boring."

"Why?"

"It's just a bunch of grownups talking about grownup things."

Fenne assembled her sweetest smile. "But Mother," she said. "I'm grown up now, remember? I'm a iarlena, just like you."

A glance passed between Lady Delle and the iarl. "I'm staying home, myself," Lady Delle said. "You won't have a chaperone."

"Lilz can come."

"Lilz!"

Lilz found herself stared at by both Fenne's parents. "My mistress, that isn't entirely appropriate," she pointed out.

"Why not? You talk all right. You could borrow one of Mother's gowns. Who'd know?"

"Sky above!" Lady Delle drew herself up, her fists clenched on the table. "You might consult me before making plans for use of my wardrobe!"

Fenne took a deep breath.

"My mistress," Lilz interjected, "I'm sure not one of Lady Delle's dresses would fit someone so shapeless as me! Even if an old one could be made to do so, I would not wear it. It's not my place."

"There, you see?" Lady Delle smiled. "I've always said Lilz has a good head on her neck."

"Grandpapa can chaperone, then."

The iarl choked on his tea. "The Dych of Summerlea, Secretary to the Privy Council, Lord Treasurer, King's Marshal, Lord of the Armies, and I forget what else—"

"Prime Lord of the Peers Assembled," his wife reminded him. "Minister of the Realm, Lord—"

"—chaperone to a giddy little girl of thirteen?"

Fenne's eyes narrowed.

"Oh, blast it!" The dych scowled at his plate. "Take the girl, Lilz. Shove her into the Hall and leave her. She'll be bored out of her mind and want to come home in half an hour. You can sit in the servant's gallery and read a book if you like—help yourself to the library. That should be good enough."

One of the serving men had melted backward through the door to the kitchen in the middle of this discussion. Lilz, still in the open doorway of the breakfast room, heard another door open into the corridor behind her and someone run down the stairs. A report to the dych, no doubt. Any of the family sitting around the table before her should know the old man would have someone ready to tell him the moment Fenne took it into her head to assert her new place.

Half an hour later, Lilz was readying the elaborate gown Fenne had decided to wear when one of the dych's men knocked on the door of the dressing room. "'S Grace wants you," he said.

Fenne, still choosing her shoes, looked up. "Lilz is my bondservant, not grandpapa's," she said. "She doesn't have to run when he calls."

The man looked confused. "His Grace did say—"

"I'm sure your grandfather won't want to see me for long," Lilz put in. "Perhaps it would be best if I go find out what he wants. You've plenty of time to dress."

"Oh, all right!" Fenne turned back to the shoe rack. "Just remember, I want you to curl the ribbons."

"Ribbons?" the dych's man asked, as Lilz fell into step beside him.

"For her hair. What concerns his Grace, do you know?"

"No. He just told me to get you and be quick about it." The man backed open the door to the dych's suite with an uncertain grin. "Ah—he's not fully dressed."

"Oh, dear. Thanks for the warning."

But the dych, while nothing covered his nether end but a pair of knit silk underpants, was having his dress shirt buttoned when Lilz was shown into his dressing room.

"You sent for me, your Grace?"

He glanced at her. "The green trousers today, Porker, and that brocade jacket I sometimes wear with them. Well, Lilz! I hear the child's determined to attend at Court without her mother, is that right?"

"It seems so, your Grace."

"Who's going, then?"

"Lord Meadowlands has asked me to observe from the servants' gallery. He believes Lady Fenne will become bored soon enough and want to come home."

"She won't." Porker fastened the waistband of the dych's green trousers and started on the fly buttons. "First chance she gets, she'll slip off with Prince Jath, if he'll have her."

"Your Grace?" Lilz said, shocked.

"You"—he pointed at her, shaking his finger at each stressed syllable for emphasis—"are to do nothing whatsoever to interfere, is that clear?"

"Your Grace, the Greencrags faction — "

The dych eased his waistband. "Lilz, you are a servant. Leave politics to one who has suckled life-long at her bounteous breasts." He glared at her. "Yes?"

"Yes, your Grace."

He slid his arms into the jacket Porker held for him and submitted to having his jabot arranged. "Go get Fenne dressed. Make sure she's well slicked up, you understand what I mean?"

"Yes, your Grace." Lilz went slowly back down the long corridor and climbed the stairs to Fenne's suite. The child had been two days married, everyone knew Greencrags had not had a night with her — what could the dych be thinking?

Hoping, she saw. For a prince's bastard to use as a block for his fortress wall, just as he had used his granddaughter. Lilz shuddered.

* * *

But Fenne did not go off with Prince Jath, though she wore her black taffeta with bands of crimson and gold embroidery in the Travaltian style; a crimson underdress with tiny golden buttons, the top two unbuttoned sometime between Lilz's sending her into the hall and her bow to the king; and black and scarlet ribbons curled through her golden hair. Prince Jath wasn't there to go off with. The prince attended upon his mother, who was still resting in her own establishment after the festivity of Fenne's wedding. Once she discovered that, Fenne demanded to be taken home.

Queen Prenta, Lilz speculated, might have matched the Dych of Summerlea move for move had she been king. But the woman couldn't shut herself up in her rooms with her son by her side forever.

"Third time's the charm." Fenne examined herself in the glass, bent forward, turned and took the hand mirror from Lilz to see how she looked from the back. "Well, aren't you going to ask me what I mean?"

"No, Fenne, I think not."

"You're such a prude, Lilz. What do you think of this color?"

"It gives you a glow."

"You're not just tired of me changing clothes, are you?"

"No, of course not." The oakleaf-green silk was the fourth dress Fenne had had on that morning. "If you would move your foot, my mistress?"

"Oh, sorry." Fenne stepped aside so Lilz could pick up the third dress—a pink and white satin stripe Fenne had declared made her look like a peppermint candy, stepped out of, and left crumpled on the floor. While Lilz put the dress on a hanger Fenne poked through her jewelry collection. "Where are those garnets, Lilz? Have I lost them?"

"No, my mistress. They're right under your hand."

"Oh." Fenne held the narrow garnet collar around her neck and turned to look into the pier glass. "What do you think, Lilz?"

"Very nice."

"It doesn't hide my breasts too much, does it?"

"Not at all," Lilz said. Her tone was far too dry, but Fenne didn't notice.

"Could you find the eardrops for me, please?" Lilz looked into the jewelry box, spotted the dark red glint of one of the eardrops and pulled it out. Wonder of wonders, the other had been clipped with it.

"Is Mother coming today?"

"I don't know."

"I hope not. Last week was just awful, wasn't it? She might as well have put me on a leash. It's not as if anybody interesting was there. Could you clasp this?" Fenne primped her hair as Lilz fastened the necklace. "What's so fascinating about hunting, anyway? I'll do that."

Fenne took the eardrops and fastened one. "I can't see charging around on a horse with a bunch of yelping hounds, getting all cold and wet just to shoot some dumb deer. And with my own brother! Men! What makes them think that's fun?"

"I couldn't tell you, my mistress." Lilz finished combing the few loose hairs out of Fenne's brush and put comb and brush into the kit to take to the palace.

"You don't suppose he'll be hunting again this week, do you, Lilz?"

"Lady Fenne, how could I possibly know what Prince Jath plans?"

Third time was the charm. Lilz glanced through the lattice of the servants' gallery to see Prince Jath standing beside his father, on the other side of the throne from the current favorite, a baron named Stormclouds whose esteem was rumored to be slipping — someone from the north, met on a tour of the country, was to be the replacement, if Coral could be believed. Queen Prenta was still not in attendance.

Lilz looked down. Below her, Fenne walked slowly toward the throne. She made a deep bow to King Guyr, was told to rise, bowed again and strolled toward the women seated on the left side of the hall. Prince Jath said something to his father and bounded down the seven steps. He stood in conversation with Fenne for nearly five minutes, somewhat closer than custom decreed, before returning to the king's side.

Fenne spent ten minutes going from one older woman to another and asking the time, as Lilz could tell by the watches drawn out of pockets and peered at. Then the new Lady Greencrags left by the side entrance to the hall, as if going to use that foul little room.

Five minutes passed. Fenne had not returned.

Ten minutes passed. Fenne had not returned.

Lilz closed her book.

Prince Jath spoke into his father's ear and left the Hall. Ten minutes passed. Fenne did not return. Nor did Jath.

Lilz counted days and got twenty-four. Fenne was fairly regular for a girl her age — she should be safe enough, so far as conceiving went. Would she bleed? She was wearing only two underskirts, and that green silk would take a stain.... But maybe Fenne would remember what happened to the other green silk and think to wear a rag.... Not that Lilz had much hope of that! She opened her book.

Normally Lilz found history fascinating, but not today. Her eyes raced unseeing over the words until she slammed the cover shut, eyelids clenched, and shook her head violently. That contemptible old man! A spider, hanging in his web, ensnaring all the careless little insects going about their insect business...but no, that was unfair. To spiders, who were merely doing what they were meant to do.

An hour later Fenne tapped on the door of the servants' gallery, her hair so disheveled that even Lilz was startled. The back of her gown was buttoned up wrong by three buttons. She carried the garnet necklace in one hand. The eardrops were gone. "Lilz, help me," she whispered.

Two of the other servants in the gallery turned, but Lilz had already pushed Fenne out of sight. She fetched the kit she had brought and led Fenne a little further down the narrow corridor that ran past the gallery into unknown territory. Around a corner, she stopped. "Let's get the dress, first."

Fenne obediently presented her back. The skirt was unstained, Lilz saw as she worked down the line of buttons, slipping each into the correct loop. Perhaps Jath hadn't gone as far as she'd expected.

"Nobody told me it would hurt," Fenne said, dashing that idea. "It still hurts, and I'm bleeding."

"That won't last long," Lilz said. "Are you wearing a rag?"

"Yes, Jath had one in his room." Fenne's voice trailed off. "I guess that means I'm not the first, doesn't it?"

"I'd think it most unlikely that you were. After all, he's nearly eighteen years old, a prince with his pick of the ladies of the Court." Lilz began brushing Fenne's hair.

"Don't bother with all the ribbons, Lilz." Fenne's breath caught. "Just get it neat. I want to go home."

Two nights later, while Lilz lay in bed shading her light so she could read while Coral slept, she heard a carriage stop in the street behind the house. The back door opened and shut. Suspicious, Lilz put on some clothes and went down to Fenne's suite. Fenne had disappeared from her bed.

Lilz gave no alarm. She waited in Fenne's dressing room until the girl returned, close upon morning, drowsy with wine.

"Where were you?" Lilz began unbuttoning as Fenne turned her back. "With the prince?"

Fenne nodded. "Don't tell Mother."

"Fenne, before this goes any farther I must talk to you." Lilz judged her mistress too tired and too tipsy to take in anything of any importance. "Tomorrow when you wake up. There are things you should know. Yes?"

"Yes." Fenne yawned. Her underdress slipped to the floor.

Prince Jath's handsome white teeth had left dozens of tiny red bruises on Fenne's small breasts, on her flanks and pale thighs.

Lilz trusted the Dych of Summerlea would approve.

Chapter Five

In the more rugged country near Miense, the way was cut into the sides of the hills. Tall elms roofed the road; beneath them huge colonies of creeper and redberry had pushed their way through years' worth of fallen leaves, as had the many bright yellow and red mushrooms that caught Lilz's eye as she passed. An occasional timid wood aster looked sick by contrast.

At one point, a dozen or more fat white mushrooms had burst their veils not ten paces from the edge of the road. Forget pharmacists, expensive powders suspiciously like talcum, ever-widening conspiracies growing more dangerous with each new recruit. Given the notion that a man must die, given heartlessness or fear enough to kill him, mushrooms would be the way Lilz would choose: one poisonous cap stewed with some harmless ones, and who could say it had not been a mistake? Those who had died of eating the veiled death often first testified that the flavor was delicious.

Switchbacks, taken at Matanda's own pace, added an hour to Lilz's ride. Dusk had begun to creep out of the hills by the time she saw the town below her. As she neared them she sat tall in the saddle, her knife loosened in its sheath, and clapped the horse into an easy trot to discourage cutpurses.

She passed her youngest brother's shop at the outskirts of Miense—deserted at this hour, of course—and approached the center of town just as a crowd was leaving a theater. Thieves would be thick among them, the going slow, so Lilz took the long way to Hasten House. Her route led her beside the Lynn estuary, Miense's connection to the sea half a day's ride away. The moon was down, the tide low. Garbage washed up on the riverbank made Matanda snort and Lilz pull her cloak over her nose. She left the waterside at the first opportunity, skirted the edge of a park where a brightly-dressed woman called out to her with an unlikely business proposition, and finally came into the courtyard beside Hasten House in the last golden hour of evening. A bell in a nearby tower sounded nine.

"Ho, Gluin," she called to the stable keeper.

"Ho, Lilz. Good ride?"

"As always." Lilz boosted herself out of the saddle and led the horse toward the stable, careful where she stepped. "Milords Ruppet and Cals may disagree, but this is the best riding horse in the stable." She patted Matanda's withers as she handed the reins to the stable keeper.

"To my mind, yes," the woman agreed. "But you know boys. They think it's more manly a ride if they may be thrown at any moment." She stroked the bay gelding's nose. "This horse knows his business."

Matanda stood still, his slotted eyes bland as ever despite this praise, whisking his cropped tail. Lilz chatted with Gluin a moment longer, retrieved her pack, and went into the house through the servants' door. She put her head into the kitchen to say hello to the cook and a kitchenmaid and went on up to the attic.

Coral was not in the room—attending Lady Delle, no doubt—and Aster was at Oakforest with Fenne, so she had a rare moment of privacy. Lilz pulled her clothing chest out from under the bed and opened it.

Her papers were still there, tucked into the back left corner: birth note and orders of servitude; a certificate showing a one-fifth share in the cottage her parents had owned, no longer valid; and a few letters from her brothers, old ones from before the oldest three had taken ship for the new lands; a few more recent from the one who had stayed behind, apprenticed; each wrapped around one or two of Sir Jen's pleas to Kav Treadwell and the whole bundle tied tightly with flimsy-ribbon. She counted the twenty-two white envelopes in the other bundle. They seemed undisturbed.

Lilz pushed the broken whizzer into the pair of rolled-up socks that held her father's signet and got out a change of clothing. Kav Treadwell, lately made Iarl of Northlands, would scarcely appreciate her appearing in the palace to ask for him still stinking of her own and her horse's sweat and clad in dust-stained shirt and trousers, no matter whose letter she brought.

Twenty minutes later, after a sponge bath and a quick re-braiding of her hair, she went downstairs and hunted up a guard to escort her to the New Palace.

When Lilz was shown into his presence, the Iarl of Northlands was at his desk, long legs stretched out with heels dug into the carpet, elbows planted in front of him, clutching fistfuls of his red hair and staring at a sheaf of paper with a ludicrous frown. "Ah, Lilz, just the one I need," he said, with an enormous grin.

"Milord?"

"I've got these papers I can't make snout nor heel of—something Jen Makeready did last year. I'm sure he explained it at the time, but—well—Lady Meadowlands says you're extraordinarily clever, and so does Fe—her daughter. Could you help me figure them out?"

"I'll do my best, milord, if that's what you desire." She handed him the letter from Fenne without comment. He glanced at it and set it on the back corner of his desk. "Milord, have you had news of Sir Jen?"

Northlands sat back. "The man hasn't sent me a word for months. First a great long complaint to tell me how stupid I am and how I'll never amount to anything without him for my brain, and then nothing." He shook his head. "It's insulting," he said, with more sadness than anger.

"Milord." Lilz, still standing, put her hand on Fenne's letter. "I believe Lady Greencrags has written a message of sympathy "

"To me?" Northlands stared at her. She could almost see her meaning take root. "Is Jen dead?"

Lilz nodded.

"When?"

"Yesterday morning, quite early."

"And no one told me?"

"I'm sorry, milord."

"That's..." Northlands wet his lips. "I'm..."

He looked around the room helplessly. It was the chamber of the king's private secretary, his most recent post and the occasion of his iarldom; what walls weren't covered with pleated brocade or the gilt-framed portraits of his predecessors were draped with deep folds of crimson velvet. The desk, an intricate marvel of mahogany and mother-of-pearl, crouched over deep shadow in the middle of a thick rug with a longer, thicker fringe. Over his head ornately carved timbers supported a ceiling of stone scrollwork. Northlands looked back at the desk. "I'm sad to hear that."

"It is regrettable, milord."

Northlands glanced at her, then again at his papers, clearly regretting his impulsive plea for help from a woman who was, after all, merely a servant. Slowly, using both hands, he lined up the edges of the papers he had been studying and set them precisely in the center of the desk. "Thank you for bringing the letter," he mumbled.

"I am happy to serve my mistress, milord." Lilz backed off at the wave of his hand and left the room. She was twenty steps down the corridor before the iarl shouted after her, "Lilz! Lilz! Wait a moment." Lilz turned to go back, but Northlands was hurrying toward her, lamp in hand, making motions for her to stay where she was. When he came up to her he took her elbow and hustled her along with him. They came to a door, which he opened into a small, square-cornered bare room.

"Lilz, how did he die?" he asked, slamming the door behind them. "He was a vigorous man. Prison shouldn't have broken him."

"Milord—"

"Don't worry, there aren't any whizzers here. My office is alive with the blasted things, so I couldn't talk there, but here should be all right." He set the lamp on the floor for better light. Like Lilz, he glanced at each of the walls and the ceiling.

Lilz went to the window slit, saw that it was five sashlengths' sheer drop to the street, and moved into a corner away from the opening. "I saw a report, milord. He wasn't in good health."

"Oh?" Northlands frowned. He looks old, Lilz thought. Much older than the open-faced, freckled youth who had come to Court in such triumph only four years before. Far older than twenty. "A report from whom?"

"A committee, milord, three representatives of the king and three of the Lord Chief Justice."

"But—" He shook his head. "No, Lilz. I haven't seen anything about a committee or a report, and I'm the king's own private secretary."

"It must have been assembled in great haste when the news came. Maybe you weren't available when it was formed," she said, as a sop to his pride.

"Maybe." The iarl paused until his brain had encompassed all this information. He did not look pleased. "You said he wasn't in good health. Did this report say what was wrong with him?"

"Most emaciated." Disbelief bunched up Northlands's mouth. "He was denied visitors through his whole term, you know. Perhaps the lack of conversation drained his spirit beyond the ability of meat and drink to bolster it."

"Well, but—" He shrugged. "Given the reason for his imprisonment—"

Lilz straightened. "Which, milord, you know as well as I had nothing to do with his religion."

Kav Treadwell bowed his head, mouth and eyes clenched. Lilz waited. "No one expected him to die, Lilz." She said nothing. "I had every expectation of seeing him released as soon as the royal commission makes its decision about Fe—about Lady Greencrags's marriage annulment. You must admit that no one could have persuaded him to alter his testimony. He would have destroyed her case."

"Indeed."

"And Greencrags really hasn't made good the marriage."

"Most assuredly."

Kav took a deep breath and looked up. "At least I can see that Jen gets a respectful funeral."

"Milord, it is my understanding that he was buried today, without public witness, in the Old Palace courtyard."

"Like a common criminal? You don't mean that." Northlands grabbed her shoulders. "Lilz! Say you didn't mean that."

"Milord, I'm sorry, but that's what the Dych of Summerlea told me had been planned."

"Told you?"

He'll leave bruises, Lilz thought, fighting not to wince. "When he sent me to tell Lady Greencrags that Sir Jen had died," she explained. Kav's fingers tightened. "Milord, you're hurting me."

"Oh, my good friend!" Not her, but Sir Jen. His grip loosened. He wiped the back of his hand across his eyes and turned away. "Alas," he said. An old word, an old-fashioned word, that seemed to Lilz to echo with loss. "Alas." Northlands turned back to her with more energy. "That old viper! What's he done?"

"Milord, I—"

"Don't dissemble with me, Lilz! You know as well as I do, he's got his slimy fingers in this somewhere. Jen Makeready should still be as healthy as I am! What happened?"

"I am not in the dych's confidence, milord."

"No, but you've got the eyes and ears of a whizzer."

"Hardly!"

Northlands gazed at her a moment. "You didn't ask who I meant. I didn't say a name."

Lilz shrugged.

"But you knew. And you say you don't know what he's done?"

Lilz smiled faintly. "I have been eighteen years in the service of the Hastens, milord. I have learned to be blinder and deafer than water, and as yielding."

Northlands let her go, at last, and Lilz collected her escort to go pay a call on Mistress Stump. A short walk from the New Palace, the house was too small to reflect the woman's very real wealth, but convenient to her profession. Lights still shone in the lower rooms, so Lilz knocked without hesitating.

The houseman allowed her into the hall, though his eyebrows rose when he saw that her clothing buttoned down the front. A few minutes later she was in Mistress Stump's receiving room—not for the first time, but for the first time as her own person and not some bodied-forth shadow of Fenne. It was a comfortable room, the furniture not carved into back-racking griffins and roses but padded and strewn with fat cushions made of a floral tapestry. Heavy velvet drapes hung at the windows and small flowered carpets overlapped on the floor. A fire had turned to coals in the grate. On the mantel, a porcelain clock with a busy tick read ten-thirty.

The costumer entered the room by a second door and glanced at Lilz. "Have you a message?" she asked icily.

"I have." Lilz took the liberty of seating herself; Mistress Stump was forced to sit, too. "One I think you may find of great interest. Sir Jen Makeready is dead."

"Oh." Mistress Stump licked her lips. "When?"

"Yesterday morning."

"I see." The woman swallowed. "Why should I be interested?"

"Because of his condition when he died, and the food you so kindly took to him while he was imprisoned."

A long silence followed. The coals in the grate shifted. Out in the street someone shouted after a friend.

"Are you threatening me?" the costumer asked.

"Threatening?" Lilz echoed.

Mistress Stump flushed. "I'll tell Fenne! I'll go back with you to Hasten House and—but she's not there. Where is she?"

"You'd best ask her grandfather."

"Does Fenne know Sir Jen—"

Lilz nodded. This was not going at all the way she had hoped. "Mistress Stump, I came to tell you Sir Jen is dead so you wouldn't be taken by surprise on hearing it from someone else, perhaps someone who would couple the news with some wild accusation. If you keep your head, nothing need be attributed to you. But you must go very cautiously."

"I—"

"For example, it would be most unwise to remind anyone of your generous trips to the Old Palace. If anyone should mention that you took him food, it would be most unwise to say that it came from Lady Greencrags—she is a Hasten."

Mistress Stump raised her bosom and chin to glare at Lilz down her nose. "You are threatening me."

Oh, dear! Lilz shook her head. "I have your welfare at heart, please do believe me, Mistress Stump. But you can't protect yourself without knowing these things. Why do you think I'm threatening you?"

Mistress Stump leaned toward Lilz with an earnest expression. "You honestly don't know?"

"I don't have the slightest idea. All I came for was to tell you what's happened, so you can plan how to meet any challenges."

"I see." Mistress Stump leaned back in her chair, frowning. "You'd best be more careful, yourself, then, Lilz." She began idly tracing the pattern of a flower on the cushion beside her. "Fenne isn't the first, you know. Her grandfather has had his displeasures, too. How do you think I got dragged into this project of hers?"

Lilz spread her hands. "You've been friendly, and she's really still very much a child. I thought perhaps she'd asked your advice—"

Mistress Stump laughed, shaking her head. "Oh, my dear, my dear! Can you really not know after all your years of service with them what Hastens are capable of? Over twenty years ago I did a favor for one of them and I've been stuck in their web ever since, trying not to struggle too boldly lest that spider of a dych finish me off!"

Lilz glanced at the draperies.

"I'm beyond caring," Mistress Stump said. "I'd be glad if the king knew what that disgusting old man is like! You hear me, whizzers? The Dych of Summerlea—"

"Mistress Stump!" Lilz whispered, horrified.

The woman closed her eyes, squeezing tears onto her cheeks. "I'm fifty-three years old, Lilz, and I'm tired. I'm tired. I'm tired. Forgive me. You'd better go."

Lilz, shaken, went out to the hall and nodded to her escort. As he opened the front door, Mistress Stump suddenly appeared in the doorway of the receiving room. "May I see you a moment longer, Lilz?" she asked.

"Yes, of course."

In a voice so low Lilz had to strain to understand although Mistress Stump spoke straight into her ear, the costumer said, "Those objects. They can be destroyed by dropping them into hot water, should you ever need to do so. I've rid myself of many just that way."

Heart pounding, Lilz drew back and stared at her. "Thank you."

"A hint I had from Summerlea himself. You may as well have one thing of value from that family. Father knows they'll take everything they see of yours." The woman went back into the receiving room. With a nod, she shut the door behind her. The click of the latch sounded far too faint to put a satisfactory end to so upsetting an interview.

A Prince Replaced

The day after she went to the palace to spend the night with Prince Jath for the first time, Fenne slept past noon.

Earlier, Lilz had taken one look at the shadows under her mistress's eyes and decided to let her rise when she would; when the iarlena came by after her breakfast to ask where Fenne was Lilz told her only that her daughter was still sleeping.

"She's not sick, is she?" Lady Delle asked.

Lilz said merely, "I don't think so."

The iarlena nodded thoughtfully and went away. Lilz wondered whether she, too, had been awake when the carriage pulled up behind the house the night before; whether she'd been instructed by her father-in-law to remain incurious—or whether, as seemed most likely, she just had her own affairs on her mind.

Lilz spent part of the morning checking over Fenne's extensive wardrobe, then settled down in the dressing room with a book. She had nearly finished it when she heard a puzzled, "Lilz?"

Book closed over her finger, Lilz went into the bedroom.

"Lilz, I've got a terrible headache." Fenne, lying back on her pillows, pressed her fingertips to her temples.

"Yes, my mistress. I'm not surprised. Do you wish some willow tea?"

"Just some water, I think. I'm so thirsty!"

Lilz went to the kitchen for a pitcher of freshly-pumped water and returned to find Fenne sitting on the edge of her bed, her bedgown pulled up, tentatively pressing at one of the bruises on her thigh.

"Lilz, he bit me," she said.

"Yes, I saw."

"Is that — ? I mean, does every — ?"

Lilz poured a glass of water for Fenne and sat on the window seat across from the bed. "No, my mistress."

"He says so. He says, look at cats. The torn always bites the quean in the act. But doesn't she always give him a swipe with her claws afterward?"

Lilz crossed one ankle over a knee, gathering words. "Do you remember last night, Fenne? I said I wanted to talk to you today."

"I don't even remember coming home."

* * *

The carriage came again that night. Lilz heard the house door
close and went down to Fenne's dressing room to wait. Once again,
cocks were crowing before her mistress returned; once again, the
girl was drunk; once again, fresh red marks of teeth had appeared
on her fair skin.

"Is this what you want, Fenne?" Lilz asked, the next afternoon.

"He's...oh, Lilz, I don't know what I want! But he's the crown prince!
Everyone would be so jealous if they knew."

"If they knew everything, my mistress?" Fenne shrugged and
didn't answer. That evening she returned early. Her monthly flow had
begun, to Lilz's secret relief; a week's respite from midnight carriages
would surely follow.

But there was Thornday's open Court to be endured.

The moment Lilz arrived in the servants' gallery she knew from
the hushed excitement that something extraordinary was in the air.
Given her own preoccupation, she stifled a gasp — had Fenne's liaison
with the prince become gossip so soon? But no, it was something far
more unusual: when she went to the lattice she saw a new favorite
standing beside the king.

"What happened to Baron Stormclouds?"

"Sent home to sulk, I suppose," the body-maid next to her said.
"This one's better-looking, don't you think?"

"Mmhmm. Younger, too."

"Sixteen, they say."

"Really!" Lilz stared through the lattice. The new favorite was a
well-built, red-haired young man with a quick grin and an aura of
eagerness that made her smile even at this distance. Prince Jath
leaned often across his father to say something; once the favorite
replied and both men roared with laughter in which King Guyr joined
as raucously as if he were their age. Lilz caught the glint of red jewels
pinned to Prince Jath's cap. Fenne's eardrops? Sky above!

"What's the new man's name?" she asked.

"Kav Treadwell. A Far-kin—one of what they call thegns, but not
a real peer. They say the king met him on that trip to the northern
provinces last summer—you know how glum the baron has been
looking ever since."

"True."

There'd be a high gale and a lashing rain from the Stormclouds
faction next the Privy Council met, Lilz thought. Unless—

"How long has he been here?"

"They say since Moonday."

Had been high gales—Lilz wished she'd been a whizzer under the
king's table at the four Council meetings since Moonday. Treadwell
would not have been there, of course; like Stormclouds and two others

before him he would be introduced to these things slowly. But surely the ousted favorite's supporters had had a great deal to say.

Some petitioner was approaching the king. While King Guyr's attention was engaged, Prince Jath made a remark to Treadwell and descended onto the main floor. He stopped to talk to a peer on the men's side for a moment, then made his way to Fenne.

Their conversation seemed to go on forever. Twice Jath touched the jewels pinned to his cap. Long before the conversation ended — not until his father called the youth away — other quiet talk had begun around them; glances darted their way; the women of Lady Delle's generation stretched their necks to see where Fenne's chaperone might be.

"That's Fenne Hasten, isn't it? The new Lady Greencrags?" the woman next to Lilz asked. "Aren't you her bondservant?"

"That's right."

The maid nodded at the lattice. "Something going on there?"

"Not to my knowledge."

"Where's Greencrags?"

"He's been sent to the university at Chrems."

"Oh," said the other servant. "Really? What will he come home to?"

"His wife," Lilz replied firmly.

Two days later, the midnight trysts began again. Lilz could only hope that her talks with Fenne had been understood, that the girl would take what precautions she could, and that the dych's hope of a connection through the royal blood would be frustrated. For a while, at least, they were.

A small noise woke Lilz. Fenne was in the dressing room. She looked dazed. As Lilz straightened in her chair, Fenne held her arms out as if to be undressed, but when Lilz went to her the girl leaned against her breast without a word.

"Fenne?"

"Help me, Lilz."

This time the prince had drawn blood in several places. Lilz got a bedgown over Fenne's head and her arms into the sleeves. It was like dressing an infant. The wine fumes were almost enough to addle her own head. No sooner did she have her mistress ready for bed than the girl threw up. Lilz held her head over the chamber pot until she was done, then changed her bedgown and cleaned up. Fenne huddled at the top of her bed, moaning. Lilz offered water.

"A little." Fenne sipped maybe a teaspoonful. "Oh, Lilz, I don't want to go to him again!"

"My mistress, I see no reason why you should."

"I'm scared."

Scared or not, Fenne went suddenly to sleep. Lilz tried to rouse her but only got pushed away in response. She turned the bed down the rest of the way and eased Fenne into it, biting her lips with anger as she thought of the dych.

Lilz counted up. Seven weeks, now; Fenne had gone through two menstrual periods without mishap. She'd have thought the prince would be tired of her by now, but maybe the combination of beauty and complaisance held him? Lilz could not imagine what the Dych of Summerlea thought he was accomplishing.

Next morning, Fenne woke a little earlier than usual. She wanted breakfast, too, for a change; creamed barley and a cup of tea. Lilz fetched both from the breakfast room, where only Ruppet was eating. "That for Fenne?" he asked.

"Yes, milord."

"What's the matter with her lately?" Lilz glanced at him, not sure what to say. "I hear a lot of gossip at Court," Ruppet went on. "She should be more careful."

"I'll tell her you said so, milord," Lilz said, and left Lord Ruppet gazing after her with blue eyes wide and his mouth open.

Fenne took the tray onto her lap and drank half the tea. "Have you told Mother about me and Prince Jath?" she asked.

"No, my mistress. You told me not to."

"Oh, Lilz, what am I going to do? He's so good-looking! How can someone so handsome be so mean?" Fenne paused to eat a spoonful of the barley. "I don't want to go to the palace ever again. I wish I could just go back to Summerlea."

She sounded so mournful that Lilz reached out and touched her hand. Fenne smiled. "You're always here, Lilz. What would I do without you?"

"I don't seem to be much help at the moment, my mistress."

"Who could?" The question was dull: she didn't expect an answer.

"What about your grandfather?"

"Grandpapa?" Fenne winced. "I'd just die. After he was so happy about me marrying what's his name, that Rovvo? He'd probably hate me if he found out about Prince Jath."

"As a matter of fact, he already knows." Fenne stared at her. "He told me he expected you to go off with Prince Jath the day you first went to Court."

"He talked to you, and not me or Mother?"

"His Grace ordered me not to interfere." Fenne blinked. "I think he considers your, mm, liaison with Prince Jath a political advantage, as it probably is. But your grandfather's a master at politics—so if anyone can think of a way out, he's the one."

"I can't talk to grandpapa." The girl shook her head. "I'd just die."

Fenne finished her breakfast. In the middle of putting on her everyday shoes she said, "All right, Lilz. I'll go to grandpapa. But you come with me, please?"

* * *

This necessitated a complete change of clothing for both of them: the dych was in his office at the New Palace, so Fenne needed a Court gown and Lilz, at the least, pants and a shirt that reflected her mistress's wealth. They waited in the anteroom, Fenne clutching Lilz's hand, for the under ambassador from Galtriva and his official translator to leave.

Vikent Quickhunt, the dych's secretary, at last ushered them into the private office. He set a gilt armchair in place for each of them. Fenne dragged hers as close to the other as it would go and plunked down next to Lilz. "Your pardon, milady," Quickhunt murmured, although his right eyebrow twitched. He went to his own desk behind a curtain to take notes, as if they were ordinary people with ordinary business.

"Grandpapa, send him away," Fenne demanded, flushing.

Frozen in the act of sitting, the vikent looked at her with both eyebrows raised.

"Out, Quickhunt. And shut the door."

Everyone watched the vikent leave, with a grave bow as he closed the door. "Grandpapa, are there whizzers?" Fenne whispered.

The dych cast a glance at the arched ceiling with its profusion of gilt plaster flowers and chuckled. "Not unless they came in with you, moppet."

Fenne shuddered and pressed her hands to her mouth. Summerlea looked at Lilz. "What's this about? You'd think the girl had a state secret."

"In a way, she does, your Grace."

Fenne started to sob. She leaned across the arms of the chairs and pressed her face into Lilz's sleeve. The dych's face went blank with surprise. "What's going on?" he asked. "Why's she crying?" He got up and went to Fenne, who sat up and buried her face in her hands. "Fenne, sweet, what's wrong?"

"He—" Fenne gasped. "He—"

"He? What he? Quickhunt?"

"No, your Grace, not Quickhunt."

The dych turned to Lilz, holding Fenne's hands. "Lilz, what is this?"

"A young man you and I discussed shortly after Lady Greencrags's wedding took the expected interest," Lilz said carefully.

"Ah." His tongue touched his upper lip as he nodded, exactly as if he had just sighted one of the Summerlea cook's lemon cream cakes. Lilz wanted to slap him.

"He has been most attentive since, your Grace," she said. "I don't know if you've heard a carriage that stops behind Hasten House most nights?"

"I wondered," the dych said.

"And returns near dawn?"

"A fine young man." The dych smiled down at his granddaughter. "Very selective, by reputation. A connoisseur of feminine beauty. You should be proud."

"I don't think he's so fine," Fenne said. "He bites."

"He what?"

"He bites." Fenne pulled up her elegant skirts to exhibit the inside of one firm thigh. "See?" Toothmarks in all stages of bruising showed, from last night's fresh red through purple to pale yellow-green. Fenne pushed her skirts back over her knees. "Lots of other places, too."

"Prince Jath did that to you?" Nevan Hasten seemed genuinely shocked: in the light from the long north-facing windows his face looked almost parchment-white. His eyes met Lilz's over his granddaughter's head. She wondered what he was thinking. The one time he had called her into his bed, Lilz had been frightened and distressed, and the old man too hasty even to notice she was still a virgin, but he certainly had not bitten her.

"Sky above!" the dych exclaimed now. "My sweet child, didn't you protest?"

Fenne nodded. "I did, but he won't stop. He says it's better. He says I'll come to like it."

"Last night he drew blood," Lilz remarked.

"Oh, my moppet!" The dych pulled Fenne from her chair and hugged her tightly. "Why didn't you come to me the first time?"

Lilz said quietly, "Think, your Grace. She'll be fourteen next month. He is the crown prince."

"Yes. Yes." The dych, stroking Fenne's hair, looked off into space. "Tonight I will meet the carriage."

"Grandpapa, be careful," Fenne said. "Didn't you hear what Lilz just said? He's the prince! He says everybody has to obey his father, and him, too. He says—"

"Jath's an imbecile. The king rules by the will of the Peers Assembled. We are not without teeth. We have chosen outside the strict succession before and we can do so again."

Lilz gasped. Jaw set, Summerlea tightened his arms. "Guyr is king by my proclamation—as Jath will never be, not by mine, not by your father's, not by Ruppet's. No Hasten will place the scepter in his dirty little hand, I promise you, Fenne. He forgets our ancestral right—"

"Grandpapa!"

"Did I squeeze you too hard? I'm sorry."

So there are limits to his tolerance and guile, Lilz thought. I hope he won't come to regret them.

Someone tapped on the door. Quickhunt opened it and leaned in. "Your Grace, the man from Godwit and Chantwell is here about that chair with the loose leg. What shall I — "

"I'll loosen your leg if you don't learn to wait for my word when you've knocked, Quickhunt! Just give the man the chair."

As she and Fenne walked toward the palace entrance they passed a man struggling to carry Summerlea's huge walnut chair. No one Lilz knew.

Of all days, that was the one on which the first letter from Greencrags arrived. Fenne skimmed it and threw it away. Later, Lilz retrieved the crumpled sheet of paper. Oh, how he must have sweated over this! she thought, reading the charming, painful declaration of love and longing. She would have to make sure Fenne replied.

Later that week, on Satingday night, the Dych of Summerlea gave a dinner party. Among those attending were Sir Kav Treadwell, the king's new favorite; his mentor, Sir Jen Makeready; two iarls from the near counties, Oakforest and Riverbend, and their wives; a rather dazed-looking Quickhunt; the Iarl and Iarlena of Meadowlands; and their daughter Fenne Hasten, Lady Greencrags, who was seated across from Sir Jen, resplendent in her black taffeta and the ruby necklace.

Nothing was spared. Lilz sat the whole evening at the top of the stairs listening to the musicians playing in the hall below, a rare treat.

As the other guests were taking their leave, she saw the dych gesture to Sir Jen Makeready to stand aside. The man stayed late.

Chapter Six

With Sir Jen Makeready dead, the Dych of Summerlea moved rapidly to secure Fenne's separation from Greencrags, as Lilz discovered the day after she had returned from House-Among-Oaks.

She was in one of the third-floor storerooms working on an inventory of the possessions Fenne had moved out of Standfast House when Coral appeared to tell her that the iarlena wanted to see her.

"She would." Lilz looked up from her dusty listing of assorted crockery. "Can't you put her off?"

"I don't think so. Lilz, there's a palace guard in the main hall."

Her heart lurched. "To do with me?"

Coral glanced behind her, as if she expected the guard to have followed her up to the storeroom. "I—Lady Delle didn't say, but she called for you right after he showed up."

"I guess I'd better wash my hands, then." Lilz tried to look unconcerned as she stood up. "Tell her I'll be right down."

Coral went down the stairs. Lilz ran back to the servants' quarters, teeth clenched against a fit of nerves. Sky above! Had someone connected the savory custards from Hasten House with Sir Jen Makeready's long decline after all, and hooked her name to the obvious inference? She rinsed the dust off her face and hands and rebraided her hair. Staring at the frightened woman in the mirror, she remembered that she was wearing her oldest clothing. She thought of the palace guard and the Hastens' reputation and pulled on a decent-looking blue shirt and trousers, and followed Coral down the stairs to Lady Delle's sitting room by ten minutes.

The iarlena sat near the window. She held a piece of stiff paper in one hand; with the other she stabbed a needle into the embroidery on her lap without looking at it or taking a stitch. The paper was trembling.

"You called for me, milady?"

Lady Delle gave her a glance of pure terror. "This is a summons." The iarlena cleared her throat. "From King Guyr. It's for you."

Lilz felt her jaw sag.

"The royal commission wants you to testify about Fenne and Greencrags."

Relief almost unhinged her knees. "Very well, milady."

"There's a palace guard in the hall. You're to go with him, right now. Oh, you'd better take this." Lady Delle held the paper out to her. "Lilz, please? Be—what's the word? Circumspect? For Fenne?"

"I'll be as careful as I can, milady."

"Oh, I know," Lady Delle sighed. "But I do sometimes worry." She looked down at the embroidery on her lap and tugged at the silk still threaded through her needle. Frowning, she touched her index finger to her pattern and set another stitch.

Lilz went out to the center hall and presented herself to the guard. He nodded, his eyes cold with boredom. They went into the street without speaking, Lilz trying to read the summons, which was written in the Old Hand and full of wherefores and whereases, as she walked. The gist was that she was to appear immediately and without preparation before the commission. She wondered whether washing her face and changing her clothes counted as preparation—but then, she'd done that before she had the summons in hand.

The palace guard strode on ahead, looking neither right nor left, trusting everyone else in the street to notice his crimson, ivory and gold uniform and get out of his way—as, of course, they did; street vendors shouting warnings to others as they scurried into the street with their barrows to clear the sidewalk before the guard's imperious stride, horsemen in the street yanking their mounts aside to avoid trampling the scurrying vendors, casual pedestrians tripping over beggars in their haste to get out of the way, beggars fleeing down alleys; even the pigeons scuttling along before his marching feet and at last wheeling into the air with a great gray flap of wings. All eyes seemed on Lilz as she hurried to keep up in the guard's wake. She kept her own gaze on his heels and wished the commission had simply sent a messenger to tell her to come.

The panel was not meeting in the Ceremonial Hall, but privately in a smaller chamber down the maze of corridors to the right. Even this chamber was large and lofty, clearly intended to impress: tall, broad windows opening onto a courtyard were glazed with leaded panes in geometrical designs recalling lace-work. Intricate velvet drapery hung behind the table where the five members of the commission sat; behind the curtains would be a desk or two where secretaries were recording the proceedings. The floor was carpeted in deep red with a small black diaper pattern calculated to draw the eye of a witness and distract his attention from what he was saying, on the theory that truth would then out. When Lilz entered, Stone, Standfast's body-man, was crouched in the witness chair.

"Take her out in the hall," called the head of the commission, an ancient, colorless cleric in a black robe. "We'll tell you when we want her."

The guard turned on his heel. Lilz had to back hastily into the hall to get out of the way. Someone inside the room closed the door.

Once standing in the corridor, the guard cast her a sideways glance, as if to say, "Nobles!" Lilz let the bait slide by. Surely more than one whizzer was stationed in the carvings of the ceiling, ready to take to the king the least critical remark.

A full half-hour passed before Stone emerged from the room, looking wrung out. He rolled his eyes heavenward as he caught sight of her, but the start of a smile disappeared when the guard raised a finger; Stone went on down the corridor without a second glance. A page put his head around the door and called for Lilz. As she seated herself in the witness chair she assessed the commission. Two of the men she recognized: hand-picked by Nevan Hasten, without possible doubt. The other three she wasn't sure of. Two were clerics, a class whose politics she knew little about. Greencrags sat to the side of the room, his secretary beside him. For what was nominally the other side of the case, the Iarl of Meadowlands lounged near the back, one foot up on the chair in front of him. He had a paper-rest on his knee, although his own secretary was also nearby.

The chairman of the commission cleared his throat and looked at Lilz as if examining something not quite identifiable found in the bottom of his soup bowl.

"You are Lilz, bond-servant to Fenne Hasten, Lady Greencrags, purchased for her service by Nevan Hasten?"

"I am."

"You have received the summons and have heard it read to you?"

"I have the summons," Lilz replied. "No one read it to me."

The cleric sighed dramatically and leaned back in his chair. "Could one of you come tell this woman what the thing says?" he asked the curtain.

"No need, sir. I've read it myself."

"You can read?"

"Yes."

The cleric raised his eyebrows and shuffled through the papers in front of him. "Ah, yes, I see—it says here that you've been educated. Most generous of the Hastens."

Lilz decided Fenne would draw more advantage from her testimony if she herself seemed less tightly connected to the family. "Your pardon, sir." She waited for his chin jerk to invite her to speak. "I was educated before the Hasten family bought me."

He peered at her near-sightedly. "And have an apt tongue, to my ear." The man to his left, one of the Hasten choices, caught Lilz's eye and shook his head. Get off this line. Some political echoes here she didn't know about?

"Yes, sir," she said. That earned a nod from the dych's man as he leaned back out of the view of his fellow commission members.

"No-ow." The chairman hunched forward and glared at her from under thick white eyebrows. "You are aware that this commission has been charged with finding whether any basis exists for the annulment of the marriage between Fenne Hasten, daughter of the Iarl of Meadowlands, and Rovvo Standfast, Iarl of Greencrags. The charge, without legalistic terminology which you cannot be expected to understand and which I shall therefore eliminate, is that Greencrags is sexually impotent and unable to consummate the marriage, which, having continued four years without penetration or issue, should therefore be declared void, returning each of the parties to the status of never-married persons free to seek other spouses." All of this was said extremely rapidly, on one breath. The chairman raised his eyebrows to look at her without raising his head. "Is that clear?"

"Yes, sir."

"Hmm." The chairman lifted his chin. "Meadowlands!"

Lilz turned to see the iarl jerk upright. The chair in front of him fell over.

"You think this girl understood all that, milord?"

"Oh! Oh, yes." Fenne's father straightened the chair. "Lilz understands everything." The cleric stared at him. He shrugged. "Everything you say to her, I mean."

Including legalistic terminology, Lilz thought, facing the commission again. The cleric sat rubbing his chin. Did he think she'd been coached?

She detected Nevan Hasten's hand in the questions that followed: she was asked to confirm that on visits to other great houses Fenne and Greencrags had kept to opposite edges of the huge beds they had occupied, but not how she knew; she was asked to confirm that at home they had kept to their separate suites and that she had been one of the personal servants with whom Fenne had surrounded herself.

"And Greencrags made no attempt to call her into his bed or to come into hers?" the chairman of the commission inquired. Lilz looked for her cue from the man to his left.

"No, sir."

The chairman glanced at Greencrags. "Most remarkable, milord," he said dryly. "Having met the lady in question and had the great pleasure of her conversation on several occasions, I find your lack of enthusiasm nothing short of astonishing."

He turned again to Lilz. "And was Lady Greencrags not upset at this failure of attention on the part of her husband, after so many years of virtuous waiting?" A nod to his left.

"Yes, sir, most distressed." She glanced at Rovvo Standfast. The young iarl met her eyes with the faintest of smiles.

With that came courage: Lilz would never have believed she could lie to a royal commission quite so calmly. She had given simple answers to questions so phrased that her answer could be indicated by the gentleman leaning back in his place beside the chairman. At the end of her testimony, Lilz could see no reason why the young woman Nevan Hasten had procured to prove Fenne's virginity would not be examined — heavily veiled and speechless with outraged modesty, to be sure — by two elderly peeresses who didn't know Fenne and two midwives in Hasten's good pay, exactly as arranged. The only time she disobeyed her cue was to say she was sure that Greencrags kept no man in his retinue for company in carriage. At the frown of the man to the chairman's left she added that she doubted any such inclination on Greencrags's part. Help rid the youth of Fenne, yes. Tarnish his attraction for other women forever, no.

But she feared no reprisal from Nevan Hasten, who while he practiced fairness only when convenient did not object to it in principle. Greencrags would soon be free. So would Fenne. That was what mattered.

An hour passed before Lilz was excused. She went into the corridor to discover that the palace guard had been detailed to flaunt his crimson, gold and ivory glory elsewhere, and she had been left to her own wit to find her way home.

Her path out of the palace led her near the Iarl of Northlands's office before turning aside. At the turn, she was surprised to find him waiting for her.

Treadwell touched his forefinger to his lower lip for silence and beckoned her to follow him into the same bare little room they had talked in the night before, now bright with sunlight. "I thought you'd never get out of there. You've testified?" Lilz nodded. "How did it go?"

"Not badly, milord."

Northlands blew a sigh up his face. "Should be decided in the next couple of days, don't you think?"

"I don't see why not, milord."

"Good." The iarl looked around the room. As last night, it contained no whizzers and no furniture. "Do you mind sitting on the floor, Lilz?"

"Sitting on the floor?"

He pulled a few folded pages out of his inner jacket pocket. "It's these—I started to ask you about them last night. You've been with the Hastens so long, you must know everything that goes on in the palace. These are notes Jen made about something—" Kav Treadwell, standing as little upon ceremony as ever, plunked himself down on the floor. "Could you look?"

Lilz hunkered beside him and took the papers. As she scanned them she realized that these were notes Sir Jen had meant no one else to see, but that he'd written in a sort of code in case someone should. "Where did these come from?" she asked, frowning.

Northlands colored. "I was going through Jen's library, looking for something he quoted to me once, and these fell out of a book."

"So...?"

He shrugged. "A couple of phrases caught my eye, you know how it is. They were so strange I stopped to read it all. And the whole thing is—look at it. I got curious."

"I see." Lilz smiled to take the edge off her frown and looked back at Sir Jen's notes. One thing seemed obvious: he'd had some kind of knowledge he planned to use as a lever to power. But what knowledge, about whom?

"What do you think he meant by 'Those who wish to remain secluded within the dawn-tinged granite circle'?"

"I thought maybe some religious order?" Northlands suggested. "He makes all those appeals to the Father."

"Perhaps, milord." Lilz felt herself frown: no. Not religious orders. The back of her mind was trying to tell her something. "Do you know of a cloister built of granite? On the east coast, perhaps? Or on a hill?"

"No, see, that's just what puzzles me," Kav said. "Generally cloisters are just thrown together with whatever kind of stone happens to be in the district, aren't they?"

"I don't know, milord."

"The ones I've seen have been limestone. Granite's imported, I think, isn't it? I've seen it in the tonnage lists."

"True, one sees it rarely."

"And what are these people supposed to be doing? I can't figure it out. It sounds like Jen was upset, though, doesn't it?"

Lilz re-read the page. *The power to speak loudly when they choose.* But what would they say? *Seeing and hearing wheresoever they will—*Ah! That must be the king, with his inhumanly loud ceremonial voice and whizzers everywhere. But the notes were personal; dates of no significance to her, abbreviations she couldn't put words to; oddly phrased appeals—no, references— to the Fathergod, senseless as they stood. An occasional word in Travaltian posed no problem; her education was broader than Nevan Hasten suspected and the words were everyday words. But the contexts seemed odd...here Makeready was talking of gates, *antranta*, in the sky?

"It doesn't make much sense to me, either, milord," she said. "At most, this phrase"—she pointed it out—"refers to whizzers, and this to the king's ceremonial voice."

"Oh, that," Treadwell said dismissively. "That's just the Jewel of the King. Jath and I played with it once, and Guyr nearly skinned us alive."

I should think so, Lilz thought. "Do you mean that the Jewel makes his voice louder, milord?" she asked, uncertain whether she had understood. "I had always understood the voice to be a gift of the Fathergod."

Treadwell nodded. "That's what the people are told, yes. But the jewel's a device anyone can use. It doesn't have to be Guyr."

"Sky above," Lilz murmured, shaken.

Now Treadwell wriggled uncomfortably. "I shouldn't have said anything, truly." No, Lilz thought. Enough to get you hanged by your bowels should Guyr find out how your mouth's running.

"Please forget it." Kav cleared his throat. "Look at the next page."

She wondered whether the Jewel also contained tiny rainbow-studded sheets of crystal or flat metal pills marked with odd symbols, and where it had come from, but a mere servant could scarcely interrogate the king's secretary. Resigned to ignorance, Lilz looked at the next page. Halfway down the page a phrase leapt to her eye: *No one comes to power without walking the blue carpet.* Ah?

She glanced up. "Milord, do you know the part of the palace with the blue carpets?"

"There isn't one."

"There used to be."

"No."

"Yes, four years ago—"

Northlands shook his head. "I asked King Guyr. He laughed at me—wanted to know if I'm colorblind, to get an idea like that. The royal color is crimson and always has been, he says."

Lilz frowned at Northlands. He seemed quite sincere; in two years she had never known that transparent face to hide the slightest feeling. "I *saw* a corridor with blue carpet, milord."

"Where?"

"Here, in the palace. After Fenne's wedding, during the masque. She needed help with her train to pee, and going back to the servants' gallery I got lost and ended up somewhere with blue carpet—"

Northlands was shaking his head. "No, Lilz. I told you. You must be thinking of some other place."

"I heard some people speaking a strange language," she insisted. "They were—or one was—surprised to see me—"

"Ambassadors," Northlands said, shrugging. "All of them were invited to that wedding. I heard all about it from Fenne, believe me. The only person present she didn't take any notice of was Greencrags."

Lilz read through the three sheets of paper again. As best she could make out, someone somewhere was using someone for some purpose without telling them, all to the discredit of King Guyr. Somehow Makeready had intended to use this knowledge to break the strength of the Hasten faction at Court, so he could consolidate Kav Treadwell's power and therefore his own. But who were these people?

"Hmmp." Lilz frowned at the page, reading it over yet again. Not the slightest clue to who they were. "I'm sorry, milord," she said, handing the document back. "I can't make snout nor heel of it, myself."

"If you think of anything, you'll tell me?"

"Yes, milord." She hesitated. "I'd keep this out of the Dych of Summerlea's hands, were I you."

Northlands snorted. "Him? I wouldn't tell him the latest price of bread in the Miense market!"

"You do understand why he's helping you with the annulment, don't you, milord?"

"Of course I do. He told me—I'm a stalking goat. But he's got a shock coming. I'm not as malleable as he might think."

No, but he's a good deal craftier than you, Lilz thought. And he has what you want: Fenne.

Lilz found her own way out of the palace. As she descended the outer steps past the magnificently-uniformed guards, she caught her heel on the edge of a tread and looked down. She was walking on pink granite.

She entered the courtyard of Hasten House to a commotion that drove all speculation out of her head. In the unpaved area beside the stable Gluin struggled with one of Summerlea's prized horses, an always-nervous creature now plunging and rearing, white-eyed, with a shrill neigh the like of which Lilz had never heard before. The dych ran from the house as she opened the back gate, followed by one of his men. Every horse in the stable seemed to be whinnying.

The old man took the lead from Gluin. He talked to the horse, loudly at first, then more silkily as the beast calmed. Lilz approached slowly. Now she saw what was wrong: a sickening curve in the left front leg where the cannon bone should have been straight and strong.

Summerlea murmured on. The horse stood still, trembling on its three good legs. The dych said something to Gluin, who went into the stable to quiet her other charges.

The dych's man handed him a pistol. Summerlea clutched the beast's halter and pressed the muzzle of the gun to its skull. The horse skittered sideways. Summerlea followed. There was a loud crack. Blood and brain flew. The horse gave one last high scream and fell. The old man danced back from the slashing hooves. In seconds, the animal was still.

"Send for the knacker, Gluin," Summerlea called into the stable. "It's over." He handed the pistol to his man, turned, and caught sight of Lilz where she stood frozen.

As he came up to her she saw tears on his wrinkled cheeks. "Lilz, my dear, I'm so sorry you happened to see that," he said softly. She couldn't respond. "I'd so rather have put him out to pasture," the dych went on. "But these breaks never heal, as you know. We just have to convince ourselves that quick and clean is best."

He put an arm across her shoulders and guided her into the house by the side entrance. "Go sit down in the back parlor, hmm?" he told her. Five minutes later the houseman came to where she sat beginning not to shiver and presented her with a large glass of brandy on a silver salver.

"His Grace says drink this and do as you please the rest of the afternoon," he announced incredulously. "What's that all about?"

Thornday, and Then

Early in the week after the dych's dinner party the weather turned cold. On Thornday morning, Lilz woke to hear sounds outdoors muffled and sparrows still quarrelling in the eaves of Hasten House, and knew snow was falling. When she looked out she saw the flakes fat and wet, already turning to slush where feet or wheels had pressed them down.

Everyone seemed as vague and lazy that morning as she felt herself. Lady Delle remarked at breakfast that she thought she'd give attendance at Court a miss that day. Fenne took the opportunity to announce that she'd just as soon stay at home, too. Lilz, at her post in the corner, thought she detected relief. Cals and Ruppet moped over their scrambled eggs and decided not to go out to the hunting lodge after all.

"You could use this time to catch up on some of your lessons, my mistress," Lilz suggested as she followed Fenne upstairs after the meal. Fenne surprised her by agreeing. They were in her sitting room struggling with the concept of percentage— Fenne to understand, Lilz to think of a hundredth way to explain—when her pupil looked up and said, "Grandpapa!"

The dych strolled into the room as if he were a regular visitor, though Lilz couldn't remember another such occasion in the past fourteen years. "What are you wearing to Court today, Fenne?" he asked. He sounded very casual. *Oh-oh*, Lilz thought.

"I'm staying home."

"Not this week."

"But grandpapa, it's snowing, and I'm behind on my lessons—just ask Lilz—"

"I think that nice dark green silk I saw you in a few weeks ago. The garnet necklace looked very sweet with it."

"The green silk?" Fenne's face blanched.

"Those eardrops were fetching. I'd like to see you wear those again, too."

Fenne sat mute with shock. After a moment, Lilz decided to speak. "Your Grace—"

The dych stopped her with one raised eyebrow. "I know where they are. She can ask for them back. Going to Court will provide the perfect opportunity."

"Today?" Fenne wailed.

"The sooner, the better." The dych held up his index finger, reducing Fenne to open-mouthed silence. "The carriage will be at the front door at one o'clock."

"Oh, Lilz, what am I going to do?" Fenne cried as the door closed behind her grandfather. "I can't just go *ask* in front of all those people! I'll just die!"

"He's right." Lilz closed the arithmetic book over the vane of her pen and went into the dressing room. "If you ask in private, Prince Jath can say he got all he wanted and tired of you. This way, everyone will know you tired of him, and perhaps think he pressed his suit further than you were willing to go."

"I don't care."

Lilz pulled the green silk out to inspect it. A light pressing was all it needed, thank heaven! "I advise you to do as your grandfather says, Fenne. Remember what he's saving you from."

Silence from the bedroom. Lilz put an iron near the fire to heat, set up the ironing board, and spread the skirt of the silk dress over it.

Fenne stepped out of the carriage at the covered side-entrance of the New Palace, still in a sulk. "I still don't see why Lilz couldn't have pinned together one of your gowns and come into the Hall with us," she said to her mother.

"Lilz, can't you do something with her?" Lady Delle sighed. "Do try to be reasonable, Fenne. You don't have to stay all afternoon—just long enough to ask for your eardrops back."

"I don't want to stay two seconds."

"Sweet—"

"Why can't I just send him a letter?" Fenne twisted her hands together. Lilz heard the seam of a glove give way.

"Your mother will be close at your side, my mistress." Lilz touched Fenne's chin lightly. "Face up, courage up, and remember—you are in the right." They reached the antechamber to the Ceremonial Hall and parted ways.

Standing at the lattice in the upper gallery, Lilz saw Lady Delle and Fenne walk slowly toward the throne. To the side, the other golden chair was also occupied. Queen Prenta was in attendance today: fate conspiring to make everything harder for Fenne. The woman surely had no idea what her son had been up to the past few weeks. How could Fenne pull him aside to ask for her favor back without risking a severe misunderstanding?

Mother and daughter bowed to King Guyr. He nodded. Lady Delle gestured toward Prince Jath, who looked away. Queen Prenta leaned forward and said something to him. Jath's face set.

King Guyr crossed his hands on his breast and made some remark to the two women standing at the bottom of the steps. They drifted toward the ladies' side of the Hall, Lady Delle frowning and Fenne with a hand to her cheek.

Prince Jath left his father's side. Lilz saw Kav Treadwell ask him a question and the prince's stiff head shake. The garnet eardrops were still pinned to his cap.

Fenne and her mother had greeted three other women and were standing in conversation when Prince Jath approached. He grabbed

Fenne from behind, spun her to face him, and kissed her hard. Fenne tried to turn her head away, but Jath had her by the hair. Lilz heard her cry, "Don't!" Jath forced her face toward him and kissed her again. The queen rose from her throne, her hands clasped at her breast.

Lady Delle began dragging at Jath's fingers, still wound in her daughter's hair. Fenne shrieked. The three women who had been talking to them stood with their mouths and eyes rounded. One began to back away. Several others noticed the struggle and stood up. Lilz heard a stir among the petitioners waiting at the back of the Hall, too close under the gallery to see what it was. Someone on the men's side of the hall got to his feet. The Dych of Summerlea. Meadowlands didn't seem to be present.

Lady Delle got Prince Jath's hand free of her daughter's hair. He rammed the heel of it into her mouth. She pressed her fingers to her face, moaning. Fenne half pulled away, but Jath twisted her arms behind her. She pushed her face into his shoulder as he tried to kiss her lips again. Instead, he kissed her throat.

Now Kav Treadwell bounded down the steps and raced up the aisle to the struggling couple. "That's enough!" he yelled. He hauled on the crown prince's shoulder.

Jath let go of Fenne to punch at Sir Kav, who ducked and came back with a blow to the prince's side. "Wait," Queen Prenta shouted. Fenne crawled out of the way and cowered behind a chair.

"The lady wishes to be left alone," Sir Kav said loudly.

"Enough!" The king's magnified bellow made the walls shiver. Everyone but Kav and Jath looked at him. For a moment the hall was dead quiet. Guyr stood up. "Enough!"

Jath took advantage of the surprise to get in a blow to Kav's jaw. Kav sprawled over some empty chairs. Jath laughed. Kav scrambled up and came back.

"Enough!" King Guyr boomed. "Jath! Kav! Do you hear me?"

The queen picked up her skirts and ran down the steps toward her son. She wriggled into the space between the two youths and pushed them apart, glaring. Fenne sobbed; Lady Delle held her mouth. Lilz had to struggle to keep her place at the lattice as the other servants tried to climb over her to see what was happening.

First Kav, then Jath took a step back and dropped his fists. Fenne said something. Jath shook his head. "Please," Lilz heard Fenne say.

Jath turned on his heel and started back toward the dais. "You heard her!" Sir Kav shouted. Jath kept walking.

Kav ran after him. He snatched the cap from Jath's head. Jath whirled and stared at him. Kav started back toward Fenne, his head bent over Jath's cap, taking the earrings off.

Jath grabbed Kav's sleeve and threw a punch that glanced off the side of the younger boy's head. Kav went to his knees. The Dych of

Summerlea started to bend toward him, but the queen pushed him out of the way to stand between Kav and her son.

Several of the men of the peerage had come to help, but only stood about, not quite daring to lay hands on anyone of the royal house. Jath shoved his mother aside.

"Enough!" the king shouted. "Jath, you whelp! Behave!" His magnified rage brought dust down from the ceiling. Several whizzers started circling under the carved stone. One hummed through the lattice into the servants' gallery, where it batted against the rear wall like any ordinary insect. A few of the maids screamed.

Lilz still gaped at the scene below. Sir Kav had sat back on his heels; he worked at the prince's cap. Blood ran from his nose, unheeded. King Guyr stood at the edge of the dais, looking as if at any moment he would take an unprecedented first step downward onto the main floor of the hall. All at once, the Court musicians struck up a lively tune.

Queen Prenta, with Jath by one ear, began to march him back to the dais. Sir Kav stood up. He rolled the prince's cap into a tight ball and hurled it at the back of Jath's head. His aim was good: the cap hit with an audible slap.

Jath turned red. He jerked away from his mother. "I challenge you!" he shouted, holding his ear. "I challenge you, Sir Kav Treadwell! We'll see what kind of swordplay they teach the thegns out in the nether provinces!"

"Jath, no!" the queen cried.

Sir Kav bowed low, accepting the challenge, ridiculous as it was. Fenne was now standing near the aisle. He turned to her and handed her the garnet eardrops. Lilz saw the Dych of Summerlea nod to himself. The music faltered and resumed.

The queen and the prince returned to the dais, while Sir Kav talked to Fenne. A smile flickered over her face. She started to fasten one of the jewels onto her left earlobe. On the dais, a hasty conference among the royal family ended with both parents on their thrones and a sullen-looking prince once more at his father's side.

"Sir Kav," Guyr boomed. "Return to our side. The first petitioner may now come forward."

Half an hour later, the cook of Hasten House stood in the back hall at a total loss. A spoon in his left hand dripped something pale yellow onto the stone floor. In his kitchen, Lady Delle leaned over the sink while Coral held a towel packed with snow to her jaw to stop the swelling. Fenne had been confined to her rooms. His Grace her grandfather paced the front hall in a fury. Lilz kept out of sight on the back-hall side of the open connecting door.

Eventually a messenger came. From the dych the news went to his son, the iarl; from her father to Fenne, and from Fenne to Lilz:

two days hence the king's favorite and the crown prince would fight a duel in the main courtyard of the New Palace.

"Papa says the queen tried to call it off, but the king said Jath can't show himself a coward because he's crown prince." Fenne sagged onto the edge of her bed and sniffled. Her lower lip was fat and her throat bruised, but for once she hadn't complained of any pain. "Oh, Lilz, it's all my fault! I feel so miserable. All I wanted was my eardrops back, and now look! What if one of them dies?"

But the duel was never fought. The next evening, news came that the prince had taken ill with a griping of the gut and the duel had been postponed for a week. Naturally the announcement was greeted with disbelief. That a Far-kin, a mere thegn, didn't know how to behave in Court was not all that surprising, but for a Prince of the Blood to cause the row they had seen last Thornday? Not a few snide comments were made when one peer or another thought himself out of range of a whizzer. What could one expect of one who forced himself upon a tiny beauty, the wife of another, in public? A week hence, a headache; the week after that, a bruised heel—anyone could see how it would go. The servants, more invisible than whizzers, took great delight in passing on each story as it arrived.

To the discomfiture of the gossips, open Court the following Thornday was cancelled. Instead, all Miense turned out with black and purple banners for a state funeral: Prince Jath died late Moonday night.

Rumors flew with the fluttering pennons—the queen maintained that Jath had been poisoned, the whispers said, perhaps by that coward, the king's favorite. That rumor was accurate: Lady Delle had been present when the Queen, raving about "monsters that surround the throne and wish us to believe them men"—rather a harsh judgment on young Kav Treadwell, Lilz thought—had been half-supported, half-carried to her bed chamber by her ladies-in-waiting. One of those ladies, Lady Meadowlands's good friend, Lady Riverside, reported further that the Queen had been given a soporific by the royal physician and woke a day later with no memory of the nerve storm.

The king's physician himself insisted that the boy had suffered a natural digestive disease. In consequence the health officers were put on alert to expect an epidemic. Rats were trapped in the alleys for close inspection. A rift opened within the Privy Council between Treadwell's faction and the queen's; at any moment the Galtrivans were expected to hear of the disarray of the throne and attack.

The disquiet continued for months. By the time the country was settled again, the rumors of poison discounted, the epidemic not suffered after all, the rift healed, and the Galtrivans shown to have placed their troops on alert for fear of an attack from Kinland, Fenne had discovered a new and more tender lover: Kav.

Chapter Seven

The day after Lilz testified, Fenne's stand-in was judged to be a virgin, as expected. The royal commission could only find that Rovvo Standfast, Iarl of Greencrags, had unreasonably failed to make good his marriage to Lady Fenne Hasten and that the union was therefore void. Tem Gudgeon, the Lord Chief Justice, issued the necessary decree that afternoon.

To no one's surprise, King Guyr proposed to give the lady's newly available hand to his established favorite, Kav Treadwell, Iarl of Northlands. Five days passed between the commission's finding and the King's announcement. During that time Lilz had little leisure to puzzle over people walking about on blue carpets within pink granite circles, or what a dead man had meant by notes made for himself more than a year before. The morning after the decision she rode again to House-Among-Oaks with the decree in hand. Then, after joining half-heartedly in a small celebration with her mistress, she organized Fenne's retinue for the return to Hasten House and packed up a small wagonload of assorted possessions for the journey.

She left Oaklands's manor by the front gate this time, jolting along in the carriage with Fenne and Aster and a housemaid borrowed from Hasten House to ease the strain of Fenne's visit on the staff of House-Among-Oaks. The four women arrived weary and seat-sore in the courtyard beside the townhouse near midnight on the Satingday before Presentation Day. Fenne had spent the last third of the journey planning what to wear for the occasion.

On Presentation Day Lilz and Aster sat together behind the lattice of the servants' gallery, a little apart from the body-maids of the girls who had already made their entrances to trumpet flourishes. Aster whispered happily about the bright, elegant gowns worn by the ladies below, *oooing* at each new glimpse. Lilz was bored. Twice while the last girl trod the white carpet, made her bow and was escorted to her seat by a redvest, she had to clench her teeth over a yawn.

Now Guyr stood. Lilz felt her pulse quicken. "Lady Fenne Hasten, come forward," the king boomed.

Fenne rose from her seat among the women of the court and went to the bottom of the stairs, infinitely more poised than she had been at her own presentation four years earlier. The king motioned to her and she climbed the seven steps to stand at his side. "My dear subjects," he boomed. "I have the great pleasure—no, joy—of announcing the coming marriage of this delightful sprite to one of my own heart treasures, Kav Treadwell, Iarl of Northlands."

Eerie! Lilz shuddered. The same words. Only the name of the man had changed. As the audience applauded, she leaned forward to look at the Iarl of Greencrags, seated in his place as a Peer of the Blood. The boy's head was tilted slightly, chin balanced on thumb and knuckle. What could he be thinking as Kav Treadwell came from his post at the side of the throne to stand where he himself had stood four years before? She glanced to her left, looking for Stone. He was smiling at the hall below, a grim little smile, his arms folded.

Again, the wedding would be on the last day of fall. Again, Jonquil the poet had been commissioned to write, not one, but two masques, to be set to music by the equally famous guitarist, Dolphin. The whole fete, so far as Lilz could see from the messages flying back and forth over the next few days, was to be a repeat of the first, but more sumptuous, more extravagant; therefore by necessity more lengthy.

Even Sweetdawn, the residence that had been assigned to Greencrags, would have been transferred to the Iarl of Northlands, had Fenne not objected that she could no more live there comfortably than a fly could swim.

"You know what I don't have, Lilz?" Fenne remarked a few days later, as she reviewed some accounts with her bondservant. "That set of opals. Could I have left them at Standfast House?"

"You'd best ask Aster, my mistress. I wasn't caring for your clothes when we moved. Unless they're in the case?"

"In the case! Why on earth would they be there?" Fenne let the ledger leaf shut and went into her dressing room. She took a handful of necklaces out of the box she kept all her jewelry in and set it on the dresser, the better to stir what remained. Both Lilz and Aster had tried to persuade her to keep each piece in its own padded case, but the empty cases always ended up tossed into a corner in a fit of impatience and the strands of gems back in this box, tangled into the amber and pearls Fenne had owned since childhood. Now Lilz bit back an I-told-you-so.

"Here's an eardrop." Fenne held the diamond and opal dangle beside her face and glanced into the mirror, then tossed it onto the heap of gems on the dresser and went back to pawing the contents of the box. "I don't see the other one, though, and I'm sure the bracelet's not here."

"Aster may know, my mistress. She should be back from her lunch any moment."

Fenne made a face. "Mistress Stump is supposed to be here in half an hour. Guyr's designed a dress for me—"

Lilz wondered whether it would be the same as before.

"I've got to have those opals, Lilz. Guyr's having a necklace made to match. Run over to Standfast House and see if you can find them in my old rooms, yes?"

"Now, my mistress?"

"Why not?"

"Shouldn't you let Lord Greencrags know I'm coming?"

"What for? Just walk in and go look. He doesn't even have to know you're there."

Lilz nodded and went down to the stable for a horse. Matanda was available; with Gluin's help she saddled him up and headed for Greencrags's townhouse.

She went in at the servants' entrance, looked first for the houseman, and found him in his shirtsleeves in the kitchen drinking tea and playing backgammon with the cook. A strong aroma of roasting fowl made her mouth water as she stated her business. "Opals!" The cook reached for the dice, shaking his head.

"A bracelet and an eardrop?" The houseman laughed. "No such luck! I'd be in the south of Travaltia by now, lounging under the palms drinking fine red wine, a fine jolly wench on my knee."

"No luck at all, it looks like," Lilz observed, as the cook rolled spider's eyes and bore off the last of his chips. "You don't have any idea about the opals, Reed? My mistress is much concerned to find them."

"I bet she is, lovey. You could ask Stone."

"Is he here?"

"Upstairs, I think."

Lilz traced an uncertain baritone singing an old folk lay to the iarl's dressing room and quietly opened the door from the hall. Stone was alone, leaning over a hard cushion to pin into shape a lace jabot he'd just washed and starched. She watched with affection.

"You've waxed the pins, I hope," she said.

Stone jumped. "Sky above, Lilz! Don't go sneaking up on a man like that." He greeted her with a long hug. But he'd seen no opals. "Doesn't Aster know?"

"I have no idea. She was eating lunch. My mistress didn't wait to ask before sending me."

Stone chuckled. "They're safe at home, you can bet on it."

"What's safe at home, Stone?"

Greencrags stood in the bedroom doorway. He raised his eyebrows at Lilz. "My mistress is missing a bracelet and an eardrop, milord," she explained, stepping away from Stone. "She thought she might have left them behind."

"Which ones?"

"The opals."

"An ill-favored gem for all its beauty, Lilz. I never did like them." The iarl touched his cheek, where the opal bracelet had left a small scar. "I don't think she left them here. None of the house servants has come into an unexpected legacy, and Stone is—well, Stone is Stone."

"If they should turn up..." Lilz shrugged.

"With sky rockets and a dozen trumpeters, I do assure you."

She grinned. "But not at midnight, if you please, milord?"

Greencrags laughed. "Have I ever disturbed your sleep, Lilz? Even with all my opportunities?"

"Never, milord."

"Let me walk downstairs with you. Did you come on foot?"

"No, milord. I've one of Hasten's horses."

"Ah, good." Greencrags held the door open behind him. Lilz reached toward Stone in farewell as she left. "Lilz, I'm glad to see you," the iarl said. "I didn't know if I'd ever have the chance again."

She raised an eyebrow at him as they went down the wide front stairs side by side.

"I saw Hasten's man dictating your answers last month. What a circus!"

"Wasn't it?"

"My thanks for the comments he found so unwelcome."

"I have my limits, milord."

"I know." Greencrags paused at the bottom of the steps, his hand on the newel post. He seemed to be considering something. "You'll have tied your horse up at the servants' entrance, I suppose." The iarl turned toward the back of the house and pushed through the door to the back hall. There was a scurrying and the kitchen door thunked shut. Greencrags glanced at Lilz, grinning. "Backgammon, again?"

"Reed's trying to win his week's pay back from the cook, I think."

"Much luck to him. He's about a year behind, by now." The iarl opened the outer door. Matanda flicked an ear their way. "Have you, mm, cleansed the horse?"

"Before I came, milord."

Greencrags untied the reins from the hitching post and ran his hand down the crest of the bay gelding's neck. He put a hand on Lilz's arm as she started for the mounting block. "Listen to me," he said, so quietly she could barely hear. "Should you ever need refuge, come to me."

She stared at him. The youth wet his lips. "I know Fenne. I'm sure she could make your life as miserable as she made mine ... or more so."

"Milord?"

"There are rumors ..." He wet his lips again. "Well. Come to me if you need me. Don't hesitate."

"Thank you, milord." Lilz swallowed hard. "But your reputation might be harmed."

"I've thought of that." Greencrags stroked Matanda's nose and leaned against the horse's neck. "But I'd risk it, to have you in my house." He smiled. "You see, I've learned a great deal about self-interest from my former wife."

"I'm afraid I don't understand."

"I mean to make my mark on this court, Lilz. I don't much care if Northlands has a place in it, but I promise you I will break the Hastens." Lilz took a breath, but Greencrags jerked his head sideways and she didn't speak. "Summerlea's a master, yes, but he's seventy-five years old and it's rumored his lungs have the bloody rot. I'm young and healthy. When it comes to politics I have three times the brain of Kav Treadwell. Still, it wouldn't harm me to have the counsel of a Makeready, especially now that the man is gone. You're easily the equal of Sir Jen."

"I am only a servant, milord."

"*Only* a servant, Lilz? I hardly think so." He smiled and stepped toward her. "Leg up?" He locked his hands against his knee. His young face had a sober, ceremonious look that added years.

"Thank you, milord." As if she were still a peer herself, she tucked her toe into his hands and swung into the saddle. Greencrags gave Matanda's shoulder a pat. "Don't discount Meadowlands," Lilz said quietly, looking down at him. "Or Ruppet. Neither is the fool he seems. Remember that Cals hasn't shown his mettle yet. Above all, there are the cousins. Säen in particular."

The iarl's mouth tightened a little; he nodded.

"Look to the future," Lilz said. "Take care not to offend Prince Oerl. Befriend him, if you can."

A pigeon landed in the courtyard and marched toward her with pumping neck and a purposeful look in its reddish eye. What had it overheard? *My dice are cast*, Lilz thought. She touched her heel to the bay gelding's side. *Let's hope I haven't thrown rat's eyes.* She guided Matanda out of the alley and onto High Street with a frown. Were rumors circulating about the way Sir Jen had died? She'd heard none herself.

Fenne would be the first suspect, but would she ever be blamed publicly? Not likely. And Fenne wasn't the only one who had found Jen Makeready a burden. A man seeing death at his heels might fix upon a defenseless alternate. Lilz shuddered.

By the time she got back to Hasten House, Aster had found the missing opals—in their case, at the bottom of Fenne's wardrobe. This Lilz learned from Aster: Fenne and Mistress Stump were elbow deep in cloth samples and patterns, their minds too full of the advantageous placement of seams and tucks to have room for the beauty of mere gems.

Sir Kav Treadwell

Lilz stood before the Dych of Summerlea, her hands folded. Vikent Quickhunt had been extracted from behind his curtain and sent into the anteroom. She was sure he had his ear to the door. Three months after Prince Jath's death, echoes of rumors about his end were still audible, if faint. Considering the scene at open Court two days before the prince had fallen sick, an ambitious—or simply careful—vikent might hope to learn something useful from a conversation between Fenne's grandfather and her bond-servant.

"Kav Treadwell," the dych said. Lilz nodded. "As before, no interference."

"Yes, your Grace."

"Unless, of course, he harms her—has he?"

"I've seen no sign, your Grace. Nor does she come home in a stupor as she sometimes did before."

The dych nodded. "He seems most direct. A healthy, normal youth." He laced his fingers together and leaned his chin on the backs of them, his elbows on his desk. His eyelids drooped momentarily. "A better choice. Given the tenor of the converse between the king and the queen, and Makeready's evident predilection for Ridehards, most useful."

"My mistress complains that they find it difficult to meet. Not every afternoon offers an opportunity like this one." Spring snow, falling thickly overnight, had marooned the royal family at a weekend retreat. Sir Kav had remained at the palace, why, Lilz didn't know, but the favorite had wasted no time taking advantage of the unexpected absence of the king. The dych's information net had functioned as efficiently as ever: not ten minutes after the carriage Kav had sent for Fenne departed, a messenger had arrived at Hasten House to bid her come. So here she stood, with wet boots and a damp cloak, enduring yet another interview with this wicked old man.

The dych sat back, grinning. "The child's just like her idiot mother. Loves dressing up. Yes?"

"She does like new clothes."

"Easily solved, then. Foster a friendship with Onma Stump, if at all possible. She's a woman of many connections."

Lilz nodded: Mistress Stump lived not far from the New Palace. She was rumored to receive guests who were then left to their own devices, at their request—for a price, payment of which ensured privacy and silence. A little service of which Lady Delle had availed herself from time to time, one of them very likely resulting in Cals, if Coral was to be believed. Certainly Riverside had blazing red hair, like the boy's.... The bill for Fenne's adventures, Lilz presumed, would be presented to the man on the other side of this desk. She cleared her throat. "Your Grace—I've asked this before. What happens when Greencrags returns?"

"Fenne would not be the first to pluck two strings at once." The dych smiled. "Often the harmony is unexpectedly sweet."

"As long as the strings don't get crossed."

"Lilz, I repeat what I said on that last occasion: you are a servant. Don't let your courtly accent go to your head. The Standfast faction is easily managed."

"And Greencrags himself?"

"A guileless boy of eighteen? Come, Lilz! Do as you're told and don't think about it."

"Very well, your grace." He flipped his fingers at her in dismissal. She went softly to the door and yanked it open. Vikent Quickhunt straightened and took a backward step.

"Quickhunt, you rascal, I hope your ears aren't so full they overflow at your tongue," the dych said. "Get behind your curtain like a good little boy."

Ahead of Lilz as she walked toward the entrance of the palace was a man who kept looking over his shoulder at her. He was dressed like a peer: wide trousers, a well-cut long jacket, the lace shirt collar spread out over the black velvet jacket collar finer than foam. He had an odd gait, Lilz thought, frowning, trying to remember where she'd seen him before.

The man glanced again at her and hurried down a side corridor toward the king's residence. Now she placed him. She was almost sure it was the same man who had run from her on the night of Fenne's wedding. What connection, she wondered idly, did he have with the king?

A woman of many connections.

Lilz remembered one of those connections, so abruptly she stopped walking. A pharmacist. What was the man's name? Clock? Clock. Evin Clock. A supplier of love-potions, female physics, and—if the rumor that had just made connections in her mind was true—of potions with darker purposes...such as might make a crown prince mortally ill, if he had shown his temper unsuited to a plan made by an old man with great power and the determination to keep it.

With so many servants in the royal establishment, surely one could be bought? If not for money, then for something else. And if anyone knew who that would be and what might move him, it was Nevan Hasten. But would even he risk assassinating a prince?

Lilz walked home slowly, not even noticing that she had forgotten to pull the hood of her cloak over her head. Someone in the prince's retinue had been fished, drowned, from the river the day after the long funeral procession. Rumors about the death had been strangely lacking, Lilz thought now. Had no one wondered how close the man had been to the prince, in what ways? Or speculated at possible sorrow, or even whether he'd had a griping gut himself, recovered, and felt remorse at the idea that he might have infected the prince?

Very odd.

"Lilz, look at you!" the downstairs hall maid exclaimed, as she pushed open the back door of Hasten House. "What was so fascinating that you didn't even pull your hood up? You're like a snowman!"

"Oh, nothing." Lilz grinned and brushed snow from her hair. "The snow's so pretty, isn't it?"

"Not on my floor! Stand on the mat, you silly."

With Mistress Stump's assistance, the affair with Sir Kav went on. Each month Lilz figuratively held her breath, and each month released her anxiety with a sigh when Fenne began to bleed. Either the girl was more careful than Lilz would have thought her capable of being, or Kav Treadwell more cautious. A year into their affair, Aster was hired to be body-maid. While this meant Lilz no longer had to wring out Fenne's rags for the laundress, she'd lost her method of monitoring. She could only hope that Fenne would come to her if she thought herself pregnant — or go to Mistress Stump, the woman of so many connections. But the month after Aster arrived Lilz saw the soaking jar set in the corner of the dressing room as usual and relaxed. She would not have to speak.

With Aster as body-maid, Lilz's duties shifted. Only the care of the wardrobe and Fenne's dressing were out of her hands, but even Lilz was surprised at how much free time that one change produced. She was still Fenne's chief tutor, particularly in those arts a lady was expected to be proficient at—singing and guitar playing, embroidery and cut-work and needle-lace (making tatty-work was for common folk; coming to it as late as she had, Lilz was not especially good at it, to Aster's amusement)—and in those fields of knowledge necessary for a woman to manage a household and engage in charming conversation with her peers.

Now she also took charge of some of Fenne's investments, studying financial opportunity with such zeal that Meadowlands came sneaking to her for advice from time to time, with such great swearings of secrecy he left her laughing. Luckily, his ventures succeeded, even the quarter of a shipload of linen fabric late in arriving at port in a distant colony and for a time thought lost at sea. Best of all, Lilz now had time to polish her own guitar technique on music far too complex for Fenne's talent or taste.

For Fenne, time passed in a round of attendance at Court, costly afternoons at Mistress Stump's establishment, tea parties for ladies and dinner parties where often her grandfather ate in the place of her husband, picnics and lawn parties and sleigh rides through deep winter snow, theatricals, winter concerts in the stuffy hall where the carved gilt seats were tiered so steeply it seemed that a listener might fall into the lap of the person in front, summer concerts on flowered barges floating down the river Lynn to the sea and back on the rising tide. She had good reason to be satisfied with her choice of lover. Kav Treadwell proved a young man of great tenderness and affection, thoroughly devoted to her and absolutely devoid of interest in Court intrigue.

Perhaps this straightforwardness was what King Guyr found so fascinating about him. Certainly it was what allowed Sir Jen Makeready to make such good, if friendly, use of the lad. Nine times out of ten, what Kav suggested, the king soon did, and what Kav suggested as his own was nearly always an idea of Sir Jen's. Sir Jen, unlike Kav, was both sensible and brilliant: by the winter after her second wedding anniversary Fenne had long been the mistress of a vikent.

Treadwell had been raised to that rank shortly after the death of Prince Jath. With the rank had come an appointment as Lord of the King's Seal, a position that gave him voice in the Privy Council. No matter that someone, seeing him walking in the king's garden with Makeready, had remarked, "Look, there's Treadwell—I see he's brought his brain along today," or that the anecdote has amused the peerage for the rest of the week. Kav's brain had little interest for Fenne. Honors, wealth, generous gifts—that was different; those Vikent Treadwell provided in good measure. Only Lilz seemed to mark the increasing frequency and passion of Rovvo Standfast's letters.

Fenne turned sixteen. Following old tradition, Meadowlands set out a great feast for his daughter. Dancing went on until dawn, when the last guests departed with sated yawns and little yelps at going out into bitter cold. Greencrags sent Fenne a birthday gift: a fine square-cut emerald flanked with peridot in a delicate gold ring she wore once and tossed into her jewelry box, where it eventually lodged in a lower back corner.

That spring the Dych of Summerlea was posted to Galtriva to conclude a peace treaty. He was to be gone for two months. Without his usual entourage, Hasten House seemed almost empty. Later, when early summer heat settled a pall of dust and humidity over Miense, Kav Treadwell was sure enough of his mistress to go with the royal family to the mountains for ten days' refreshment. Sir Jen Makeready was left behind to deal, as usual, with all of the favorite's glittering responsibilities.

Ruppet, Cals, and their mother retreated to Summerlea, leaving the iarl and his men, Fenne, Lilz, Aster, and the house servants in town. Fenne lay about in a state of utter boredom, without even the energy to embroider. The iarl tended his own and the dych's business in the afternoons and went out to drink or play cards with his friends almost every evening. The weather grew hotter and muggier; the maids kept to the cellar and fanned themselves; the horseflies in the courtyard turned vicious. To Lilz, lying with a book propped on her knees in the heat under the roof tiles each night, it seemed as if something were gathering, twisting, about to kink like yarn wound too tightly. Heat lightning sometimes flickered in the dim night skies, but the weather would not break.

Then, in what Lilz thought an unbearably apt act of nature, a thunderstorm lashed the streets the night the real storm broke: Greencrags came home.

Chapter Eight

This time Guyr had designed Fenne's wedding dress to set off the opals. Their shifting fire was echoed in the myriad tiny pearls embroidered onto the white watered silk of the outer gown; the underdress was a thin brocade of many colors mixed with white and gold, giving much the effect of an opal become a transparent sheet and laid upon silk. A matching headdress let Fenne's hair hang free past her waist, an open proclamation that the elderly peeresses had found her to be a virgin, worthy to marry again unwidowed. As a subtle additional reminder, the dress had been styled to emphasize the flatness of her belly.

As before, the formal ceremony of the marriage was short, the priest of the Fathergod rapidly shuttled out of the way and the festivities begun. An enormous banquet had been set up at the back of the hall. Tempting aromas rose to the servants in the gallery above, who could only sit with their mouths watering and watch the guests repair to the tables from time to time to refresh or stuff themselves. Guyr on his throne and Queen Prenta on hers offered toasts to the health of the lucky couple. No one mentioned Greencrags. It was as if he had never existed.

At last, at a signal from the king, the musicians began playing loudly, the lights dimmed, and the masquers entered.

"All hail our master Priapos," they sang, the traditional opening verse. Some of the peers began to sing along. In the gallery, where Lilz and Aster sat together among the servants, a couple of Treadwell's men also began to sing, to be shushed by a maid or two. Lilz, looking through the lattice, saw a familiar silhouette enter the hall by the side door. Sky above! *Greencrags?*

She said nothing to Aster. The young iarl slipped sideways along the wall toward the back of the hall. In a few minutes he reappeared on the other side, now holding a well-loaded plate and a fork. He leaned against the wall, eating, watching the masque. Lilz watched him with increasing puzzlement. As one with the right to stand in the hall he'd been invited, of course, but why had he come?

After a few minutes, the players captured Lilz's attention with their antics. When she glanced at where Greencrags had been, he was gone.

The masque continued, to much laughter from the audience. Lilz heard the door to the gallery open and looked back. One of the redvests appeared with a basket of food and bubbling wine for the servants, four huge bottles of it. Treadwell's body-man, Swan, popped the cork and began to pour the wine. Lilz accepted a glass and sipped. The servants offered toasts of their own, to the happy couple and, more vigorously, to each other.

Down on the floor of the hall the first act of the masque was over. The players darted or tumbled out of the bright lights and disappeared behind the dais. A space was cleared for dancing. The orchestra struck up a tune. Lilz watched idly for a moment, then tried to find Greencrags again. She saw him, with one of his men, back in the same place, now with a glass in his hand. The light caught the curve of his cheek. He was grinning. She turned again to watch the dancers.

Fenne's bright hair swung as she skipped through the figures of the first dance. The Iarl of Northlands looked delirious with joy. Lilz could see him squeeze her mistress's hands each time they met. At last the dancers stopped to catch their breaths.

"More wine?" someone asked.

Lilz accepted a brimming glass. The man pouring—a redvest, of all people, a blue-eyed man with a short beard—looked somehow familiar. She couldn't place him. He stopped to chat, a man with an odd cadence to his speech—provincial, probably, although Lilz couldn't place the accent, either. The dialect marked him as landed gentry recently risen to the minor peerage. One of Treadwell's folk? Behind her, the musicians tuned their instruments.

"Lilz!" Aster tugged at her sleeve. "Look at Greencrags! What's he doing?"

A new, slower dance was beginning. Rovvo Standfast had acquired a partner, a girl a couple of years younger than Fenne. They had joined the figure at the edge of a pattern that would leave him the partner of Fenne—Lilz's eye raced ahead, calculating as Greencrags must have done—in the center near—no, at—the end. She chuckled. "I think he means to dance."

"But just look at where he'll end up!"

"I don't doubt he planned it, do you?"

"How can he *do* that?"

"With more aplomb than I'd have credited to him." The music had begun. Fenne had not yet noticed her former husband, who had led his chosen partner into the first steps of the figure. Lilz watched the glittering headdress of the bride as it wove among the dancers. Now Fenne came even with Greencrags; she was small enough that without glancing up she would see only the finery of his shirt—and after she passed she looked back with a jerk, faltered in the pattern and had to run two steps to catch up. He must have said something.

Those guests not dancing began to realize what was happening and crowded closer to see. Fenne's face, what Lilz could glimpse of it, was set in anger. Rovvo Standfast smiled at each lady as he raised her hand and twirled her about, as if his whole being were concentrated at that moment upon that woman. Each seemed to sparkle. Watching from her throne, Queen Prenta threw back her head and laughed—perhaps at something one of her ladies-in-waiting had said.

The music beat on. At the end, Greencrags did not take Fenne's hand, as the figure decreed; he merely bowed, made some small remark, and sought his original partner.

"She could set limestone on fire, let alone opals," Aster groaned. "Sky above! What got into him?" Faster music started; Standfast and his partner joined a new figure. "Oh, dear heaven," Aster continued. "I don't know how I'll face undressing her tonight!"

"You'll find out what he said," Lilz pointed out.

"I'm not sure I want to." Aster stopped to consider for a moment. "At least, not straight from her, not that soon."

Lilz had not removed her gaze from Greencrags. Now, only a few exchanges into the figure, someone tapped his shoulder to take his place. He graciously bowed out. She followed his unhurried retreat to the side of the room, where he joined his men, and their slow exit, before looking back at the dancers.

"You want to know what he said?" Aster sat down on the edge of the bed and yawned widely.

Lilz rolled over. "Oof, it's chilly! What?"

"First, when she passed him at the beginning, he said, 'Ah, milady, I see we meet again.'"

Lilz laughed. "Shame on him. And at the end?"

Aster grinned. Her accent shifted, just enough to suggest the iarl's. "I had hoped to dance at your first wedding, madam, but find this one far more to my liking."

Lilz almost choked. She pulled the blankets back over her cold nose, still laughing.

Aster sobered. "What now, Lilz?" She started to unbutton her shirt. "Do you think milord Kav will challenge Greencrags?"

"Not unless Fenne puts him up to it."

"Do you think she will? I never know what she'll do next."

"We'll just have to wait and see."

"I don't know why, but I'm frightened." Aster pulled her bedgown over her head and loosened her pants to step out of them. She turned down the lamp. It went out with a pop.

Greencrags

"Lilz!" Fenne pounded on the door so hard it rattled. "Lilz!"

Lulled by the patter of the rain, Lilz had been dozing in the warm attic room. The book she'd been reading earlier that evening slid from her lap and slammed to the floor as she rushed to open the door.

Fenne stood in the narrow dark passage, fists clenched, eyes staring, breathing hard from her run up the stairs. Lilz couldn't recall that she'd ever come to the servants' attic before. "My mistress, what is it?"

"He's here," Fenne whispered. "He wants to take me away."

"What? Who? Take you where?"

"Greencrags," Fenne gasped. "The houseman just came up to tell me. He's down in the south reception room and he wants to see me. He's going to take me away—oh, Lilz, why?"

"Probably because you're his wife." Lilz returned to the side of her bed, pulse slowing, and picked up the book. A corner had been bent. She touched it with regret.

"But he can't! What right does he have? He wants to take me with him to that place, what's its name—I don't remember— but I'm sure it's just like Summerlea, dull, dull, dull! Oh, Lilz, I'll just die! What will Kav say?" Fenne pressed her hands to her cheeks. "Oh, sweet heaven, what if that monster wants to go to bed with me? Kav will leave me, you know how jealous he is—"

I know how jealous you try to make him, Lilz thought. She set the damaged book on her bed. "What do you want me to do?"

"Go down there. Tell him—I don't know, tell him anything, tell him I'm already in bed—no, don't tell him that—tell him I'm sick—just make him go away." Fenne swallowed and gulped air. "Tell him I can't see him before tomorrow."

"My mistress, I think you might—"

"Nevernevernever." Fenne shook her head, eyes clenched shut. "Oh, why isn't grandpapa here? Even papa's out somewhere—" Fenne's eyes popped open. "Oh, Mother of All! You've got to get rid of him before papa comes home!" She started pushing Lilz toward the stairs. "Who knows what papa might do!"

"Fenne, please! Let me put some decent clothes on."

"Oh, *hurry*!"

Lilz, not slowly but not hurrying, took off her bedgown and pulled on the shirt and pants she'd worn that day, replaced her socks and stepped into her shoes. She went down the stairs at a dignified pace. Fenne stood in the middle of the second floor hall, wringing her hands, as Lilz went on down the front stairs.

Greencrags and two of his men sat in the large south reception room. They looked damp, travel-stained and weary, especially in contrast to the room itself, with its elegant white brocade walls above gilt wainscot and the pale golden carpet patterned in vines and flowers, brought with a boatload of raw silk from the eastern edge of the known world.

"You're Lilz." The young iarl sprang to his feet with a huge smile. "I'd know you anywhere! Where's my wife?"

Lilz smiled; no mere human could help smiling at that eager grin or the pride in that voice. Rovvo Standfast might remember her, but

had they passed on the street she'd never have recognized him. He'd
lost no weight, but he'd grown more than a head—he was a full hand's
breadth taller than she was, now, and wide across the shoulders.
As the dych had predicted, his skin was clear. Not that he'd become
handsome: his eyebrows were set a little too low over his light brown
eyes; his nose was too sharp and his cheekbones too flat, but youth,
good humor and a well-trimmed reddish-brown beard went a long
way toward making him attractive.

"Milord, I'm sorry. Lady Greencrags wasn't feeling well and retired
early this evening. I'd hate to wake her."

"Should she have a physician? I'll go—"

"Oh, no, no. Nothing that serious." Lilz forced a smile. "I'm sure
she'll be better with a little rest. But since you've waited this long,
surely tomorrow would..." She trailed off. How crestfallen the poor
kid looked!

"A good idea, if you ask me, Rovvo," said the older of the two men
with him. "I'm sure Lady Greencrags would rather see you cleaned
up and dressed in finer garb."

Greencrags made a helpless gesture. To Lilz, it said, *I've thought
of nothing but her for days.* He twitched a smile at her. "Tomorrow,
then. Would ten o'clock be too early?"

"Ten?" At least it's Aster who'll have to blast her out of bed, Lilz
thought. "No, I don't think so." She heard the front door open and
someone come into the hall, the voices of the houseman and Fenne's
father.

"There's Lord Olen," Greencrags said, brightening. He started for
the hall.

Fenne's father appeared at the doorway. His eyebrows shot up.
"Greencrags?" he said. "Sky above, you've grown! I wouldn't have known
you if not for Merrow, there. What say, Merrow, good journey?"

Merrow. That would be Merrow Strengthen, Dych of Lealands.
Lilz took good note of him for the first time: a man with no hair on
his pate and what he did have gray, but still vigorous at what must be
about sixty-five years. A man my father's age, she thought. I wonder
if they knew one another before the banishment?

"Not bad," Strengthen was saying, "but long, long, long. Four weeks
riding, and the rain followed us every step of the way but coming
through the pass at Hekluit. We met snow in the mountains." The
older man nodded at Lilz. "Your daughter's bond-servant says she's
not feeling well."

"Not well? Fenne? She was in fine fettle at dinner." Meadowlands
looked from one man to another in the sudden stillness. "Oh. Well." He
ran a hand through his pale hair. "She's a shy thing, and whomever
you sent ahead didn't deliver the message. Give her time."

"I'd thought to apply to you for her custody." Greencrags tilted his
head to one side. "She's of age, now. As am I."

"Well, of course you'll have custody," Fenne's father said. "No question of that. Where are you planning to live?"

"At Sweetdawn, at least at first. It's closer to Miense than Greencrags; I thought she might like to come into town from time to time." Greencrags paused, his eyes watchful. "From her letters, she seems to *enjoy* society."

Meadowlands glanced at Lilz. She would hear about this, though his embarrassment was scarcely her fault. "Ah, yes." The iarl rocked awkwardly onto his heels and back. He'd been drinking. "Yes, she does," he added, with the tone of a man who has just made a momentous discovery. "In a shy sort of way."

"If you'll excuse me, sirs, I think you can better converse in my absence," Lilz said. Meadowlands waved her away.

"Where did your father find that woman for sale?" she heard Lealands ask as she started up the stairs. "Sounds for all the world like a Peer of the Blood!"

Rovvo Standfast, too, now sounded enough like a Peer of the Blood that Lealands should feel no compunction at his comment about a servant. Chrems certainly worked a marvel, Lilz thought. I wonder what else the boy learned there. She knocked at Fenne's suite. The door was snatched open.

"What did he say? What's happening?" Fenne whispered.

"He's talking to your father."

"Oh, *no!* I told you to get rid of him before papa saw him, didn't you hear? He'll ask for my custody!"

"He already has."

"Oh!" Fenne flopped onto a padded lounge and beat her fists against it. "*Why* did grandpapa have to negotiate that stupid treaty! He's never around when I need him."

"Calm down, Fenne." Lilz folded her arms. "Rovvo Standfast is coming tomorrow morning at ten o'clock to see you. Attempt to be civil if you can't be pleasant. It is important to your grandfather to keep the Standfast faction under control. *You* are his instrument of control. He will not appreciate your making his job harder."

"Oh, politics! What's that got to do with life?"

"With yours, everything." Lilz sighed and smiled. "You'll be surprised at the change in your husband, my mistress. He's taller than me by this much, *very* nicely built, and his skin is clear and his speech far smoother than when you saw him last."

Fenne snorted.

"Give him a chance."

Fenne shook her head. "Lilz, don't you understand? I don't care how much he's changed. The only important thing is that he isn't Kav!"

The interview the next morning was stiff and formal. Fenne insisted that Lilz sit beside her, with Greencrags two sash-lengths away across the room. Fenne's father excused himself, pleading urgent business at the New Palace, as soon as an agreement had been reached. Greencrags was visibly baffled, disappointed beyond measure. Lilz slipped out of sight as he was taking his leave, to give the boy a chance to speak personally.

"Fenne, don't you know how I've dreamed of you?" she heard him ask her. "Haven't you read my letters? Your own were so sweet—"

"Milord, I— I didn't expect—"

"I love you! I said so, so many times! Your image in small was the light of the whole three lonely years. I told you that, too. How could you not expect me to want to make you my true wife?"

What Fenne replied, Lilz didn't hear. Standfast sneezed. "The journey from Chrems was wet and nights in the mountains chilly," he said, in answer to a murmured question. "I've taken a little summer cold. Nothing to worry about."

"Don't let it work in you," Fenne said, the first interest in her husband as a person Lilz had heard all morning. She went with him to the front door and stood in the opening watching as he untied his horse and rode away. "At least he dresses well," was Fenne's comment, giving Lilz hope she might become resigned.

Fenne would stay at Hasten House until her husband had inspected the manor at Sweetdawn and seen that everything was ready for them. He'd rest a day or two at Standfast House and start for Sweetdawn the next weekend. Lilz, Meadowlands told her, was to begin packing and make the arrangements with the carters.

Thornday evening the Dych of Summerlea returned from Galtriva. The house rang with the returning entourage. Servants seemed to be everywhere. Fenne greeted her grandfather with dancing joy. "Why so happy to see me, moppet?" he asked.

"Greencrags is back."

"Ah! Improved with age, has he?"

"Improved, yes, but grandpapa, you don't understand. He wants to take me to live in that place King Guyr gave him."

The dych laughed. "Wonderful!"

"Not wonderful!" Fenne stamped her foot. "Grandpapa, he thinks he can treat me like a wife!"

The old man's eyebrows rose. "You are his wife."

They moved from the hall into the dych's suite, then, so Lilz heard no more. Fenne emerged an hour later, sullen and snuffling, her eyes red. Lilz presumed she had been made acquainted with the relationship of politics to life. Fenne sulked in her room until the next evening, when a messenger came from Standfast House to tell her that her husband's cold was worse. He was too ill to ride out to Sweetdawn that week—but surely he'd be well enough to go the week following. She wrote a polite little note of concern and sent it back with the man, asking Lilz for a few coppers to tip him.

At first it seemed Greencrags would quickly recover, but on Moonday a second messenger brought a letter of love and sadness to say that his cold had gone into his liver and he was seriously ill.

"Good!" Fenne said. "Good, good, good!"

Well, at least the girl had had the sense to wait until the messenger left before saying that! Lilz thought. "Fenne, you're talking about a decent young man, your own husband." She walked around to look into Fenne's face. "Can you really be wishing him such ill?"

"I wish he were dead! That would solve everything. I'd inherit his property and be free to marry Kav."

In fact, it soon looked as if Greencrags might die. The dych summoned Lilz to his suite one afternoon when Fenne was visiting with Mistress Stump. "I want you to go over to Standfast House, Lilz," he said. "Make sure this fellow isn't malingering."

"I'm sure not, your Grace. He didn't seem at all that sort."

"Go." The dych's eyelids drooped slightly. "I want to know exactly what shape he's in."

"Very well, your Grace." Lilz hesitated. "Wouldn't it be more appropriate for Lady Greencrags to go? He's her husband, not mine."

"Fenne go! Sky above, Lilz, where's your head? Don't I have enough trouble with the Standfast faction as it is? Heaven only knows what she'd say!"

"They might think—"

"You think too much, Lilz. Or not enough! What if Fenne caught whatever he's got? No, you go. Besides"—he grinned—"you're a lot harder to fool than Fenne."

So Lilz put on her best shirt and her only skirt and went to call on the Iarl of Greencrags. On the way she stopped at a stand and spent two weeks' pocket money on a huge bunch of flowers, to have something to give the boy from his wife. The houseman at Standfast House looked surprised to see her, but took the flowers and went away. He came back with permission for Lilz to go up to the iarl's chamber.

He was in bed. Merrow Strengthen sat in a chair near the window, reading silently. Another young man, whom she didn't know, sat on the other side of the bed.

Greencrags slept. His face was thin and yellow, fragile looking against the white pillowcase. Lilz felt her own face fall; she blinked back the start of tears. "He's very sick, your Grace," she said to the Dych of Lealands. Her voice was hushed.

The man nodded.

Lilz turned away from the bed. As she did, the door opened, and the iarl's body-man—Stone, was that his name?—came in. A bowl of soup steamed on the tray he carried. He caught sight of her, nodded without smiling, and set the tray on the table next to the iarl's bed.

"My master," he said softly.

Greencrags's eyes opened a little. The whites were yellow.

"My master, I've brought some good soup." Stone sat next to the bed, in the chair the younger man quietly vacated. "Lady Greencrags sent it. She made it with her own hands."

Lilz stiffened with shock. She tried to catch Stone's eye, but his attention was on the youth in the bed.

"Try to eat a little. I'll help you."

Greencrags shook his head weakly and turned his face away.

"Don't press it on him if he doesn't want it," Lilz advised. "You can always warm it up again."

"He must eat, miss." Stone must have forgotten her name, if he ever knew it. "He must get his strength back."

"Sleep helps, too. As the playwright said a few seasons ago, it darns up the torn sleeve of affliction."

His shoulders slumped, Stone clasped his hands between his knees. "I could leave it here." He glanced at her. Dark-eyed, as she remembered. "Maybe he'll want it in a little while, and one of these gentlemen—"

"Cold soup?" Lilz produced a shudder with little difficulty. "Ugh. Let's take it down to the kitchen. I'm sure his Grace will send for the soup the moment milord calls for nourishment."

"Let him be, Stone," Lealands said. "Take it away."

The body-man picked the tray up reluctantly. Lilz went to the door and held it open for him. "I'm sorry," he said, as they passed into the hall. "I know I've met you, but I don't remember where."

"At the wedding. I'm Lilz, bond-servant to Lady Greencrags."

"Oh! Oh, of course! I beg your pardon." Stone pushed through a swinging door onto the back stairs. "I'm so—my mind's elsewhere, I'm afraid—"

The houseman squeezed past them on the stairs, with the flowers Lilz had brought arranged in a silver vase. Lilz followed the body-man down to the kitchen. He set the tray on the table. She picked up the bowl and poured the soup down the sink.

"What on earth?" he said angrily. "Lady Greencrags sent that for my master—"

"Stone—it is Stone, isn't it?—I don't know who sent that soup, but it was not Lady Greencrags."

"Not Lady—?" He shook his head, his face slack with confusion. "But—The messenger said she'd cooked it herself for my master—"

"Lady Greencrags can't cook!" Lilz took the lid off a pot on the stove and found more soup like what had been in the bowl. She poured that into the sink, too. "I doubt she could make herself a cup of tea without two people to help. When did that stuff come?"

"Not a quarter hour ago," Stone said.

"Then it didn't even come from Hasten House. I stopped in the kitchen just before I left to walk over here—don't you think the cook would have sent it with me, rather than hire a messenger?" She turned the pot over and pushed it at him. "Look here. All Hasten House pots have an H.H. on the bottom. This one's blank."

"I didn't look—"

Now she'd made him feel guilty. "Of course you didn't," Lilz said more gently. "Who would, with the thing full of soup? What else has come here with Lady Greencrags's name on it?"

Stone frowned down at her, his tongue compressed between his lips. "A pair of roast doves, and other soup—there was a pastry, I think—two. My master ate one of the fowl with much gusto. At the time he seemed to be getting better—"

"What happened to the other?"

"The next day he was too sick to want it." Stone passed his hand over hair already graying, although he wasn't more than a few years older than Lilz—forty, at most. "The day after that, I threw it away. It had stood in the sun and I was afraid it had taken contagion—"

"And how are the rats in your alley, Stone?"

Stone's face went as gray as his name.

"You've been at Chrems for three years and out in the back provinces before that," Lilz pointed out. "But I've been at Court. Don't you know your master's the center of a faction opposed to two others, securely allied only with one, and, lacking children, only marginally connected with the Hastens?"

He was quick to understand, at least. "Oh, no," he said under his breath. "Oh, no. I carried—"

"Hush."

Stone met her eyes. He motioned to her to follow him out of the kitchen and out the back door. They crossed the courtyard together. Stone unbolted the gate into the alley, where the trash and cooked garbage were left for the cleaners to pick over and take away.

Mingled with the sour odor of the garbage was the sweet metallic scent of rotting meat. Lilz and Stone went in opposite directions, peering among the piles of refuse, some scattered or loosely stacked, some in oozing barrels. "Here it is," Stone said. "It's a cat."

Lilz walked over to where Stone was standing. The cat, a brown tabby, had been dead for some days. "I hope it enjoyed the leftover fowl," Lilz said. They left it where it lay and went back into the house. "Feed him only what comes from your own kitchen," she told Stone. "Only what the cook buys himself at the market. Your master's young. He started out healthy. Let's hope he recovers."

"Oh, Lilz!" Stone sounded sick. "I served him that fowl myself. And the other soup, and a custard—"

"It's not your fault." She grabbed the man by the shoulders and tried to look into his eyes. "It's not your fault, do you understand that? You couldn't know."

"Since before he was two years old," Stone whispered.

"Shh." She patted his back. "It's all right, now. Everything will be all right, yes? Stone?" Stone, one hand to his face, nodded. "But you must tell his Grace, the Dych of Lealands, what's happened. I'll make sure Lady Greencrags sends nothing to eat, so you won't destroy something healthful by mistake. Yes?"

Stone nodded once and sagged onto a bench by the stove. Lilz left him in the kitchen and started back for Hasten House. On the way, she decided to tell the Dych of Summerlea only that Rovvo Standfast was genuinely, seriously ill.

Greencrags lingered near death for two weeks. Twice during his illness, while Fenne was occupied at Mistress Stump's, Lilz went unbidden to see how the young iarl fared.

The first time he seemed much like the last, but weaker, when a maid showed Lilz into the room. No one was with him but Stone, who was trying to spoon soup into his loose mouth. "I could weep when it all runs out," he said, without any greeting.

"Maybe he could suck it from a napkin," Lilz suggested. "At Summerlea the dych had us feed some kittens that way, when their mother was killed by a dog."

"Or a handkerchief?" Stone went into the dressing room. He came back with a fine white linen handkerchief bordered in Travaltian lace. "Let's sit him up. Can you—?"

Lilz sat on the bed and wriggled her shoulder behind Greencrags's head. He groaned. Stone folded the handkerchief into a thin triangle. He dipped the tip into the broth and pushed it between the boy's lips. "Ah, thank all fates that be," he said, as Standfast began to suck. The houseman came into the room to set the new bouquet of meadow flowers where it could be seen from the bed and stood watching Stone dip the handkerchief into the soup and poke it into his master's mouth for a few minutes before leaving. Not long after, the young man who had sat by the bed on Lilz's first visit came quietly into the room and took the chair near the window.

Half an hour went by. Standfast had swallowed the best part of a cup of soup and fallen asleep. Stone wiped the dribbles from the boy's beard and Lilz laid his head back on the pillows. "I'm late," she told Stone. "I have to go."

The body-man nodded. As Lilz left the room, the youth sitting by the window got up and followed her out. "Much thanks," he said. "I'll write to Meadowlands and tell him how you helped."

"Please don't!" At his blink of shock, she added, "I'm not even supposed to be here."

Lilz left the man standing in the hall still looking puzzled and ran all the way to Hasten House. She'd just dashed through the back door when Fenne's carriage pulled up to the front entrance.

Chapter Nine

As the king's favorite, the Iarl of Northlands had lived in the New Palace since coming to Miense. As a bridegroom, he would divide his time between the palace and his wife—for whom the king had given him lodging.

Lodging, in this case, was rather more than a roof over Fenne's pretty blonde head. Lilz had known the mansion by its outer walls for several years, had gazed at its ornate white facade while riding past more times than she could count, never dreaming that she herself might one day live there. Built, as Lilz understood it, on private terms for a nobleman married to a commoner, who had therefore died leaving no son to succeed him, the property had reverted to the Crown and for years had been a royal guesthouse, seldom used.

The name of the house was Waterside. It occupied a large plot on the south bank of the Lynn, half an hour's ride upriver from the New Palace. Unlike most of the town houses, it was set back from the road a few dozen paces. Ornamental trees had been planted in that space. In spring, Lilz had seen hundreds of pink and white tulips blooming under the clouds of crabapple blossom, but this was winter; a few dark evergreens near the house and some shriveled red fruits still clinging to the black twigs of the crabs were the only color. A white brick drive led through a high iron gate into the central courtyard, from the other end of which a second brick drive led to the river landing. Like most other large houses in town, Waterside had a good-sized kitchen garden and a small ornamental garden suited for strolling or lazing on summer afternoons—not that Lilz expected to do much of that—and a large patch of scruffy grass where the horses could be led out for exercise if needed.

For the third time in less than two years, Lilz was in charge of moving Fenne's possessions. The collection had grown, yet again. At Northlands's request, King Guyr lent a few palace guards to augment the armed men the Dych of Summerlea could supply, to protect the groaning carts of valuables as they snaked through the crooked streets of Miense to their new home.

"We'll need live-in guards as well," Fenne said, the morning of the move. "Has anyone thought of that?"

"There are two," Lilz said.

"Get a couple more."

"I've put in a requisition at the hiring hall," Lilz told her. "But I've insisted upon men who can post bond."

"Oh, good idea. Aster?" Fenne went into the dressing room. "Where is she?"

"At Waterside, my mistress. Don't you remember? You sent her there to receive your clothing."

"How long can that take? She's been gone over an hour."

"My mistress, I wouldn't expect her back for at least five. Not if she stops to check each trunk off the carter's list and secures the jewelry."

"Oh, really? I had no idea. Come put up my hair, then." Fenne sat at the dressing table and smiled at Lilz in the mirror as she came up behind her. "It'll be like old times. Just a woven braid, Lilz. I won't see Kav before dinner."

Fenne's curls were snarled, but Lilz found that her wrist remembered the years of learning how to comb without pulling. She worked in silence on the long golden fall for a few minutes.

"Lilz?" Fenne glanced at her in the mirror. "Remember Prince Jath?"

"Oh, yes!"

"He turned yellow before he died, did you know?"

Lilz put the comb down. "No, I don't think I'd heard that."

"Kav told me, just a few days ago...that report you brought to House-Among-Oaks, about Sir Jen? I never read it. Did he turn yellow, too?"

"Not that anyone mentioned."

"I didn't think you'd said so." Fenne sat staring into the mirror as Lilz began braiding at the top of her head. "That's funny," she said.

"Oh?"

"I thought he probably had."

Lilz let her hands do the braid, catching in a little extra hair with her pinkie each time she made the crossover, for an even zigzag pattern down the back of Fenne's head. *Makeready turn yellow? Because Prince Jath had? Why?* "Not that I know of," she said. "Do you want a full braid, or just down to a bow at the nape?"

"Just the bow, and then make the rest twirl, like you used to. Aster never has got the hang of that. Did you arrange with the Waterside cook for dinner day after tomorrow?"

"I told him sixteen."

Fenne's lips moved as she counted on her fingers. "That's about right. You did send the invitations?"

"Yes, my mistress."

"I want it all to be perfect. Perfect, perfect, perfect!" Fenne stood as Lilz put the comb back into its case. "Isn't life going to be wonderful now, Lilz?"

"It would seem so." Lilz pointed out that she, too, was needed at Waterside, but that Coral was available for emergencies, and excused herself.

Is she like that because that wicked old man made her his favorite? she wondered, going down the back stairs and out to the stable. Or is she his favorite because he recognized a kindred spirit, before she could even talk?

Prince Jath. Rovvo Standfast. Sir Jen Makeready. Mistress Stump could be the link...but the food sent to Greencrags had Fenne's name on it. Surely the costumer, no more than the dych, would not betray Fenne's trust that far...or was that thinking one layer of intrigue too shallow?

Waterside had a staff of twenty-nine, not counting the two guards. Even with the stable lad and both kitchenmaids pressed into service and Aster and Lilz to help, they were sorely put to unpack all of what the head hall maid called "milady's little knick-knacks" before the dinner party.

All the work had to be done so that neither Fenne nor her many callers would notice the scurry and bustle. A parlormaid serving an unflurried afternoon snack to Lady Northlands and her three friends, sent back to the kitchen for a fresh pot of tea, became a crazed woman with the soft *thuck* of the door behind her—another drawer could be filled, another layer of straw torn from a barrel and the china under it transferred to a shelf, while the teapot was refilled for her to carry back to the calm of the front of the house. The houseman shifted in an instant from a wild-eyed maniac to a creature of imperturbable dignity with the ring of the front doorbell. The stable lad carried a barrel of straw out of the house to dump straight into stalls as bedding for horses, and dashed back to the house to unpack trunks of bedding for peers. Not even Lilz knew where everything was.

Nevertheless, dinner the next night was "perfect, perfect, perfect." Lilz and the houseman congratulated each other with what was left of the brandy when the gentlemen were done drinking. Raising her glass, Lilz predicted a harmonious meshing of duties for the foreseeable future. Grinning, the houseman agreed.

"Of *duties*," Lilz repeated.

Spring came, and with it the tulips Lilz remembered poked out of the ivy groundcover. Crabapples budded; in the kitchen garden fresh herbs emerged from the mud. The first warm day arrived, with an enervating softness in the air. That afternoon Lilz, in the tiny second-floor room where she kept track of Fenne's finances and tried to plan each week's demands on the house staff in the face of Fenne's whims, opened the window wide. A breeze smelling strongly of freshly-turned earth ruffled the pages of her ledger.

Somebody tapped on the door.

"Come in," she called. She turned to the last used page of the ledger and picked up her pen to look busy.

"Fenne's not with you?" Kav Treadwell stood in the open door, looking uneasy.

Lilz put the pen down and stood. "No, milord."

"Do you know where she is?"

"I'm sorry, no. She's gone to call on someone."

"She didn't say who?"

Lilz put a hand on the open ledger, half to keep the pages from blowing, half out of sudden fear. "No, milord."

Northlands narrowed his eyes at her. "It wouldn't be her great friend Onma Stump, would it?"

Sky above! Lilz widened her eyes in genuine shock. "I don't know, milord. I'd hardly think so."

"Sit down, Lilz." Northlands came into the room and shut the door. Besides the one at the desk, there was one other chair in the room. He sat on it. "We're not getting along, I suppose you know."

She had had some suspicions, though nothing so concrete as to lead her to conjecture that Fenne had resorted to Mistress Stump's renowned services. "My mistress doesn't discuss you with me, milord."

"Oh, milord, milord!" Northlands shook his head, his mouth tight. "I'm only a thegn with pretensions, Lilz, and you know it."

Lilz began to protest, but Kav shushed her. "Northlands! What's Northlands? No place at all, just a name to hang a title on. There's a real iarldom vacant, did you know?"

"Is there?"

"Darkforest. Hasn't been a Iarl of Darkforest for nearly thirty years. Why couldn't I have that?"

You're not good enough. Lilz looked down at the ledger, chilled. "I don't know, milord. Have you asked?"

"Oh, I asked. Impossible, Guyr says. No further discussion. Stop, the end. So I asked Summerlea," Kav went on, severely aggrieved. "He just gave me that glassy brown stare and said there were good and sufficient reasons which he was not free to tell me. Jen would know what to do. I'd never have thought I'd miss Jen as much as I do, back when he was infuriating me with all his advice, as if I couldn't think far enough ahead for myself to open my fly before pissing."

Her lips met to say, *Milord?* Instead, she sat still.

"The man was brilliant." Northlands lifted his chin at her.

"So it was said."

"Brilliant, clever, sensible and *right*. It was folly to set myself against Jath—the queen will never forgive me for his death, even though I had nothing to do with it."

Lilz folded her hands on her desk.

"His brother hates me."

Oerl was now the crown prince: Kav's favored place would vanish with the king's death. "A difficult circumstance, milord."

Northlands laughed through his nose. "When I eat in the New Palace, I make sure I'm always served from a common bowl, I'll tell you that!" He leaned forward. "Lilz, you've lived among Hastens almost nineteen years. What do you think of the Dych of Summerlea?"

She looked at the wide-open window. Pigeons *kroo-kooed* outside on a ledge. Spies? The ceiling over her head, supported with beams carved with dragons and flowers although this had never been intended as anything but a storeroom, drew her gaze upward. Northlands stared steadily at her. Waiting. She would have to form some answer. "He has always abided by the terms of my bond papers, so far as I know."

"You think you'll find your bond-money ready to draw on when you reach seventy?"

"I do hope so."

"Good luck!"

Lilz silently formed the word 'whizzers' as clearly as she could. Northlands shook his head. "Not here. Guyr promised."

"But did *he*?"

Kav shrugged. "I'm not sure he has any say in them, Lilz—but even if he does, he needs me. He needs all the routes to the king's ear he can find. He intends to take Jen's place as my advisor—*has* taken Jen's place whenever he's well enough—so he can run the country as he pleases. To his advantage, of course. Fenne's my consolation prize, just like being made Keeper of the Keys was supposed to pacify Greencrags for losing Fenne."

Keeper of the Keys? Had he been! "Why are you telling me this, milord?"

Northlands took a folded sheaf of paper out of his inside jacket pocket. "Remember this?" He handed the three worn pages across the desk. Makeready's notes. Lilz nodded and set them down. "When I understand all the information in these"—he slapped his hand on the papers—"I will run the Dych of Summerlea. Not the other way around. *I'll* be the chief power in Kinland."

Lilz glanced down at the notes. "Will these be enough?"

"Oh, yes. Hasten hasn't eliminated everyone Jen helped bring to power. The Lord Chief Justice, for instance."

"Gudgeon?" Lilz asked, interested. "Isn't his mother a Ridehard? And isn't he married to a Ridehard cousin? I thought they'd seen to his appointment."

Kav smiled. "Not quite. Jen turned the last key, a year before Fenne and I were married. His lordship will be delighted to help me put old Hasten down. Fenne won't want to spend any afternoons at Mistress Stump's then, will she?"

"All for Fenne?" Lilz asked, almost involuntarily.

"She is beautiful," Kav reminded her, for a moment looking even younger than his twenty-one years. "And pleasant and lively company, as long as I have the wealth to keep her." She nodded. "Keep those notes. Study them. Let me know what you can figure out."

"If I can decipher them, milord."

"You will. I have faith in you." The Iarl of Northlands left. Lilz got up and closed the door after him, leaning her forehead against it. Kav Treadwell, sweet, conceited, naive, utterly knuckle-headed Kav, the chief power in Kinland? Solely to get enough money to keep his insatiable wife? By putting down her beloved grandpapa, of all idiocies?

She sat at the desk, took three sheets of paper from the drawer, dipped her pen, and began a careful copy of what Makeready had written. Stone might be in the gallery at court any day the peers met. Next chance she got, she'd hand him a letter for his master.

Nor would it hurt Greencrags to be reminded to investigate the ancient functions of the Keeper of the Keys, ceremonial as the post had been allowed to become. He should enjoy his unexpected entry to the Privy Council. The study of history has its uses, Lilz thought. She smiled as she folded the letter.

Sweetdawn

On the third visit Lilz made during Greencrags's long illness, the young iarl looked far better.

This time Lilz had stopped to buy a large basket of sweet cherries, the first of the season. She gave them to the houseman saying they were from her mistress, and when she saw Stone told him the cherries had come straight from the market.

"They're safe, then." Stone glanced behind him. "Other foods have come with messengers saying they were from Hasten House," he whispered. "A venison pastie, very tempting, and soups and a cobbler. It hurt my heart to throw them away."

"Be glad you did. Where they came from, I don't know, but they were not from my mistress."

"Several rats were found dead in the alley. The health warden came to look at my master to be sure he didn't have the plague." Stone caught his lip under his teeth. "He doesn't, of course. I'm relieved to hear that none of the food did come from Lady Greencrags."

Today the iarl was quite up to eating cherries. He wrote a note of thanks to Fenne and gave it to Lilz with a grin.

"Dry the pits for a tossbag for Lealand's grandson," he said to Stone. "Bring me shears and an awl and that old suede bag with the hole in it—that'll be perfect. Good, soft leather with lots of use in it still. I'll stitch up a tossbag myself."

* * *

Making a toy for his guardian's grandson must have been good for Standfast's liver. As summer drew to a close word came that his health was mended. Two days after Presentation Day, the Iarl of Greencrags and three of his men took horse for Sweetdawn, to be sure it was suitable for habitation after being left to the servants for three years.

For the first time in her life, his wife had lost a contest of wills: her grandpapa had finally called in her debts. She'd come from his suite wailing, "Oh, why couldn't he just die? Why isn't he dead?" but there was no more argument. All the wedding gifts, most of the elegant clothing, stood ready for transport. Word came within the month to begin the move.

First, the caravan of household goods. Despite the guards, at Fenne's orders Lilz rode with it, her knife at her waist.

The three-day trip seemed endless. The first day was a market day. A light rain fell. The roads were crammed with jostling carts and people in foul temper slogging on horse or shank's mare through the mud. One of the teamsters let his off mule sideswipe a farmwife's pannier—or she side-stepped her horse into the mule, as one preferred. The pannier was full of eggs every one of which seemed broken. Lilz sat her horse in the cold drizzle, haggling over the price and number of the eggs and the cost of cleaning the mess out of the basket, beyond upending the thing and strewing yolky shell over the road as the farmwife did to demonstrate her loss. Settled on a price only mildly outrageous, Lilz went on in bad humor, not improved when the same teamster got his cart stuck in a pair of ruts too far apart for his wheels.

Rain fell on the second day, too, equally chilly, but at least fewer people were on the road. Lilz was riding a skittish white mare new to the Hasten stable, a beast who saw ghosts behind every tree and had an iron mouth besides. Most of the time she stepped sideways down the track, while Lilz hauled on the reins as if pulling a bucket out of a bottomless well and used her stick more in a mile than she ordinarily did in a month. By the time the caravan drove into the courtyard of the next inn, where two of Standfast's men were supposed to be waiting but weren't, she was ready to take an ax to the animal's skull.

The third day improved enormously: Standfast's men had arrived in the night, the sun rose into a sky laced with cool white clouds, the rain of the preceding two days kept the road dust down, and the mare settled into an easy walk by mid-morning. Late in the afternoon, Lilz had her first sight of Sweetdawn.

The house faced south, a little away from the road. "An old place," Lilz exclaimed, on seeing the plain facade.

"Two hundred years, miss," said the guard Standfast had sent.

"Pretty."

Yellow stone, elegantly proportioned. A large terrace to the east came into view as they approached along a curving drive. The manor stood near the northwest, highest corner of a broad, sloping meadow bordered with chestnut and red maple trees just coming into brilliant fall color. In front of the house and curving around the terrace was a formal garden still filled with bloom. A happy-looking house, Lilz decided; with luck, it would work on Fenne and make her content.

Inside, the house was no disappointment: the same simplicity, the same elegant lines; rooms filled with light. Greencrags eagerly showed her where everything should go. He'd thought to put Fenne in a west-facing suite so the sun wouldn't shine into her windows and wake her earlier than she wanted. His own suite connected through the two dressing rooms. Lilz herself was given a small snug room for a desk and a chair, a place to keep her records to make running Fenne's part of the household easier. She noted the thickness of the door with pleasure. A good place to practice her guitar? "How thoughtful of you, milord!" she said.

"It was Brook's idea, really," the iarl confessed. "He's the houseman. I asked him what I could do to make everyone most comfortable, and he suggested you'd find such a room convenient." Lilz made a mental note to discover the houseman's heart's desire and bring it from Miense, if at all possible.

"One more housemaid!" Brook, found in his pantry, laughed. "Or a round of sharp yellow cheese—I'd settle for that. I do like my toasted cheese of a winter's night."

Lilz spent a day seeing everything as settled as it could be in that short time, got Brook's assurance that all would be ready a week hence, then climbed back on the skittish white mare to return to Miense. She rode into the courtyard at Hasten House on the third day with hands cramped from keeping a tight rein on her mount, but hours early—the mare had taken off at a good gallop each morning, and Lilz had given her head until the kinks were run out. So she now knew four inns along the route, and what to expect of each. Fenne should be comfortable on the road, at least.

They set out the next morning. Under the carriage seat Lilz had tucked a large sharp cheese for Sweetdawn's houseman, and in the sash wrapped around her waist with the money for the journey was a promise from King Guyr of one more housemaid: Nevan Hasten had his uses. A last cartload of possessions, things Fenne absolutely couldn't do without for a week, followed the carriage. Both spare teams were hitched behind the cart. Four retainers armed with pistols rode with them, two ahead and two behind. Their cheerful shouted conversation penetrated even into the closed carriage.

Although the sky was a painful blue and the air mild, Fenne slumped in a corner, staring out the window as if it were the gloomiest of winter mornings. Lilz couldn't blame her. Lady Delle's idea of sending her daughter off to take up married life with a man she'd barely met had been to remark, "Really, Fenne, he's turned out so much better than anyone could've guessed, I don't see what you've got to complain about."

"Exile," Fenne had moaned.

"Don't be absurd." Her mother had laughed. "Three days' easy ride, exile?" She was still chuckling when a servant slammed the carriage door and the driver clicked his tongue to the team.

The leaves of the maples this close to town were most of them simply tarnished, but every so often a whole tree blazed red on the side of the road. Lilz wished she were outside, riding, despite the dust whipped up by a breeze. Maybe the next day she would do that. Surely the carters needed supervision? One wouldn't want a repeat of the egg incident.

Aster cleared her throat. "What a beautiful day!" she said brightly.

"Shut up."

"I beg your pardon, my mistress, I only meant—"

Fenne glowered. "How would you like to walk back to Miense and find yourself some other lady to dress?"

Lilz touched Aster's arm. She slowly relaxed, while Fenne glared at her for a moment or two before going back to the window. No stranger could have guessed that Lady Greencrags was famed for her gaiety and light spirit.

Knowing where to look, Lilz was the first to spot their new home through the trees. She pointed it out to Fenne.

"Sky above! Look at the place!" Fenne flounced back on the seat. "Guyr gave us that? It's almost an insult."

"It's a beautiful house, my mistress." Lilz tried to catch Fenne's eye, but the girl wouldn't look at her. "Don't judge it before you've seen the inside."

Fenne snorted and settled back in her corner. The carriage jolted along. "Greencrags could have fixed the road," she said.

"This is the king's highway." Lilz watched Fenne, wondering what that face would show when they took the final jolt and ran onto Sweetdawn's smooth drive, as they did a few minutes later. The girl blinked; her finely arched eyebrows lifted; she nearly smiled; she said nothing. Perhaps there was hope?

Sweetdawn disappeared behind the trees as the drive passed along the edge of the estate, then reappeared as the fringe of trees became sparser. Sunlight flashed from its tall windows. In the week Lilz had been gone the woods that framed the house had lost half their leaves, but the garden was still filled with color.

Aster touched Lilz's arm and pointed to the flowers as the drive made its curve toward the front of the house. "Yes," Lilz said quietly. "There are more in back."

"You have something you want me to know, Aster?" Fenne demanded.

"No, milady."

"Something about those flowers, maybe?"

"I thought they were pretty. I didn't want Lilz to miss them."

"Lilz has eyes. She's been here before."

Dear heaven, thought the woman with eyes. *What* is she going to say to Greencrags?

The carriage drew up by the wide front steps. Rovvo Standfast dashed down them, smiling. He opened the carriage door himself and let down the folded steps. "Fenne!" Joy lighted his whole face. "Oh, Fenne, it's wonderful to see you!"

"Have you no servants, milord?" Her voice was cold. "Must you open carriage doors for your guests with your own hands?"

"I am always *your* servant," the young man said gallantly. "Never anyone else's."

Fenne went down the steps. Greencrags put an arm around her waist and tried to kiss her, but she turned her face away. "Dinner will be at half-past seven," she said. "I will see you there. In the meantime, the houseman can show me to my room."

By seven-thirty, the carpenter had been called from the stable to board up the door between Fenne's bed chamber and the iarl's. Fenne called her servants to her side. All three women went down to what the iarl had evidently planned as an intimate dinner with his bride. Aster and Lilz were ordered to sit at table. Lilz ate little, in an anguish of compassion for Standfast and fury with her mistress. Aster, nearly weeping with embarrassment, ate less.

Fenne had chosen to wear a dark blue silk gown with a deeply cut decolletage. Her breasts were pressed up into smooth white mounds above the edge of the silk. Eardrops of opals with small diamonds tucked between them dangled beside her slender white neck. Every comment Greencrags made, every attempt at conversation, she greeted with scorn. A storm coming, Lilz thought. She felt as powerless as if a whirlwind were bearing down upon the house and she alone had been deputized to stop it.

Fenne waited until Brook was serving her husband a slice of roast beef to announce that if he hoped ever to share a bed with her he would have to cut off his cock.

Greencrags stared at her. "I beg your pardon, milady?"

Fenne repeated her remark. Everyone else in the room went red, including Brook-—who, trying to efface himself, tripped over the fringe of the rug and dropped the roast with a clatter of metal and china.

Greencrags ignored the noise. "It seems you have a few things to learn about becoming a man's wife," he said, still staring at Fenne.

"I doubt I could learn any of them from you."

"Only for lack of wit."

Fenne was wearing a bracelet of opals and diamonds set in heavy gold. She snatched it off and threw it at her husband. It struck his face.

Stiff silence followed. "Lilz, fetch me my bracelet," Fenne said calmly.

Blood welling drop by drop from a cut under his right eye, the iarl finished his meal without another word.

The first week proved that Fenne meant what she had stated as ground rules: she would see her husband at meals, in the company of her servants—his, too, if he liked—and at no other time. She even hired two of the armed escorts who had accompanied the carriage as body guards to enforce the arrangement. Occasionally, as the Iarl and the Iarlena of Greencrags attempted to move through the house without coming face to face, Lilz found the situation unbearably comic. More often she could scarcely stand to look at the pain in either young face. More often still, she imagined with guilty pleasure the Dych of Summerlea suffering a death usually reserved for traitors—gutted alive and hanged by his bowels until dead. Even that sometimes seemed too merciful.

The fifth night, after Fenne retired to her rooms to write some letters with Aster on guard, Lilz escaped for a moment's relief. She carried a candle down to the kitchen, thinking to find it empty and make herself a cup of tea. Stone was ahead of her, sitting at the scrubbed wooden table with a mug of steaming dark liquid. When she opened the door he looked up, with so woeful a face she began to back out.

"No, come in," he said. "There's more hot water. The servants' tea is in that tin box on the left end of the bottom shelf."

"Thanks." Lilz pinched about a spoonful of tea into a mug and poured water over it from the kettle muttering to itself at the edge of the big iron stove.

"Is my master so repulsive?" Stone asked, when she sat down on the other side of the table.

"I don't think so."

He offered her his spoon. "Then what's the matter with her?"

What to say? Lilz stirred the tea. "She's a spoiled brat who'd rather be at Court flirting with all the dandies."

"I've always thought my master a fine young man." Stone licked his fingers and thriftily pinched out the flame of one candle. "At the time they married, it's true, he seemed arrogant, but that was just over-flexed shyness. I know he's not handsome, but he's not ugly, either—or is he?" Stone glanced up at her.

"To my mind he's quite a pleasant-looking youth."

"Then what can we do?"

"I don't know." Lilz sipped at the tea. Still too hot. "I don't think we can do anything right away. She's stubborn. If we try to push her she'll just—" She shrugged.

"—Stand fast?" Stone inquired, with a smile jerking at one corner of his mouth.

"Refuse to budge." Lilz smiled, too. "But if she shows signs of wavering, then perhaps a judicious push... It's hard to say. I've had almost seventeen years of her, and I still don't know."

"So many sleepless nights." Stone didn't sound as if he were talking to her. Lilz reached across the table and touched his hand.

They had been at Sweetdawn about ten days. As usual, Lilz woke early and watched the room grow light. Fenne and Aster still slept—Fenne in the center of the big bed, Aster on her other side. Lilz slipped out of bed and went to the window. The sun wasn't yet up. A milky haze covered the field between the window and the nearest trees.

I have got to get out, she said to herself. Half an hour can't hurt. Fenne will never know I was gone.

Lilz dampened a cloth in the pitcher standing ready in the dressing room to wash her face and dressed quickly. She went down the back stairs—no one else was stirring—and out into the kitchen garden. Rows of seasonings and pot herbs stood covered with fine droplets of dew, frozen in low places into glittering rime. A few bright stars still shone in the west. It occurred to Lilz that the terrace to the east must have been built as a place from which to watch the sun rise—why else call the house 'Sweetdawn'? No one about, unless the sounds from the stable were the keeper feeding the horses. Not even the cook had yet come down to shake up the banked fire in the stove. She would watch the sun rise from the terrace.

Gravel crunched under her feet as she followed a path along the back of the house. Too noisy? She stepped to the side to walk on the grass so she wouldn't wake anyone. An opening between the broad stone balustrade and the northeast corner of the house admitted her to the terrace.

But the terrace was occupied: not three sashlengths away the iarl himself leaned against the heavy stone railing that divided it from the garden, apparently lost in thought. Lilz stepped back, onto gravel.

Greencrags looked over his shoulder. "Don't go away," he said. "Come watch the sun rise."

As she approached, Greencrags looked again at the garden. "Isn't it beautiful, Lilz?" He waved to include the whole panorama before him.

The sun was the merest sliver of brilliant red peeping through distant trees whose lower trunks were swathed in mist. The sky above it was brushed with the softest of yellows and oranges, decorated with wisps of cloud, shading into an intense deep blue above her head, and the whole meadow between the trees and the low box hedge that edged the formal garden was white with dew.

"That color!" Greencrags levered himself up to sit on the damp stone rail, still absorbed in the view. "I think the shading of a perfect peach must have been designed to remind us of the luminosity of dawn. Think how sunrise would taste if we had the palate for it, Lilz!"

Lilz, her hands still politely folded, cocked her head to look at the boy. His wide smile, directed at the rising sun, made her smile herself. "Delicious indeed, milord," she said, hearing her voice warmed by her smile.

He glanced at her and back at the meadow. "See? The least blade of grass is spangled along each edge with tiny crystal globes. What wouldn't a jeweler give to work something so fine!"

Greencrags sat dreaming for a moment. Lilz thought she'd best remind him she was there. "You should write poetry, milord," she said. "To circulate as manuscript, if nothing more."

"Oh, I haven't the extravagance of mind."

"You have the eye."

"Do you think so?"

"Fresher than the famous Jonquil's."

Greencrags chuckled. "Small trick that! Look there." He pointed with his chin. Three deer had come from the trees to the left and stood in the meadow, heads lifted to sniff the still air. One stepped forward and started to graze. The other two continued to test for scent, large ears swiveling. After a few minutes they, too, began cropping the long grass, and then a few more slipped from the trees to join them.

As the sun topped the tree line the white dew of the meadow turned orange in a flooding wave sparked with tiny rainbows. Lilz heard a small gasp from the boy beside her. "You see?" he said a moment later. "I could never capture that in words. Could you?"

"Not I, milord."

"I feel sorry for the man Guyr evicted. I don't see why he couldn't have lived here at least until I came back from Chrems."

"Your prestige would have been less."

"Oh, prestige!" Greencrags snorted. Someone in the house behind them raised a window. Every head in the meadow came up. Lilz watched the deer drift back to the trees and vanish.

"If people are getting up, I'd best go back, milord."

"Guard duty?" Greencrags looked down at her, his smile twisted.

"I'm sorry."

"Isn't there something you can do? Stone says you've known her all her life."

"No." Lilz gazed at the tightly-laid paving of the terrace. "At least, not yet. Be patient, milord."

"Patient! What about Chrems?"

"I know how hard you must find it." Lilz smiled faintly. "I've got four older brothers. None of them was ever too careful of how he talked around his younger sister."

"Shame on them," Greencrags said.

"Years ago, milord, and no harm done. It taught me caution, sometimes useful, as you can imagine." She bowed and left the iarl sitting on the railing, looking again at the meadow.

As she stepped through the back door she heard the cook curse the stove and one of the kitchenmaids screech at the other about something said to a stable lad.

At least some of life at Sweetdawn was normal.

Chapter Ten

For a woman noted for lightness and laughter, Fenne could become remarkably shrill when she liked.

Her second husband could bellow in kind: it was no secret from any of the servants that he thought her unfaithful—and probably not from anyone riding past in the street at the right moment, either.

Lilz wasn't sure. She could see Northlands's point. It must be difficult to trust a wife you'd won from another man, especially if you'd slept with her under her former husband's nose three or four times a week and knew of others who had shared her favors before you. But Lilz thought it more likely that Fenne was simply starved for attention: without Makeready at his elbow, without the older man's intelligence and experience to balance his own slowness and artlessness, poor Kav Treadwell was almost overcome by the responsibilities the king had placed upon him—responsibilities Makeready had handled easily, and that, to be truthful, most men would not have found so daunting. As Treadwell knew. And now that the Dych of Summerlea seemed to be failing, Kav had nowhere to turn.

Fenne herself was no thinker. She would never understand that Kav was scrambling as hard as he could to keep from falling over a cliff. To her mind, just as she needed him most, her precious Kav had deserted her.

A week past the longest day of the year, Nevan Hasten took a turn for the worse. Fenne came to Lilz as she was working on the accounts to tell her. "Papa says he's coughing up blood." Fenne blinked back tears. "I think I'd best move into Hasten House until—until he's better." She sat looking out the window for several minutes. She had picked up Lilz's abacus when she sat down. The beads clicked steadily as she toyed with them.

"Do you want me to come with you, my mistress?" Lilz asked, when Fenne didn't seem about to continue.

"No...no. You stay here. I need someone I can trust in the house." She looked down at the abacus and pushed the beads to the center one by one. "But be ready to come if I send for you."

"Very well." Lilz smoothed the vane of her pen. Fenne and her grandpapa. Eighteen years. How quickly gone! For no reason she could imagine, a picture presented itself: eleven-year-old Säen sitting in the fishpond at Summerlea bawling his head off, his blond hair plastered to his head and neck with dirty water. Fenne had tired of his teasing and pushed him in. On the other side of the pond, the dych applauded while Säen's mother, the widow of his youngest and least favorite son, scolded him. Lilz smiled briefly.

"What's amusing?" Fenne asked.

"I don't know why—I just thought of the time you pushed Lord Säen into the fishpond."

Fenne laughed. "Oh, I was angry! And oh, how good it felt to see him soaking wet and green with duckweed!" She sobered. "I don't know why either, but I've been thinking a lot about Summerlea lately, too. When grandpapa—When the crisis is over, I think I'll go there for a while. Would that be nice?"

"Who'd stay here?"

Fenne pressed her lips together in a wry little smile. "Kav."

When Fenne left, Lilz sat for some time with her hands clasped on her desk, staring out the window. The sun had swung away, leaving only a narrow shaft of light streaming into her room. Lilz watched it slowly disappear. She heard the carriage drive past the corner of the house. A few minutes later Aster looked around the door to tell her she and Fenne were leaving for Hasten House. "We'll be gone overnight," she said. "Maybe two. I've packed up some clothes in case she decides to stay longer—they're in a case in the middle of the dressing room floor."

"I'll send them on whenever you say," Lilz promised.

"Thanks. You're a love."

Lilz went down to see Fenne off and returned to her room, still thoughtful.

Stone. He'd stood in the shadows in the gallery over the Hall with his hands behind him. "It's not from her, is it?" he'd asked, looking at the letter she'd tried to give him as if it might blister his fingers if he touched it.

"No, it's from me."

At that, Stone had unbuttoned a button, taken her letter and tucked it inside his shirt. Back, when next they met, had come a worn-looking reply from Greencrags thanking her for the copies of Makeready's notes and promising her any service he could do. Now Lilz thought he could do one. In the back of the drawer of the desk was a flat tin box she'd once kept some ledgers in. Lilz took it out and went up to the room she shared with Aster. Although it was late afternoon and the other servants would be busy below, she closed the door before she dragged her big wooden box out from under her side of the bed.

The key to the tin box jingled inside it. She took the key out and put the loop of string it was tied to over her head before she opened the larger box and set her clothing aside. What should she send for safekeeping? She settled on her birth note and orders of servitude, her father's signet and the whizzer she'd broken at House-Among

Oaks—sky above, almost a whole year ago? The rolled socks wouldn't fit in the flat tin box. She opened them out and folded them separately around the signet and the whizzer to keep them from rattling.

Plenty of room left for the poison.

Lilz undid the twine holding the envelopes together and counted them. Twenty-two. The pharmacist's seals were still intact—all but one: Lilz had been too curious about what the stuff looked like not to investigate—the quantities dispensed and the dates they'd been sealed were written in Clock's angular hand. Mistress Stump's note still covered one side of the first envelope: "Sweet Fenne, here is the powder your grandfather asked me to fetch for you. May it work to your good." On the other side, under Clock's notations, in Fenne's neat round letters, "Lilz: You are to put this into a custard and send it to the Old Palace for Sir Jen Makeready. It will keep him healthy."

Food, medicines fetched by Mistress Stump from old Clock, and Fenne's burning hatred of Sir Jen had made a combination a blithering imbecile would suspect: the custard Lilz had sent to the warden had been as innocent of unknown powders as any ever cooked.

Each of the first ten envelopes had a similar notation—one cautioned against using too much, "in case it turns the food bitter and he doesn't eat enough." The rest had only the pharmacist's date and seal. Lilz knelt by her bed with the envelopes in her hands. Surely, a year after Sir Jen's death, Fenne was safe? And with Fenne, she herself?

But Nevan Hasten was dying of lung rot. Who knew what might come, whizzer-like, out of the wainscot? Mistress Stump, maybe. Or even the warden of the prison, installed by Summerlea for the precise reason that he could be depended upon to keep Sir Jen incommunicado. And why? Because he'd "done a favor" and never gotten loose, like the costumer?

With a sigh, Lilz put the envelopes into the tin box. Makeready's letters, wrapped in the ones from her brothers, took too much room. She left them behind. Locking the box, she dropped the key inside her shirt. Now to think of a way to send a letter.

The difficulty was the forty-five minute ride to Standfast House. With Fenne apt to send for her at any moment, Lilz couldn't leave Waterside even for an hour. To ask a house-servant to carry a note to Fenne's ex-husband was clear folly. Nor could she send for a messenger: anyone registered with the crown, anyone trustworthy, would then have on his books a record of a letter from Waterside to Standfast House. Sooner or later the record might be scanned. No. The last thing she wanted was to bring anything down on Greencrags's head.

Lilz, still kneeling, let her face come to rest against the bed. She could think of no one even remotely able to help. Perhaps her brother? But how much could she ask of a man her service had permitted her to see fewer than a dozen times in twenty years?

Besides, it was midsummer. He'd be touring the provinces, taking orders and making repairs. She'd just have to hope a call to Hasten House would come shortly, and be ready to take her chances when she got nearer the center of Miense, as she had with the last letter.

The dych improved somewhat. The crisis passed. Fenne came back to Waterside, and with her Kav Treadwell. Two afternoons later, while Fenne entertained a few friends downstairs, Northlands tapped on the door of Lilz's room and walked in. She looked up from the book she was reading and flushed with guilt.

"Busy, I see," the iarl said. "Don't get up. I wondered what you'd found in those notes I gave you."

Lilz closed the book and put it on her lap. She sighed. "Not much, milord. They're so personal, I'm afraid they might as well be written in cipher."

"Frustrating."

"Yes." Lilz drew the originals of the notes out of her desk. "A challenging puzzle, however."

"It's getting more urgent." Northlands leaned back and adjusted his shoulder blades to the carvings in the chair, arms folded. "With Summerlea sick, the whole government goes into suspense. I want to be ready with any information I can get."

"Why not talk to your father-in-law?"

The iarl laughed. "Meadowlands? What would he know?"

Probably every single fact or speculation the old dych thought useful to secure the family position for generations to come, and a great deal more. Remembering Kav's own ambitions, Lilz thought better of saying so. Northlands was a man good for show: handsome, red-haired, with those deep greenish-blue eyes. Dressed as he was now in a gray tapestry jacket, teal green trousers, green brocade vest and a shirt trimmed with particularly delicate lace, he looked the epitome of a kitchen-maid's view of what a peer should be. But king's favorite or not, he lacked the knack for intrigue. Failing that or a keener brain, a certain steadiness of character might have done for advancement, but Kav Treadwell was a man run by his passions.

"I've been thinking about the blue carpet," he said. "You said you'd seen some in the palace?"

"I thought I might have. Years ago, milord."

"At Fenne's first wedding, wasn't it?"

"Yes."

"That's what I thought you'd said. I went looking."

"And did you find blue carpet, milord?"

"No. I found something much stranger." Treadwell got up and closed the window. Lilz raised her eyebrows. "I know, I said there aren't any whizzers, and I'm sure there aren't, but you know the expression, 'a little bird told the king.'"

Lilz nodded. "What did you find?"

"A door that bites." The iarl came back and sat on the edge of his chair, leaning on the desk to whisper. "I put my hand on the knob, and it bit me." He rubbed the fingers of his right hand as if trying to squeeze something out of their tips. Lilz remembered rubbing her own fingers exactly that way, the night Fenne married Greencrags.

"How do you mean, it bit you?"

The iarl sat back. "I—yes, I guess that does sound funny Not with teeth, of course. With a kind of tingle, and a snap, like you sometimes get when you touch something in the middle of winter? But this was just last week, when it was so sultry. And the feeling was much, much stronger than just a little spark. I held on anyway, but the door was locked."

"How strange! Where was this door?"

"I think it might be where you found the blue carpet. I tried to trace your mistake, you see? I've spent almost a month at it, late at night, whenever I could get away. I made a map." Kav reached into his jacket and pulled out a battered sheet of paper, which he spread on the desk. "This is the Ceremonial Hall, here, you see? And these are the corridors that go off. I wrote them all down as I went through them. Some of these doors here were locked...but I think they're all rooms, see the square empty places left?"

"Yes." Lilz felt the thrill of the chase begin to build. The map was crude, but readable; Northlands had even thought to mark the distances in paces. He must have spent hours—

"This door here, at the end of this corridor." Marked with a wiggly line. "That's the one that bit me."

Lilz examined the map. She'd gone by instinct to her left—yes, about there—and there was where she had recognized where she was and found her way back. Yes. That might well be the door that had bitten her, too.

"Do you think it might lead to the blue carpet?" Northlands asked.

How earnest he looked! How hopeful! Lilz gazed down at the map. "I'm sorry, milord. I couldn't say for sure. But I don't think so. The door to the carpet didn't bite me when I went through it."

Northlands sighed. "I thought I might be onto something."

"Leave the map with me. Maybe comparing it to Sir Jen's notes will help," Lilz suggested.

"I'll need it. I've got more exploring to do."

"I could trace a copy now, milord, against the windowpane, and add to it as you discover more."

"Good idea. I knew you were clever. Shall I hold the inkwell for you?"

"Thank you, milord, but I'm afraid that might blot. I'll use my writing lead." Lilz took another sheet of paper from her dwindling supply and held the two sheets against the window to trace. She would have to find some way of replacing the paper she had used; it was expensive and Fenne would want an accounting. Nor would this be the last theft. Greencrags might make something of the map—she'd copy it for him, but a neater job, and not against the window where she could so easily be seen at work.

Finished, she glanced through the glass before she turned away. Someone had drawn a boat up to the landing and was rolling a barrel through the courtyard gate.

Ah. If she could somehow arrange to meet Standfast there, and hand him the tin box herself?

The New Housemaid

A few snowflakes had drifted out of a sky the color of pewter that afternoon, but if they had been the edge of a storm it had missed Sweetdawn. Just after dark a messenger rode up to the house with a packet of letters. Brook, the houseman, called Lilz downstairs to take Fenne's. She sorted through them, noticing with pleasure a thick letter from Lady Riverside: surely that would contain a few poems of Sir Jen Makeready's, which Fenne would pass on to Lilz to read so she could pilfer some intelligent comment to make in reply to her mother's best friend. One addressed in Kav Treadwell's hand Lilz slipped into her pocket in case Greencrags should appear. While she still stood in the hall the messenger asked the houseman for a night's lodging before going back to the village with any replies. Brook sent him off to the stable to sleep in the loft with the lad—good accommodations, warmer than the servants' attic and close to the frozen privies.

Fenne brought a few of the letters to the dinner table. During the soup, at which she turned up her nose, she sat breaking seals and skimming the contents of the notes. Aster, Lilz, and Stone sat tensely along the sides of the table, as usual feeling too constrained to talk to one another and having no cause to talk to their mistress and master. The three had agreed among themselves that dinner guests were most welcome at Sweetdawn.

Today there were none, so here they sat. The meat and bread arrived at table. Fenne ate while continuing to read. Lilz, sitting straight in her chair, cut into a slice of perfectly-roasted lamb. She ached to be in the servants' hall eating the wrong end of yesterday's roast, amid the laughter and talk. In the iarl's private dining room there was only the clink of cutlery against china, an occasional *hmmch-ch* from Brook—who had a cold—at the sideboard, the crinkle of Fenne's letters, and the soft sound of genteel chewing.

"Here's an invitation to Riverside for the week before the annual meetings begin." Fenne tossed the letter across the table for Greencrags to look at. "Then ride up to Miense together for the gala. I think we should go."

Her husband scanned the note and glanced up. "You do realize we'd be expected to share a bed," he reminded her.

"The four of us should be quite cozy, then, shouldn't we?"

"Four of us?" Greencrags looked from his wife to her servants and back. "You don't seriously mean to take Lilz and Aster to bed with us, do you?"

"To bed *between* us." Across the table from Lilz, Stone put down his knife and fork and stared at Fenne.

"Oh, I see." The iarl's voice was so edged, Lilz winced. "Well, let's have Stone, then, too, shall we? No reason he should shiver alone in his cot when he can have four healthy bodies to warm him!"

"All right," Fenne agreed casually. "We'll have Stone, too. He can sleep next to Aster; he should enjoy that."

"No."

Stone had spoken the first word from any of the servants in the whole month they had sat at table. Everyone looked at him.

"You're not insulting Aster, are you, Stone?" Fenne asked.

"Your pardon, Aster. But I will not share a bed with three women and my master. It's just not right."

"Suit yourself," Fenne said. "I'd have thought you'd jump at the chance—but maybe you'd prefer a night with the messenger. He's down in the barn."

Stone's lips paled. A patch of color bloomed on each cheek. "You, milady, have a sweet face," he said stiffly, "but it hides an evil heart. The worst day of my master's life was the day King Guyr chose you for his bride. And you, my master, if you descend to her level you can do nothing but harm to yourself."

Fenne laughed. "Stone has spoken!"

"Yes, Stone has spoken!" The body-man glared at her. "And not nearly soon enough. You treat your husband like the dirt on your shoes, but you aren't worthy to be the dirt on his! You—"

Oh, Stone, Stone, watch out! Lilz thought.

Fenne had drawn herself erect. "Greencrags, curb your servant!"

"Curb him?" the iarl said. "*Curb* him? What, madam, do you think he's a horse? No, I won't curb him."

"Out," Fenne said to Stone. "Get out."

Stone remained sitting. He looked to the iarl.

"Do you hear me?" Fenne shrieked. "Get out of this room! You have no right to be in this room!" Stone took a long, shaky breath, but he stayed where he was. Lilz slowly put down the forkful of stewed carrots she'd half raised to her mouth, hoping Fenne wouldn't notice the motion.

"You are not my mistress." Stone's voice was shaking, too. "I obey my master's orders, but I do not obey the orders of some callous wench who happens to show up at the front door, whether she calls herself his wife or not."

"Oh, you horrible man! How dare you speak that way? Out, out, out!" Fenne rushed to the side of the table to pull at Stone, who didn't move even when she twisted his ear. "You filthy-mouthed perversion! Who are you to call me a wench?"

"Let go of him!" Greencrags jumped up and pried at the fingers Fenne had clamped on Stone's ear. Tears stood in Stone's eyes, but he kept his seat. Fenne's grip came loose. Stone put a hand over his ear. Lilz dug her nails into her palms to keep from crying out.

"You may go, Stone." Greencrags grabbed his wife's wrist as she raised her hand to slap the body-man and clamped her arms to her sides. Probably it is the first time he has held her so closely, Lilz thought, still rigid in her seat. Beside her, Aster was trying not to weep. Small choking noises gave her away.

Stone rose from his chair, bowed to the iarl, and left the room without hurry. Lilz saw blood on his ear. Brook glanced at Fenne and followed Stone out.

"Let go of me, you barbarian!" Fenne said through her teeth.

Greencrags let go. Fenne ran from the room, shouting for her bodyguards, leaving Aster and Lilz still at the table. The iarl resumed his seat. He looked at them for a moment, his face blank.

"If you'll excuse me, milord," Aster whispered. She jumped up and ran out of the room. She'd forgotten to curtsy.

The iarl shut his eyes and sighed. "Finish your meal if you like, Lilz."

"Thank you, milord, but I don't think I can. Please do excuse me." Lilz stood, bowed, and went, not to the door to the main hall, but to the door to the back of the house. There she stopped and looked at the boy sitting motionless at the table, alone in the room. "Milord," she said. "You shouldn't descend to my mistress's level. Stone's right about that."

"Is he?" A dull question, requiring no answer. Lilz let the door close behind her. She found Stone perched on a stool in the houseman's pantry, his elbows on his knees, one hand over his injured ear, the other across his eyes.

"I think our iarl needs service," she said to Brook, who hurried into the dining room. "Stone, I'm so sorry." The man didn't move. "Are you all right?" He nodded. Lilz stood looking at him for a minute or two. "Let me see that ear?"

Stone let his hand drop, still hiding his face. The ear was purple with trapped blood and swelling badly. Fenne had left a deep, bleeding scratch on the innermost whorl. "It could do with some ice," Lilz said.

"The skivvy's gone to the fishpond to get some."

"And a leech or two."

"Brook will send someone to the village pharmacist first thing in the morning."

"Good." She put an arm across Stone's shoulders. "I don't know how you've restrained yourself so long," she said. "For me, I have to remind myself constantly that she controls my whole life. But she doesn't control yours."

"Oh, she does!" He sighed.

"I'm a coward, Stone," Lilz said, near tears. "If I could stand up to her better, maybe she wouldn't be so—"

"Wicked," Stone supplied.

"No, it's not Fenne who's wicked." She wished Stone would look at her. "It's her grandfather. She's just willful and spoiled. I'm afraid it's partly my fault."

"Wicked or willful, it comes to the same thing."

"Lilz," Fenne shouted, from somewhere upstairs. "Lilz, where are you? Come here!" Stone made a little dismissive gesture. The under kitchenmaid opened the back door, her apron loaded with chunks of ice.

"Break that small and wrap it in a towel before you put it on him," Lilz told her. "And get a little whiskey from Brook to wipe that scratch." She hurried up the back stairs as Fenne shouted again.

A few days after that incident the promised extra housemaid arrived—in a carriage, to everyone's startlement. She spoke Kennish with a thick accent, very fast, as if she thought herself fluent. The day she came, Greencrags and two of the local gentry had gone on a hunt with several servants apiece. The successful party rode into the stable yard near dusk. The usual racket—hoofbeats, whinnies, yelping hounds, shouting men and an exuberant blast or two on a hunting horn—announced their arrival. The deer, a handsome buck with enormous antlers, gutted and bled and tied to a pole by its legs, was carried through the back door just as the new housemaid reached the bottom of the stairs a sashlength away. She screamed.

Lilz had come to the kitchen to collect a tray for Fenne, who was boycotting meals after Greencrags's defense of Stone and refusal to discipline him. She ran into the back hall to see what was wrong—but what was it? The two servants carrying the deer stood just inside the open door, equally confused, while the housemaid cowered against the stairwall, her hand pressed over her mouth.

The man at the lead end of the pole dropped his burden, but the man at the rear end held on. The deer flopped sideways onto the floor. The liver fell out. The new housemaid crouched against the wall, eyes squeezed shut, and made retching noises. The cook pushed Lilz aside to rescue the fine, fat liver and began to berate first the servant who had let the pole fall, then the one who had not. Both defended themselves loudly while Lilz gaped at the bizarre behavior of the housemaid, who now crept back up the steps toward the second floor.

"What's wrong?" she asked, running up the stairs after the woman.

"Thing," said the maid.

"Thing?" Lilz, recalling the difficulties she'd once had with the Travaltian tongue, was careful to speak as slowly and distinctly as she could. "The deer carcass, you mean?"

"Deer carcass," the woman said, as if she had never heard the words before. "Yes. In the hall below."

"But it's dead. It can't hurt you."

"Why bring to the hall?"

Why? Lilz stared at the woman. "The cook has to finish dressing it so it can hang."

The strange housemaid was now sitting on a step, with Lilz crouched beside her. "Dress? Hang?" Her lips moved: trying out a sentence before she said it, as Lilz had done as a young girl touring Travaltia. "For use as decorative object?"

"What?" Lilz ran the sounds over in her mind and deciphered the words. Decorative—sky above! "No. To make it fit to eat."

"One eats this carcass?"

Lilz felt her jaw sag. "Haven't you ever heard of venison?"

"Oh, yes, venison! It comes from this carcass's corpse?"

Lilz began to feel as if the world had come a little loose from its moorings. "A carcass *is* a corpse," she said, as carefully as if she were explaining a ghostly noise in the night to herself. "The animal is called a deer."

"Oh, the *animal* is the deer. As the pork animal is the hog?" Lilz nodded. "How is it meant, the verb *dress*, in this case?"

Mindful of the shriek that had followed the loose liver into the hall, Lilz braced herself. "It means to take the insides out and remove the hide—the skin—and to trim the waste parts—"

The housemaid nodded vigorously. "I understand. Is it possible to watch these interesting doings?"

"You could ask the cook," Lilz said doubtfully.

The maid appeared to take a grip on herself. "I ask."

"You'd better check with the head hall maid, first."

But the new maid didn't seem to hear. She got up and started back down the stairs. Lilz stared after her. Where could the woman come from, that she didn't know how deer were dressed out, but knew what venison was? Even someone as coddled as Fenne knew all about that! This woman was her own age, mid-thirties, at least. No. The hair at her temples was beginning to gray and she was running to fat—maybe middle forties. And first to scream when the fresh deer came into the hall, then to want to watch the cook prepare it?

Aster came down the steps from the second floor. "Oh, Lilz, there you are! Fenne wants her tray. "

"Yes." Lilz stood up, shaking her head. "I was just getting it. Aster, have you noticed anything odd about that new maid?"

Aster rolled her eyes. "Who hasn't! She's been here three hours and everyone's talking!"

The next afternoon Aster darted into the hall from Fenne's dressing room as Lilz passed on her way from the sitting room to fetch some records. "Lilz," she whispered. "You won't believe this. That maid?"

Lilz didn't have to ask which one.

"She didn't know where to empty the chamber pots."

"You're joking."

Aster started to cross her hands over her breast and turned the gesture into folded arms. The remnant of Mothergod worship was innocent enough; every child did it, but best to avoid even the suggestion of lawlessness: Lilz, too, glanced about for a whizzer. The bodyguard on duty was sitting on a chair outside the door to the suite, mending a cloak. Aster's back was to him. "I swear I'm not," she said.

"Maybe she's fallen aristocracy," Lilz mused. "A captive from the Galtrivan war too shamed to go back?"

"Oh, come, Lilz! Even Fenne knows where to empty a chamber pot!"

"True. Not that she's ever done it."

"No, but she could if she absolutely had to. And listen to this. That maid didn't want to share a bed with anyone. She went to Brook about it, you can imagine how far that got her, and then she went to Greencrags!"

"Sky above! What did he do?"

"Oh, she didn't get past Stone, of course. He sent her away, told her what's good enough for the rest of us is good enough for her, and she'd appreciate her company when the wind came through the roof tiles. *Then* she said she'd prefer to have a room to herself! Stone about fainted, I bet."

Lilz chuckled. She could imagine Stone's bland face stark with surprise, his indignant retelling of the incident, and his wry little smile when he was done.

"She asks the *dumbest* questions!" Aster continued. "Oh-oh, here she comes."

The new housemaid came along the hall with a feather duster in her hands. She seemed to be examining the way it was constructed. At a side table outside Greencrag's suite she stopped and soberly wiped the *side* of the duster across its surface, pressing too hard, and came on toward Aster and Lilz.

"Here, let me show you." Lilz stepped forward with her hand out for the duster. The maid frowned, but she gave it to her. "The top of all this wainscoting needs to be dusted," Lilz said. "So you go along the hall like this, using the tips of the feathers, you see? Just whisking."

"Whisking?" The maid looked confused. "As with drink?"

"Drink?"

"In a bottle downstairs is a drink—"

"Oh, *whiskey*. No, no. Nothing at all to do with that. I mean, brush lightly—"

Aster watched the lesson, laughing. The housemaid looked at her with her lips compressed in puzzlement, but went on down the hall dabbing awkwardly at the wainscot.

"Dear heaven," Lilz said. "Whiskey."

"Lilz." Aster frowned. "Whiskey's a gentlemen's drink. It must be in the sideboard, mustn't it? How does she know what's in the sideboard? Doesn't Brook keep it locked?"

"I'd think so."

Fenne opened the door to the suite. "Lilz, what's keeping you? Can't you find those certificates?"

"I'm sorry, my mistress," Lilz said, as Aster vanished into the dressing room. "I got delayed. I'll be back in a moment."

After the conference with Fenne—who laughed just as hard as Aster had at the antics of the new maid—Lilz went down to the dining room. As she had thought, the sideboard was locked. Brook was not in his pantry. She glanced about the room but saw no keys, or any pegs they might hang on when not in use.

Peculiar.

Other gossip soon flew about the new servant. Each of her outlandish questions seemed to top the last. She had a genius for the most distressing topics—once insisting that Lilz tell her the names of every relative she could remember, although Lilz explained that she was a bond-servant and had sold her connection to family. The woman hadn't seemed to understand. It had taken Stone, through welcome providence coming along the second-floor hall, to rescue Lilz from her attention.

The woman wrote in a plain book each night, and at times during the day, "a hand so crabbed I can't make out a single word," according to the maid who shared her bed. She neglected or misunderstood her work, and was often found where she didn't belong. No one missed any possessions—she was never suspected of theft—but no one appreciated her furtive searches of their belongings, either.

The day Lilz surprised the new maid poking through the papers in her own desk in her own snug room she had Fenne send one of the guards into the village to buy a tin box with a key. That afternoon she put her ledgers into it to keep them away from prying eyes and hung the key around her neck.

Chapter Eleven

Late summer turned cold and wet. For three or four nights rain drummed on the roof tiles so loudly sleep was fugitive; a raw damp seeped through even the wool blanket Lilz shared with Aster. A few chilly days of light sprinkles followed. Then hard rains returned, a month earlier than usual. Gardens turned to sloughs, roads to ankle-deep channels of clinging muck. Three nights in a row brought frost. Fear of a poor harvest hung like the mist in the air, even in urban Miense. But at Waterside that fear was less immediate than the worry over what the weather might do to the Dych of Summerlea's lungs. Fenne moved back to Hasten House, as before leaving Lilz behind to manage her household.

The tin box still sat at the back of Lilz's desk drawer. To its contents she had added the copy of Treadwell's map she had made for Greencrags, faithfully amended each time Kav came by to report the results of his nocturnal palace explorations. She had seen no way of sending Greencrags either the map or her letter.

With Fenne gone, Waterside suffered no crises. Therefore Lilz had only to shepherd her mistress's investments and confer briefly with the houseman each morning, leaving her long stretches of free time to read or play the guitar. This she did in Fenne's suite, to avoid being gossiped about by the other servants: she was no longer tutoring Fenne in literature or music and had lost her prime excuse for either activity.

Two weeks went by. Lilz found herself pacing the house, too tense to throw off the traces she'd hitched to her problem and find a new route to the answer.

Nevan Hasten himself provided one.

At the end of the second week a messenger came to Waterside with a note from the dych asking Lilz to attend him that afternoon. She hurriedly added a few lines to the letter to Greencrags, explaining her difficulty with communications, folded in the map, and sealed the packet before ordering a horse saddled and riding across town with the messenger.

At Hasten House, Lilz stopped for a moment to chat with Gluin while turning over the horse to her care. The stablekeeper clicked her tongue as she ran her hand over his side. "Feel that!"

Lilz ran her hand along the wet side and felt the ripple of ribs.

"I'll slip him some corn while you're in the house," Gluin said. "Any bit of fat for winter will help, and with the old man sick nobody's checking each measure of feed."

"They say the ears are heavy in the fields, if only the weather would dry," Lilz remarked.

"There's that, but some householders will take any excuse to be stingy." Gluin narrowed her eyes at the horse Lilz had been riding. "Be thankful if you get your own bread."

Lilz reminded herself to have a short talk with the Waterside stablekeeper, who had ample funds to buy feed for the winter even if the price should double. She went into the house and presented herself. A new maid hung her cloak on a peg in the back hall and showed her up to the dych's suite. No one was in the sitting room, but the door to the dych's bedchamber stood open, so Lilz looked in. Summerlea was in his bed, Fenne at his side, as was her father.

"Ah, Lilz," the old man said. This set off a frightening fit of coughing. Fenne pounded her grandfather's back, glancing at Lilz as if to ask her for help. "Thank you, moppet," the dych wheezed at last. He spat blood-stained phlegm into a handkerchief. "Go wait in the sitting room while I talk with Lilz, there's a good girl."

"What do you have to say to Lilz that you can't say to me?" Fenne objected.

"Fenne," said her father. "Just go."

Fenne went. "And shut the door," the dych added. Pouting, Fenne swung the door shut. Lilz was sure she wasn't more than a handsbreadth away from the thick walnut panel. Much luck to her—Lilz had never succeeded in listening at any door in Hasten House.

"What's it been, Lilz?" The dych raised his eyebrows at her. "Nineteen years?"

"Yes, your Grace."

"Half your life with me, woman! What do you think of that?"

Lilz groped for an answer. "A long time, your Grace," she said after a moment. "But mostly spent with Fenne, as you know."

"The money that's kept you was mine. I've a question for you, Lilz." The dych stopped. Lilz thought he was about to cough again. She'd have said the man wasn't long for this world, if he hadn't rallied so well a couple of months earlier. He was pale, his cheeks a feverish pink and his eyes glistening with an unhealthy luster; she thought he'd lost flesh since she'd seen him last, a month or so before. The coughing fit, when it came, was lighter than the last.

"I've a question for you, Lilz," Summerlea repeated. "But first, come here. Sit by my side."

She started to sit in the chair Fenne had just left, but the dych waved her onto the edge of the bed. She perched on the turned-down lace border of the top sheet. He took her wrist between his fingers. "Where's your heartbeat?" he muttered. "Ah, there." He chuckled. "For a moment, I thought you were dead."

"Not yet, your Grace."

"Skinny but hale, eh?" His cold fingers were firm on her wrist as he bantered with her a moment longer. "Now, tell me. How many Kinlands are there?"

"How many Kinlands?" Lilz blinked. "The country? One."

"Just one?"

"How could there be more?"

"Can't you think of a way?"

Lilz was silent a moment. "Only if you mean that each of us has his own view of the world? Then there are as many as know of it."

"Maybe, maybe. A good answer." The dych released her wrist and turned to his son. "Steady as a trotting horse, Olen. You need do nothing about her."

"Your Grace?" Lilz said, bewildered.

"I should have known, of course. This may surprise you, Lilz, but I do know what honor is. I'm a suspicious old fellow, though, and couldn't help myself."

"Your Grace, I'm afraid I don't understand."

"Afraid!" He grinned and started to chuckle. Something about the sound sent a tremor down her spine. The chuckle turned into a cough. She pounded his back until he hawked and spat. "Afraid! No, Lilz, be glad. Glad is how you should feel. Go on home, now."

"I hope your cough improves, your Grace," she said, standing.

"Oh, it will be gone entirely soon enough, Lilz, soon enough." She was at the door when he said, "Wait."

Lilz turned. A sick old man in a huge bed hung with silk, in a room darkened by deeply folded blue velveteen draperies drawn across the usually bright windows. How absurd it seemed to think that he could ever have intrigued as he had, or inspired a thrill of apprehension only a moment before...and Meadowlands, sitting in a cushioned chair near his father's bed, wasn't he just a man, a somewhat foolish man as he looked, with no real effect on anything?

"You'll thank me for those years one day, Lilz," the dych said. "Not now, but one day. And I thank you for them, on the moppet's behalf, since she hasn't the wit to see what you've done for her."

"I've always done my best, your Grace."

"Have you, Lilz? I sometimes wonder. Go away, now."

She went into the sitting room. Her heart had been steady for the dych's odd question, but that last remark had left it hammering. Could he know about her contact with Greencrags? She thought she'd been discreet. A scrap of conversation between the old man and his son, overheard on that visit a month ago, came back to her: his Grace remarking, "Either he's much brighter than we thought, or he's got a new advisor." Both sets of brown eyes had turned to her as she tapped on the bed chamber door. "Merrow Strengthen has never had that much imagination," the dych had continued, grinning and motioning to her to enter. Perhaps meant for her ears? Lilz wondered now.

Or had he guessed about Makeready, who had not turned yellow?

Fenne was near one of the rain-gorged windows, her hands clasped at her waist. She looked as if she hadn't moved for several minutes. "What did grandpapa want?" she asked.

"He wanted to know how many Kinlands there are."

"You see?" Fenne shook her head. "His mind's wandering. It won't be long, now."

"No, I think not."

"Oh, Lilz—" Fenne came across the room and slipped her arms around Lilz's waist. "What shall I do?" She rested her head against Lilz's chest and started to cry. Lilz rocked her gently in her arms until Meadowlands came to the door and asked Fenne to come back to her grandfather's side. He gave Lilz a long, sober look she couldn't quite understand.

"You've no idea how lucky you are," he said, and escorted his daughter back into the dych's room.

At Standfast House, cold water poured off the roof tiles into the courtyard as if defending the windows. Lilz tied up the horse and dashed through the deluge to slip into the house by the servants' door.

The houseman walked out of his pantry to see who had come in. "Well, Lilz! You've missed me that badly, have you?"

"Pining away, Reed, my dear, as you can see." She showed him her broadest grin.

"Couldn't resist sneaking back for a quick tumble, I know, I know." Reed made as if to steal a kiss, all a sham, and laughed when she presented her cheek. "What does bring you?"

"Message for your iarl." She handed over the letter.

"Will you wait for a reply?"

"I'm told none is needed, thanks." She'd just denied herself a half hour's toasting beside the kitchen fire and a hot cup of tea to fortify her for the cold ride back to Waterside, but she couldn't steal any more time. Ducking back through the torrent pouring off the roof, she swung into the saddle and walked the horse smartly out of the yard.

Aster caught a terrible cold, which settled in her lungs. Hot and raving, she was clearly unfit to work, so Lilz returned to Hasten House four days after the interview with the dych to act as body-maid for Fenne until Aster recovered.

The dych was no better, but no worse: Fenne had resumed her normal social life. When Lilz walked into her mistress's suite she found her talking with a friend, looking less well-turned-out than usual—Coral must have been rushed that morning, with both Fenne and Lady Delle to dress and most probably Aster to see to, too. "Lilz!"

Fenne exclaimed, with every appearance of great pleasure. "Look at what Benina's brought. There's a new poet."

"Oh?" Lilz took the sheet of manuscript, caught the guest's twitch of an eyebrow out of the corner of her eye, and said, "Thank you, my mistress."

"What do you think?" Fenne turned to her friend and said, "Lilz is really very clever. She taught me to cast a rhyme."

Lilz was scanning the poem: not bad. Certainly one of the better things going the rounds since Makeready...a couplet caught her eye: *Men/Should rather fear the thousand tiny deaths / That filch their lives in daily, unmarked breaths.* That had a familiar ring.

"There's no signature, my mistress," she said.

"No, isn't it exciting? Nobody knows who it is."

The Hasten taste for intrigue and mystery, brought to Fenne's level. Lilz handed the page back with a smile. "Nicely turned. Are there more?"

"A few." Benina shifted uncomfortably. She couldn't be used to conversing with servants. "I don't have any with me, though."

Fenne reread the poem, frowning. "Copy this out, would you, Lilz?" She passed her the page. "I think I'll keep a few and see if you can figure out who wrote them." Lilz took pen, paper, and ink from Fenne's desk and went into the dressing room. As she sat down at the dressing table she heard the guest remark on Fenne's "odd servant" and Fenne make some off-hand reply.

I could tell her who it is right now, Lilz thought, reading the poem once more before starting to copy. What would she say if I told her she'd once been married to the man? Smiling with her secret, she uncorked the ink and dipped her pen.

The next day, a Thornday, the dych insisted against all protests that Fenne attend at open Court. "He says he needs me there," Fenne reported to Lilz. "I just don't understand it at all. Why shouldn't I stay here with him?"

"Politics," Lilz said. "He needs the family to put up a good front, so the vultures don't gather yet."

"Vultures? What vultures?"

Lilz sighed. "A figure of speech, my mistress. He wants to put off the dealing for power that will surely accompany his death until your father's place is secure."

"Oh," Fenne said. "Oh. I see. Is mother going?"

"I'm sure she is."

Aster's fever had broken but she could scarcely stand unaided, let alone work, so it was Lilz who dressed Fenne and would accompany her to the palace. She made sure to share a large pot of tea with Coral before they left: she'd need her out of the way for a minute or two should Stone be in the gallery with a reply to her letter.

She was in luck. Stone greeted her with a slight lift of his eyebrows as she stood in the doorway scanning the faces of the other waiting servants. Coral didn't appear to recognize him; she stood on tiptoe making her own search and left Lilz's side with a whispered hello to another maid at the lattice. Stone caught Lilz's eye again and touched his shirt as she went to join Coral. She nodded.

The tea took forever to work. She must have a bladder the size of a mare's, Lilz thought more than once before Coral at last excused herself to run downstairs to the servants' latrine. Stone wasted no time. He was at the back wall of the gallery before Lilz, to stand between her and the others. "Whizzers?" Lilz asked silently.

In the Hall, Guyr announced something in his booming ceremonial voice and a round of applause sounded.

Stone leaned close. Lilz caught his scent, coarse soap and the man himself. She felt it spread over her like a protective cloak. "I'm supposed to arrange what you want of my master," he said under cover of the applause. "Could you bring it here?"

"No, it's too big. I can't carry it hidden." Guyr was making another announcement. "Do you know the place called Waterside?"

"Yes," Stone said into her ear. Now the peers were cheering over something.

"Could someone trustworthy come to the watergate and take a tin box from me, late at night?"

"I'll see. I'll find a way to tell you."

"Not right away. I'm at Hasten House now—Aster's sick. When you see her here, I'll have returned to Waterside."

"I hope she's not in danger?"

"She was, but she's better now."

"Can you give her my good wishes?"

"Why not? We've met by chance, haven't we?"

Stone grinned. "To chance," he said, and embraced her briefly. They returned to their places as someone down in the Hall got to his feet to speak.

"What was all the noise about?" Lilz asked the maid next to her. "I couldn't hear."

"He's given the Iarl of Riverside some new post," the maid said. Lilz blinked; she could understand applause for that, but cheers? She said so.

"Can't you see? The sun's come out—that was the cheering." A light bright enough to create vague shadows on the floor of the Hall streamed through the high windows. It brightened as Lilz watched; the faces of the peers turned toward it like sunflowers while the king listened gravely to a petitioner. "Not a minute too soon, either," the maid continued. "I've been juggling a hole at the edge of milady's umbrella the best part of a month, and will she have the silk replaced? Or even patched? Not with the water falling on my head, she won't."

When Coral came back and asked about the clapping and shouts, the other maid was still complaining.

Toasted Cheese and a Journey

"The finest cheese I've had in many years." Brook bent down and adjusted the rack in front of the kitchen fire, where a slice of the cheese was just beginning to bubble on a slab of bread. "Let me tell you again, I do appreciate it."

"I told the merchant it was for the Dych of Summerlea."

Brook grinned at Lilz. His face was red from the fire, where an occasional drop of water hissed into the coals from the chimney—it was snowing lightly tonight, a wet snow that melted as it fell. For the first time in days, Lilz was happy: the kitchen was warm, Brook friendly. With the iarl gone hawking for the best part of a week she wasn't expected to guard Fenne's side all night. Meals were peaceful and her stomach content. She was darning one of Fenne's stockings. Her mend was all but invisible, the sort of small mindless perfection in which Lilz took pride.

"Too bad you couldn't have got me a maid fit for a dych."

"That, I'm sorry about."

The houseman shrugged. "What could you do?"

"At least she's learned where to empty the chamber pots and how to dust a hall!"

Brook snagged his toasted cheese onto a plate with a fork and carried it to the table, where Lilz sat with her tea. "Lilz, have you ever wondered..." He broke off and looked about the room. So did Lilz. Any oval object in a shadow could be a whizzer, and no way to tell it from a large blackbeetle unless you caught it or it flew.

His meaning was clear enough. Probably every servant in the house had wondered whether the woman was the king's spy. "A very clumsy one, if so," Lilz said. "Though I suppose it's not strictly necessary to be adroit at it."

"But why here?" Brook asked.

Lilz shrugged. "Who knows?"

Brook looked straight at her. "I've wondered about you, too."

"Me!"

"Because of the way you talk."

"Oh." Her happiness, already dimming, vanished. Lilz bent her head over the stocking as if to see better. "I can't help that."

"What's your real name?"

"Lilz."

"Your whole name, I mean."

"It's Lilz." Brook kept looking at her. He had bright blue eyes that reminded her of her father's. Her father's hair would be as gray as

Brook's by now. He was about as tall. He might even be as portly, though last she'd seen of him he'd been as skinny as herself. "I'm a bond-servant, Brook. I sold my name years ago."

"Was Lilz your first name to begin with, at least?" She nodded. "Mine's Jen." He looked at her expectantly.

"Just Lilz. I'm glad you like the cheese, Brook, and I'm sorry about the maid." She started to get up.

"No, sit down, I'm out of line." Brook cut his snack in two. "I apologize. It only just dawned on me what your way of speech might mean—forgive me if I embarrassed you." He held out the plate with half of the toasted cheese pushed toward her.

Let him think her the illegitimate daughter of some careless woman in the peerage. She could scarcely refuse his peace offering, although she didn't care much for sharp yellow cheese. She took it with thanks.

Neither spoke until the snack was gone. Brook cleared his throat. "Swear you're not one of those?"

Lilz set the needle and put her hands palm to palm, as if called to witness at a trial. "I swear."

"Stone said he didn't think so...." The idea that Stone and the houseman had discussed her was as irksome as a burr up her pants leg. Brook leaned forward. "Help me figure out what this new housemaid is."

"How?"

"Maybe you could ask her some questions—she's always asking questions. There's no reason she shouldn't answer a few."

"Worth a try." Lilz automatically scanned the greasy stone walls of the kitchen. The lamplight was too dim to reach into the corners, but she saw no large bugs.

"Tomorrow, then." Brook fetched the kettle from the stove to warm his own cup and silently offered to fill hers. She watched the liquid rise and pale against the white china.

What about that book the woman wrote in every day? Lilz hadn't seen it: the maid who shared a bed said it was such bad writing it was impossible to read. A private code? Or was the woman just a foreigner? Maybe from the same land as the men who had talked behind that door in the palace on the night of Fenne's wedding? Maybe that was a good question to start with: what land are you from?

The next morning was busy: the trip to Riverside was only a few days off. Lilz had been helping Aster with Fenne's wardrobe all week. The gowns their mistress would take had to be spot-cleaned and pressed and put into trunks with a cushioning of fine linen; her underdresses and drawers had to be washed and ironed, each point of the lace pulled out to show the design; the jewels she'd decided on—a different set every day, naturally; Aster was ready to give up on them and on Fenne—sorted out of the tangle Fenne kept them in and polished, their individual cases found and filled and tucked into a strongbox for the journey. And of course Fenne had to have casual clothing for daytimes, pants and shirts and knitted pullovers, all of which had to be in perfect condition and which were distinguished from those of her servants not just by their perfect, generous cut but by their luxurious fabrics, all of which required the most delicate laundering.

All this flutter, designed to impress, had left Lilz secretly amused. Anyone knew Riverside had come by his title through the back door. The next to last Iarl of Riverside had been a Breedwary; the current iarl's grandfather, a Clerkwell of not nearly as refined a pedigree, had somehow gotten into a violent quarrel with the iarl and been killed. Law of inheritance decreed that should one peer kill another, the victim's children received the murderer's titles and positions as if they were his own issue, while the hapless sons of the killer got nothing. An outmoded remnant of a more bloodthirsty age designed to keep tempers in line, yes—but the Clerkwells had profited with unseemly good cheer and the Breedwarys fought civil court and king in vain. Lilz herself would accordingly have foregone this fuss, whether the Riversides were her mother's friends or not.

"Brook wants me to ask the new housemaid some questions." Lilz took a warm iron from in front of the fire and exchanged it for the cooling one Aster handed her.

"Like, 'Why don't you just shut up and do your job?'"

"In short, I suppose. He wants to know where she came from and why she's here."

"Doesn't everyone!"

"Can you manage without me for an hour?"

Aster placed the iron on its stand and grinned at her. "Sure. Put milady in a barrel and stop up the bung and I'll have leisure to spare. I can't *wait* till we get to town and she's got Sir Kav to distract her."

"Shh!" All she needed, a quarrel between Fenne and Aster as cap to the past two months!

Lilz went into the hall, wondering how to begin questioning the strange housemaid. She needn't have. The woman was standing outside her counting room, apparently on the watch for her.

"Why don't you come to this room so often as you did?" she asked, without so much as a good morning.

"I have other things to do."

"I wish to ask you about this music I sometimes hear you play. Some is of a type I have not heard before."

Lilz gazed at the woman, determined not to show her annoyance. One of the pleasures of this small room was that she could practice her guitar technique in private, on the premise that she was instructing Fenne in music and had to keep her own hand in. That Fenne was too ill-disciplined to learn more than the melodies of the latest songs and a few flourishes for effect both women knew and pretended not to notice, a small gift from mistress to servant. It would be just like the new housemaid to dig that out and ask all about it. Privacy was not among her concepts.

The current songs Lilz learned mostly for Fenne's sake. Lilz preferred a classic, complex interweaving of melodic line with melodic line to the current plaints—although she was perfectly capable of providing the rollicking chords of the servants' hall with equally keen enjoyment, and often had. Why she shouldn't mind strumming away as accompaniment to that ragged chorus but found the prospect of discussing more intellectual music with this preternaturally intense woman so loathsome, she couldn't say. But she did.

"What do you want to know?" she said dutifully, thinking of her agreement with Brook.

As Lilz had feared, it was the old music the woman wanted to know about, in infinite detail. To her surprise, the woman had a good ear—she hummed a few examples in the course of her questions—but she seemed totally ignorant of any sort of music other than what might be played at the palace on feast days. Shifting from one foot to the other, Lilz tried to answer a series of questions that jumped from theory to history to technique to emotional significance in no particular order, each of which seemed to begin with, "How is this different from..."

"Honestly!" Lilz burst out, after twenty minutes of this. "Where did you come from?" The woman looked shocked. "Sometimes I don't see how you and I can have grown up in the same world!"

"I—why, but of course I—" The maid squinted. "Tell me, what is your concept of a world?"

"I'm not going to answer any more of your crazy questions," Lilz said heatedly. "You answer mine. Where *did* you come from?"

"Uh—a, a v-village north of—ah—ah—"

"The palace? Didn't you come from the palace? The only music you know anything about is palace music! Is that all they play in 'a village north of Ah'? Confess it! Aren't you sent by King Guyr to spy on us, like whizzers and small animals and birds?"

"Whizzers?" The maid's forehead knotted. "Small animals?"

"Whizzers." Exasperated, Lilz moved her hand past the woman's eyes, rubbing her fingers together to indicate flight. "Little things like insects that spy on us and fly back to the king to tell him all the things the galloping stars can't see."

"You've seen these whizzers?" the maid asked, blinking.

"Sky above! Everybody's seen whizzers," Lilz exclaimed, shocked. "Where *do* you come from, the moon?"

"Small animals, you believe they spy too?"

"Everybody knows—" Lilz caught herself shouting. She closed her eyes. Down the hall a door opened.

"Lilz?" Aster called.

"Excuse me, I have to go." She left the strange housemaid standing in the middle of the hall and hurried back to Fenne's dressing room.

"Lilz, what's wrong with you?" Aster pulled her into the room and shut the door. "Standing in the middle of the hall yelling about whizzers! And to her!"

"I snapped." Lilz sank onto the dressing table stool, her face in her hands. "I just finally snapped. Between Fenne and Greencrags snarling at each other at every meal so normal people can't even eat and this woman and her stupid questions every single day and Brook thinking I'm a spy because I don't talk like a servant, and going to Riverside and who *knows* what'll happen when we get to town—"

"Brook thinks you're a spy?" Fenne stood in the open door to the bedchamber. "For Guyr?"

"Excuse me, my mistress." Lilz willed her head erect. "Yes, he said last night he thought I might be."

"I'll tell him he's wrong."

"No," Lilz sighed. She wiped her face, surprised to find she'd been crying. "It doesn't matter."

Fenne brought her a handkerchief. "Don't worry about town. It's all arranged. And grandpapa has an idea for making us happy, so you don't have to worry about that."

Not worry! About one of grandpapa's ideas? Dear heaven! Lilz squeezed her eyes shut. "Thank you, my mistress," she said.

Dusk came early at this time of year. All day, Lilz had kept to Fenne's suite, not wanting to face Brook and confess her disastrous failure, but now she was sent to the kitchen for a tray of tea and cakes. She found the door of the suite ajar and no guard posted—without her husband in the house, Fenne must have given the guard some time off—and entered the corridor silently. The lamps had not yet been lit.

At the other end of the hall was the new housemaid. Lilz stood still. The woman was talking. Not to a person. To a wall. The words were fast, urgent, but at this distance indistinguishable. Lilz recalled the old women she had sometimes seen at Summerlea Manor, creeping along back passages in the dark in that ancient house. Something about the woman's speech reminded her of the strange soft songs sometimes heard there. Could this woman be a priestess of God the Mother? Would the Dych of Summerlea arrange to send a priestess to Fenne, out in the country?

Not that unlikely, once one thought of it.

The woman reached out to the wall and seemed to pluck something off it. She started for the back stairs. Lilz crept after her.

On the stairs, lamps had been lit. The woman went down quickly and out to the yard. Lilz ran down after her and looked out the open door in time to see her standing cloakless in the freezing twilight. She seemed to loft something into the air, as one might release a small bird. Lilz thought she heard a high-pitched hum. A whizzer?

She is a spy! But why is she here? Lilz almost staggered into the warm kitchen.

"What's the matter with you, Lilz?" the cook asked. "You look as if you've seen a ghost."

She fashioned a smile somehow. "Nothing so pleasant. My mistress sent me down for tea and cakes."

"She's in a foul mood, is she?" The cook moved the kettle to the center of the stove. "I'd take a ghost any day, myself."

Lilz heard the outside door close and footsteps going up the stairs. "I'll be back in a minute," she said. She found Brook in his pantry. At the sight of her he stood up so quickly he overturned his stool: she must look awful. "Brook," she whispered, leaning against the closed door. "I just saw the new housemaid put a whizzer into the sky."

Brook righted his stool, took her by the shoulders and sat her on it. "Did you ask your questions?"

"No. I—I'm afraid I lost my head."

"You?"

"It's been a difficult two months." Lilz took a deep breath. "This morning, before I could even say hello, she started in on me about music. Just on and on and on, you know how she does. I got sick of her questions and accused her of spying. Then she wanted to know about whizzers, she said, but I just saw her talk to one upstairs and bring it down and let it go outdoors."

"Where is she now?"

"She went back upstairs."

Brook chewed at his upper lip, staring out his window. "I wish Greencrags were here, or even just Stone."

"Now I'm not even sure it was a whizzer," Lilz said unhappily. "She just did this—" She spread her hand and moved it swiftly upward a handsbreadth or two. "I thought I heard one, but it could have been the wind...or my imagination... Before that she was talking to the wall, upstairs."

"Maybe she's just crazy. I've heard of craziness like that."

Yes. Come to think of it, that might be the most logical explanation. A craziness...or she might be one of those who suddenly forgets everything they ever knew... Why hadn't she thought of that before? A lot of the woman's behavior made sense in that light. Maybe a little of everything was true: an aristocrat from Galtriva, the shock of capture driving her mind astray, trying only to learn how to live? Lilz felt a fleeting pity. "What should we do?"

"Keep quiet, obviously, and just give the most harmless answers to her questions we can think of."

But there were no more questions. The housemaid moped about her chores for the next three days. Lilz saw her once, talking to one of Greencrags's men, but he didn't have the trapped-beast look most people got when talking to her, so Lilz paid no more attention. On the fourth night, after the house was dark, a carriage stopped on the drive. In the morning the maid was gone.

Greencrags notified the palace by messenger that the housemaid had disappeared, of course, but beyond that the chief reaction at Sweetdawn was one of relief. With the coming trip to Riverside Lilz had other things to think about. Fenne now saw fit to nag Stone about the state of her husband's clothes, with which no one else on earth could have found any fault. The result was that Stone went about in constant silent fury. Lilz did her best to placate him.

The trip began. To everyone's joy, the weather was fine and the roads firm: Greencrags and Stone and the guard rode outside the carriage, Aster and Lilz and Fenne within. A trunk occupied the opposite seat, others were lashed to the roof, but somehow Fenne this time had contrived to need so little with her that no carts had to be hired. Lunch at an inn early in the afternoon was even pleasant, Fenne at her most cheerful and Greencrags clearly basking in her mood. They arrived at Riverside late that evening.

Weary of being bounced about and aching with the involuntary effort of bracing herself for the ride, Lilz unpacked while Aster changed Fenne for a late supper with her hosts. Stone had taken a few things out of his master's single leather case and repaired to the bed chamber to help him change with his lips pressed together as if he thought his tongue might burst.

"Lilz," Aster said, when a smiling and gracious Fenne had gone downstairs on Greencrags's elegant arm. "Do you think she meant it? About all of us sleeping in the same bed?"

"Do you doubt it?"

"The way she's been today, I guess I hoped...who's going to sleep next to him?"

"I will, if you like. He's not likely to mistake a long sack bones like me for Fenne."

"You hope."

Lilz shrugged. "If he does, I'll pinch him, poor boy."

A maid knocked on the dressing room door with the offer of a supper in the kitchen, and they walked out of the room leaving everything exactly as it was. Two hours later, Aster was undressing Fenne in the bedroom with Lilz standing against the door to the dressing room, where Stone was getting his master ready for bed. As Lilz had expected, only Stone would sleep alone.

Chapter Twelve

Rovvo Standfast was far more audacious than Lilz, as she learned on the Thornday following her return to Waterside. In midafternoon the houseman sent a maid to tell her a messenger from Lady Northlands was waiting in the back hall. When she went downstairs it was all she could do not to gasp: the messenger was Stone!

"Miss Lilz?" His tone was so much that of a man addressing a stranger that for a moment she doubted she really was looking at a man she knew so well. Stone wore a messenger's official crimson cap. Where on earth could he have acquired it?

"I am Lilz." Shock made her sound properly reserved.

"A letter for you from Lady Northlands." Stone held it out, still playing the stranger. "I'm to wait for a reply."

"Yes, surely." She slid her thumb under the seal—marked with Fenne's crest—and looked at the note: *Give this man the gift we talked about.* The writing was Fenne's and the signature hers. Uncertain, she glanced at Stone, who winked.

A ruse of some sort, then. "Just a moment," she told him. He nodded. Lilz went back up the stairs.

She put the letter into her desk for later examination and took out the tin box. It was already locked. Dripping some wax into the lock as a seal was a matter of a minute; by the time handed the box to Stone she thought she had figured out Greencrags's method of forgery.

"No written reply will be necessary," she told the mock messenger. The houseman was standing a couple of steps behind her, so Lilz dropped a few coppers into Stone's hand to maintain his disguise. "I'll see him out," she said over her shoulder. "You don't have to bother."

She walked with Stone to the door, where he had tied up a nondescript horse. As he mounted, Lilz marveled at Greencrags's thoroughness: the saddle was plain, the saddle pad not the bright green of Standfast House but dingy undyed wool, easily one a messenger might use. Stone tipped his cap to her and rode away with everything of value to her life in a scuffed canvas satchel at his side.

Back in her counting room, Lilz closed the door and leaned against it, weak with relief. She had reconstructed the whole plan, now: Standfast was undoubtedly at open Court. Stone had gone up to the servants' gallery and seen Aster there. Following some sort of standing instructions, he had ridden out to Waterside with the messenger's cap and boldly presented the letter Greencrags had forged.

Where might the houseman of Waterside have crossed paths with the Iarl of Greencrags's body-man and so recognize him? Nowhere!

That was what Greencrags had seen and she had not. By now the cap was in Stone's satchel and he was just another horseman going to town; when he got to Standfast House he'd switch horses or saddle pads and return to Court to wait on his master as if nothing had happened. Lovely.

Lilz sat at her desk and took out the note. The seal had been prized from one of Fenne's letters to Greencrags and stuck to this one with a drop of fresh wax the same color: she could see the doubled curve where old wax joined new. Fenne's hand, Fenne's signature, yes, but examined at leisure the writing looked stiff: traced word by word from one of those other letters. The faint gray mark of a writing lead still showed at the very edge of the paper, where Greencrags had missed a spot in rubbing his guideline off. No one could be fooled for long by the trick, but no one had to be fooled for long: just the houseman, who wouldn't give the thing more than a second's glance, if that. Perfect!

I'd never have thought of a plan like that! Far simpler than trying to slip unnoticed past the house guards to make furtive use of a Watergate in the small hours, when the relative silence would magnify every step or splash.

Lilz shook her head, smiling. She felt rather proud of Greencrags. Only downstairs, watching the wax of the seal flare up in the kitchen fire as the paper blackened and curled, did she wonder why the young iarl might have saved Fenne's letters.

She hoped it was not because he still loved her, after all.

Autumn continued, golden and warm: Summerlea's lungs held out, though it was clear he would never improve. The bed chamber, even the sitting room of his suite, developed an unpleasant odor, as if he had already died and hadn't noticed.

Fenne stayed at Hasten House, but Lilz felt now free to accompany Waterside's cook to the market as she had before the crisis. Fall vegetables at last filled the stalls. Sprouts the size of small cabbages appeared on the servants' table at Waterside, tough from standing too long in the fields, but cheap. As the cook remarked when a guard complained, the sprouts might have split after all that rain, but on the other hand they were considerate enough to provide their own toothpicks. Hard squash, carrots, cabbages, and turnips stood in the sun for an afternoon before going into the cellars. The loaves of wheat bread vended from the backs of the bakers' donkeys returned to their normal size: Kinland rejoiced.

Twice a week Lilz rode into Miense to go over accounts with her mistress and hear the latest news. Occasionally she found Fenne talking with the dych. He was growing slowly weaker, but after that one day of wandering his mind had seemingly recovered.

On one of these visits she was shown into Fenne's sitting room to find her reading a letter. "Oh, Lilz, hello!" Fenne's dark eyes sparkled. Lilz was about to be teased.

"Here, you've got sort of gray eyes, maybe you'll like this." Her mistress rummaged through the papers in her desk and handed Lilz one of the manuscripts often circulated among the peers. "It's by that new poet, the one that won't sign his name."

Lilz took the paper, curious to see what Greencrags had done this time. The poem had the format and rhyme scheme of a standard love-lies-longing complaint:

TO HIS WISE LADY

Stand beside me there once more—behold
The sun expend his sap upon the dew
The dew respond with rainbow passion, you
Of the cloud-gray eyes, who never told
A syllable of how you supped that view
Paired to my own. Tell now, within that bold
But silent brain was there no thought to scold
Him whom you gazed beside? What should I do?
For I was raw to life that morning we
Stood separate beneath the peach-flamed skies;
Knew naught of how men come to agony.
How, were we there again, could I devise
Ways to deflect the path of destiny,
O lady of the tear-pale eyes?

Sunrise at Sweetdawn, the meadow as if afire; Greencrags comparing the sky to a peach. But why agony? *He suspects that Makeready was poisoned. Has he broken into my safebox?* Lilz scanned the page again. *He wants advice.* Oh, dear. How?

"It's passable, though I don't know how you'd 'sup a view'," she said, "and the last line lacks a beat." She extended the paper to Fenne. "It doesn't make an awful lot of sense."

Fenne giggled. "Oh, Lilz! You have no romance at all. Obviously the poor dope's in love with some girl who won't have him—that's what Benina says. Keep it and read it again."

Lilz put the paper into her satchel and drew out the household ledger. Yes, the poem would leave exactly that impression with most readers, given the form.... Even cleverer than she'd thought at first. She opened the ledger on her knees.

"Have you guessed who it is yet?"

"No, my mistress, I haven't. After all, there've been only five poems. Three of the others had been only fairly competent verse, so far as she could tell, but buried among the quatrains of the fourth had been a message for Lilz alone:

Impostor, trickster though he be
Bearing sham words falsely sealed
Count him my kestrel: know that he
Has brought your gift, and stands your shield.

She thought it a strange method of communication, possible only in one direction. Lilz could see its roots: her own suggestion that he write poetry to circulate in manuscript; possibly also Makeready's acrid verse of the winter before. That Greencrags would think of it, knowing that in time any manuscript going the rounds would come to Fenne and that Fenne would show it to her bond-servant, that he'd alert her by using phrases out of their conversations, proved to her again that he was bolder, more intelligent, and far more devious than most gave him credit for. And yet she trusted him as she had never trusted any of the Hastens, or even Kav Treadwell.

"Well, you'd know who was writing if you saw five letters, wouldn't you?" Fenne said.

"Perhaps not, if they weren't signed and I didn't know the person who wrote them," Lilz pointed out. "One thing these poems do have in common is that they tend to be, shall I say, somewhat opaque."

"That's just what the older ladies say at court. But that makes him more interesting, doesn't it?" Fenne sighed. "I'd love to meet him."

Kav Treadwell had better pay a lot more attention to his wife in a hurry, Lilz thought. Today it's an unknown poet who can scarcely pose any danger, but tomorrow, who knows? She closed the ledger over one finger. "The houseman at Waterside has a number of complaints about furnishings," she said, consulting the list that had marked the place she was keeping with her finger. "Loose joints in a drawer in his buffet, front hall tabletop water-stained—he says because of a peer's wet gloves, but it looks like a vase-ring to me—bed in the blue-and-gold guest room has some broken pegs—"

Fenne tittered. "That was Oakforest."

"And he wants some shelves rearranged in his pantry. Shall I send word to Godwit and Chantwell to send somebody out?"

"All but the shelves. He can do without that."

Nevan Hasten lingered into the beginning of winter. On the last day of her grandfather's life, Fenne sent for Lilz, saying he was failing fast and she was to come right away, in a carriage. Anticipating a houseful of mourners and consequent formality, Lilz put up her hair and wore her best Hasten blue shirt and skirt. When the messenger was sent, the dych had been sinking fast but still living. By the time the carriage pulled up in the courtyard of Hasten House nearly two hours later, all the shutters had been closed and black banners hung over the doors. Lilz steeled herself.

She went up the back stairs to Fenne's suite. Northlands sat at Fenne's desk, sorting through some letters. He glanced up as Lilz paused in the doorway. "She's with him," Kav said, and continued to scan each letter before folding it away.

"What are you doing, milord?" Lilz asked.

Northlands smiled at her. "Reading my wife's letters. She seems to get a great many."

"I doubt you'll find what you're looking for."

"What am I looking for, Lilz?"

"Power."

"With Summerlea dead, so's everyone."

Lilz tilted her head. "Milord, I've served the Hastens nineteen years. I think you'll find arrangements have already been made to distribute every influence his Grace held to those whom he wished to have it."

"Yes, but will that stay arranged? There's the question." Kav's greenish-blue eyes narrowed. "You've failed me, Lilz. I thought you'd have made sense of those notes I gave you before this."

"I told you, milord, they're meant for the man himself. Or, just possibly, as notes intended for someone who would know what he meant by pink granite circles and blue carpets. "

"Nonsense, Lilz, nobody writes in riddles but the new poet. Jen was always perfectly direct."

Yes. Even when he did construct riddles, as in those disastrous poems two winters ago, Makeready's meaning was always obvious. But maybe this time Sir Jen had been indirect, in prose? Maybe his notes had been made to help him compose a message. A message that had led to his death?

"That's something I know nothing about, milord," Lilz said. "If you'll excuse me, I'd best go to my mistress."

"Go on, then." Northlands took the papers out of another pigeonhole of Fenne's desk and put his feet up to read them.

Lilz shut the door and started down the hall. So far as the new poet was concerned, she had yet to devise a way of finding out what he wanted. She's just have to let him tell her himself.

Standfast House

What the servants learned the night the Standfasts came to Riverside, their hosts knew in a few more hours. As Lilz soon discovered, before dressing for dinner Lady Riverside drew Fenne into a heart-to-heart talk designed to ferret out what vicious behavior the young iarl had indulged in to make his wife place her servants between them in bed. Fenne emerged from the older woman's sitting room in a fury and slammed into the dressing room to glare at Aster.

"I will not have my body-maid gossiping about me," she snapped. "You're dismissed."

Aster froze with her hands on the hanger she had been about to insert into the dress she'd just finished pressing. "Milady, I swear, I never—"

"Then how does Lady Riverside know where you and Lilz slept last night?"

"I—I don't know, milady, I—" Aster went pale: Fenne's low, controlled voice was far more terrifying than her usual shouts could have been. She backed away, stopped by the closed door to the bed chamber where Greencrags was dressing for dinner.

"How does she know?" Fenne insisted.

"Milady, I haven't breathed a word!"

Fenne slapped Aster's cheek. The maid cowered against the door, her hand over the red finger marks her mistress had left.

"Fenne!"

"Stay out of this, Lilz."

"My mistress, you have no call to slap Aster or to dismiss her," Lilz said vigorously. "She's telling the truth."

"*You* went to Lady Riverside?"

"No one went to Lady Riverside—at least, neither of us. Calm down." Lilz waited for Fenne to relax a fraction. "My mistress, Aster and I are only human. We can't sleep down here and upstairs with the other servants at the same time. They surely noticed our absence. Don't you remember the maid coming in with your breakfast tray before Aster even had a chance to dress this morning?"

Fenne gave Aster a sullen glance.

"She came early to find out what was going on. Do you think servants have no eyes or ears or curiosity? Especially about a young woman as beautiful as you, a Peer of the Blood so extravagantly married and so wealthy? I'm quite sure the person who discussed you with Lady Riverside was her own body-maid."

Fenne plopped onto the dressing table stool. Someone knocked on the bedroom door. "I'm not ready!" she yelled. "Go away!"

"You're right," she said after a moment. "Lilz, what can I do? I can't ask Greencrags to sleep with the servants! Neither of us would ever live it down. But I absolutely refuse to sleep alone with him. What if Kav found out?"

"What did you tell Lady Riverside?"

"To keep her big fat nose out of my business or I'd bite it off."

Lilz sighed. "Oh, my."

"That wasn't very diplomatic, I guess, was it?" For once, Fenne looked genuinely contrite. "Now I suppose mother will take me aside for a talk, too. Oh, why did grandpapa make me marry that clod?"

She smiled wanly at Aster and got up to pick up the hanger the girl had dropped. "I'm sorry I slapped you, Aster. That old bitch made me so mad, I couldn't think. Is the burgundy silk in here, or is it in the bed chamber?"

"It's here."

"I'll wear that, then. And the garnets."

Sky above! The burgundy silk and the garnets? Kav Treadwell's favorite outfit, worn for no one else. The carriage Lilz had heard pull up to the house half an hour ago must have been his. Surely he wouldn't return to Miense tonight? She gave Fenne a horrified glance, but Fenne was fluffing her pale curls in the mirror.

Lady Riverside couldn't know. Risk Greencrags discovering Kav with Fenne? She'd never invite such a scandal upon her own house!

Aster, her cheek still red, got out the burgundy dress. The ivory underdress came out without asking; outfits had been discussed for days before they left Sweetdawn. Fenne beamed. With that sign of approval, Lilz felt it was safe to leave Aster alone with her. "If you'd excuse me, my mistress?" she murmured. Fenne mumbled something from the depths of the underdress Aster was pulling over her head. Lilz fled the dressing room. Dear heaven! Should she warn someone? How? Of what?

She found Stone pacing along the hall and raised her eyebrows at him, hoping she looked less upset than she felt.

"He's ready. He's just waiting for her."

"And you?"

Stone shrugged. "I'm waiting for you." He jerked his head at the dressing room door. "What was that about?"

"Milady didn't conceive that Riverside's servants might gossip about her sleeping arrangements. She thought Aster had told them. It's all straightened out, now."

"Nothing's straightened out." Stone began pacing again. "What happens when we get to town, Lilz?"

Lilz sucked in her lower lip, letting her fears tick on until Stone again glanced at her. "I think that will depend upon Nevan Hasten," she said. "I'm told he has something in mind, but I doubt it's anything you or your master will like."

"What is it?"

"I don't know. But I do know him."

She stood chatting with Stone about less dangerous topics for several minutes. The door of the suite opened. Fenne came out, with Aster walking behind her and ahead of Greencrags. Fenne's mouth was pinched into an angry line and Aster's head was down.

Stone gazed at the procession severely. "Much joy of her," he muttered, as the young couple started down the front steps and Aster headed for the back stairs. "If they stay together, I'm beginning to think I'll take ship for the New Lands."

Lilz slipped her hands into her pockets and leaned against a door jamb, surprised to be distressed at the thought of his going. "How long can it last, Stone?" she asked. "They'll have to come to some kind of truce sooner or later."

"Not soon enough." Stone looked toward the steps Greencrags had just descended. "Six months, and I'd bet you'd come with me."

"I just might." Stone blinked at her: he'd only been grousing, she saw with relief. "Three of my brothers went to the colonies, years ago."

"Did they do well?"

"I've not heard from them since."

Stone lightly touched her cheek. "I'm sorry."

"I've one more." Lilz felt unexpectedly forlorn. "He's close by, in Miense, a tradesman. I see him from time to time."

"A long while between times, by the sound of it."

"True."

Stone glanced away. "Servants can't afford to love," he said. "Not even their own kin."

That night, with Standfast breathing softly beside her, Lilz felt the bed shift. Fenne went into the dressing room and didn't return. Lilz tried to stay awake, but the day's emotions had worn her out and she was soon drifting, half dreaming, half alarmed, not able to resist the descent into sleep. She felt as if she had slept a long time when the bed shifted again and she realized that Fenne was back.

Lilz caught a whiff of her rose-scented douche. As Fenne rolled over and snuggled under the comforter, a rooster crowed.

The afternoon they arrived at Standfast House, Fenne ordered the carriage and drove off without saying where she was going.

"Mistress Stump's, I imagine," Lilz told Aster.

"Sky above! Couldn't she wait ten minutes?"

"Apparently not." Lilz took a deep breath to calm herself: if Greencrags should ask her where his wife had gone, what should she say? She put off the moment by going downstairs to introduce herself to the house servants.

The houseman she'd already met, on the visits she'd made while Greencrags was sick the summer before. His name was Reed.

Stoutness was an occupational hazard for housemen. Reed had not escaped. A bald man of about Lilz's height, he had a professional air of offended melancholy that evaporated with a step into the back of the house. He was in the kitchen when Lilz walked in, playing backgammon with the cook. "Ah," he said. "Lilz, isn't it? Just the lass I need. Your bones and my bulk would average out to a likely couple, now, wouldn't they?"

"You think so?" Lilz grinned.

"Let's see if we can shake them together," Reed suggested in a loud whisper, making the cook laugh.

"He's all talk," a kitchenmaid said.

"All talk! All talk!" Reed patted his paunch. "What do you call this, then, child?"

"Nothing that ought to be on a man."

"Miss Pert! Shall I put one on you?"

"You see?" The kitchenmaid stopped scraping carrots to appeal to Lilz. "He's been saying that two years, now, but I ain't yet seen his pants come down."

What Reed would have replied, Lilz never knew: the front hall maid burst into the room to tell her she was wanted upstairs. "Right this minute, she said," the maid added.

Lilz ran up the back stairs and into the hall. Fenne was standing outside her suite. "Do you know what he wants?" she shouted, while Lilz was still ten sashlengths away. "Can you imagine what that hick husband of mine plans to do now?" Lilz came up to her, breathless. "He wants to go back to Sweetdawn! All the way up here for one gala and a few stupid meetings of peers and then straight back to that hut in the country!"

Now Lilz saw Greencrags standing in the doorway to Fenne's rooms. "You could invite your friends," he pointed out mildly. "There's plenty of room in the hut."

"Oh, yes! Invite my friends to lurch along those country roads for three days out and three days back so they can spend a few days bored to death." Lilz heard a door quietly open: Stone looked out of Greencrags's dressing room.

"Why not?" Greencrags asked.

"Why not? Why not! *My* friends are accustomed to Court, Master Standfast! Insult them by marooning them out there with all those yokels running around in the woods with nothing to do but shoot deer and get drunk and puke on the carpet? As if my friends had nothing more important to do!"

Lilz was relieved. Taking the steps two at a time, she'd imagined she'd be dealing with a Fenne Kav had rejected. Apparently something else had brought her back to the house.

"Sweetdawn's a pleasant place, my mistress," she said. "And I don't believe any of the hunt soiled the carpet in any way at all."

"Pleasant? Sweetdawn pleasant? Are you out of your mind? The blackest cellar of the Old Palace would be paradise compared to Sweetdawn! Where's Aster?"

Aster now came out of Fenne's dressing room holding out a pair of long black kid gloves. "I'm so sorry, milady, I didn't notice your gloves until the carriage—"

Fenne snatched the gloves and in one motion turned and slapped them across Lilz's face. The sting made her jaw sag. Fenne slapped the other cheek. "You idiot! How dare you take his side?"

"Hold on," Greencrags said. "You do entirely too much slapping, Fenne."

"Call me 'Fenne' again and I'll slap you!"

"Apologize to Lilz."

"Apologize to a servant?" Fenne turned a deep red. "My dear Master Standfast, a iarlena does not apologize to a servant! Where did you learn such fine etiquette? Out in the pigsties?"

"Go to your room," Greencrags said. His voice was steady, but his fine lace jabot trembled.

Fenne spat at him. "As to you," she said to Lilz, "I don't ever want to see you again."

"My mistress—"

"Don't you 'my mistress' me! If you can't be loyal I won't have you. I'm leaving"—she turned, glaring at Greencrags, a dare he didn't take— "and when I get back you'd better be out of this house with all your pitiful little bits and pieces, Miss Lilz No Name, or I will have your hide!" She ran along the hall and down the front staircase. "Reed!" echoed her shout in the stairwell. "Come get this door open this instant, you fat buffoon!"

Lilz let her face sink into her hands. "Where will I go?" she asked herself in a whisper.

"This is my house," Greencrags said. "A detail my wife seems to have forgotten in the heat of the moment. You're welcome to stay as long as I live here."

"She'd have you out of it in a week if you let me stay, she and her precious grandpapa." Someone put a warm arm across her shoulders. Stone.

This is what it's like to be gutted alive, Lilz thought.

Stone's arm tightened. "Hush," he said. "It's nowhere near as bad as that." Did I say that out loud? Lilz wondered. She felt the shape of the words still in her mouth and knew she had.

"Let's get out of the corridor," Greencrags said. "I hate having an audience." Stone led her somewhere, just a few steps, but Lilz stumbled. A door closed. Here, the air felt safe. Stone put both arms around her and guided her head to his shoulder.

"By the time she comes back, she'll have changed her mind," he said. "You know that."

"Oh, Stone," she started to say, and sobbed.

"It's all right." He laid his cheek against hers and rocked her gently, as she had rocked Fenne so many times. "It's all right."

"She will, you know," Aster said. "She's dismissed me a dozen times in the past two years, I'm sure."

"But never me! Never me! Almost seventeen years—"

"Why can't I ever keep track of a handkerchief?" Greencrags muttered. "I know I had one." Lilz heard a drawer slide. Stone's arms loosened. He dabbed at her face with lace-edged linen. She gulped and thanked him and took the handkerchief to wipe her own tears.

"I'm so sorry," she said. "I'm so sorry."

"Shh." Stone gazing at her as if he, too, might cry in a moment. Greencrags sitting on Stone's cot with slumped shoulders and worried face. Aster standing by the dressing room door with her hands clasped under her chin.

"I guess I did it this time," Lilz said.

But Fenne, while still so far as anyone knew a iarlena, came back a few hours later with an embarrassed, tearful apology for her bond-servant Lilz — still vowing to spend the whole winter in Miense.

At Standfast House there was no nonsense about sleeping arrangements. Fenne had a suite to herself; Greencrags had his, Stone his cot in his master's dressing room. Aster and Lilz shared a tiny room and a bed under the roof, like any other servants.

"How long do you think it will be before he figures out she's sneaking out at night?" Aster asked, the third day they were there.

"Correction," Lilz said. "Afternoon is when she sneaks out. Nights, Kav sneaks in."

"Sky above," Aster said weakly into the dark. "Is she crazy?"

"She's a Hasten."

"Sometimes I think that's the same thing."

Wicked or willful, Stone had said. *It comes to the same thing.* Lilz thought of Standfast's face smooth with sleep in the early morning light at Riverside. A good thing he had Stone. Rock-solid Stone, the boy called him, with a smile lit with affection. The sheer smell of the man was a comfort.

What could Nevan Hasten be planning? she wondered.

An annulment.

The guitar between her knees, Fenne tightened a tuning peg ever so slightly. Lilz watched from behind her desk, still blinking with shock. "See, grandpapa says that since he hasn't, what's the word, completed the marriage — "

"Consummated?"

"That's it, consummated the marriage, we can have a commission declare it void."

"Just like that?"

Fenne shrugged. "There're some details. There'd have to be a hearing, and they'd have to make sure I'm a virgin."

"Forgive me if I seem overly skeptical, Fenne, but might that not be a somewhat bothersome thing to prove?"

"No, not at all. We'd get a girl who is. To take my place, you see? Somebody about the right size, and she could be so upset by the whole idea and so shy, she'd have to have a veil, and we'd get people who never met me to do the examining, and the girl could sob a lot so the voice wouldn't be a problem. One of my cousins might do. Isn't it a beautiful plan, Lilz?" Fenne struck a chord on Lilz's guitar and added a flourish.

Lilz looked down at the account book she and Fenne had been reviewing before Fenne picked up her guitar. Standfast, unsuspecting Standfast, was about halfway back to Sweetdawn at that minute. He was to pack up an enormous list of things and bring them to Miense, to Standfast House, having agreed after much wheedling to spend the winter season in town with his wife. Lilz suspected the final cajolery had been the prospect of a normal marriage, although Fenne would not precisely promise what she had no intention of granting. She had a small child's, or a bureaucrat's, knack for providing herself with hairs to split.

"What does Greencrags have to say about this?"

"He doesn't know yet. D'you think he'll much mind being proven impotent? Grandpapa says he might give us some trouble over that."

"Yes," Lilz said. "That's possible."

But Fenne was impervious to irony. She bubbled on, thrilled with the plan her grandpapa had devised for making everyone happy: that is, for cementing his own relationship to the king and the reins of power. Lilz could hardly find anything to say.

With her husband gone Fenne threw herself into life at Court with every bit of her old relish. Music and dancing and gossip filled most of her hours. She reported flirting with an ambassador from one of the Silk Countries, pushing the outside corners of her eyes up with her thumbs and pulling the inside corners down with her index fingers while imitating his sing-song pleasantries, making Aster sputter with laughter. Sir Jen Makeready was amusing the ladies with verses caricaturing court personalities, some of which Fenne brought home for Lilz to chuckle over—as she did, though she thought one of them so fiendishly precise it might make a mortal enemy of Ven Jonquil the Famous Poet.

Lilz, too, while she had enjoyed the stay at Sweetdawn, was happy to be back in the city. The servants at Standfast House were every bit as congenial as the ones in the country, and the relief of having Fenne herself in such high spirits was more than she could have imagined.

One morning Lilz collected some letters from a messenger and took them up for Fenne to read over her breakfast tray. She'd gone into the dressing room to ask Aster to check the seams of the dark blue silk to see if it could be recut to this year's fashion when she heard a shriek of outrage from her mistress.

"Lilz! Lilz! Will you look at this!"

Lilz rushed into the bed chamber. Fenne, red with rage, was shaking a letter at her. "The minute I'm dressed, I'm going over to the palace and have it out with this man. What business is it of his whether I stay married to that oaf or not? Just because I want to share Kav with him? You'd think he had a certificate of title!"

For a horrified moment, Lilz thought Fenne was talking about King Guyr: certainly the king could expect all the attention he wanted from his favorite. What could Fenne be thinking? But no, the letter was from the Iarlena of Oakforest, Fenne's mother's good friend, always inclined to put a word in when she thought Lady Delle wasn't holding up her ideal of motherhood.

Now, she advised "just a tad more discretion, my dear. You see what's going the rounds these days."

Lilz looked at the second page. A copy, in Lady Oakforest's beautiful script, of a poem:

FOR F., FROM HER LOVER K.

My lady bright of face and foul of heart
Practices each day deception's art,
Flaunts scheming virtue for the world to see—
Creeps from her husband's house to dart to me.

Pleasant indeed her smiles, her wiles, her touch!
Her sleek white breasts and fanny divert me much!
But I desire a long and sunny life—
Father, preserve me e'er from such a wife!
—Sir Jen Makeready

"Oh, dear," Lilz breathed. The same pun on her mistress's name that had earned young Säen a swim in the fishpond some years ago, and other indignities since. "That is rather near the bone."

"He'll be sorry," Fenne said through clenched teeth. "He will be *sorry*."

Chapter Thirteen

No one in the dych's sitting room noticed Lilz poised in the doorway. The door to the dych's bed chamber was shut. A cold draft crept across the floor to her ankles: windows had been opened. She heard a bump from the inner room. The washers must already have come to prepare the body for burial. A scented candle burned on a table under one of the shuttered windows. Most casual visitors might think it had been intended simply to improve the air of the room, but Lilz recognized an herbal blend from Summerlea Manor, one she associated with the elderly strangers, the women who seemed so shy. Not perfume, but incense.

Fenne was curled up on a brocade loveseat with a handkerchief to her eyes, her mother beside her patting her shoulder with a vacant expression. Neither of her brothers was present, but Lord Säen had crawled out of some wainscot or other and sat leaning his forearms on his thighs with his hands clasped, looking utterly bored.

It was Meadowlands who drew Lilz's attention. He sat on the opposite side of the room from his wife and daughter, on the front half of his chair seat. His back was straight, his legs crossed at the knee. He had laid his hands one over the other on his knee and gazed at a spot a couple of sashlengths in front of him, his head tilted as if he were listening to something. Lilz found herself cocking her head to try to hear what it might be, but aside from Fenne's sniffles there was no sound in the room.

Of the family, Meadowlands was the only one who had changed into mourning clothes. Seeing him in black, with a ruffled purple jabot puffed between the lapels of his jacket instead of the far less formal shirts he usually wore in her presence, Lilz was struck by how much he had aged. It was no longer clear how much of the lightness of his hair was due to Hasten blondness and how much to gray. She was used to thinking of him as a man of about thirty, as he'd been when she first met him. He was closer to fifty, a fact she only now fully took in.

Meadowlands suddenly looked toward her. "Hello, Lilz," he said. "Come in."

"Thank you, milord."

Fenne glanced up and nodded toward a chair near her. Lilz sat tentatively. She couldn't think of the right thing for a servant to say on the death of a family member, but she had to say something. After a moment she simply murmured the phrase she'd been taught, though it was more appropriate to a Peer of the Blood than to a bond-servant. Lord Säen blinked.

"Shall we tell her now?" Fenne asked.

Her father glanced toward the bed chamber door.

"They'll know anyway."

The iarl nodded twice. The motion had a mechanical look. "My father's last request was that you walk in his funeral procession." His dark eyes moved toward Lilz. "Just ahead of the hearse."

"Milord?"

"We'll have some clothes made...a black dress..."

"She doesn't have to do it," Säen said. "Just because he asked for it? He won't know, and nobody else would dream of such a thing."

"Immediately ahead, milord?" Lilz could not believe it. To be asked to walk where Meadowlands himself would ordinarily expect to be?

"That was his request." Fenne's father regarded her soberly. "He was very clear. He repeated it three times and made me say it back. You're to lead the horse."

"Milord, I...I don't know what to say."

"She doesn't have to," Säen insisted. "Who will know?"

"I will know." Meadowlands turned his slow stare on his nephew. He had barely moved any part of his body but his head since Lilz had entered the room. His immobility had begun to wear on her. "I will know I did not carry out my last promise to my father."

"Well." Säen shrugged. "Obviously he wasn't in his right mind. What will people think?"

"And Lilz will know."

Säen laughed silently, shaking his head, as one did over open lunacy unexpectedly revealed.

"If there should come a day...there might come a day that it will matter. She will walk where he wanted her to."

Lord Ruppet came into the room, wearing black, his purple jabot slightly askew. "Hello, Säen," he said. "You got here fast. Where's Cals?"

"Coming." Lady Delle got up to hug her son. "I sent a message."

"Ruppet, Lilz is to walk in the procession," Meadowlands said. "I promised father."

"You should learn to keep your mouth shut, Uncle Olen." Lord Säen sounded disgusted. "The fewer who know about it, the easier it will be not to bother. That's five who didn't have to know, now, counting me and her."

"Directly ahead of the hearse, with the horse," Meadowlands told his eldest son, as if Säen hadn't spoken. "I'll walk beside her."

Ruppet looked at Lilz as if he had never seen her before. The blue of his eyes seemed to brighten. "I don't see why she should."

"I told you." Olen Hasten still had not moved. Lilz folded her hands. She wanted to rush across the room and drag him to his feet. "I promised father. He says—he said—it was a promise he made himself, and that if I want to be Dych of Summerlea and you, Ruppet, Iarl of Meadowlands, we will do as he said."

Everyone stared at him. That the eldest son of the Dych of Summerlea would be the Iarl of Meadowlands, and that on the death of his father he would rise to the dychdom, was not something anyone in Kinland would think open to question. Summerlea did not serve at the pleasure of the king. He owned his dychdom by the loins of his father, as the official phrase went.

"Milord, perhaps simply offering the place, as you have, would fulfill the promise," Lilz said quietly. "If so, I'll decline."

"There, you see, she's got some sense, at least," Säen remarked.

"You're a generous woman, Lilz." Meadowlands let his eyes fall shut, as if the effort of keeping them open were beyond him. "I've always liked that about you. Be generous once more, and do as he wished."

"I've already sent word to Onma Stump," Fenne added. "She's coming to measure you before dinner."

Four days later, Lilz the bond-servant walked along the cobbled High Street of Miense, a few sashlengths in front of the black horses that drew her late owner's hearse. She led a seventh black horse with an empty saddle, a beast hired for the occasion, docile to the edge of torpor. Several paces to her left, the Iarl of Meadowlands kept step. They headed a long procession. Lilz walked with her head bowed under the wide-brimmed black hat someone had found for her, wearing a dress that, while black and of a good warm wool, buttoned up the front as a servant's clothing should. Four days was a short time to sew up such a dress, even for a workshop as skilled as the costumer's. Mistress Stump had apologized for the hem, pressed into place and held with stitches invisible on the outside but as long as her thumb on the inside, and for the buttonholes, eight fully worked and the rest plain slashes in the fabric.

None of this slap-dash work was visible from the curb. Lilz heard the speculation in the whispers of the crowd that lined the street. Who could help but wonder who she was and why she was part of the funeral of the man who had been most powerful in Kinland, other than King Guyr himself? She could have told them her birth name, but that was all.

Behind her, the hearse rattled and the hooves clopped and the harness jingled and the dych's guards' saddles creaked and the Summerlea pennons they carried popped in the breeze. Behind them rolled the carriage with Fenne and Lady Delle and Lord Säen's widowed mother and Ruppet's young wife; farther behind came other carriages with other women of the family; along the sides of the procession the Hasten men walked well outside the line of travel of the horses.

Following the Hastens were thirteen drummers with their *tat, tat, rat-a-tat-tat* endlessly echoing off the stone of the nobles' townhouses and their shuttered windows. Last came the remaining Peers of the Blood. After a time nothing seemed quite real to Lilz, except that her feet burned in her new black shoes.

Lilz entered the cemetery behind the Old Palace with tears of pain streaming down her cheeks. As arranged, she handed the reins of the riderless horse to Fenne's father at the gate, but stayed with the procession until it reached the Hasten mausoleum. Someone had found some greenhouse flowers to stand on the steps, white carnations wilting with cold, on which the hired horse browsed while a priest of the Fathergod offered the appropriate prayers. Meadowlands made no move to stop it.

After a short speech by King Guyr and a full hour's eulogy by the priest, the coffin was carried into the vault, the vault sealed, and the procession reformed with Meadowlands now mounted at its head on the horse Lilz had escorted. She thankfully joined her mistress and the other two women in the carriage.

"Please heaven that's over!" Lady Delle said. "Lilz, how are you holding up?"

"Well, thank you, milady."

"I kept thinking of your new shoes, all that long way."

"I'm bound to admit I thought of them often, myself," Lilz said ruefully.

"Was there talk in the crowd?" Fenne asked.

"A little."

"Why on earth do you suppose he wanted you to walk ahead of him with father's horse?"

"I have no idea, my mistress."

"Probably he wanted you to look out for potholes," Ruppet's wife said, and was stared down.

Whatever his reason, it was a full week before Lilz could walk comfortably again.

With all the colors of the realm displayed, with ceremonial and feasting equal to Fenne's second wedding, but without the masques and dancing, Olen Hasten was raised to Dych of Summerlea.

"Arise, Olen Hasten, and come before our knee," King Guyr intoned in his loudest ceremonial voice, once the murmuring of the Peers had slackened. Lilz, in the gallery, watched with the hushed audience as the head of the family that owned her moved forward, head bowed, to stand before the king.

"As you came into this world by the power of the loins of the Sixteenth Dych of Summerlea," Guyr continued, "We count it our pleasure that you leave this world as the Seventeenth dych..."

A ripple of closer attention passed over the assembled Blood.

Lilz, too, pinned her gaze on the rite played out before her. She had a sense of the long history of Kinland being sustained at this moment, in this scene she had never before been privileged to witness, and felt in some peculiar manner both honored by the thought and indebted to her forebears and to generations to come.

"Let the feast begin," Guyr intoned at last, and the nobility of Kinland dashed ravenously for the tables of elegant food.

Immediately upon his father's assumption of the dychdom, Lord Ruppet was raised to Iarl of Meadowlands. Most of the posts Nevan Hasten had held devolved upon his son. Ruppet inherited a few cast off by his father. It seemed to Lilz that the Hasten grip on Kinland's government was as firm as it had ever been. True, two or three posts of minor significance and infrequent responsibility were given to the Iarl of Northlands, but no one believed that Kav Treadwell was anything more than the puppet of his father-in-law, for all his efforts to appear to be his own man.

The winter turned harsh. No fires, no close-draped windows, could drive the chill from any but the smallest room even in the townhouse. Seeing the steam of her breath as she readied herself for bed, Lilz thought of the servants in drafty Summerlea Manor and wondered whether in the absence of the Hastens they'd had the gall to move from the attics into the downstairs rooms, as plain common sense should command.

Fenne gave a party for her nineteenth birthday, subdued because the house was still in mourning. She came upstairs midway through the evening. Lilz was in the dressing room with Aster, keeping warm by the fire, and heard her mistress rush into the bed chamber. She opened the door. Fenne was standing at the foot of the bed, hugging herself, as if with the cold, but Lilz felt something more was wrong. "Fenne?" she said.

No response. "Fenne?"

Fenne looked up. She seemed dazed. Lilz brought her into the warmth of the dressing room. "What's the matter, my mistress?"

"Elm."

"Elm?" Lilz frowned. Oh, yes, the warden at the Old Palace.

"He's said Jen Makeready was poisoned."

Lilz felt her heart cool. Was all of that to fall upon them now, after so much time?

"He's said he thinks I did it. He's said he thinks I was angry because of what Sir Jen said about me, so I caused deadly viands to be transported to him in his imprisonment."

Someone else's phrase. "But you never even visited Sir Jen."

"He's said things came for Jen to eat and he once ate a bit of a veal pie Jen was too sick to want but it was too spicy so he gave it to his dog and the dog died." *Veal pie?* "He's said the mice in Jen's cell all died that summer. He's said—I don't remember what else he's said.

They're all talking about it down there. And it's my birthday! Lilz, I don't know what to do!"

"Do nothing until we can consult your father." Veal pie? Lilz racked her brains. Surely she'd sent only custards and soups? No, there was that one roast fowl—

"But I have to *say* something!" Fenne sank into the chair Lilz had been sitting in and stretched her hands out to the fire. She smiled briefly at Aster as if she'd only just noticed her. "You member those horrible poems. People say he dropped another out of the window at the Old Palace, saying I was killing him—oh, I will have that warden's hide! *No* one was supposed to have any word from Sir Jen, not even his family!"

"Say you did not wish Sir Jen ill." Lilz marveled at the calmness of her own voice. "Remind them that the king's physician saw him often and did not dispute the death. Say Elm is mistaken, or someone else did the poisoning. Remember, *nothing* went to the Old Palace with your name on it. You sent no veal pie. Say that these are serious accusations and you are affronted."

"Lilz, he was supposed to be safe! Grandpapa said he was safe!"

"The warden?"

"Yes, one of ours, so he could be trusted—or at any rate, one of grandpapa's. But now he's sick himself and he's saying all these things, he says he wants to clear his sins from his heart before he dies—oh, Lilz, what shall I do?"

Patiently, Lilz began again. "Do nothing."

Makeready's Error

"Sky above, Lilz, where did it all *come* from?"

Lilz stood beside Stone's horse, watching as the carts drove into the courtyard of Standfast House with Greencrags supervising. "Wedding gifts, most of it," she said. "Isn't it odd? The wealthier people are, the more others want to give them more riches."

"Give me room to dismount—that'll be wealth enough for me at the moment." Stone swung to the ground as she stepped back. The horse suddenly whinnied in response to a call from the stable. Stone twitched a shoulder against the sound. "How did you ever get it all down to Sweetdawn so fast?"

"I had over a month's warning," Lilz reminded him. "You've done well. Three weeks, start to finish? I'm not sure I could have managed it."

"Ah, well, but my master's a hard worker. Most of the china he and I packed together."

"He'd best not tell his wife. One cracked plate and she'd cut his throat with it."

Stone half smiled in agreement. He led the horse across the yard, circling to avoid the carts. Hugging herself for warmth in the chill of an early-winter afternoon, Lilz watched him go. As Stone reached the stable she went back into the house and shut the door on the cold air, if not on the noise: why couldn't men ever get anything done without shouting at each other?

She went up the back stairs to Fenne's suite to report. "If he hasn't got it all, he's brought a few carts too many," she said.

"Good." Fenne had just threaded a needle. She drew it through the last few stitches she had made and continued the outline of a flower in the cut-lace napkin she was making. "Is he with them?"

"Yes, my mistress. He'll probably come up in a few minutes. Just now he's getting all the carts into the yard."

"How does he look?"

"Splendid."

"Can't anything touch his health?" Fenne asked testily. "I thought that rain day before yesterday would at least give everyone colds."

"Stone's sniffling, if that's any consolation."

Fenne sniffed herself and held the napkin up for Lilz's inspection. "What do you think? Will that mistake I made yesterday show?"

Lilz spread the work out in her hands to see the full square. Fenne had mis-stitched the stem of a leaf. "White on white, in a napkin...no, I don't think anyone will notice."

"Stay here with me." Fenne looked around the room. "What's a reasonable thing for you to be doing? Play the guitar."

Lilz got Fenne's instrument out of its case and gave it a badly needed tuning. She had barely finished when someone tapped on the door.

"It's him." Fenne closed her eyes and took a deep breath. "Come in?" she called.

Greencrags opened the door. He looked a little surprised to see Lilz sitting by window with Fenne's guitar, but he nodded and smiled at her and turned to his wife. "Hello, Fenne," he said.

"Hello, milord." Fenne held aside a loop of thread with her thumb and pulled the needle through the cloth.

"Is that all the greeting I get?"

"Did you bring everything?"

"All but one small silver candlestick no one could find." The iarl sounded annoyed.

"Lilz is just playing some music for me," Fenne said. "Why don't you go change from your travel clothes?"

"Sky above, woman! Is that all you have to say to me?"

"Woman? Who taught you to address a lady as 'woman'?" Fenne made another stitch. "I won't answer to that."

"Fenne Hasten, Lady Greencrags," the iarl said with heavy sarcasm. "Do you greet a husband gone a month with nothing more than 'hello, go change your clothes'?"

Fenne smiled. "That's how I greet you."

The battle, icily polite, still raged when Stone looked in to see what had happened to his master.

Lilz was an early riser, though at this time of year that meant leaving her warm bed before dawn. Once up, she wanted activity. In good weather she often took a horse along the river for the exercise, and was back and the horse rubbed down and fed and her own fast broken before Fenne even dreamed of waking.

The day after Greencrags returned she saddled the dappled gray the stablekeeper had told her needed a stretch. As she led it into the courtyard, the iarl appeared from the dimness. "Where are you going with my horse, Miss Lilz?" he asked cheerily.

"Milord, I beg pardon—"

"Don't beg pardon. Should I be paying you as an exercise boy?"

"No, milord. It's only that I enjoy riding, so sometimes—" She shrugged.

"Hold on. I'll ride with you."

A few minutes later Greencrags led the way out of the courtyard. They clopped through trash-strewn alleys toward the riverside, where a broad riding path along the straightened bank led under unpruned trees. A light fog blurred the black trunks and dripped from the bare twigs onto the hood and shoulders of her cloak and rustled the dead leaves beside the path. Lilz could hear waves slapping the stone flood wall: the tide was in. The mist smelled of manure and damp smoke, but the usual reek of garbage was absent.

"At high tide the river's not so high," Greencrags said over his shoulder. Lilz dutifully laughed at his wordplay and reined her mount into line behind him. "No, come even with me," he said. "How can I talk to you if you're halfway back to Standfast House?"

Lilz brought the gray abreast. "Well?" Greencrags said.

"Well, what, milord?"

"She's up to the same tricks. I could have sworn she'd promised to change her behavior, but now it seems misplacing that silver candlestick's to be held against me."

"It doesn't exist, milord."

"What?"

"There is no such candlestick."

"Lilz..." He reined his horse to a stop. "Dismount." When she reached the ground he rested a hand on her shoulder. "Do you mean to tell me my wife put that candlestick on the list so that everything could go on just as before?"

"Yes, milord. If I'd known of it, I'd have warned you. I find her behavior toward you abominable."

"Brave words from a bond-servant." Greencrags led his horse off the path and tied it to a small tree. "There's a wall here, somewhere. We can sit on that to talk."

Lilz tied the gray to another limb of the tree and joined the iarl on the river wall. "You know, when I first came home from Chrems I thought I loved her," he said.

After awhile, Lilz said, "But?"

"But what I loved was a small board, a few daubs of paint, and a colossal dollop of my own imagination."

"Most men do without the board and the paint."

With icy fingers, Greencrags turned her face toward him. The light had grown strong enough to see him clearly; it was so late the gulls were mewing. "How did you become so cynical?" he asked.

"Life."

"With Fenne, yes. That whole family is enough to sour one's stomach for living, I can see that." He sighed. "You must know about the little deaths."

"I'm sorry, milord?"

"The little deaths. At Chrems, all those learned men discussed the nature of death and whether a brave man should fear it and so forth and so on. It's all the nibbling little deaths before the last one a sane man should fear." Lilz sat still. He'd lost the tone of conversation. "Like the ones she deals out to me. Little daily deaths that steal my pride, my life—" Greencrags glanced at her. "Did it ever strike you, Lilz, that only two breaths are ever held important? Of all the thousands, tens of thousands, millions of breaths you or I may take in our lifetimes, only the first and the last are marked."

She nodded. Cold had made her draw her knees up and hug her legs to her. Greencrags put a hand on her arm. "You're shivering. Let's go back. I'll race you."

The gray was the better horse, but Greencrags the more reckless rider. He beat her handily.

Later that morning, Stone stopped her in the hall to ask if she had time to talk to his master. Lilz hesitated.

"I'll tell Aster to cover for you, if *she* calls," he suggested. "She can say you're downstairs and offer to go for you."

"All right." She tapped lightly on the door of Greencrags's suite and was bidden come in. Lilz had passed through this room before, on her visits to the iarl in his illness, but she had not particularly noticed it. For nobility, it was a rather plain room. The carpet was magnificent, one of those brought from the east, in pale green silk with somewhat geometrical flowers worked into it. Dark blue draperies framed the windows. But the walls were simply whitewashed, and the furniture looked as if it had been assembled over a number of years by someone who bought whatever he liked with no thought to impress. Probably Greencrags's father. What he'd liked was comfort. The iarl was sitting at a writing desk in a windowless corner. One of his dogs, a slender red setter, lay at his feet. It raised its head as the boy turned to sit sideways on his chair.

"Speak plainly to me, Lilz."

Lilz glanced automatically at the walls and gessoed ceiling. "Milord, if I speak plainly, how many ears will hear?"

"In this room, only mine. Stone and I go about checking every once in a while, and the windows haven't been open since fall."

"What do you wish to know?"

"Sit down, Lilz." She perched on the nearest chair. The dog came over and laid its head on her knee. Greencrags narrowed his eyes and pursed his lips for a moment. She was beginning to think he had changed his mind about whatever it was when he asked slowly and deliberately, "Who is the man?"

"Man, milord?"

"There must be a man!" Greencrags pushed back from the desk and cocked his head at her. "I go off to Chrems leaving a bride so far as I know willing to be mine, dream of no one but her for nearly three years, write and receive passionate letters, and when I come back—you know what our life has been. What could the cause be, other than that she's made a liaison with some man at Court?"

Lilz fondled the dog's ears for a moment, looking into its soft amber eyes. "Milord, you told me to speak plainly."

Greencrags nodded. "Please."

"Then may I say that your manner is not the most refined—you don't yet know Courtly ways. And your speech, while far softer than when you went away, is still rough." The iarl made an impatient gesture. "Then, too, while you are far from ugly, you are not strikingly handsome."

The iarl ran the tips of his fingers over his face, as if learning for the first time that he had one. "These things matter?"

"To my mistress, they matter."

"But why?"

"Milord, you've married a shallow, vain girl who lacks both the wit to look beyond what's fashion to see what a fine young man she has for a husband and the sense to understand how fortunate she is to have him."

Greencrags smoothed his beard. "You speak with a courtly tongue," he mused. "How did you learn?"

For the first time she could remember, Lilz felt loss at the idea that her father had been banished and she and her brothers brought up as secret peers, only to become uneasy commoners. Annoyed with herself, she said, "I have an apt tongue, and have been seventeen years in the service of the Hastens."

To her relief, the iarl accepted her answer with a nod. "Lilz, you were open with me by the river this morning. Tell me, what are my chances? I can't go on warring with my wife. If I polish my tongue and learn Courtly manners, will she come to me?"

No, no, a thousand times, no, Lilz thought. But how can I tell him that? It would be just another little death. Beyond his left shoulder, the door to his bed chamber stood ajar. How sick he had been, just last summer! And Stone...

"Milord," she said reluctantly, "I don't think she will ever forget that you were so carelessly raised that you didn't know the figures to dance at your own wedding."

He considered that for a moment. "No, in other words."

Her hand on the dog's head, Lilz gathered her courage. "To speak plainly, as you asked, you were better rid of her. Were I you, I'd petition for an annulment on the grounds that she refuses you, and find a wife who will recognize your good heart."

Greencrags smiled. "Someone like you, Lilz?"

"Me!" She laughed. "Milord, I don't think your faction would find the match a very good bargain."

"I don't find the one I've got a very good bargain!"

Lilz shrugged. "It's politic."

"Politic? Yes, it's that. But she's so beautiful..." The boy looked so sad, Lilz wanted to take his hand, as she might a child's. "Lilz, my tongue may be rough and my manner rude and my face less lovely than hers, but she can't complain of the way I've treated her."

"Indeed not, milord. You have been a model of restraint. Some might say, too much so."

He sighed. "Any idiot can rape his wife or beat her until she submits. I want Fenne to come to me of her own desire."

"You may wait a very long time."

Greencrags folded his arms on the back of his chair, looking out the window across the room, while Lilz waited to be dismissed. He touched his cheek again, looked at his fingertips, touched his forehead. "Lilz, if I'm not handsome, who is?"

Deaths. Tiny deaths. Large deaths. But, like pouring whiskey on a wound, maybe pain suffered now would make for less pain in time to come. Lilz took a deep breath. "Prince Jath was handsome while he lived. Sir Jen Makeready has a certain attraction, though not of late. Many have said for two years or more that the king's favorite, Kav Treadwell, is an exceedingly handsome man indeed."

Greencrags met her eyes. She gazed at him steadily.

"Sky above." She barely heard him. "You're right. I'm best rid of her."

With Greencrags's return came a round of entertaining such as Standfast House had not seen in a good many years —"Since our old iarl died," according to Reed. Fenne kept her guests amused with her gaiety and light spirit. Even her husband essayed a few jests and drew laughter. Music returned to Lilz's life, if only from the top of the stairs or rising through the ceiling of the newly-repainted ballroom to sound through the servants' quarters. She found she was hard at work more often. Even that was welcome.

But still Fenne refused her husband her bed and flaunted the liaison with Kav under his nose. Whether he'd realized his current rival was the king's favorite, or thought Lilz had been speaking only of his face, she couldn't tell. Stone, she thought, might have guessed, but he said nothing, not even to her.

Not so Sir Jen Makeready. Had Treadwell's mentor been content to stop with a single stinging poem, Fenne would never have forgiven him but he might have saved his life. He wasn't. The next was entitled "K, from her Husband, R." Fenne shredded the page and stamped up the stairs leaving the hall floor strewn with confetti for a housemaid to pick up, but Lilz, ever curious, gathered it herself. She resurrected the page on her own desk and read,

How harsh to have a wife I'll never ride:
For though she makes the hearts of all men sing,
To me she will remain a virgin bride,
But one, I think, who's stretched her wedding ring.

Indeed, it's stretched so far I've lost all count.
I see no reason she'd have need of me.
So, did she offer, I might too soon dismount
And find a woman with more loyalty.
—Sir Jen Makeready

"Dear heaven," Lilz murmured. "The man's gone crazy." She screwed up the bits of paper and threw them into the fire.

Over the next couple of months, while the old dych was moving forward with Fenne's annulment arrangements—no one had told Greencrags yet, so far as Lilz knew—Makeready became all but rabid on the topic of wifely purity. The Iarl of Greencrags and his wife continued their social round, with Fenne preserving wifely purity on visits to other houses with the tested expedient of keeping her servants between herself and her husband at all times. Makeready did not relent. As winter deepened, both Aster and Fenne came home from Thornday courts complaining that Sir Jen was calling her names, suggesting that she'd slept with half of the peerage, spreading rumors even more obscene and salacious than the first, which had merely been that she'd made a lover of the king's own favorite, and the king having the taste for young men that he did...

Power. He was about to be thrown from his own horse, Lilz thought. And a great steed it had been for a mere benighted thegn, however able. Poor Makeready: he'd chosen Kav Treadwell early, as a lad likely to appeal to King Guyr, a young man of stunning face and body, just ambitious enough and not overly bright; made a friend of him; put him forward when the king seemed to be tiring of...what was that imbecile's name? Stormclouds; and rapidly and cleverly consolidated his position. How hard he must find it to believe he had been thrown by so well-schooled a mount!

His pride in his brain must be wounded, too. Many of the latest royal rulings had come from Sir Jen Makeready through the medium of the favorite. On the whole, a vast improvement over what Guyr did in Summerlea's bridle, in Lilz's opinion. The struggles among the factions were becoming more even. Only last fall a man named Tern Gudgeon had been appointed Lord Chief Justice, a boon for those led by the Ridehards and a blow to the Hastens.

And that was why Nevan Hasten was moving to acquire Treadwell. He saw the Hasten grip on government threatened by Makeready's shadow ascendancy. So he sat and schemed, and the victims of his scheming thought they acted of their own free wills, while Makeready raved.

Early that spring, as the first yellow crocuses came into bloom in the formal garden of Standfast House, someone brought to the king a notarized accusation against Jen Makeready: he was formally charged with adherence to the old religion and thrown into the Old Palace to await a trial.

Oddly, no one seemed to know who had accused him. The paper from the notary disappeared before reaching the files of the Lord Chief Justice. Though the notary was advertised for, he did not come forward. Not long after Makeready had gone into the Old Palace, protesting innocence and threatening revenge, a new warden was appointed to the prison, a longtime Hasten adherent named Senvar Elm. Two weeks later, Sir Jen was declared incommunicado. Fenne had already moved back to Hasten House and filed her annulment petition. Everything was in place: the path Lilz would take to House-Among-Oaks six months later had been paved.

With the first sealed white envelope Fenne gave to her Lilz saw the road clearly, knew what her feet had been set upon, and refused those few steps she could.

Chapter Fourteen

"Does it seem to you that those awful rumors are dying?" Fenne asked. "I haven't heard anything since Elm went into the country for his health, have you?"

"No, my mistress, I haven't."

A weariness had settled into Lilz. Hasten machinations were becoming more than her spirit could bear: she knew quite well that Senvar Elm had gone to the country "for his health" more because he thought it threatened by the new Dych of Summerlea than that the purer air would heal him, and that if the rumors were dying it was because of Fenne's father's fierce campaign of repression. Her own thirty-eighth birthday was fast approaching. While no one else had marked any of her birthdays for twenty years, Lilz had only once forgotten one herself. She viewed this one's arrival with a sensation of defeat.

"Oh, I almost forgot." Fenne set her embroidery aside and went to her desk. "Benina brought another of those anonymous poems yesterday. He's still on about gray eyes. Do you want to see it?"

"Is it interesting?"

"As much as any of the others."

Three months had passed since the love-lies-longing complaint asking advice. Lilz had yet to find a way to talk to Greencrags. She took the poem Fenne handed her and held it toward the cold light of windows all but sealed to vision by frost, expecting to be upbraided for ignoring a plea for help. Instead, Greencrags addressed his lady of the tear-pale eyes in the title, and asked why she no longer rode upon the fog to tame his despair in the mist-net of her words.

Lilz smiled briefly and handed the poem back. "If she won't have him, at least she must have talked to him once," she remarked.

"Benina says it's better than the others. Is it?"

"He's got fourteen full lines this time, and nothing so outrageous as—what was it? Sipping a view? No, supping it. Yes, I'd say he's gaining strength."

"I wish I knew who it is. Both of them." Fenne returned the poem to her desk and sat down with her stitchery. "I've looked at all the ladies of the Court, I think. There're only six with gray eyes, and they're all at least forty years old. *Much* too old to be getting poems written to them."

How one sentence could plunge her into heartsickness these days! Much too old to be loved, in just two more years? Lilz bent her head over the underskirt she was embroidering. But if I thought it a real complaint addressed to me, wouldn't my heart beat faster? she asked herself. Wouldn't I still respond to an admiring eye?

"Maybe there's a daughter at home," Fenne speculated. "Can you think of anybody presented in the past few years who isn't married yet?"

Lilz raised her gray eyes to stare at her mistress. "Need she be single?" Her tone was mild, the thought venomous.

"No, I s'pose not."

Aster tapped on the open door. "Milady? Those ribbons you wanted curled? I'm sorry, but the sugar-water discolored the blue ones."

"All of them?"

"Yes'm."

"Oh, honestly, Aster. Those were Travaltian! Where will I get more before I want to wear the dress?"

"How discolored, Aster?" Lilz asked.

"The dye's leached out."

Lilz sighed. "No help for it, then. Shall I go to the market, my mistress, and see whether the draper has any to match?"

"No...no. Let's see them, Aster, maybe I can still wear them after all."

Lilz completed an eyelet in the fine linen underskirt. No ribbons. One more chance to stop at Standfast House gone by. She smiled faintly. Now, it didn't matter. She'd been given instructions.

Her early morning rides into the country were ridiculed among the Waterside servants, who between that and her insatiable appetite for the written word thought her extremely strange. So did Fenne, but at least Fenne didn't care. The rides had been infrequent lately, not only because of bitter weather but because dejection had kept Lilz later in bed than usual. She was distressed to think that Rovvo Standfast might have been waiting for her on those cold mornings while she had lazed under her blanket, too dispirited to think of the obvious. No help for that.

The next morning Lilz rode only a couple of hundred sashlengths along her usual route. Here, there was a bridge across the River Lynn; she took it and turned back along the other bank. The air was bone-chilling, as it had been over the past couple of months. Clouds of steam drifted from her own mouth and the sorrel mare's. For twenty minutes, Lilz let her thoughts drift with no more direction than the steam's as she rode through the last of darkness, guided by sputtering lamps at the street corners. Then she took a second bridge across the river.

Not far from the Miense end of the bridge, her horse whickered. An answer came from close by. She reached the spot and found a horse tied to a tree. In the meager light she couldn't tell whether the blanket it wore was Standfast green. Loosening her knife in its sheath in case it was not, she dropped out of the saddle and tied up her own mount.

"Welcome, gray-eyed lady." Standfast ducked under a branch and came toward her. "I've had a long vigil, I must say."

"Good morning, milord." Lilz pulled her cloak snugger. "I didn't see the poem until yesterday. I hope you aren't frozen."

"Only every morning for the past five weeks."

"Dear heaven!"

"They say cold air's good for the lungs." He was well bundled against the raw morning, Lilz was glad to see; at least his voice sounded warm.

"We should find a faster way to communicate than manuscript, milord."

A temblor near the top of the mound of wool and furs before her was doubtless a nod. "It does present certain problems," the mound agreed. "Frozen fingers, frozen toes, frozen you-know-what, and frozen nose."

Lilz chuckled. "You've caused a great deal of curiosity among the ladies of the Court, milord, did you know? My mistress, for one, pines to meet the wonderful fellow whose love won't have him."

Greencrags laughed. "Someday, I'll have the pleasure of telling her who it is," he said. "Oh, that's funny. Stone will be rolling on the floor."

"How is Stone?"

"Well. He sends his fondest regards."

"Take mine to him, please?"

"Gladly." The iarl untied his mount, the gray she'd ridden herself that other morning. "It's getting light," he pointed out. "Bring the horse back to the wall, or someone will see the blankets and wonder what Standfast House can have to say to Northlands. How long can you talk?"

"Not over half an hour."

"I've only got a week's worth of questions to ask," Greencrags sighed. "Starting with the state of the Hasten faction, but let's leave that aside for now. We can meet again, can't we? Somewhere warmer?" He went to the right around a small tree. "First, the question on everyone's lips two months ago," he said, when they'd fixed a place and possible times. "Why did you lead Summerlea's horse?"

They'd reached the river wall. Lilz draped the mare's reins over the nearest bush. "You know as much about that as I do."

"He gave no reason?"

"Not that the new dych divulged. Even Fenne's mystified."

"It was the old dych's idea? How very strange." Above the frost-coated scarf wound over his mouth, the iarl's eyes narrowed. "Lilz, I've heard rumors that my former wife may have had something to do with the demise of the man whose verse jigged along so censoriously two years ago."

Shivering, Lilz pulled her cloak close. Greencrags turned her to face the wind and stood to protect her from it. "She would have, if she'd had her way."

"What happened?"

"She left me in charge."

"And you?"

"Sent the foods she ordered, but spiced more blandly than she desired."

The young iarl nodded. "I thought as much, long ago. Lilz—" He stopped and looked about. Not far away, several starlings picked at the withered berries of a rowan tree. He waved his arms until they flew. "When I was ill—"

"I don't think so, milord. Nothing went from us to you, though things arrived at Standfast House that had her name on them. My own thought was that the name was someone else's inducement for you to eat. Possibly her grandfather's."

"Of course, she could have sent them from elsewhere."

"I don't think so." How to convey her sense of Fenne to this man? "She's too self-centered. She may have wished you dead as a convenience, but I can't believe she'd poison a man who adored her. The annulment was much more in her line, although not her devising. More, if she had had the cunning to have someone else do murder in her name, I'm sure she'd have asked me to arrange it, as she did later."

The boy sighed so heavily Lilz felt the warmth of his breath on her cheeks. "She was certainly direct about everything else! What did she send, besides the flowers and the cherries?"

"Nothing, milord. Not even the flowers or the cherries."

"I see." Greencrags put a foot on the wall and leaned on his knee. "My thanks for both, and for giving me the will to live on. Did you write her letters for her, too, while I was at Chrems?"

"No, milord. That she did herself."

"The woman plays a deadly enough game when she likes." The iarl glanced at her. "Lilz, if I could buy you, would you come? If not for me, for Stone?"

She looked out at the ice-choked river. Leave the Hastens? How often she'd dreamed of just that! But even with old Nevan dead, they... "I don't know, milord. I might prove extremely expensive, not just in money. Maybe you'd best not even inquire."

"Not at all?"

"I'm useful to them." She looked at the rowan tree. The starlings were back. "Once the question of that death is settled, perhaps," she said finally. "It's too dangerous before then. I know too much."

"Think about it, Lilz. Find out the likely terms, if you can do it on the quiet. You'd be the best investment I ever made."

"I'll think about it, milord."

"Please do. You'd be surprised how much Standfast House misses you. What's in that box you sent me?"

"Some papers, important only to me. It's too bad you couldn't have used Stone to contact me again, milord, and saved yourself some shivering. That was clever."

Standfast's eyes half closed with a grin. "I thought so, myself."

"He was superb!"

"Stone always is. We'd better go. Do you need to warm up before you ride back? I could sneak you into my kitchen for a few minutes."

And have every servant in Miense know about it within three days. "That's kind of you, milord, but I'm afraid I can't take the time."

They were back on the bridle path and mounted when Greencrags said, "What do you think of my poems, Lilz?"

"Not bad. Getting better. You should try to be—or at least sound—more direct."

"Did you read the one called 'To his Wise Lady'?"

Lilz nodded, smiling. "The memory was sweet, milord. The poem—" She shrugged. "You broke the thought two lines too soon, the last line lacks a beat, and 'supping a view' is a dreadful metaphor. Makes me think of hills of porridge."

"Porridge! Oof! But it had to rhyme." The anonymous poet leaned over to put a mitten on her arm. "I do wish we were there again, Lilz. I'd find a way to keep you with us, sharing as many sunrises as we pleased." He clicked his tongue to his horse and rode away, leaving her looking after him with astonishment.

Air softened. Ice softened. Earth softened. At Waterside the tulips sprang from the ground in a blanket of pink and white. Lilz rode back one morning and reined up merely to watch the low sun tip each blossom with light, as it might the ripples of a pond.

She had just left Greencrags at a country inn. Stone had been with him, a frequent pleasure. Not much to discuss—they'd managed to talk on several occasions, and the young iarl had his strategies well-mapped—but each time she rode to him hungry for the glint of a real mind against her own, each time returned home light with satisfaction.

Today she was less happy. A trip to Summerlea Manor was in the making. Given Fenne, no telling how long it would last. Greencrags had again urged his purchase plan upon her, with Stone's initial support.

"Milord, it's not possible," she'd said. "Do you have any idea how valuable I am to her? I run her household as she should herself, I'm in charge of her investments—you can imagine how much wealth that entails—she interposes me between herself and anything she doesn't want to deal with, just as surely as she used to put me in bed between you. And there's the question of the man who displeased her. That surely hasn't gone away forever. "

Stone had put his hand to his ear at that. "My master," he'd said. "Lilz may know too much for them to let her leave. I'm sure it has never occurred to them that any offer might be made. But if it is, and by you? Accidents are so easily arranged...."

"Good point." Greencrags had smoothed his beard for several minutes, frowning. "Good point."

"And I'm of more use to you there," Lilz had added. "None of them thinks of a servant as having ears. Or mouth or heart, for that matter. Not even me."

"True." The iarl had glanced worriedly at Stone. "Oh, Lilz, I have such a premonition of danger! Those rumors—I'd be so much more comfortable knowing you were safe."

As would I, Lilz thought now. She turned the horse over to the stablekeeper and went into the house with her muddy boots in her hand. Sounds from the servants' hall told her breakfast was still in progress. Her own belly was full of fine country eggs, backfat fried brown, real tea fit for a iarl and bread slathered with fresh butter. Greencrags had offered her oat porridge with a huge spoonful of cream clabber, but by that time she'd felt her eyes were popping, so Stone had eaten it.

Aster came up the back stairs behind her. "Good ride?"

"Oh, very fine. Did you see the tulips in front of the house?"

"No, are they out? I'll take a peek later."

"Is she asking for me yet?"

"She's sleeping in. Northlands stayed overnight, don't you remember?"

"No, it had slipped my mind." Aster went through the second floor door and Lilz went on up the stairs to the attic. A bad case of spring fever, she thought, slowly removing her mud-flecked trousers. Lucky Fenne, to have even one whole night with a man. Lilz ran her hands down her bare flanks and thought: Stone.

Immediately a wave of depression hit. She put on her house pants and started cleaning her boots. Each time she blinked, tears fell, though she couldn't say why she was crying.

"Lilz, what's the matter?" Aster had stopped in the doorway, balanced as if she didn't know whether to step back or come forward.

"Nothing, really. Spring and age."

"Oh." The younger woman sounded unenlightened. "Onma Stump's downstairs. She's got an appointment. Fenne's not up yet. What shall I tell her?"

"Where's Northlands?"

"I don't know."

"Check with Swan. If our iarl's in his rooms, go wake Fenne up. If not, better stay out of the way. I'll go talk to Mistress Stump."

"Are you—I mean, do you mind?"

Lilz shook her head and dried her eyes. "I'm better off doing something," she said. "I'll just finish getting the mud off these and be right down. I'm almost done."

Onma Stump was drumming her fingers on the arms of the chair Aster had offered her when Lilz walked into the back reception room a few minutes later. "Ah, Lilz," she said. "Where's your mistress?"

Lilz smiled. "Her husband found himself free of other duties last night, Mistress Stump. I'm afraid Lady Northlands has overslept."

"It's not fair," the costumer said. "She ought to wear out, really she ought. Takes after her mother, just as Jen Makeready said. It must pass with the blood."

"Shh," Lilz cautioned.

Mistress Stump shrugged. "There's a lot of talk about. If she has any sense, she'll treat us well."

"Will she?" Lilz sat beside the costumer. "You must know by now how little foresight she has."

"True. How old is she now? Nineteen? She hasn't changed a whit from the moment I first saw her" Mistress Stump cocked her head at Lilz. "It's you that made her so, you know. If she couldn't say, 'Lilz, do you mind? Lilz, if you would? Lilz, I'm too lazy, so if you?' she wouldn't be such a bitch."

Lilz glanced at the door.

"You're far too competent," the costumer continued. "You do everything for her. Everything but bed her men. *That* you may be sure she does for herself, as if the sap didn't rise every spring until the tree dies! Unless, of course, you kept Greencrags happy for her?"

Lilz shook her head. "Where Greencrags found his happiness, if any, I couldn't say. Please, Mistress Stump, I know it's annoying to be kept waiting, but there's no reason to blame me for it."

Onma Stump jumped up and paced across the small room. "It's these stories. They make me nervous. Clock, too. He's been at me to get a paper from her saying what she bought from him was just for rats, but I don't dare ask. Whoever heard of a iarlena buying her own rat poison? That's the houseman's job. Can you imagine what she'd say?"

Unfortunately, Lilz could. "Lady Northlands thought the rumors were dying down," she remarked.

"That's because people have become more guarded in her presence, thanks to her father." Mistress Stump stopped pacing in front of Lilz and grimaced. "Actually, the stories are improving. There was Greencrags, you recall. And Prince Jath. Both in her way, and most conveniently taken ill. Not that I believe for a moment that she was responsible—she was so clearly inexperienced about the other."

"I think you can rule them out," Lilz said.

"But people talk." The costumer plumped back into her chair. "It's true, Lilz, the old viper's not running our lives any more, but we don't have him to protect us, either. What will we do if someone decides the rumor is strong enough to investigate?"

"You will be quiet, and I will be quiet, and Clock will be quiet, and the new dych can try his hand at protecting his family from scandal."

"I s'pose that's the best solution anyone can offer."

Lilz pursed her mouth, gazing at the costumer. How had Nevan Hasten kept guilt from working in her so many years? Now it was loose, and eating away at her tongue-strings. Lilz had the urge to tell the woman that all her conniving had gone for naught, that the poison she had obtained for Fenne sat unused in a tin box less than an hour's ride away, but caution stopped her. As it was, she had the uncomfortable feeling that they should be inspecting this small room for whizzers with the aid of Mistress Stump's suggested pot of water. She glanced at the ceiling. The dark object nestled in the curl of a plaster wave was an ordinary spider.

The costumer followed Lilz's glance. Without a word, she got up and began a search. Lilz closed the door and joined her.

If there was a whizzer in the room, they didn't find it.

Chapter Fifteen

Two days later Lilz set out for Summerlea Manor, to make sure everything would be in readiness for Fenne when she arrived—a week after Lilz, if all went as planned. The journey would take most of two days. For convenience, Lilz was to carry the next several month's maintenance for the house in gold coin, so at Olen Hasten's insistence she chose a guard to take with her: Raven, a blue-eyed, blond-bearded young giant well over a sashlength tall, broad in proportion, and as skilled with a pistol as with a sword.

Near sunset they stopped at an inn, although a fat yellow moon hung in the eastern sky and they could have ridden on by its light. Lilz dickered over the room while Raven saw to the horses. He met her in the aleroom, where she had already ordered two dinners and was defending a chair for him against a noisy party from a nearby manor.

"Lilz," Raven said, over the last of the meal. He turned a bright red. "Er, I don't know why, out of all the guard—that is—"

Smiling, Lilz leaned forward to be heard over a drinking song now being attempted in what was probably meant to be only four part harmony. "My dear Raven, I guarantee you a peaceful night."

"I don't mean to say that a man who lusts after women might not find you—" He shrugged.

"Precisely." Raven had come to the Hasten's service from that of a vikent who'd kept him as company in carriage until he grew too large and hairy for the man's taste. "That's why I chose you."

Raven looked somewhat disgruntled. He might not care to bed a woman, but surely he was accustomed to their admiration. Even Fenne had flirted with him, if that counted. Lilz caught the eye of the serving wench and pointed into her mug with two fingers.

"It's a settled vice with me, you know," Raven said. "It won't help to get me drunk."

She smiled tightly. "If I thought it would, Raven my sweet, it's the bung I'd have in your mouth, not more ale."

The girl came with full mugs, collected her payment, and stopped to tug playfully at Raven's beard before taking the empties away. He laughed but made no move to snatch at her, as the other men were doing. "You're a shy one!" The server rolled her eyes at Lilz. "Ain't always, I bet, eh? Enjoy the night!"

Raven's eye followed her until caught by someone more interesting. "We'll want an early start tomorrow," Lilz said, "So don't even think of the lad with the broom."

Raven flushed again and drank off half the ale. Three more mugs followed, paid for out of Lilz's pocket. He was a cheerful drunk, luckily. Lilz barred the door to their room with no misgivings, helped him off with his boots, and laid him down in the bed. By the time she'd shed her own boots and climbed in beside him, he was snoring. In the morning she found he had thrown off the blankets and was twined around her for warmth.

"Raven," she said softly. "Raven? Time to get up."

He opened his eyes. They focused on her face. "Oh, shit," he groaned.

"No, dear heart, it's Lilz."

Raven sat up, holding his head. "Shit," he repeated.

"Headache?" Lilz asked. "I did try to make you drink some water last night, but you weren't having any."

"I drank enough something." He got up and stumbled to the corner. Lilz turned her back and pulled on her traveling boots while Raven pissed long and hard into the chamber pot. He straightened his clothes and combed his hair and his beard with his fingers. "I'll order the horses."

"Leave time for breakfast," Lilz told him. "I don't start without it. Meet me downstairs?"

With Raven gone, Lilz barred the door. She counted the coins in her money sash to be sure none had escaped into the sheets. She washed her face. Yawning, she replaced the few things she had taken out of her saddle pack and looked out the window. A few clouds caught the light of the still invisible sun with a pink glow. If the clouds would thicken a bit without dousing them, a good day to travel.

"Is that it?" Raven pulled up to look across the meadows at Summerlea Manor.

"That's it." Lilz, too, pulled up. The house caught the afternoon sun on its carved stone facade and on the tall windows of the front rooms. From here, the sweep of the drive disappeared beyond a low rise where last year's flattened dead grass had given way to this year's new growth. The five statues plundered from some ancient monument far to the south and set along the drive looked a bit dull. Probably black moss had started to spread on them again and they'd need scrubbing.

She felt oddly neutral as they rode toward the house. Weeds between some of the paving blocks. The gardener would need a nudge. Her gaze drifted again over the building, her home for sixteen years. Lilz had expected the lift of her heart she'd had on other returns to Summerlea. Instead, she felt only this peculiar blank.

As they trotted around the curve, the rambling nature of the house revealed itself. "I didn't know it was this big." Raven sounded awed.

"Most of it's empty."

The sweep of lawn looked ragged. No one had taken a scythe to it this spring. Cherries were in early bloom, the thickly-set peonies near the front entrance loose-budded. "We'll go around back," Lilz said, when the drive forked.

A tow-haired young man came out of the stable as they neared. He shaded his eyes. Lilz waved and got a two-handed wave in return. "Who's that?" Raven asked.

"Stablekeeper's son."

"Do I detect a resemblance to our employer?"

"You do."

"I see yet another advantage to my way of doing."

"For some." The young man went into the stable. He reappeared as Lilz dismounted, and took hold of the reins.

"Ho, Lilz, we've not seen you for two or three years," he said. "Is your mistress arriving today, too?"

"Not today, Vole. Next week."

"Phew!" Vole rolled his eyes up. "Wait till you see the house."

Lilz laughed. "I doubt they'll have done anything I didn't expect!"

"It was a bitter winter, remember. Who's this?"

Lilz started to introduce Raven. In time, she realized the lad was asking the name of her horse. "Alyia. And that's Morgeen, and the man on her back is Raven. Come along, Raven. Let Vole take care of the horses—that's his job. You and I will have a look at the house."

She led the guard across the stableyard and through the kitchen garden to the servants' door, which she found standing open, as she expected. "Ho?" she called, walking in. A skivvy popped her head out of the kitchen and squeaked with surprise. "Where's the houseman?" Lilz asked.

"I don't know." The girl stood in the kitchen door as if hiding the room, so Lilz walked up and looked past her. The cook had moved his bed downstairs over winter. Here it still was. Beside the table, the bed's owner was looking more than a little flustered.

"Sky above!" said Raven, behind her.

"Lilz?" The cook swallowed and attempted a smile. "It's been a long time. Is—ah—everyone with you?"

"Just Raven." She reached for the guard's wrist and pulled him forward.

"Are you checking the house?" The kitchenmaid sounded faint.

"Indeed I am. Oh, I'm Lilz, bond-servant to Lady Northlands, the new dych's daughter. She'll be here a week from today." Lilz looked at the cook, who was still standing by the table where she'd surprised him and now puffed his cheeks out in relief. "Lord Cals will come, too. The Iarl of Northlands is staying in town, as, I believe, is his Grace. Lady Delle hadn't yet made up her mind when I left, nor had Lord Ruppet or his wife. What the cousins may be planning is somewhat less clear. Be prepared for a crowd, but don't count on one."

"Everything as usual, then," the cook sighed.

"Do they allow his bed in the kitchen?" Raven whispered, as Lilz poked her head into the houseman's pantry. Empty.

"No."

"Then what—?"

"Cold weather, Raven, don't you recall? You guards complained loudly enough when his Grace had you stand out."

The table in the informal dining room, a room with narrow windows easily made snug with rags, had been shoved to the wall and the chairs piled on it to make space for two beds. Lilz glanced at the belongings scattered over the room. Four people slept here.

"Sky..." Raven said.

In the back hall she met the head hallmaid, who greeted her with a sick smile, a twin of the cook's. "One week," Lilz said. The smile broadened into a relieved grin accompanied by a hug.

"A long time, Lilz! It must be two years, if not three. How long are you staying?"

"Lady Northlands hadn't decided when I left, so it's anyone's guess. Where's the houseman? Is it still Hammer?"

"No, Hammer went back to his village to care for his old mother. The new man's called Byre. I saw him in the cellar a little while ago." The maid's smile faltered.

"Not into the wine, was he?"

"No one ever put much past you, Lilz, not for long." The maid sighed. "Yes, he's into the wine, if there's any left after the winter."

"Sky..." Raven said.

"When the master's away, the house servants play, Raven my lad." Lilz grinned at him. "Don't say you haven't yourself!"

"Lilz, if you'd give me a day before you look at anything else?" the maid asked nervously.

"Of course. Is there a bed in the attic for either of us?"

"Mmmm. Not likely."

"Sky..." Raven said.

"But you'll each have one before evening," the maid added firmly. "Shall I see if I can get Byre into shape for you?"

"Just tell him I'm here, and that Lady Northlands will arrive in a week, probably with more of the family. I'll lecture him in the morning, when he's sober. Oh, this is Raven. With his jaw up, he's a house guard." She opened the door that led to the rest of the house. "Come along, Raven."

"Where are we going?" Raven whispered, when they'd traversed several twists of back corridor under the benign painted gaze of departed younger sons of Hastens.

"To wake up the dych's house servants. It's a separate staff, though I imagine that if he comes he'll take meals with his family in the room you just saw."

"Sky above!"

"Never mind. It'll be ready." She laughed, feeling cheerful at the prospect of catching Quern, the self-styled perfect houseman, with his collar undone. She was too late, of course: the faster way to the dych's apartments was through the gardens. But at least she had the satisfaction of finding the place in a mess.

Walking back to the main kitchen with Raven, Lilz had a sudden idea: why not look at the Summerlea ledgers while she was here, to find out exactly what the terms of her bondage had been?

The next day, Raven was put to work moving furniture, a job for which he used one hand where most men needed two and two where most men needed help. Byre was tearfully glad to have his assistance.

To Lilz, it meant that Raven was out of her way. When the cook complained that Byre was too busy to drive into town with him to restock the delicacies Lady Northlands and her brother were sure to demand, she suggested he ask Quern to go. Somewhat to her surprise, Quern went. She stood at the window beside the front entrance to watch the cart turn from the drive and disappear behind the ancient trees lining the high road. Quern gone. Raven was on his way up the front stairs with a bedstead on his back—Byre had decreed the back stairs too steep and narrow to struggle with, so long as only servants were in the house. Lilz ducked through the door under the front stairs, the shortest route through the house to the other end. No one else was about. At the dych's apartments, she found the inner door open. Pleased, she walked boldly to the library without meeting a soul.

Quern had made entering his house accounts simpler in the dych's absence: this door, too, was unlocked. Lilz stepped through and closed it. Sunlight poured through the dust-hazed doors to the west lawn. In the meadow beyond, a dozen still-shaggy cows were grazing, kept in bounds by the invisible sunken fence.

She had last been in this room nearly six years before. The old dych had sat at the desk in casual blue tunic and trousers, his arms folded behind his head, grinning at her. His son, now the new dych, had stood at those doors staring over the meadows— the glass had been polished to invisibility then; no one would have dreamed of allowing it to be otherwise—while they discussed the marriage of his daughter to the Iarl of Greencrags. How little of what had happened since she had anticipated, even knowing then how headstrong Fenne could be!

Lilz sighed. No one had made any more attempt at putting the room into logical order than on her last visit. Ledgers and journals were stacked in every corner and even on two of the chairs, some looking rather precariously balanced. She'd have to be cautious.

At least she had light. Lilz moved softly across the room to ease back the bolt on one of the glass doors. She tried the handle. With a whispered groan, the door opened inward. She pushed it shut. The moment's rush of air had stirred a cloud of dust that swirled in the sunlight.

Maybe if she bolted the inner door, someone coming to wash the windows would think it simply locked? Would that make time enough for the dust to settle after she'd escaped? Or would she just send someone speeding around the house to catch her? She decided to leave the door on the latch.

The most recent books were bound in the brightest leather, Lilz soon found. A few had been marked with dates on the spines. A quick survey showed that they were not in any order she could define. She'd just have to start at one side of the door and work her way around the room, hoping to find the volume she was looking for before Quern returned.

She found something far more interesting first: a book bound in crumbling once-blue leather, dating from the earliest years of King Lehrr's rule. Curious, Lilz turned a few pages. Accountants of that time were not content to write brief descriptions of transactions and note the figures. It was still an age where barter was the mainstay of commerce. Rambling tales of the sources of and reasons for various trades filled these pages, the ink faded to sepia, the neat archaic hand almost unreadable to Lilz's modern eye. Here was a description of a farm-hand's wedding, complaining of the bride price, but remarking that it was "yet a semely Compact, for the Wench has the lad gladly and hir Stiches be most fine." Immediately after, a comment that King Lehrr "has bid construct upon that Site a Palace of Travaltian Granitt, as if our oun Native Stone fares not so Sturdy as to stand an Age!"

Reluctantly, Lilz set the volume aside. Time was too short to indulge herself in history.

An hour later she found the ledger she was looking for. She turned the pages, scanning entries for the fall of the year before Fenne was born for her name. And here it was, in Nevan Hasten's spiky script:

"Lilz Chantwell, daughter of Dilyn Chantwell Peer of the Blood, Iarl of Darkforest in banishment, came to the House of Hasten today as hostage for her father's solemn word."

Hostage? Lilz felt her face drain. Not bond-servant, but hostage? What could that mean?

Not a line about money paid in trust to her account, she noted. Not one line, in a ledger kept to the quarter-copper.

Not bond-servant. Hostage. Soon to be twenty years a hostage! With no idea why, or for what—

Not a copper set aside for her old age, never mind the sum she'd thought had been agreed—

Quern went by in the hall, talking to someone. Moving in a daze, Lilz found a penknife on the desk and cut the page with her entry out of the ledger, close to the stitching. The other half of the sheet skewed in the book. She could not make it line up with the remaining pages. She pulled it out. Was there more?

Hastily, she went through the rest of the book, crouched in the shadow of the desk lest someone come up to the glass doors and look in. *Lilz Chantwell...Lilz Chantwell*...wherever she saw her name, she took out the full sheet, not stopping to read. For the last twenty, there was no mention of her...no, here, the very last page. She ran the knife blade down the gutter between the pages and pulled this last sheet out. Quern's voice stopped in the hall just outside the room. She folded all the pages she'd removed together and pushed them into her shirt. As silently as she could move, she put the ledger back and replaced the rest of the stack on top of it, matching the dust mark on the cover. Quern's voice rose as if the person he'd been talking to were walking away.

Lilz stepped through the outer door, pulled it shut behind her, and sprinted for the ha-ha into which the gardener had disappeared six years before. She leapt over the edge, jarred hard on the ground beyond. On hands and knees, the breath knocked out of her, she waited for the sounds of chase.

Chapter Sixteen

Lilz had placed herself in a predicament only slightly less urgent than had Quern found her in the dych's library. The fieldstone wall of the sunken fence faced southwest. To her left, it ran almost to the king's highway, to end in a turn and an ordinary split cedar fence as high as her shoulder; to her right, it ended behind the stables, again in a split cedar fence.

The cut into the hillside was deeper to the left, but it curved with the drive and might bring her into sight from the manor before she reached the shelter of the trees beside the high road. In any case, it was a long walk, with a consequently long absence to explain.

To the right, the cut turned shallow: she might soon have to crawl to remain concealed. Like all cows, the ones in this field had spent much of their time pacing the boundary of their enclosure. A band of well-manured mud beside the stone wall was the inevitable result. The mud she wore now might be accounted for by a slip and a fall, but she'd be coated in more muck than anyone could reasonably excuse if she took the second, far shorter route.

One of the cows decided to investigate this creature who had dropped so abruptly into her domain and plodded toward her. A few of the others lifted their heads.

She could scarcely trail this nosy cohort all the way to the highway without attracting someone's notice. A blessing she hadn't landed on one of those broad backs, to be bucked off in full view! Or worse yet, skewered herself on a pair of horns! Shuddering, Lilz rolled the bottoms of her pants and started for the stable. For the first thirty sashlengths she bent over, still shielded by the wall. She'd heard no chase, but Quern might simply wait to see who appeared beyond the ha-ha: she had no misconceptions about his intelligence, just because he irritated her.

Soon she would be forced to crawl. At this distance surely she could take a small risk? Lilz crouched and slowly raised her head above the wall, tilted back to present the smallest possible area to view. No one stood outside the dych's end of the house. Two maids were beating an extraordinarily dust-filled carpet in the courtyard, but their backs were to her.

Lilz climbed the wall and headed for the stable, where she used the stile over the fence into the back stableyard. One of the dogs barked violently. She startled it into silence by growling. The dog wagged its tail; she walked past without looking at it. With a handful of straw she wiped most of the mud from her house shoes, then stopped to rinse her hands at the watering trough pump.

Vole came down the loft ladder as she walked through the stable toward the house. "Lilz, what on earth were you doing?" he asked.

"Oh, no. Did you see me?"

"Yes, from up in the hayloft. You came flying out of the dych's end of the house and went over the ha-ha without missing a step. You didn't come up and didn't come up—I'd just decided to go see if you were hurt."

Lilz made a face. "I suppose Quern saw me, too. I was pulling a prank on him."

"On Quern?" Vole grinned. "Good. I've been longing to put a burr under that old fart's saddle most of my life. But mother would have me taken out and shot."

"Not quite, but she'd make your life a misery, I'm sure." Lilz turned toward the open stable door.

"Lilz, no, wait!" Vole took a step after her. "Tell me what you did."

Did? Oh, to Quern. "I fixed one of his cupboards for him." She grinned at the idea. "Everything will fall out when he opens it. The best part is, he's let things get so out of hand over there he'll spend the next week wondering whether it was a prank or his own fault. But he nearly caught me."

"If I'd known, I'd have kept him longer when he brought back the cart."

"I'll remember that, next time," Lilz said. "I'd better get back to the house, though. I've been gone too long as it is."

"Lilz?" Vole called as she walked into the sunny yard. "Thanks for taking Sussu out—he really was stablebound. I'm sorry he threw you."

"No damage done," she called back, by way of thanks, as one of the maids turned from beating the carpet to glance at her.

No one greeted her with any interest in where she had been, so Lilz trusted to the maids beating the carpet to repeat Vole's handy excuse for the mud on her knees. She hurried up the back stairs to the attic, where she now had a whole bed and her old room to herself for the next few days, changed her trousers, and finished cleaning her shoes. The pages she'd cut out of the dych's ledger she shoved into her open saddlepack. Three tries, and the cloak she draped over the pack to hide them looked as if it had been tossed there with no special attention. She walked out of the room and nearly collided with Raven and the four chairs he had under his arms.

Raven had an interest in where she had been.

"I am a trained house guard," he yelled. "Will you please inform that excuse for a houseman that I am not a donkey? I'm sick of toting things around! These jerks got all their junk down the stairs, why can't they get it back up?"

"They had longer to move it down than they have to move it up." Lilz took one of the chairs and set it in the doorway of her room. "Believe me, Raven, they appreciate your help."

"Yes, we do," said the maid behind him. "Just put the chairs anywhere, we'll straighten them out later."

Raven ruffled his yellow mustache with an exasperated breath. "Tell me where they go—I may as well put them there. Just so you remember I'm not a carter by trade."

Lilz left the maid to her useless blandishments and carried her filthy trousers down the back stairs. She dumped them by the back door while she checked progress. Things were shaping up: the front hall and the two most often used reception rooms were clean. Windows looked clear; draperies had been taken down, the dust shaken out. The carpet being whacked in the courtyard belonged in the informal dining room, where a housemaid had just finished scrubbing the stone floor. Lilz carried her dirty trousers to the laundry house and pumped some water to put them to soak.

Late in the afternoon she went to have another look at the records she had stolen.

A hostage for her father's solemn word. What could that possibly mean?

She looked through the other pages she had cut out. Here, a sum charged to bringing a witness to the house to see that she was in good health. A representative of her father, disguised as a guest? Someone who had simply come to observe her from afar? After nearly twenty years, an event unmarked at the time would scarcely come to mind. She had no way of knowing what it might have been, or even whether it had really had anything to do with her or had simply disguised some other expense.... This entry was for clothing. That she did remember, the first pair of trousers in Hasten blue. For some incomprehensible reason she'd felt as if that one piece of apparel had sealed her fate far more securely even than losing her virginity to the dych.

Hostage.... Lilz stared at the grimy wall, seeing instead the cobbled street, the walls of the nobles' townhouses, hearing the drums and the horses and wheels and the whispering crowd. Had Nevan Hasten demanded that she lead the ceremonial horse to show that she was still under his control, even after his death? Did that mean her father was still alive? She sighed and looked back at the bed. Who would have thought, even this morning, that she'd be sorry that evil old man was dead, and his tongue with him?

What to do with the pages now? She couldn't be found with them. Fenne would be here in less than a week, Aster with her, all her privacy gone. If by some chance the new dych....

Sky above! That old ledger! She'd left it lying on top of one of the piles, after finding it half buried!

I'll have to go back and replace it. Seized with a yen to read about the New Palace built by King Lehrr—that palace with a biting door —Lilz looked at the papers scattered on her bed. *I'll steal it.* Might as well be slaughtered for a lame courser as led to the knacker for an old nag. And I'll put the penknife back...unless Quern did go into that room?

Carefully, she folded all the ledger pages into a packet no larger than her hand. With that in her pocket, she went to inspect Lady Northlands's suite.

Fenne was to have her old rooms. The cleaning crew had been through. Everything a noblewoman could reasonably want had been furnished. Lilz shut the door on the hall and pulled out a drawer of the desk at which Fenne had written out so many of her lessons.

She opened the leather folder lying in the drawer and took out two sheets of thick paper. One wrapped around the ledger pages made an innocuous enough looking packet. Flimsy-ribbon and wax were ready to hand. Lilz tied the bundle tightly. The partly-used stick of wax she put into her pocket; she'd seal the letter when she could light a spill at a fire in private. That left only one full stick, but Fenne wouldn't notice.

Ink in the well, sharpened pens laid ready. Lilz picked up one of the plumes, dipped it, tapped the excess ink away, and wrote, "Dearest Stone." Must remember not to use the blotter.

The house was silent and the moon high. Lilz stole down the back stairs in the dark, close to the edge of the treads, pausing for half a minute after every creak. She reached the servants' door still in the dark. Beside it three lanterns hung ready. A fine fat candle met her fingers as she checked the first she took. Matches were kept in a safe on the wall beside the row of lanterns in case the kitchen fire had gone out. Lilz took two and felt for the doorknob. The key was in the key-hole. As she started to turn it, old memory flooded back and she leaned against the door to free the bolt so that it wouldn't squeal as it moved. Sky above, but it was hard to turn! Not as Hammer had kept it.

She pushed the latch down, straining to lift the door against its hinges so that it would not creak.

The door had been left unlocked. She'd locked it.

Lilz turned the bolt back easily, put the key in her pocket and slipped through the door. The kitchen garden lay before her, bleached of its color by the light of the moon. An angle of the house cast a shadow to her right. She went cautiously along the wall, the hood of her cloak pulled well over her head. At the corner, she stopped.

Her plan was to cross the side lawn to the drive leaving as few footprints as possible, turn right, and walk along the drive past the front of the house. No one was likely to see her. All the servants kept to the back of the house; not even in winter had they moved into the front rooms. The dych's apartments were angled toward the rear of the main house. Lilz wasn't sure about the servants' arrangements there, but the third, top-floor windows opened toward the back.

The moon was ringed with the faintest of rainbows. Within its circle the sky looked bruised. An omen? But of what? Of rain, surely, but what else? Success? Failure?

> Full moon ringed with light
> Goodwife, take fright.

One night past full. A quibble that fed her resolution. Lilz tiptoed on, clutching the dark lantern.

As she reached the drive, one of the stable dogs growled softly and yipped twice. Though Lilz was stepping quietly, her boots on the stone blocks of the drive sounded as sharp as hoofbeats to her ears. The dog must have lost interest. It barked no more.

Lilz cast another glance at the moon with its bright halo and screwed up her courage. She would walk around the house and try the glass door. If it was open, she would return the penknife and take the old ledger: she could picture exactly where she had laid it down. If the door should be locked....

One month's maintenance in gold coin was still wrapped in her sash awaiting her judgment that Byre could be trusted with it.

Run away? *Not possible.* Lilz could not think of it. She'd never been mistreated. Five more months, and she'd have spent twenty years in the service of Hastens, bond money or no bond money. None of them had any reason to suspect her of deception. Fenne would not agree to punish her on no more evidence than that her name had been cut from a ledger and a door found with the bolt drawn back. And what was to say that it was her name cut away? The old dych might have decided those pages were incriminating in some other way and removed them himself. Who was to know? Why would anyone even want to look at a twenty-year-old record book?

Nevertheless her heart was pounding when she tried the door.

Unlocked.

Quern had not noticed. Or Quern sat in the dark, waiting for someone to come back. Which?

Ready to run, Lilz struck one of her matches and lit the candle. The flame flared and steadied as she closed the lantern door and opened the shutter over the lens. Teeth clenched, she swept the light across the room. No one.

She let out the breath she had held in a long sigh. The door squeaked faintly as she pushed it open. Lilz skimmed her light across the dusty desk to match the penknife to its mark, picked up the old ledger, and skinned through the door, pulling it shut. Blow out the light. Close the lantern.

Now, back the way she had come, with the book clasped to her chest beneath the cloak. Her shadow beside her seemed too black, the cherry blossoms too snowy, the dark fountains of the peonies like grotesque beasts crouched and waiting for something Lilz couldn't imagine. How glad she would be to gain the shadow of the house!

What about the dog?

Lilz stopped under the cherry trees and looked down the drive. Half the lawn had been scythed that afternoon. Two rabbits fed in the uncut part, ears flipping toward her from time to time. Spies?

Spies here, the dog at the back of the house. She could explain away the missing pages of the newer ledger, but if she were caught with this one?

Ditch it. Retrieve it tomorrow.

In the long grass beside one of the statues? No, the gardener would be back with his scythe soon after dawn. The trees along the highway? Too far away. The cherries!

She looked into the dappled splendor over her head. Who knew what feathered spies roosted in those branches? *Where?* Surely in all of Summerlea there must be a place to hide a book only as wide as her hand could span and twice as tall!

The rabbits?

Whizzers! Whizzers in the dych's library. No. He'd kept the doors shut, even that golden afternoon when they'd discussed Fenne's wedding—

Don't panic, Lilz.

Never a whizzer at Summerlea. She remembered old Pearl looking at her the morning Fenne was born, saying, "These are the Hastens."

Lilz swallowed. The book. She couldn't leave the book outdoors. What if it did rain? No, the book would have to go in with her. But if the dog barked?

What would Greencrags do?

Greencrags would pound on the front door until somebody came to open it and walk right in, like the iarl he was. Lilz almost laughed. Walk through the front door of Summerlea Manor in the middle of the night like a Peer of the Blood?

Why not? Byre had been careless about the back door, far more often used. Why not the front?

She walked up the steps and pushed down the latch. The door swung inward. Lilz stepped into the house. As she did, she heard the dog in the stableyard bark. *Good ears, it's got,* she thought.

Home without mishap. Lilz went confidently through the front hall into the back one, needing no candle: here, order had been restored to what it had been for the past twenty years. She hung the lantern on its nail and thrust the key into the back door lock. As she turned away the door opened and bashed her elbow.

The cry of pain or fear that rose to her throat came out as a crowing sob. A man, a huge man, grabbed her by the head, his hand over her mouth.

"Who are you?" he demanded.

Raven. Lilz made a small noise. He let go of her mouth. "Raven, it's me, Lilz," she whispered.

"What are you doing wandering around at two o'clock in the morning?" he whispered back.

What, indeed? "And you?"

"I heard a dog bark. I'm a guard. So I guarded. You're no guard, Miss Lilz. You've no call to come down."

Miss Lilz! Dear heaven! Her mind seemed to bat like a fly at a windowpane. Buy him off? She had nothing to offer in exchange for his silence, not even the classic last resort of a desperate woman, the use of her body.

"I couldn't sleep," she whispered, to gain a few seconds. "So I got up and went out for a breath of air." Guilt riding. Unhorse it. Let innocence ride. What would an innocent woman say? "Did you see the moon? It has a circle."

"Does it! Isn't that good fortune?" Raven shut the back door and turned the key in the lock. "I'm glad you didn't lock me out."

"I found the door unlocked," Lilz said. "Come look at the moon. It's really a sight. Wait, I'll open the hall. You can see it better from the front." Oh, yes, Lilz, she thought as she made for the door between front and back halls. Any normal woman would go out to gawk at the moon carrying a huge book under her cloak. Stands to reason.

Moonlight reflected from the polished floor of the front hall made a faint light. "Come on."

Opening the front door, Lilz bowed and gestured for Raven to go through. The motion served to hide the corners of the ledger under her cloak. Raven stood on the top step to look at the moon. The ring was even brighter, though a few clouds had mounted the sky to the west. Moonlight turned them into bands of beaten silver.

"There, now." Lilz stayed behind the guard, the ledger now pressed to her side. "Wasn't that worth it?"

"I think it's good fortune," Raven mused. "Or is it ill?"

Ill. If the moon's full. "I don't remember. Lock the door when you come in." Lilz made her escape while the guard was still entranced.

What to do with the ledger now? If only she had her clothes box! But that was back at Waterside, strapped up ready for Fenne's carter to bring. She lifted her mattress and balanced the book across the ropes. Ten to one it would work loose and thump to the floor some night, waking Aster. She would have to find a better hiding place sometime in the next five days.

A few minutes later the back stairs creaked under Raven's weight. Lilz heard him go along the corridor outside her room. A door closed.

She was still awake when the rain began, a soothing rush against the tiles over her head. At last she slept.

Chapter Seventeen

By morning, the rain had slackened into a drizzle. Lilz had thought to take one of the Summerlea horses out for exercise, a nice long ride across the spring-green meadows that would include the inn beyond the manorlands, seldom visited by anyone from the house. There she had planned to give her letter to Stone to a king's courier, despite the danger of having it appear on his register. She had addressed it to Sweetdawn, where Stone would arrive in a couple of days, if Greencrags hadn't changed his plans.

When she went out to the stable she found the stablekeeper talking to the farrier, who was to reshoe all of Summerlea's horses. The farrier's son, a child who had somehow grown into an over-sized replica of his father in the few years since she'd seen him last, was starting a coal fire in a shed that opened on the back stableyard. Vole worked the bellows.

Lilz watched for a few minutes as the three men eased the anvil out of the farrier's cart and set it near the fire. Instead of her ride, she arranged for Alyia and Morgeen to have their shoes checked and any problems attended to. She went back to the house with Stone's letter still in her pocket. Tomorrow, or if the farrier's work lasted two days, the day after, would be time enough. Only guilt was making her so fretful.

"Absolutely not!" Raven was shouting as Lilz opened the door. "What do you think I am?"

Byre cowered against the wall. Raven glared at him, feet spread and chin jutted forward. The guard's face was pale with fury.

"What's the matter, Raven?" Lilz sighed.

"This—this bum-wart wants me to scrub floors! As if I hadn't already shifted every piece of furniture in the house! You'd think he'd thank me, but no, it's go fill a bucket and get rid of that mud we've tracked in." The back hall floor was splotched with mud, she saw. "Tell him I'm a trained guard, not some woman with calluses on her knees!"

"He's a trained guard, Byre," Lilz said dryly. "I can't speak for the state of his knees, but with that beard, I doubt he's a woman."

Byre, trembling—more likely from lack of drink than from fear, Lilz thought—said, "I didn't mean to insult you, sir, it's just that time's getting short and we're so far behind."

Lilz sighed again. "This floor, Byre?"

Raven came to her half an hour later, as she knelt on a pad of rags to push a brush losing its bristles over the worn stone of the back hall. "I'm sorry," he said. "I didn't mean for you to do this."

"Someone has to," Lilz said, still scrubbing. "Otherwise it'll be all over the carpets."

"But you're a bond-servant, not a housemaid."

"So?" A whole tuft of hog's hair came out of the brush. Lilz tossed it into the bucket of yellow-brown water. Raven stood watching her work for a moment or two, and left.

Five minutes later he was back with a bucket of fresh water and a mop to take off the film of dirt the brush left behind. He started swabbing the floor without a word.

"What you should do is put on your Hasten blue." Lilz didn't look at him. "If you keep going about in ordinary clothes Byre won't think of you as a guard—just as extra hands."

"Um." Raven squeezed out the mop.

They worked in silence until the hall was clean. Raven took the buckets out and sloshed their contents over the already sodden yard. Lilz watched him pump up more water and rinse them out. "Thanks," she said, when he returned.

He handed her the buckets. "I've got nothing else to do." At lunch, he was wearing blue and eyeing the farrier's son, which would gain him nothing at all.

The only way Lilz knew to avoid impressed labor was to take herself out of sight, so after the meal she went up to the room she would soon share with Aster. She closed the door and wedged the back of the one chair under the knob to lock it as best she could before pulling the old journal out from under the mattress.

"Ruppet Hasten, twelfth Dych of Summerlea," was written on the flyleaf in the same archaic hand as the rest of the journal. That must be the man the present Ruppet was named for, Lilz thought. And what she had, she decided after leafing through the book, wasn't an account book after all, but a personal record of what had interested that other Ruppet well over a century ago. Even better.

She began at the beginning. The old Ruppet had started his record in the spring: the first entries had to do with lambing. The weather had been foul. This dych wasn't afraid of hard work. He'd ridden out to help his farmers find their sheep in an early spring blizzard, bloodied his hands with the birth of their lambs, carried a weak one to safety draped over his horse's withers. As ever, the ewes with the hardest births hid in the farthest thickets while those who scarcely noticed the process plodded up to the byre to drop their lambs...not that Summerlea Manor still kept sheep. Lilz was remembering her father's stories.... As she read on, Lilz found the hand growing clearer to her eye, began to anticipate the dych's eccentric notions of spelling.

Here was that farmhand's wedding, the one she'd read about, and the acid comment about the granite used in the New Palace. A few sentences to do with the weather and the sweating workmen building the palace followed. The old Ruppet had a gift for word-pictures, Lilz thought. Then...Lilz felt the hair begin to rise on her arms, despite the mild day. She sat up tailor-wise on the bed to read again:

Those who duell in the Place Beside do demand of us Two Dors, or rather, they demand Dorways twain, for the Dors they will bild of theyr own Cunning, that None may pass threw by Chance...

The Place Beside? Lilz examined the word. Clearly it was *place* and not *palace*. What on earth did the man mean by "the place beside"? Beside what? Hoping for enlightenment, she read on.

....We, too, have Locks, I told them, and did show the One the Key to our Manor, the which I think to be wrought most Fyn. But they declare their Locks better, for they have within them Imps as it were to nip the Fingers of a prying Hand....

Almost a century and a half past, this man was writing about the same kind of door that had stung her own fingers six years ago, and the fingers of Lord Northlands only last summer! Lilz rubbed her hand at the memory. "I praied of King Lehrr that the Carpette they wish might be Blu, for twas I who first brot them to him," his Grace continued. Here he veered maddeningly into an exquisitely detailed description of the cultivation and preparation of indigo. Evidently he had invested a large sum in a cargo that had been lost, and wondered whether he might grow the stuff "even in this Land of Rym and Snou."

The next entry began with a census of calves born at one of the farms subsidiary to Summerlea. Not for another month did an allusion to the New Palace occur. There the dych merely remarked that construction was nearly finished on the Great Hall and the area west of it. After a detour into the astonishingly manifold vices of a servant he wished to have out of his house, he added, "Those from the Place Beside are much intrigued by the Gallerie, for in theyr Land have they no Servants and needs must ask of us a Thosand, yea, Ten Thosand childish Questions."

Ten thousand childish questions. Her hands on her knees, the book open on the bed, Lilz stared again at the wall. The housemaid sent to Sweetdawn must have come from the place beside. Beside what? she wondered again. Beside us? How?

How many Kinlands are there? Nevan Hasten had asked.

An idea, a concept she had never before encountered, nudged at the edge of her mind, but Lilz couldn't quite grasp it. The dych had written for himself, as Makeready had written for himself. Without knowing what either man was writing about she could make no sense of it. Except that Makeready had thought King Guyr was collaborating in some venture that should bring him shame, and old dych Ruppet was talking about someone from the Place Beside demanding doorways to fill with doors equipped with imps to nip one's fingers.

Early morning psalms...elderly women who came and went without notice given to the servants...blue carpets in the New Palace. Lilz couldn't put it together.

Old dych Ruppet rambled on, now writing about the statues he'd bought from a pirate to set along his renovated drive and now about saplings growing up along the king's highway that he'd decided not to cut. Weather was noted, as a farmer would do. Lilz's eye raced along the faded words. She was no longer enjoying the sense of a history continuous with her own. She wanted more about the palace, and no more was being given!

Winter came to Summerlea that hundred and forty-odd years ago. The diarist measured icicles. He planned to add to his house—Lilz realized suddenly that the house the twelfth dych had inhabited could not have been more than a third the size of the one in whose attic she was sitting. The attic itself had not existed. "I, too, shall have an *Antran*," Old Ruppet declared. "As soon as this Addition be finished, for Provision shall be made in the Cellar thereof tho Lehrr knows naught of it."

Lilz spread her hands on the book to hold it open and read the words again. She knew where this "antran" must be. In one of the half-deserted rooms in the middle-aged parts of the house she had seen a trap to the cellar. Other doors led to the cellar, of course, but this one she had never known to be used. Often a rug lay over it, undisturbed for years.

Antran. Travaltian for gate. Gate to what? Or was "antran" a coincidence, a word from another language with an entirely different meaning? Not quite bold enough to find out by herself, Lilz decided to invite Raven to help her explore.

The drizzle had stopped and the sun had come out. Not finding Raven in the house, Lilz went out to check the back stableyard. Sure enough, the big blond guard was holding a half-hobbled horse while the farrier's son clamped a hoof between leather-clad thighs and hammered nails into a shoe.

"Used to be a skivvy," that youth was saying between taps of the hammer. "What a woman! When I was fifteen I couldn't *wait* to come along on a Summerlea job. My dad about flayed me alive when the girl had a whelp—he liked her too, see—but I swear it wasn't me. Wrong timing, see? I'd bet it was Sawan Vole, myself, with that blond hair. Or the old dych, or maybe even the new."

Raven cast a morose glance at Lilz.

"Mind you, if you're desperate there's always Lady Delle, as I s'pose you know." The horse tried to kick its trapped hoof. The farrier's son wrestled it still. "Isn't she arriving in a couple of days?"

Lilz cleared her throat.

"Uh," said the boy. "Um. Hello. We were just talking about, um—"

"Finding employment?" Lilz suggested.

"Um." The farrier's son banged the last nail flush with the shoe and let go of the hoof. "Something like that."

"Raven, if you're not needed here, may I speak with you?"

"Er, Raven," the youth said. "This isn't a likely one."

"Well do I know," Raven replied, glum. "What is it, Lilz?"

"Sawan?" the farrier's son shouted. "Come hold this stupid horse of yours while I clinch the nails!"

Lilz led Raven through the stable and into the kitchen garden, where she gestured him onto the cook's bench and sat beside him. "Are you bored?" she asked.

"Am I bored! I'd stick my head under a cart wheel just for the excitement."

"Can you keep quiet for the sake of a small adventure?"

Raven cocked his head. "It wouldn't endanger the family?"

"Oh, no. Of course not. Don't forget, I'm their bond-servant."

"How big an adventure?"

"Very small." Lilz plucked a sprig of thyme from between the flagstones. She crushed it between her fingers and sniffed its sharp scent. "Just a little exploring I'd like to do while the family's not in the house. But I don't want the servants to know, either—you know how they gossip. So I'll have to go after dark. I'm not very brave. It would be a comfort to have a guard along. A trained guard."

"What kind of exploring?"

"There's a trap door in one of the rooms," Lilz said. "Nobody ever uses it. I've been wondering what it leads to ever since I came, almost twenty years ago. Now's my chance to find out."

"Sure, I'll come." Raven sounded eager. "Tonight?"

"If you don't find anything better."

Raven snorted. "Here? I'm not ready for Byre, not yet."

Lilz had no idea what an "antran" might be, but she did not want to be left in the dark with it. The candles she and Raven carried were protected from drafts by lanterns. A clock somewhere in the front of the house struck eleven as they went quietly along a back hall to Old Ruppet's new section of the house.

"Here," Lilz whispered. She opened the door to the room, again feeling guilty for no particular reason. "It's about there." She pointed. "Help me move the rug."

Raven took one corner of the carpet while she took the other and they folded it back. As Lilz had remembered, a trapdoor interrupted the planks of the floor. A large iron ring nested into a square of iron in its center, all fitting flush with the surface of the boards.

"You'll never lift that," Raven said. "Let me." He straddled the opening, hooked a finger under the ring to raise it and pulled the trap upward. It came free, nearly over-balancing him. He grunted.

Lilz helped him shift the trap to the side. Much heavier than she'd expected: Raven was right. Without him she'd have been stymied right here. Below the opening she saw stone steps.

"You want me to go first?" Raven picked up a lantern.

"No, I will. But you be right behind me."

Her own lantern held high, Lilz went down the steps. Cold air seeped into her clothes. At the end of the steps, she sniffed in disappointment. All she saw was a square doorway in the stone and a small room beyond, in which stood nothing but a plain table and a chair.

"That's strange," Raven said. Lilz walked into the room. There was scarcely space enough for the two of them. Raven backed into the entrance, still holding his lantern high. Lilz set hers on the table.

They were not the first in the room. A battered tin candlestick beside her own held a rind of congealed dripping and the burnt end of a wick. Let burn to the socket. Lilz frowned. Who'd go back up those dark stairs without a light? Why hadn't the candle been carried away?

Tightly laid cut stone around her, the joists of the floor over her head. Arms stretched out, she could easily touch opposite walls. No openings she could see. Had this been a prison of some sort? She sat in the chair to feel for secret drawers in the table. Nothing.

Standing again, Lilz moved the tin candlestick. Not quite a plain table, after all. Someone had inset a small flower, in what looked like brass and copper for petals and leaves, a mother-of-pearl disk for the center. She touched the disk and was startled to feel it yield to her pressure.

"Transposition request acknowledged," a voice said, a calm woman's voice that sounded somehow mechanical.

Lilz jumped. In a cold sweat, she looked past Raven. No one on the stairs.

"It came from that room," he whispered, staring.

"But there's no one else here!"

"Transposition begins in fifteen seconds," the voice said. "Fourteen. Thirteen."

"Lilz, a door's closing," Raven gasped. A smooth dark panel edged with irregular cut stone had thrust itself out of one side of the opening to the stairs and now moved slowly across the doorway. Raven braced himself against it. "I don't think I can hold it open."

"Eleven," said the woman's calm voice. "Ten. Nine."

Terrified, Lilz dived under the guard's legs and scrambled up the steps, Raven right behind her. Together they turned to watch the door shut tight, just as the woman's voice said, "One." A humming noise came from behind the door.

The humming noise stopped.

"What *was* that?" Raven wiped shaking hands on his pantslegs.

"I don't know." Lilz stepped into the upper room. "Help me cover this up."

They shifted the trapdoor into place and settled the carpet over it, hurrying by unspoken consent. "Father of all! Raven, I left my lantern down there."

"I'm not going back for it."

"No, no." Lilz pressed her hands to her cheeks to stop her teeth from chattering. "I—did you hear something odd down there?"

"A woman, but I couldn't see her." Like Lilz, Raven whispered.

"I didn't, either. Where was she?"

"A ghost?"

"I...it *was* cold down there. Aren't ghosts supposed to bring drafts?" Lilz folded her arms around her middle, shivering. "But she sounded so—so—"

"Businesslike," Raven said.

"It was only a voice." Lilz wished she could stop trembling. But Raven was still trembling, too. "No, it can't have been. Voices don't just sound out of thin air! They come from people. No one was there but us." She glanced at Raven, saw his eyes gleaming in the candlelight. "Did you hear...did you hear anything else?"

"A sort of humming after the door shut. As if the room filled with bees."

"I'm glad you heard it too."

Raven didn't answer.

"And that door." Lilz stared at the carpet where it covered the trapdoor. "How did it move?"

Raven said nothing.

"A counterweight." At the idea, Lilz felt a small relief. "It must have a counterweight. We tripped it somehow—doors don't shut of their own volition."

Raven flexed an arm and felt of his muscle. "That one did."

"Did you lean against its edge?"

"I—I don't know. I don't think so."

"Could you swear to it?"

"Swear? No."

"Then that's it." Lilz tucked her cold, still shaking hands into her armpits. "There's a counterweight and that closed the door. The rest of it...we must have imagined the rest of it."

"Both of us?"

"What else could it be? A voice coming from an empty room? Who ever heard of such a thing?"

"Lilz, my dear woman, our minds don't run at all alike!" Raven paced off to look out the window at the moonstruck garden wall. "How could we both imagine the same...the same...." He leaned against the sill for a few minutes, while Lilz tried to convince herself that she had not seen and heard what she had just seen and heard. Raven laced his fingers over his belly. "That door didn't just move by itself. It was *pushing*. I almost split my gut trying to hold it open." Raven looked at his arms. "And that voice was real. That I will swear."

"Maybe a speaking tube," Lilz said. "But so clear...and who? She said 'acknowledged.' Did she think she was answering us?"

"I'm finding out." The guard came back across the room.

"Raven, no."

He turned back the edge of the rug, planted his feet on either side of the trapdoor, and heaved the square of planking up and forward. "Come balance this thing," he grunted. "Before I drop it and wake up the whole house."

Lilz squatted beside the cover and helped him push it further onto sound floor. "Raven, there's a light down there."

Raven started down the steps. "It's only your candle." Lilz crouched on the top step while Raven felt the edge of the stone entrance to the room. "Come get your lantern," he said.

"You get it."

"You left it."

Still weak and shaking, Lilz supported herself against the cold stone wall and went down. She took the one necessary step into the room and retrieved the lantern.

"Give me some light here," Raven said. "I've left the other candle upstairs."

Lilz held the lantern high. Built into the stone was a pair of lines, not parallel and not straight, that might fit the shape of the end of the sliding door as she remembered it. The edges were chiseled roughly. She couldn't tell if the fit was looser than between other stones.

Raven pressed on each part of the doorway, leaned against it as naturally as he could. "No use," he sighed. "What did you do in that room to start the door moving?"

"Nothing."

"No, Lilz, you must have done something! Touched something?"

"I sat down." She frowned, trying to remember. "But the door didn't start then, did it?"

"No."

"I felt along the edge of the table. It's just a board." She'd moved that old candlestick—yes. "The only other things I touched were the candlestick and that little flower inlaid in the table top."

Raven went to the table and picked up the candlestick. After a moment he set it down and touched the flower. "Transposition request acknowledged," said the woman, exactly as before. Lilz pressed her fist to her chest. A small shifting sound came from the door as it began its creep across the opening. "Transposition will begin in fifteen seconds."

"Raven, come back!"

"Fourteen."

The guard turned toward her. "This is my job," he said. "I'm paid to protect the Hastens."

Lilz lifted the lantern. Sweat glistened on Raven's forehead. "But it can't be a danger," she objected. "The family must know it's here!"

"Eight. Seven."

The door was halfway shut. Lilz tried to push it back, without result. She leaned to look around it. "Raven, please!"

His eyes closed. In the last of the lantern light she saw his beard glint as he bit his lips. "Raven!"

"Two. One."

The door shut. Lilz sank onto the bottom step. She put her head on her knees and hugged them tightly. The humming began.

Good-wife, take fright.

Chapter Eighteen

The door had opened by itself the first time, surely in less time than this! Why didn't it open again?

Because the trap door hadn't been closed? Lilz carried her lantern up the stairs and examined the opening, but could find nothing unusual. It looked like a hole in a floor. Joists and headers framed it, like any other trap. Cleats at each end took the weight of the trapdoor. She set the lantern down and tried pushing down on each of them with all her weight. Downstairs, not a sound.

She left the opening to heave at the rug. When she judged that she'd cleared the floor over the little room Lilz knocked on the bare planking. Raven was more than tall enough to reach the other side of the planks to knock back. He didn't. She tried again. Still no response.

Was he unconscious?

Lilz went back down the stairs, lantern in hand. She noticed a strange effect of the candlelight on the walls, a sort of shimmer she had never seen before. For a moment, she could neither move nor breathe. The shimmer intensified. Staring, she understood suddenly that it came of her own trembling as she held the lantern: the reflector behind the candle flame trembled, too. Relief washed over her and instantly died. Raven was still in that room. She tried prying at the edge of the door that had slid across the opening. Nothing moved. Even the blade of her penknife wouldn't push into the crack. The half-formed image of a crowbar once seen in the stable faded. She couldn't gain purchase to lever the door open. Lilz closed the knife and returned it to her pocket. Her hand thrust into the spaces left by the disguising blocks of stone was stopped by a smooth wall before she was wrist-deep in any opening. None of spaces had any trips for the counterweight. She rested her head against the door. Cold. Cold as a grave.

Shuddering, she sank onto the steps. What now? Olen Hasten had never seemed as scheming as his father, but he was every bit as much a Dych of Sunimerlea. Cutting pages out of his ledger. Stealing a journal kept by his three-greats-grandfather. The comfortable life she had contrived for herself sagged away from her in every direction Lilz could imagine.

Raven.

A candle had burnt to the socket in that room. He must have air. She'd wait to see what happened, for a little while at least. Maybe the door would decide to open.

Shivering now with cold, Lilz kept her vigil until her candle flickered out. She felt her way up the steps and found the candle in the other lantern also guttering, the room silvered by the first light of the next day. She sat on the edge of the floor—how warm the wood felt, after the hours on stone—with her feet on the top step, wondering what to do.

Something had to be done. Soon. But what? Tear the floor up? She'd need help. Vole and the gardener or his lad and maybe a carpenter if one could be found...Byre would have to agree to it first. She'd have to confess her theft of the journal, describe the strange consequences. But who would believe a tale as wild as the one she had to tell? She scarcely believed it herself!

Except that Raven was gone.

Lilz was about to go upstairs to shake Byre out of his sleep when she heard the humming sound again. At the bottom of the stairs the stone door slid back into its place. Raven started up the steps.

She stood, all the terror of the night returning at once. Raven came on. In the gray light Lilz saw the flash of his teeth. He was smiling at her. She grabbed his arm as he reached the top step. "Raven, what happened?"

He shrugged and stepped onto the wooden floor. "It's just a little room down there with a table and a chair in it. Nothing very interesting."

"No, what *happened*? You were gone so *long*—"

Raven chuckled. "Come, Lilz, you know it won't do you any good to flatter me. Let's get this lid down."

"Flatter?" Feeling numbed, she guided the trap as he lowered it into its opening.

"How long was I gone? Two minutes? You can live without me two minutes. You've done it every day of your life."

"Raven, you were gone far longer than two minutes!" Lilz grasped the edge of the carpet as he motioned to her and helped him straighten it out. "Almost the whole night."

"What are you talking about?"

"That room! Don't you remember? We both went down, and there was a woman talking—" She stopped as she saw his expression: total bewilderment. "She counted backwards, and a door came out of the wall," Lilz went on, less rapidly. "We came upstairs. Then you decided to go back—"

"I think you must have been dreaming," Raven said.

"No! I—" *He doesn't remember!* Lilz glanced toward the trapdoor, glad the rug was over it. *He just doesn't remember!* "What do you think happened, Raven?"

"Yesterday you invited me to go exploring, so we met here at cock's crow. We got the trap up and I went down first to see what was there."

"With what for light?"

"A candle, of course."

Lilz snatched up one of the lanterns. "Look, Raven! How much would you see with a candle like this?"

"They *were* pretty short."

"And they're both *upstairs*. You came out of that room in the dark. How did you see what was down there?"

Raven frowned. "No." He sounded less certain. "I'm sure I had a lantern in my hand as I came up the stairs."

"Raven, we came down here last night." *How to make him remember?* "I heard the big clock in the blue room strike eleven just before we came in here. We picked up the trap and went down. We both saw the table and chair. There's a tin candlestick, too." Raven was shaking his head. "Yes, there is. And the table has a little flower inlaid in the top. Copper and brass and nacre. I touched the flower and a woman we couldn't see started talking—"

"You dreamed it," Raven said.

"No, I didn't. We were both scared. A door started coming out of the wall and we ran up the stairs—"

Raven was still shaking his head.

"Then you decided to go back—"

Raven took her by the shoulders. "Lilz, you're crazy. Now, I can see that you'd like to find something thrilling and secret—so would I—but all that's down there is one little room with a table and chair."

"It's not what's down there that I'm arguing about. It's what *happened* down there." Something hurt her chest. Lilz looked down. She was still holding the lantern, clutched so tightly the edge of the base dug into her ribs.

Raven very gently took the lantern away. "I think you must be confusing something you dreamed with what we did this morning. Truly, Lilz, I was down there two minutes. Maybe three or four. I should have had you come with me, then you'd know. "

How to make him remember? "What about the candles? They were new. "

"All candles are new sometime." He grinned at her. "Maybe you're up too early. Maybe you should go back to bed."

"Maybe so," Lilz said, giving in. She took both lanterns to return them to the storage room before Byre missed them. Raven held the door open for her and she went into the hall, now more thoroughly frightened than at any time over the long night.

In her room, Lilz checked carefully for whizzers. Finding none, she took the letter to Stone out of the journal, where she had hidden it. Should she add last night's story before finding a messenger to take it?

Stone would think she was crazy. She wasn't all that sure she wasn't. Voices in thin air? Doors that close of their own desire? All from touching a design in a tabletop? Already it seemed half nightmare. No, save the story for when she could talk to Stone face to face, convince him and his master the tale was true.

Doors in the palace that nip. Men who look frightened and speak strange languages. A place beside. How did they connect? Would the woman in Summerlea's cellar warn the men in the palace that a young man had found her hiding place?

The journal would have to go, just as fast as she could get rid of it. Return it tonight. No. How could she give it up forever? The proof of her horrid night was preserved in that ancient book. She thought of wrapping it up and sending it to Greencrags, but the shape of the thing—

Change the shape.

She put the letter back into the book and the book back under the mattress and went down to breakfast.

Once again, it was afternoon before Lilz could find time for herself. She told Byre at lunch that she had her mistress's accounts to work on and would be upstairs if anyone should need her. With this announced intent she boldly supplied herself with paper, ink, and pens and carried them up to her room. No one was likely to interrupt, but she braced the chair under the doorknob again to have a chance to hide what she planned to do before anyone walked in on her.

If any whizzers had sneaked through her closed door and window during the morning, Lilz couldn't find them.

Poor Old Ruppet, she thought, as she pulled the journal out of her bed. What would he have said if he could have seen what would happen to his diary so many years later? Opening her penknife, she slit the endpapers and taping away from the binding. The cover fell off. The pages were sewn together, held with cloth tapes across the back. These, too, Lilz cut. The bundles of pages came apart. She numbered each sheaf with her writing lead so the book could be reassembled in order. A shame, that she wouldn't be able to read the whole thing. Unable to resist one more glance, she flipped through the loosened pages, reading here and there, before going on.

About two thirds of the way through, the word *antranta* caught her eye. His Grace was much put out: "For they pass whensoever they do Please, but We, should We pass, shall call Naught of the Passing to Mind, but shall be strateway dumped back where We began, all Mind of it erased as Chauck from Slate. I proved that yestereven with Wyllym and find it Tru, to my Grate Angre."

So Raven had passed, and now called naught of the passing to his mind. Passed where? To the Place Beside? That much seemed obvious. Was it another Kinland? How could that be?

Lilz began rolling the first signature tightly, pressing hard against the top of the small table that held her basin and pitcher. When she had finished, she added the second, then the third, and so on, making a long thin cylinder of what had been a large rectangular book. She tied it with flimsy ribbon and turned her attention to the cover.

Last night she'd been too excited to remember to fill her pitcher. Now she hid the pieces of Old Ruppet's journal and went down the back stairs to pump some water. Byre stopped her as she came in, to ask about Lady Northlands's preference in meats. Sky above, she thought. Fenne will be here in three more days! Would she have time to rid herself of all these things she'd stolen?

The conversation with Byre done at last, she went back to her room and re-braced the chair. First to soak the leather from the boards. While the broken cover floated in her washbasin she wrote a note to Greencrags explaining what the cylinder of paper was and pointing out that parts of it must refer to whatever Makeready had discovered. She wrapped it around Old Ruppet's journal and stitched both up in a piece of tightly woven muslin ripped from an old pair of underdrawers.

The parcel would have to be entrusted to a messenger. Lilz could see no way around that. But to send a letter *and* a parcel to Stone? She could scarcely send it to Greencrags. Her eye fell on the chair, an old one with loose stretchers.

Her brother.

Last summer she had hesitated. This was a far greater emergency. Lilz cut a stout nib in a goose quill and printed Greencrags's name and Sweetdawn's directions on the muslin. With a sharper pen she started another letter, this one to her youngest brother. How seldom she'd seen him! But she'd never asked such a favor before—

After the ordinary greetings, she explained her request: "These papers by rights belong to the Iarl of Greencrags. I want to return them, but my mistress is so spiteful still I dare not do so on my own name. Could you send them by king's courier? It shouldn't cost more than the silver I've sewn into the packing." What an easy liar I've become, she thought with shame. But why drag Clâes into this any further? She hesitated. "Clâes," she wrote at last. "I have discovered something strange. I am not listed in Summerlea's records as a bond-servant, as I've believed these nearly twenty years, but as a hostage for our father's solemn word. I have no idea what this may mean, have you? I'm probably at Summerlea until fall, but when next I'm in Miense, I'll find a way to stop at the shop to talk to you. Meanwhile, tell no one." She finished the letter, rolled it around the package for Standfast, and covered both with another layer of double-stitched muslin. This she addressed to her brother at Godwit and Chantwell, Cabinetmakers. She'd have to think of some plausible object the package might hold, in case the new dych should find out about it and ask.

By midafternoon she had the leather off the boards. Cut into pieces and twisted into irregular cylinders, it looked remarkably like turds even without being thrown into the privy, as she planned to do when twilight fell. The boards of the cover she might shave into tinder; they were fine old cedar, perfect for the purpose.

By the end of the afternoon Lilz was exhausted. She ate her supper noticing with envy that Raven seemed much as usual and pled a headache, a real one, to excuse an early bedtime. But tired as she was, she slept fitfully. One by one the other servants came up the back stairs and padded along the hall. Each time she woke and stiffened until she recognized the tread: what those in the place beside might have discovered from Raven she didn't know. She was glad to have the other servants near, even though she had again wedged the chair under the doorknob to keep intruders out. What if one should come to see that she, too, called nothing to mind?

Stone. How she wanted to lie in Stone's arms! How safe she would feel, with Stone's warmth against her, Stone's scent in her nostrils. It wouldn't hurt to have his master in the next room and the stout walls of Standfast House around her, either, Lilz thought, now growing drowsy. But even if Stone were just here....

Her sleep was shattered by a scream.

Others heard it, others sprang from their beds as she did, others fumbled to find a precious lucifer or touched spill to nightlight to light a lamp or candle. Lilz dragged the chair aside and went out into the passage, where two of the men already stood and a few of the women peeked out of their doors. "It's the guard," one of the men said, as a high, thin whine of agony came from the room at the end of the passage.

Lilz followed them. Someone opened Raven's door. He lay on his bed, raised on his elbows, looking stupefied.

"What happened?" the cook asked.

"I..." Raven shook his head as if to clear it. "I think a nightmare... I think, yes, a dream." He flopped back on the bed. "It's all right. Go back to bed. I'm sorry I waked you all up."

Lilz stood aside as the cook, swearing, went back to his room. Down the hall, the others began closing doors, settling down. Raven lay with his mouth agape, staring at the ceiling. She went into the room and lit the candle beside his bed from her own.

"I thought you might want light."

"Thanks. Yes. Thanks." He held a hand out as if warming it at the candle flame.

"What did you dream, Raven?" Lilz sat on the edge of his mattress.

"I...I don't...something bright. Something shining." He was sweating in the cool room, as he'd been sweating down in the cellar just before the door closed on him.

"Something shining?"

"Shining and moving...I know, it sounds odd...I'm not supposed to remember..."

"You're not *supposed* to remember?"

Raven looked at her. He seemed puzzled. "I mean, I don't want to remember."

Maybe it's better if he doesn't, Lilz thought. One less complication to worry about. Her curiosity protested. This time she held it in check without trouble: last night should be lesson enough! "Can you sleep?" she asked.

"I'm afraid. So many eyes—"

Raven broke off. He looked at the door. Lilz turned to look, too, but no one was there. The hall was dark. Thirty steps away, her own door had been left open. "I'll stay until you doze off, if you want," she offered.

The guard reached for her hand. His grip was almost painful. His eyes, too, clenched shut. Lilz sat watching his face in the glow of the candle. Twenty-one or -two years old, she guessed. What if she had sent him to his death, instead of costing him a few hours of memory?

At last his eyelids smoothed. The hand relaxed. Raven's breathing deepened and slowed. When she was sure the guard was sound asleep Lilz gathered every bit of courage she had and went back to her own bed.

The room was empty. She braced the chair and checked under her mattress. The parcel addressed to her brother was still there.

The next morning she rose early, although far from rested. She dressed quickly, with riding boots and cloak, and went down to the kitchen. The cook had just shaken down the fire and added a couple of chunks of coal.

"Can I get a cup of tea?" she asked.

He shook the kettle. "It's not very hot."

"I just want a little breakfast before I take my horse out for some exercise."

"Yesterday's bread? There's a little left."

"Good." Lilz hung her cloak, weighted with the package and the letter, from a hook in the back hall. She returned to the kitchen, where the cook was sawing a thick stale slice of brown bread from a loaf. She chewed it down, chatting with the cook as he went on with his morning chores. By the time she had managed to swallow it all, he had brewed a cup of tea, which she drank with thanks. She went out to the stable.

Vole, still yawning, saddled Alyia. "Going far?"

"Just out to stretch her. I may be gone awhile, if the ride's good."

"She's had half an hour at her hay."

"I'll walk her, don't worry. She can graze later."

"I'll give her a measure of feed when you get back."

"How are the meadows? A pleasant ride?"

Vole smiled sleepily. "Blooming. Don't let her eat daffodils."

"Vole, my dear child, have I ever brought you or your mother a horse with a tummy full of daffodils?" Lilz mounted, flipping her cloak clumsily into place. Vole, yawning again, went back into the stable.

The ride across the meadows was cool and sweet. A mist rose out of the grass after yesterday's rain. The daffodils Vole had warned her against stood like small pale stars in drifts under the occasional clumps of trees. As the eastern sky colored more brightly Lilz thought of Sweetdawn. Greencrags should arrive there that afternoon, and with him, Stone.

Alyia took up a steady slow pace. Lilz didn't urge her. Her eyes hurt, after the shortened night and the sleepless night before that, and all her muscles ached. What would it do to Raven, she wondered, to have that piece taken out of his memory? She wished she had read further in Old Ruppet's journal, to find out if anything untoward had happened to—what was his name? Wyllym.

As she entered the woods on the other side of the meadows Lilz began to have the feeling that she was watched.

Guilt rode her back, or a small spy perched in a tree. Nothing to worry about in either case, she told herself. She was only a woman riding a mare needing a stretch. If she gained the road, as she would in a few minutes, what of it?

The sensation continued. Eyes, somewhere behind. When she reached the highway, Lilz strained her ears to hear whether another horse followed, but the only hoofbeats were Alyia's, and the mare didn't whicker. The air was still. Scent might not carry. Lilz shifted her weight to signal Alyia to pick up the pace. Now that she rode the rutted muddy track, that was natural enough.

The highway wound down the side of a hill and crossed a rushing stream, where a wooden bridge rang hollow under the mare's hooves. If anyone followed, she'd surely hear that, Lilz reasoned. She listened hard as the road climbed a slow incline on the other side of the stream and ducked out of the woods into a small tongue of lealand. Just as she re-entered the woods, just as she relaxed, she thought she heard a muffled clump like the strike of a hoof on wood. She turned in the saddle, but the bridge was out of sight.

Don't panic, Lilz.

She picked up the pace again. If only she had Matanda! He could go forever at that ground-eating stride of his. This was a decent mount, but to get Matanda's speed she'd have the mare blowing in no time. She didn't want to enter the innyard like a fugitive, her horse out of breath and her own eyes staring—

The road twisted again. Far ahead, she saw a cart pulled by a pair of mules.

Any port in a storm, her oldest brother used to say, meaning something quite different. Lilz caught up to the cart.

"Ho, carter!" She thought she sounded hearty.

"Ho, miss. A good morning."

"May I ride beside?"

"A good notion, miss. There are highwaymen about." Lilz bit her lip. She'd forgotten her knife. "Traveling far?"

"Only to the next inn, to give a letter to the courier, if I haven't missed him."

"Oh, nay, you haven't that. The inn's but ten minutes off, and the man doesn't leave until noon."

Alyia settled into stride with the mules. Lilz chatted with the driver, to find he was a farmer with Summerlea holdings. She wondered idly whether he was descended from that other farmer, the one whose wench had him gladly and sewed a fine seam. The ten minutes passed quickly. She turned into the inn's courtyard—the farmer drove on—and dismounted.

Five minutes passed, and ten, much more slowly than they had with the farmer for company, but no one else rode by. She must have imagined the eyes, or they were only those of some small spy that could report nothing of value. She went into the inn.

"Yes, miss, and what can I do?" the landlord asked cheerfully.

"I've two things for a messenger."

"Let me call him." The landlord stepped from behind his tall desk at the door and bellowed a name. A few minutes later a sleepy man appeared, pants on over his nightshirt. The size of Raven and twice as old, he looked toughened by travel.

"Much of value in here?" he asked, when Lilz had produced her parcel and letter.

"Nothing at all."

"I'm taking no gold these days. There's a robber about."

"If he steals these, he'll be sorry he wasted his time," Lilz was pleased to say in the landlord's hearing—nine times in ten the highwayman was the innkeeper's partner. She handed parcel and letter over. "When are they likely to be delivered?"

"This one to Miense, I'd guess in three days." The messenger spread his register on the landlord's desk and began to write in it. "That one's big. It'll cost you eight coppers. Sweetdawn..." He sucked in his cheeks. "That's a transfer. I couldn't promise you less than two weeks."

"I was hoping nearer one, but two will have to do."

"For three extra coppers, I could put a speed notice on it."

"No." Lilz was tempted, but she wanted as little attention called to the letter as possible. "It's not that urgent."

"That one will be seven."

Lilz gave him a silver and three coppers to make up fifteen and dropped an extra two into his hand as he'd expect. Not too much, not too little. He'd be less likely to remember her.

That left enough of her pocket-money for eggs and sausage and tea and a piece of toast, which she ate with relish before climbing back on Alyia.

Chapter Nineteen

The ride back to Summerlea manor might have been pleasant, had the feeling of watching eyes not been so strong. After a time Lilz decided the "eyes" were only her own guilt and apprehension, but that decision didn't make them go away, even when she rode into the now-sunny meadow and the manor itself came into sight.

She turned Alyia over to Vole with an assurance that the mare had not nibbled so much as a stem of grass on the ride and went into the house.

"Good ride, Lilz?" the cook asked, as she passed the open kitchen door.

"Splendid, thanks."

"A messenger come while you was away. Byre has what he left."

"Oh, dear. I wonder what that is?"

Cloak over her arm, Lilz tapped on the closed door of Byre's pantry, but got no answer. She went up the back stairs to her room and found three fat sealed envelopes tossed onto her bed, addressed in Fenne's round script. Business, she thought, and sat down to pull off her riding boots.

Business, yes. The first letter was from a shipping company, to announce with sorrow the loss of a cargo of salted veal in which Fenne had bought a tenth share; Fenne had written a note in the top margin to ask whether the cargo had been insured, and if not, why not?

"Of course it was insured," Lilz muttered. "Does she think I'm an imbecile?" She made a note on the envelope to compose a letter demanding payment as soon as Fenne was present to sign it. Sending the reply to Miense for Fenne to sign wouldn't do: it would pass her on the road. A bill for eight pairs of ladies' silken slippers could be paid with a draft on the Bank of Miense, again as soon as Fenne arrived. The third contained an estimate for a portrait of Lady Northlands by the most fashionable painter of Kinland, to be copied twice in small. Fenne's note expressed surprise at the cost and asked whether Lilz thought it reasonable and if so, whether she could afford it.

"The man can ask any price he likes," Lilz sighed, wondering what it would be like to have a natural gift people gladly paid well to see exercised. Fenne, on the other hand, could afford any price she elected to pay. That, too, would be an interesting position in life to occupy. Lilz tucked the letters into her saddlepack and went back downstairs to help Byre plan the last details for Fenne's arrival the day after next. She'd forgotten to remind him not to perfume the iarlena's room with lavender. Only rose would do.

The rest of the day, and the next, passed in swift routine. Lilz saw Raven a number of times. He seemed much as usual.

Again, she felt watched.

Lilz closed the book she had borrowed from the guest library and lay back on her bed, scanning the walls in the yellow light of her lamp. No small dark ovoids. She sighed and got up to search.

Twenty minutes later, she felt sure that if a whizzer were in the room it might hear, but could not see her. She reopened the book and began reading where she had left off, in the middle of a drama several seasons old. The action soon caught her up. Half aware, she heard the other servants mount the stairs a few at a time, their goodnights and occasional laughter. Silence worked its way into the night, only to give way to the rhythmic creak of somebody's bedropes, heard through the thin partitions. That, too, soon quieted. Someone—Byre?—snored in the room to her left.

Lilz finished the play, unsatisfied. She lay against her pillow with the book on her raised knees, thinking it over, then went back and read a snatch here and there to see how the story had been fitted together. The spoken word must empower parts the printed word did not, she decided. That might explain the popularity of the play. Far off downstairs, the clock in the blue room struck a solemn midnight.

As she was about to turn down her lamp someone came up the back stairs. Lilz couldn't place the tread.

Someone from the place beside, coming through the *antran* to see that she, like Raven, would not remember?

Don't panic, Lilz. The trap had a carpet across it, she reminded herself.

The steps stopped outside her room. The door moved inward. Stopped by the braced chair, it settled back into its frame.

Now someone rapped lightly.

Lilz went to the door. "Who's there?" she asked through it.

"Summerlea."

Summerlea! Lilz pulled the chair out from under the doorknob and opened the door. Fenne's father stood in the narrow passage. He held a candle at waist-level. Shadows moved over his face as the flame flickered, making his features look not quite substantial. He seemed in shock.

"Your Grace?"

He didn't move. He didn't smile.

"Your Grace, what's wrong?"

"Come."

"Just a moment." She left the door standing open, jabbed her feet into her houseshoes, and pulled her cloak over her bedgown. In the passage, Summerlea stood exactly as before. Lilz took up her lamp and joined him.

The new dych turned and went along the passage. Lilz followed. The night air was even cooler than she'd expected. She was glad of the cloak.

Summerlea said nothing as he moved before her down the stairs, along the back hall and into the front. Still silent, he opened the door under the front stairs and led her toward the part of the manor that had been his father's and was now his.

When did he arrive? Lilz wondered. She couldn't remember hearing a carriage. Why no warning? Why hadn't Fenne mentioned in one of her notes that her father would be coming?

They passed the room with the *antran* hidden under the floor. Guilt. Portraits of Hastens long dead stared from the walls to accuse her. Lilz bit her lips. Had he been told somehow about her adventure with Raven? Almost as bad, had he learned of her parcel and letter? No. No one could ride to and from Miense in that short time...unless a whizzer...Sky above! Did he plan to assert his bed right? At this phase of her month? Lilz thought of flaxen-haired Sawan Vole and swallowed. *Please, no.*

Hasten opened the door of his sitting room and walked in. His candle and Lilz's lamp were the only lights. The dych went to the mantel and lit all ten candles of the candelabra standing in front of the mirror with his own. His reflected face was blank.

"Your Grace?"

Both Lilz and the dych turned toward the door. Olen Hasten's body-man stood there. He, too, was still fully dressed. His face was taut with exhaustion.

"Go to bed, Garden," the dych said. "I'll change myself."

"Thank you, your Grace."

"Send Quern in here with two glasses and a bottle of whiskey."

"Right away, your Grace." Garden shot a quick glance at Lilz and bowed as he closed the door.

"Sit down, Lilz." Hasten took the lamp from her and set it on a small table near the door. He circled the room, lighting the candles in the sconces on the cream-colored walls, then came to stand over Lilz where she sat on the front half of the straightest chair. By this lavish illumination she saw that the dych had ridden hard to get to Summerlea: his sweat-stained clothes were caked with dust, his lace jabot drooping and dirty. A day's growth of blond whiskers glittered on his cheeks as he pursed his lips. The *antran*, she thought uneasily. Yes. The woman down in the cellar had sent a message to the king—

There was a long silence while Lilz tried not to squirm under the dych's inspection.

"How old are you, Lilz?" Olen Hasten asked.

"I was thirty-eight last winter, your Grace."

Hasten nodded twice, gazing at her. "You've been with us almost twenty years."

The door opened. Quern, looking rosy with sleep, came in carrying a tray bearing two glasses and a bottle of amber liquid, which he set down next to Lilz's lamp. As he turned she saw a wisp of his normally sleek hair standing up at the back. Why that should scare her—

"Give her a good shot, Quern," the dych said. "And me double."

Quern cast a sympathetic glance at Lilz, who clutched her cloak around her. "Not too much, please, Quern." Her voice came out in a whisper. She cleared her throat. Quern poured about a finger's width into one glass and three times that into the second. He presented the tray to Summerlea with a precise little bow, and to Lilz as neatly.

"You may go, Quern," the dych said. "Go back to bed. Sorry I rousted you out."

"Thank you, your Grace."

"Leave the bottle." As the houseman closed the door behind him the dych downed a third of his drink in two swallows.

"Drink, Lilz, don't be shy."

She sipped at the whiskey. The flavor was sharp and smoky, a taste she had never acquired and had no wish to. Fenne's father stopped pacing in front of the cold fireplace and tilted his head at her.

"What do you know of Evin Clock?"

Clock! Her heart seemed to flop in her chest. "Clock? He's a pharmacist."

"Go on."

"Much used by the peers, your Grace." Only Clock. Not the *antran.* Not the damaged ledger, not Old Ruppet's diary, not her messages. Surely Clock was less danger? A mild relief emboldened her. "Your father, I know, had recourse to him for medicines for his lungs from time to time."

"Go on."

Go on? Lilz tried to think of something more she could say. "He's known for love philters and for, um, potions to insure the faithfulness of a mate, said by some to be efficacious."

Summerlea turned away and put his free hand in his jacket pocket. "Has my daughter dealt with him?"

Her relief vanished. "Fenne?"

"Has she dealt with him?" He sounded almost violent.

"Yes, your Grace."

"For what?"

Even under her cloak, her skin cooled. *Don't panic, Lilz.* "You know that she refused Greencrags her bed, your Grace."

He turned and frowned. "No, I didn't know that."

"I thought perhaps your father had told you...she had a long liaison with Lord Northlands while Greencrags was still at Chrems and when her husband returned she did not wish to lose Lord Northlands's admiration. So she wrote to Onma Stump from Sweetdawn and asked her to see that Northlands swallowed a philter, to keep him faithful to her."

The dych snorted. "Superstitious rot."

"Nonetheless, it comforted her to think it might work."

He sighed. "I suppose it would. She's no brighter than Delle. You're not drinking, Lilz." She took a dutiful sip. "Is that all Fenne got from Clock, then?" the dych asked. "One philter for Kav Treadwell?"

"No, your Grace. She bought several, all much the same. And after we returned to Miense she sent for some, um, concoctions she thought might increase his, um, pleasure. At least once, I'm fairly sure twice, she ordered a dose of that powdered root from the Silk Countries."

Hasten downed another third of his whiskey. "What powdered root is that?"

Sky above! Could the man have reached his age and eminence and not know about the powder? "It's a female physic, your Grace. Safer and quicker than bryony tea."

He frowned, working it out. "Do you mean to say my daughter has deliberately spilled my grandchild short of life?" Lilz nodded. "Sky above! When?"

"The instance I'm sure of was about a year before Greencrags returned from Chrems, your Grace. Perhaps again last summer, not long before the annulment commission met."

"Who was the father?"

"I assume it was Kav Treadwell, your Grace. There wasn't anyone else, by then."

"By then! The child was fifteen years old! What do you mean, by then?"

"There had been Prince Jath."

"Jath! He was dead three months after her wedding!" Olen Hasten sprawled into the chair across the fireplace from her. "Who else?"

Lilz pressed her lips together.

"Who else, Lilz?"

"Possibly Sir Jen Makeready, your Grace."

"Makeready!" The dych groaned. "What did I do, Lilz?" He shook his head and stared into the empty grate. "What could I possibly have done in my last life to deserve this one?"

"Your Grace?"

His dark eyes met hers. "Fathered by a conniving devil, married to a woman of exquisite beauty with the wit and moral sense of a biddy hen—and now it seems the only child I'm sure I sired inherits from both!" The last two fingers of his left hand flicked the words away. He's dissembling, Lilz thought.

"Her ladyship has many good points, your Grace," she pointed out softly. "She's excellent company when she wishes to be, she—"

"Oh, hush!" Hasten jumped out of the chair and began to pace from one end of the room to the other. He stopped at the tray to refill his glass. "You've heard all the rumors, I suppose?"

"Rumors, your Grace?"

"Don't play dumb with me, Lilz." He came back across the room and stood over her. "Did my daughter poison Sir Jen Makeready?"

Lilz took a deep breath. "No, your Grace. Fenne did not poison Sir Jen Makeready."

"Fenne didn't try to poison Sir Jen? You can swear that to me?"

"I can swear that Fenne did not poison Sir Jen Makeready."

He plopped again into the chair opposite her and gazed at her with half-lowered lids. "And Evin Clock? Have you ever gone to him yourself? For one of these imported powders, perhaps?"

"I have never dealt with Evin Clock, your Grace."

"Hmm."

For a moment Lilz thought she had slipped through his snare. The dych tilted his head, pursing and unpursing his lips, eyes narrowed in thought. "I see," he said. "I see."

Lilz pulled her cloak around her.

"She bought the poison. You were to give it to him. Maybe you even agreed to. But you didn't."

"Your Grace?"

"Isn't that the way it went, Lilz? Isn't that what happened?"

What could she say? Her silence was speaking for her while she tried to make up her mind.

"Did you throw it away?"

"I...throw what away, your Grace?"

"Listen to me, Lilz." Olen Hasten sat forward in his chair, suddenly looking very much like his father. "I have got to know the truth. I can't protect any of us without knowing the truth. Who bought the poison?"

"I don't believe Fenne ever bought any poison, your Grace."

He stared at her a moment. "Then it was Mistress Stump."

"I can't speak for Mistress Stump, your Grace." Even to herself, Lilz sounded unsteady.

"Onma Stump bought the poison and gave it to Fenne. Fenne gave it to you with instructions to poison some delicacy and have it delivered to the Old Palace for Makeready." His eyelids drooped again. "You see, Lilz, I have a great deal more experience with the Peers of the Blood than you do. That's how it was, wasn't it?"

She felt her head nod.

"The question is whose idea it was."

Lilz sat rigid with fear. *Not mine!* she wanted to shout. *Not mine, never mine!*

"Drink up, Lilz."

Obeying to the extent of sipping a third time at the glass, she recovered enough to ask, "What makes these rumors a crisis now, your Grace?"

"Crisis?"

"You've ridden hard to get here." His eyelids flickered. She felt on more solid ground. "No one came ahead to prepare for you. You didn't come in carriage. You rode, with Garden and perhaps a guard. Garden looks weary. So do you. You must have started last night and ridden through without stopping."

The dych went to the tray. He brought the bottle back to his chair and poured at least three measures of whiskey into his glass. "It's the warden. Elm."

Lilz waited. Fenne's father took her glass out of her hand and half-filled it. He thrust it back at her, splashing some on her cloak. "Drink, damn it," he said.

She sipped.

Hasten plumped down in his chair and picked up his own glass. "Elm went to the Lord Chief Justice with his story about Makeready."

"The same one he was telling last winter?"

"Exactly." Hasten looked at the glass in his hand. He shot a glance at Lilz and drank. "He's got hold of a letter the bastard wrote to his father, saying he had such pain in his belly he thought he was being poisoned, and he's shown it to the parents—now they're determined to see somebody hanged for his murder. How Elm got the letter, I don't know, but it's apparently in Makeready's hand—or at least that's what old Gudgeon believes."

"Oh, dear."

The dych laughed. "Oh, dear! Oh, dear! Sky above, Lilz, can't you think of something stronger than 'oh, dear'? Gudgeon's a Ridehard, you know that! And it was Makeready's nudge that got him appointed—that's exactly why Father was so anxious to have Fenne rid of Greencrags so she could marry that nitwit thegn Guyr dotes on! Can you imagine the old fish will let her go? A fine fat Hasten worm like Fenne, with no hook in her?"

"None, your Grace?"

Olen Hasten sprawled in his chair and stared at her for a long time before saying, "Evin Clock has been summoned to testify. He has almost as many friends as there are Peers of the Blood. As does Mistress Stump."

"Who'd've thought it?" the dych mumbled. Somewhere in his apartments a clock struck two. "I al'ays knew 'ese rooms'd be mine someday. Bu' I'm still 'spectin' Father t'walk through that door." He nodded at the white-painted door he had closed on one of his tours of the room earlier in the morning. "What, Olen, making free of my whiskey, are you?" he said, somewhat sloppily but so accurate a mimicking of his father that Lilz jumped. "Go drink your own." The dych giggled. "You're not drinking, Lilz," he added in his own voice, more slurred.

She sipped again.

"Ah, Mother'v All! Wha'm I goin' t'do wi' th' ol' scapegrace's moppet?"

Lilz raised her eyebrows. "I'm sure I don't know. But you must be more prudent in your speech, your Grace. You've already pointed out that should a Hasten come to trial the Lord Chief Justice may well bring the matter of religion into—"

"Pssh. Carefu' wi' you? You know all 'bout us b'now."

Sky above! Lilz put her glass down on the table beside her. "I hope you choose your drinking cronies carefully, your Grace," she said, eyeing him.

"Hunh."

He was drunk enough to remember nothing in the morning, surely? "You know, I've never understood that about the Hastens," she went on, her eyes narrowed. "How it is that you cling to the old religion, despite your closeness to the throne, and yet no king has ever accused you of doing so, although every one of them from Lehrr on down must at least have suspected."

"Tha's 'cause 'tsa 'sper'men'. Royals know all 'bout it."

"Spermen?" Lilz turned the word on her tongue once or twice, not sure what it was.

"'Sper'men'." Articulating with great care, the dych added, "Like the nachral ph'los'phers."

"Natural philosophers?"

"Uhn. Like—wha'sa name a' th'fellow? One 'at writes all the letters t'Guyr?"

"Letters?"

"Tell 'im how t' run th' country. Gammon."

Gammon...? Oh, *experiment!* How did it go? Observe all factors, change one and observe the effect...something like that. "What's an experiment?" Lilz asked. "I don't understand."

The dych sat up straight, his eyes wide. "Nothin'," he said. "Nothin'. I di'n' say anythin'."

"What is the experiment, your Grace?"

"Shu'p. I di'n' say." Fenne's father lurched to his feet and stumbled toward the tray Quern had left the whiskey on. "Where'sa bo'le? Wha' happ'n 'e bo'le?"

"It's over here, your Grace." Lilz stood up. The dych propped himself on his hands, elbows locked, and mumbled something about the missing bottle. She went to him and led him to a settee beneath the front window, sat him down, and pushed him onto his side. He keeled over with a moan. "Time to sleep," she said.

"Thought I'd s'eep wi' you."

Lilz nearly laughed. "Not tonight, I think, your Grace." She pulled off his riding boots and bent his knees to tuck him onto the settee. The man was asleep before she finished.

The hall was dark, her lamp long empty. Lilz took a candle from one of the sconces and lit it at one of the seven that hadn't burned out in the dych's sitting room. As she did, Hasten snored.

The room was chilly, but he shouldn't suffer. She blew out the rest of the candles. At the door, she hesitated. A shred of moonlight came through the front window of the room, silver on the back of the settee. The dych was in shadow, invisible, still snoring. The room stank of extinguished wax, damp chimney, whiskey, and sweat. Lilz shut the door.

Experiment. What could the dych have meant? Shielding her candle with her hand, Lilz went toward her own side of the manor, wide-awake despite her exhaustion. She wished she still had the journal she had sent to Greencrags. If anyone could tell Lilz Chantwell, hostage, what this "experiment" might be, it was sure to be that cheerful record-keeper, the Twelfth Dych of Summerlea.

Old Ruppet! Lilz stopped in her tracks, eyes narrowed. A small fact bubbled out of the Kennish history she had learned nearly a quarter of a century before. That Ruppet's sister— also named Fenne—had been Lehrr's queen, the last direct royal link to the Hasten family.

But not the first. The first had been a younger brother of a king generations older than Lehrr, the source of the ancestral right of the Dych of Summerlea to place the scepter in a new king's hand. Lilz went slowly on. *Royals know all about it.* Olen Hasten had included himself in that small circle, she was sure.

Lilz slipped through the door under the front stairs, wondering about the morass of ill-will across which King Guyr and Queen Prenta seemed to regard one another. Prenta wasn't Kennish. She must have been raised in the old religion. Then why the gem-covered book of prayers given to Fenne?

Aimed not at Fenne, but at her grandpapa? Even more spiteful than Lilz had thought. Or had it been a protest against hypocrisy discovered at the heart of her husband's rule?

Eventually she slept, and sleeping, dreamed. In the morning she recalled only one image, a genuine memory of the chuckle with which the old dych had announced the name he had chosen for his new granddaughter—and his son's startled frown.

Chapter Twenty

"Lilz? One of the maids from the other end of the house poked her head through the servants' hall door. "'S Grace wants you."

Sighing, she got up from her lunch and went with the maid to the dych's library. "He's in a nasty mood," the girl warned her.

"Thanks." Lilz smiled, a wan smile, and tapped on the door. Olen Hasten opened it himself. He'd been shaved and dressed tidily, but a stale odor of whiskey from the night before lingered about him and he moved his head with the exaggerated care of a man whose whole skull pounded.

"Good afternoon, your Grace," Lilz said. "You sent for me?"

The new dych gestured for her to enter and stalked to the chair behind his desk. "Shut that damned door."

Lilz closed it quietly and waited to be told whether to sit down. Fenne's father gave her an impatient sign. She sank onto the nearest chair.

"I talked to you last night."

"Yes, your Grace."

"About what?"

"You wanted to know whether Lady Northlands has dealt with a pharmacist named Clock," Lilz said. "You explained to me a number of circumstances surrounding the death of Sir Jen Makeready that have led to suspicions of your daughter's complicity in what may be his murder. You speculated over likely outcomes of Evin Clock's testimony on the matter to Lord Chief Justice Gudgeon."

Hasten nodded. "What else?"

"Nothing much, your Grace. Not that made any sense to me."

The dych gazed at her. He looked aged and tired in the clear light that poured through the glass doors, an effect of his hangover and the hard ride of the day before, no doubt. "Such as?"

Trap. "I'm sorry, your Grace, but it made so little impression that I just don't recall." The dych's eyebrows twitched: not good enough. Lilz gave the first excuse that came into her head. "I think I'd had too much whiskey." Hasten stared at her. *He must remember urging it on me.* She felt herself color. "You did say you wanted to sleep with me, but—"

"I was drunk," Hasten muttered. "All right, Lilz, you may go."

She went back along the twisting corridors wondering what would have happened to her if she'd asked the questions that had kept her awake much of the night. A sudden illness, perhaps? One that would turn her skin yellow? Without someone like herself to intercede, without a caring heart like Stone's to guard her, she would never recover. A minor snarl in the Hasten scheme of things. She would have to get the more damning of Makeready's letters into safe hands to protect herself, or they'd surely be turned against her. As soon as Fenne brought her clothes box, she'd find a private time to set them aside. If Fenne should ask about the letters, after all this time? Lilz sighed. She'd just have to hope her mistress wouldn't miss those few. She'd probably forgotten them all, truth be known.

Byre met her with a distraught stare as she came into the hall of the main house. "The forward rider's just come," he said. "Lady Northlands's carriage will arrive in an hour. She's bringing her mother and her aunt with her. Do you think we're ready?"

"Of course we are," Lilz assured him, and went into the kitchen to see if she could get anything more to eat.

From the moment of Fenne's arrival the mood of the whole house changed. Even sour-faced Byre was seen to smile—one morning as she was passing through the hall Lilz saw him come down the front staircase and greet the girl dusting the bannisters without making the slightest objection to her singing at the task, ordinarily a matter for his sternest rebuke. Lilz herself went on humming the sprightly tune, that of a song still half in the old tongue: *See the lasses dancing,/ Crazy every one*, the maid had sung, *They think to pass the summer/ Without a single man!*

Whether that was Fenne's intent or not, Lilz didn't know. The new Dych of Summerlea went back to town a week after he'd come, taking his personal servants and Raven with him. Lady Delle stayed on. An assortment of cousins drifted in and out of the house as in the old days. Bright afternoons saw lawn parties and picnics; one stormy day the whole lot of them played hide-and-seek through the entire house with a great deal of scuffling and giggling in dimly lit corners, Lady Delle even rowdier than her daughter. On other occasions, Fenne went to visit at one or another of the great houses nearby for a day or two or three, taking Aster with her and sometimes, if she expected musicians or players to entertain, taking Lilz too, as a treat.

After one of those trips, Byre handed Lilz the messages that had arrived while they were gone to take upstairs to Fenne. She flipped through them as she went up the front stairs. One fat envelope had been shoved into the stack upside down and showed only a plain seal with no crest. Lilz turned it over. The letter bore her own name. The writing was Stone's.

Sky above!

Byre might have warned me. What if I'd handed that to Fenne?

Lilz slipped the letter into her shirt to read later and delivered the rest to her mistress. She was in luck. The second of Fenne's many messages required Lilz to look something up in a ledger left in the office Fenne had wangled for her use on this visit.

Safe in the tiny room, Lilz broke Stone's seal and eagerly scanned the letter. "My sweet," he addressed her, and signed with his love and his first name, Beor. Lilz smiled. Toss the envelope into the fire and no Hasten would have the slightest idea to whom or by whom the letter had been written. But every word was clearly for her and clearly his own, though he must have been encouraged to write by Greencrags: the plumpness of the envelope had been due to a second sheet of paper, "a few verses handed to me yesterday, which I thought you might find amusing," copied out in Stone's hand but bearing the unmistakable stamp of the anonymous poet. It seemed his lady had provided the youth with "much to ponder of our aching history." The parcel had arrived.

Lilz slid the letter under a pile of Fenne's papers, folded the envelope small and stuck it into a pocket, and took the ledger back to her mistress's suite hoping Fenne wouldn't hear the happiness bubbling in her heart. She'd stash the letter in her clothes box and burn the envelope first chance she got.

Spring gave way to summer. The peonies faded. Among their burnished green leaves silvery drifts of lychnis bloomed a violent pink. One warm afternoon Lilz stood in a second-floor window watching Fenne on the lawn below. Her mistress was rolling a hoop with her cousin Lord Säen, her skirts tucked up like a child's. Even at this distance, their unheard laughter made Lilz smile.

Motion at the end of the drive caught her eye. A van drawn by two chestnut horses had turned off the high road. As it came closer, Lilz recognized the driver and put her hand to her chest.

Clâes.

He pulled up sharp as the hoop rolled into the drive. Lord Säen chased after it. Lilz saw Clâes say something, probably a warning. Säen responded with an arrogant jerk of his head, but Fenne put soothing hands on his arm and glanced over her shoulder at Clâes, her usual flirtatious glance, at which Clâes tipped an imaginary cap. The van turned aside at the fork and headed for the stableyard. The lettering on its side—Godwit and Chantwell, Cabinetmakers and Repairers of Fine Furniture—seemed a little faded. She hoped that didn't mean her brother's income had faded, too.

Lilz ran down the stairs and out through the kitchen garden. Her brother met her at the gate.

She always thought of Clâes as a youth just turned twenty, as he'd been when she'd first come to the Hastens, like their father the instant darling of every woman who laid eyes on him. At forty, he was still a handsome man, with their father's bright blue eyes and dark hair. Like Lilz, he had inherited his lanky shape from their father. That shape was a trifle more heavily padded than when she'd seen him last, four? No, five years before. His grin was as broad as ever, though, and his hug as bone-cracking.

"This is the life, eh, Lilz?" he greeted her. "Free as a bird to wander over the countryside. Why not come with me?"

She laughed. "You know why. The moment the Hastens caught up with me it would all be over."

"Come as far as the wagon, at least," he said. "I've got my oldest boy with me this trip."

"Wonderful." Lilz followed her brother across the stableyard. A boy of fifteen sat on the tailgate of the wagon with a book. "Sky above, is that Aust?" she exclaimed. "How he's grown!"

"Ought to've. Eats enough for an army."

Her nephew greeted her as he might a stranger, but graciously put up with a kiss on the cheek and made room for her to climb into the wagon and sit on a tied bedroll. Clâes sat across from her and glanced about. "I think we're clean," he said softly.

"We'll have to be quick, here."

"I know. About that parcel...I sent it on, of course, and asked for a return receipt, which I did get."

"I must owe you—"

"Forget it. Your pocket money can't be much and it was little enough out of mine."

"Thank you, then. Clâes, I'm sorry, but could you do the same favor again?"

"More of his papers?"

"Mine, this time." She hesitated. "Have you heard any rumors about my mistress?"

His eyebrows shot up. "Are they true?"

"Nearly. I've got some letters that would protect me should she decide...you can imagine." Clâes nodded. "They'd be safe with him."

"I could keep them myself."

"No, no." Lilz lowered her voice and glanced toward Aust. "Too obvious. I don't want you involved any more than I can help. The new dych is his father's son in more ways than you'd think just to look at him. So if you'd send...?"

Clâes, too, glanced at his son. "Whatever you think best." He sighed. "About the question you asked in your letter...I was only ten when *it* happened, you know. Nobody told me a thing, then or since. I don't really remember much more than you."

It, in Chantwell parlance, was the banishment. Lilz shrugged. She'd hardly expected a complete explanation.

"All I really remember is that there was never any money. So when the time came I was sent to old Godwit as apprentice. You were what, eleven? The Hastens were his good customers long before I went. I was surprised when they bought you, but I thought it was just my good luck that I'd see you once in a while."

"Didn't you ever wonder if there might be a connection?"

"No." Clâes sucked in his lips, one of her father's old habits. "Mother said I must never refer to *it*, or to life before *it,* in old Godwit's presence, which seemed only reasonable." Lilz leaned toward him to hear better. "I never had any cause to think the reason for *it* had anything to do with your old dych. Why did you walk in his funeral procession, by the way?"

"I don't know."

"He just asked you to, and you did? Didn't you ask why?"

"He ordered his son to give me the horse to lead. I'm not sure, but I have the impression the new dych has no more idea why I was there than you or I do."

Clâes tilted his head at her. "You were on exhibit."

"I thought so, too, but for whom? Father?"

"Ah, Lilz." Clâes looked out the back of the wagon at his son, named for their next older brother. "I think he must be dead, don't you? Not to contact either of us, his children? I'm sure he'd know where to find us."

A heaviness settled onto her shoulders. "Have you ever heard—?" Her throat closed over the question.

"I had one letter from Aust just after he reached the New Lands, but none since, nor ever any from Dilyn or Milas."

"I haven't even had that."

Her brother sighed. "This I hate to say to you, Lilz, but I think I must. The letter from Aust said he hadn't been able to find anyone in Newton who'd ever heard of Father or either of our brothers."

"I thought—"

"Milas found father's name on a passenger list to Newton and they went to look for him, yes. But Lilz, that letter from Aust was so—how to say it?—so worn-looking, creased and dirty. The letter Mother got from Father was fresh, you remember?"

Lilz nodded.

"As if it hadn't been carried far. But she couldn't have been deceived by someone else's hand, surely? I think she faked it, to keep us all hopeful, just as they had us all tutored."

They sat in silence until the boy on the tailgate turned to look at them, a full two minutes later.

"Well." Lilz roused herself. "I'd best get back. The house can give you a fair amount of repair, if you can persuade Byre to have it done. I might be able to help with that—the man's drunk all the wine the new dych had laid down, though I don't think that's come out yet. A little blackmail—" She shrugged.

"All small jobs gratefully accepted."

Clâes followed her into the house, where Lilz introduced him to Byre as the Hasten's usual cabinetmaker. "Perhaps the dych will want a new wine cupboard constructed," she murmured. "Since the old one seems faulty."

With Lilz at his shoulder, Byre discovered a good many loose joints and sagging hinges in Summerlea's furniture, although of course none were in the servants' attic. Clâes stayed four days and left well-compensated for his work. As was Lilz: she and her nephew Aust were now on comradely terms.

Almost as important, in Lilz's view, the half dozen letters in which Sir Jen Makeready warned his protege against his liaison with Fenne Hasten and complained that he thought he was being poisoned were on their way to Greencrags.

Summer flowed sluggishly on, with little to mark one day from the next, like a green stream where not a ripple shows what may live in its black depths. By the time Fenne started talking about returning to Miense for Presentation Day and the new social season, Lilz was as eager to go as her mistress. The night of the *antran* had become dreamlike; unable to make any sense of the experience she pushed it to the back of her mind and declared the various other puzzles she had encountered unsolvable without more information. More immediate was the permanent ache in the largest joint of her right thumb, developed by pushing a needle through the heavy stuff of a chair seat Fenne had decided must be embroidered with hundreds of thousands of tiny cross-stitches in the newest, intricate floral style. With luck, in town the project would be forgotten.

They arrived at Waterside almost a month ahead of time, so that Onma Stump could cut a new dress for Lady Northlands. This would be silk faille the color of claret, embroidered in gold and seed pearls. Mistress Stump and Fenne considered each seam with the eager assistance of Aster, while Lilz sat in the corner of the dressing room, dazed by the long discussion. Finally everything was agreed upon. A silence fell. "Milady, if you could excuse your body-maid?" Onma Stump said, after a moment.

"If you like. Go away, Aster."

Blinking with surprise, Aster left the dressing room. Mistress Stump went to the door a few seconds later and snatched it open, but Aster was not to be seen. Gone to the hall door, Lilz thought, or waiting to hear this one open and shut.

"What's the matter?" Fenne asked.

"Evin Clock." Mistress Stump licked her lips nervously. "He's in the Old Palace. It's said that at night the guards take him back to his shop to copy out his records."

"That's silly," Fenne said. "Why don't they just seize whatever they want?"

"They say he has a secret code—"

"He could set it over to Kennish outside his shop, surely."

"Lady Northlands, don't you understand what's in those records? Lists of those who've had poisons supplied—"

Mistress Stump stopped speaking as Fenne smiled, a sweet little smile that made Lilz shiver. "That doesn't include me, though, does it, Onma?" Fenne said. "Only you, since you've been so kind to me."

The costumer went white. She opened her mouth and closed it again. She did give Fenne's name, Lilz thought. Mistress Stump glanced at her, where she still sat in the corner. Lilz shook her head, not more than half a finger's breadth, just as the Hasten man on the annulment commission had signaled her, so long ago.

"I would pray that you be kind to me, milady." How wretched the poor woman looked! Lilz glanced at her own hands, clasped in her lap and tightened with sympathy.

"Oh, I shall, Onma, I shall." Fenne's smile widened. "I shall be just as kind as I can afford to be. This will be a stunning dress, won't it? You're so clever at design." As if she thought she'd smoothed everything over, Fenne went on talking. A few minutes later Onma Stump took her sketches and measurements and departed.

The costumer had left the door ajar. Lilz pushed it shut. "My mistress, you'd be wise to keep Onma Stump in good humor," she advised.

"What, Onma? She's just being absurd."

Lilz watched Fenne gather up the jewelry she had decided to wear to the Presentation Day gala and toss it back into the box. "I think you've missed her point," she said. "Evin Clock has been talking about poisoners among the Peers of the Blood. You remember last winter's rumors. It can't take much wit to place them side by side. Should Clock stand for trial, I'm sure he'd say all he knows to gain a few more days of life in hope of pardon."

"Foolishness," Fenne snorted. "What does that have to do with me?"

"He did supply the poison to Mistress Stump, remember."

"So?" Fenne sat on the stool in front of the dressing table and gazed up at Lilz. She looked about fifteen years old, fresh and naive and pure of heart. "She's not me."

"Fenne, do think! If Clock accuses Onma Stump, she, too, will stand for trial, and she, too, will say all she knows to gain a few more days. Don't you think the Lord Chief Justice would promise her life if she could help him bring down a Hasten? His mother's a Ridehard. So's his wife."

"Politics!" Fenne laughed. "You seem to think I'm Ruppet! Grandpapa explained it all to me years ago, Lilz. *My* part in politics is to be a sweet and cheerful wife to the right man. Then it was Greencrags. Now it's Kav. Other than that, I can do just as I please."

"Not quite, my mistress."

"Grandpapa said so." Fenne turned to the mirror with a little pout. "I'm going to need a fresh underdress to go with this new silk, Lilz. Onma and I were thinking of a needlelace edging, and you're so good at it—how wide a piece could you work by the day, do you think?"

Lilz pressed her lips together. What on earth could be going through her mistress's mind? Even a woman like Fenne could scarcely believe what she'd just said! "How long a piece?" she asked at last.

"Oh, a couple of sashlengths. Where's Aster?"

Mistress Stump was waiting in the back hall when Lilz went down to the kitchen to fetch her mistress's lunch.

"Sky above, I thought she'd never let go of you," the woman whispered. "What did you do all morning?"

"Lady Northlands's bidding."

"Did you hear her?" Mistress Stump shuddered visibly. "I wouldn't have believed it. As if some other creature, something evil, spoke out of that innocent mouth! "

Lilz sighed. "I've heard it before."

The costumer pressed her hand to her collarbone and shook her head. "Dreadful! I don't know how you live with it! Why did you say not to tell her I'd given Clock her name?"

"Does anyone else know?"

"Only Clock."

The cook looked out of the kitchen and asked what all the whispering was about. Lilz pantomimed eating and pointed upward. "Oh, the tray. Half a moment." He went back to the stove.

"Write it all down, as much as you can remember," Lilz advised the costumer. "If you've got proof of what she asked for, put it all together. Give everything to someone you can trust to hold for you."

"I don't understand."

Silly woman. "Then you can tell her that if anything happens to you, your friend will see that your proofs go to the king," Lilz explained. "As it is, Fenne learns some sorts of lessons all too well. You're alive only because the old dych foresaw a possible use for you and told her. As am I," Lilz added, to forestall any notion Mistress Stump might form that she herself would be a good repository for her proofs. "She'll probably claim that she had nothing to do with any of it and anything done in her name was done without her knowledge."

"Oh, dear!" The costumer wrung her hands. "I've thrown away most of her letters. I put so much faith in her grandfather! I thought it was all over and done."

"Well." Lilz touched Onma Stump's fingers, to stop her from shredding her fine lace gloves. "Do what you can."

"He couldn't prosecute her, could he? Old Gudgeon?"

"That's his job."

White showed all around the woman's faded blue eyes. "He can't. He *can't!*"

"Shh!"

"Don't you see? It's not just Fenne and the old man. He'd have us in, too! The scandal! What would become of my business?"

The cook came to the kitchen door with Fenne's lunch on a tray. Mistress Stump cast it a glance of pure despair—wishing she could season it with a dash of Fenne's own salt, no doubt—and went into the front hall to be shown out.

It might have been coincidence that Evin Clock's pharmacy burned to the ground, taking half the block with it, the following afternoon. Lilz was inclined not to think so.

Chapter Twenty-One

Over the following week Lilz took no early morning rides. She ate from a tray and paid only the barest necessary attention to Fenne's financial affairs. Certainly she played no guitar. Every possible moment was consumed in producing a froth of ivory linen to peep under the hem of the Presentation Day dress.

At least she'd persuaded both her mistress and the costumer that the width of embroidery-in-air anyone could produce in the required length given the time available would be intolerably skimpy. Instead, Lilz had suggested fine hookwork, an idea she now rued. The constant unaccustomed flicking of fingers and wrist had left her with aching joints no sleep, no balm, no overnight wrap of knit wool, could ease. Soaking in salts took waking time; Lilz hadn't tried that remedy.

She'd made a little over half a sash-length of lace as wide as her hand was long by the end of the week, sitting with Fenne hours at a time—most of the iarlena's friends were still out of town—sometimes enjoying, sometimes stupefied by the younger woman's prattle.

A drenching rain now fell. The fire in Fenne's sitting room popped and crackled as mistress and servant sat together after lunch, Fenne opening a few messages the houseman had just presented on a silver tray, Lilz chaining and catching up stitches in a pattern she saw with equal clarity whether her eyes were open or shut.

"They've finally come through with that insurance payment," Fenne remarked. "Record it when you've got a moment, yes?" She tossed the bank's letter onto the table beside her and glanced up as the door opened. "Hello, Kav. What are you doing here?"

Lord Northlands came into the room, followed by Olen Hasten. Lilz stood. The lace spilled from her lap and the ball of thread rolled toward the fire. She gathered the lace up with her free hand as she curtsied to the two noblemen. Their faces stopped her from retrieving the thread.

"Stump's been arrested," Kav said.

"Who?" Fenne's pale lashes opened wide.

"Onma Stump, the costumer."

"Arrested?" How she can act, Lilz thought. "For what? What about my new dress?"

Her husband tossed the idea of the dress away with one sharp motion. "For obtaining poison from Evin Clock."

"Sky above! Who would have thought it?"

"Sit down, Lilz." Summerlea turned a side chair and straddled it, arms folded on the back. "We have something to discuss."

Lilz sank back into the armchair she'd been sitting in as Kav drew up a second side chair. "With me, your Grace?" She was sorry she'd asked: alarm had made her voice brittle.

"All of us." He stared hard at his daughter, the muscles of his jaw working. "Fenne, I want the truth. Did you have Sir Jen Makeready killed?"

"Did I—Papa, how could you ask such a thing?"

"The rumor has been going the rounds since Father died. I can't say I appreciate the assessment of my own capacity that implies, but I recognize it. I also recognize the danger." He glanced at Lilz. "I had an interesting discussion with your bond-servant last spring, Fenne. She has a nicety with words and a commendable loyalty to you, but I formed the impression, which I believe to be accurate, that you had Onma Stump buy poison from Evin Clock, just as he said, and that Lilz agreed to see that Makeready got a good dose in food you had sent to the Old Palace."

His mouth was grim. Fenne glanced at her father, then at her husband, whose scowl could have frightened a palace guard.

"Lilz, I want to see your ledgers for the time Jen Makeready was jailed. Go get them, right now. Kav, go with her. See that she touches nothing but the covers."

"My mistress?" Lilz turned toward Fenne.

"Go on," she said. "We'll thrash this out, don't worry."

Lilz put the lace on the floor beside her chair. Hoping she looked less frightened than she felt, she led Lord Northlands to the small office where she kept Fenne's books and unlocked the door.

"I want Jen's notes back," he said. "And your copy of my map."

"Yes, milord." She opened the desk.

"If you say one word about them to Summerlea, I will have your life, do you understand?" Treadwell's greenish eyes met her own, the color darkened with emotion. "You'll disappear into the Old Palace so fast no eye will follow and not even your bones will come out."

"I understand, milord."

"Don't think I can't give the order, and don't think the Hastens can protect you. Guyr does as I say. He dotes on me too much to do anything to cross me."

Lilz found the papers he'd asked for and handed them to Northlands. He folded them into an inner jacket pocket. She gazed at him steadily. "If I may caution you in friendship, milord, it might be best not to let the king hear of your speaking of him in that manner."

Kav gave her an insolent smile. "The ledgers?"

"There's only one." Lilz sorted through the slender books in the deepest drawer of her desk, found the one with the right gummed paper label on the front cover and handed it to him. Northlands checked the first and last entries. He jerked his head for Lilz to follow him and strode back to Fenne's suite.

Fenne and her father were sitting where they'd been when Lilz left, but Fenne had rolled up the thread and the lace and held them in her lap. She handed them to Lilz. "You may as well get some of this done while they blather at us."

"Very well." Lilz looped the thread over her index finger, where the leather shield she wore had a groove chafed into it from the week's labors, and began hooking.

Summerlea opened the ledger, "Where's that list of dates?" he demanded. Kav Treadwell produced a slip of paper from a jacket pocket and handed it to him. Summerlea began leafing through the ledger, glancing at the list from time to time, the book and the paper held almost at arm's length for better viewing. Lilz kept hooking. No sound in the room but the pop of the fire, Summerlea's angry breathing, the soft thrum of the rain against the windows.

The ledger closed with a snap. "To Onma Stump, for sundries. I suppose you could scarcely write 'poison,' could you, Lilz?"

"Your Grace—"

"It's none of your business, papa, but it happens that I made use of Mistress Stump's establishment for entertainment purposes," Fenne broke in. "Would you rather Lilz had written, 'To Onma Stump, so Treadwell could bed Fenne in peace'?"

Lord Northlands flushed.

"Unusual coincidence, isn't it, Fenne, that every single time Clock recorded selling you poison, a day or two later you met some lover at Stump's?"

"I paid for that," Lord Northlands said.

Fenne took a breath. Her eyes narrowed. She said nothing.

"Or at least, I paid for my share."

"Who sent you to Stump for those services, Fenne?" her father demanded.

"Lilz."

The two men stared at Lilz, who stopped hooking. "At your father's urging, your Grace, long before Greencrags returned from Chrems."

Northlands began to say something, but Fenne's father hushed him. "Save that for later. These expenses aren't large enough, unless Fenne got a quantity discount. The other coincidence that catches my eye, Lilz, is the notation of some item of food to be sent to O.P., always the day after Onma Stump provided whatever those sundries may have been. May I take it that 'O.P.' stands for 'Old Palace,' and not some person's name?"

Fenne didn't answer. Nor did Lilz.

"Where's the famous veal pie, Lilz?" Summerlea demanded. "The one that killed Elm's slobbery old hound?"

"I sent no veal pie, your Grace."

"Ah." Summerlea's eyes narrowed. A trick of the dark day and the firelight made him look exactly like his father. The illusion fled as he jutted his jaw. "I asked you a question at Summerlea, Lilz. Only this morning it occurred to me that you never did give a satisfactory answer." The dych glared at her. "Did you or did you not save the poison?"

"I have no poison, your Grace."

"A nicety of words, I think I said. Where does she keep her personal stuff, Fenne?"

"She's got a box with some clothes in it upstairs, I think."

"Good. Send for it. We'll search it right now."

Makeready's letters. Lilz nearly jumped out of her chair. "Your Grace, I protest! That's completely unwarranted, an intrusion you've no right to make."

"Oh, let him look." Fenne sounded disgusted.

"My mistress, I have every right to privacy in my person and property, bond-servant or no bond-servant." Please, she thought. *Remember!*

Summerlea was already at the door, calling for a guard. "Stay here," he said to Northlands. "I'll go up and make sure nothing's taken out of the box before we get a look at it."

Left behind, the three glanced uneasily at one another. "What's in the box, Lilz?" Fenne asked.

"Only my clothes, and some letters I've been saving." Her hands started hooking again, almost by themselves. Lilz watched them in dismay. Why wouldn't Fenne understand? "I prefer not to have it all on display," she continued. "In male company—"

"Pff, Lilz, you're always such a prude!" Fenne laughed. "Ever seen my bond-servant's underdrawers, Kav? Think you'll find them titillating?"

Lilz bit her lip. "Please, my mistress. Ask your father not to turn my things out, or read the letters I've saved. I've served you well. Can't you do this one small favor?" I should have given all of them to Clâes, Lilz thought. She'd never have missed them, after all.

"Do you have poison in the box, Lilz?" Treadwell asked, as if it were a matter of minor curiosity. She shivered.

"No."

The door banged open. Summerlea marched in, followed by a guard with Lilz's clothes box on his shoulder. "Just put it anywhere and go get the other," the dych ordered. The guard set the box in the middle of the floor with a glance at Lilz, whether of curiosity or sympathy, she couldn't tell, and left. Summerlea flipped the box lid back. Her sewing case was on top. The dych opened and closed that and put it on the floor.

Everyday clothes next. Lilz watched him start to set them aside in a stack, but with a swift glance at her the dych changed his mind and shook out each shirt, her sweater, each pair of pants, the plain muslin underdrawers Fenne had laughed about. "She doesn't provide you with much, does she?" he commented, unfolding her skirt.

"Quite sufficient, I do assure you, your Grace." Her voice again betrayed her tension: Fenne's father glanced at her and pulled the black dress made for the old dych's funeral from the box.

"Do you know the reason for this?"

"No, your Grace."

"Just as well." He ran finger and thumb over one of the unfinished buttonholes. "The Stump woman knows how to write a bill, I'll say that for her. She should have docked her price for these. I'd put odds she didn't." He was shaking out the dress as he spoke. He plucked at the side seams, but the dress had no pockets. In the bottom of the box were the letters. The dych reached instead for a little tin box with a slide top, opened it, dumped her hairpins out into his hand, and replaced them.

The guard came back with Lilz's guitar. While Summerlea opened the case and peered through the soundhole of the instrument, Northlands reached for the one letter not tied up in flimsy. He stood with his back to the fire and glanced at the first page. "Who's Beor?" he asked. Fenne raised her brows at Lilz.

"A solid thegnly hand, I'd say. He thinks you'd like verse, does he?" Northlands continued, grinning. "Who do you s'pose sends poems to servants?" He scanned the second page. "Ah, our friend of the last couple of seasons! The man's still not signing his name. Is it this Beor?"

Lilz swallowed. "I haven't read the letter, milord," she said.

"Not read it?" He turned to his wife. "Is it yours?"

Fenne examined her fingernails and pushed back a bit of cuticle. "I don't know any Beor."

Summerlea returned the guitar to the case and closed it. Northlands had turned back to Stone's letter.

"Oh-ho-ho-ho!" he exclaimed. "Not likely yours, Lilz, no. Now, if Fenne got a letter like this..." He narrowed his eyes. "Well, dear wife?"

"Not mine. Let's see?"

Kav held the letter behind his back. Lilz saw what was coming and inhaled slowly for strength, the hook steadily looping, looping, looping. Northlands tossed Stone's letter on the fire. The hook continued in unbroken rhythm. Fenne made a little gasp as the paper flared up.

"Yours," her husband said.

"No, I swear not!" Fenne protested. "I just wanted to read it."

"Not hers, milord," Lilz said. "Given into my keeping, but not by my mistress."

Summerlea had opened his penknife and cut the ribbon on one of the packets of Makeready's letters. "Clâes Chantwell," he read from the return address of the top one. The rest of the bundle he tossed into the box. "Let's see what he has to say." One page—her brother's letter—unfolded, revealing another. The dych let the first fall.

The hook stopped. Lilz closed her eyes.

"My one master, dear friend, Sir Kav that was, milord that is," Summerlea read.

Fenne jumped at her father. She snatched the letter out of his grasp and threw it toward the fire. The page caught the air and sailed to the side. Her husband pounced on it. Fenne tried to grab the paper back, but Treadwell hunched over it. She twisted his ear with one hand, reached with the other, clutched a corner of the letter only to have it slip from her fingers as he wrenched away. Fenne grabbed his arm. He overbalanced. They fell over the chair she'd been sitting in. She sprawled on his back, prying at his hands. Paper tore.

Lilz sat like marble, unable even to breathe.

Summerlea forced his daughter's hands apart. Treadwell crawled away. Redfaced, screaming, Fenne fought her father's arms. She kicked the ledger. It spun across the floor to Lilz's feet.

Pick it up? Hide it? Summerlea would surely miss it at once. He'd wonder.... She eased it under her chair with her heel.

The dych hauled his daughter onto her feet and stilled her in a hug. One of the guards opened the door and looked in.

"Come here and hold her," Summerlea ordered. "Keep her quiet."

The guard approached uncertainly.

"This is my house, mine!" Fenne shrieked. "Go away."

"No, Lady Northlands, it's my house." Kav, on one knee, got up. "Do as his Grace ordered," he told the guard, and bent to pick up the piece torn from the letter his father-in-law had started to read.

Fenne lurched in the guard's big arms, still squealing, trying to get teeth into flesh. Aster came to the doorway, her eyes huge.

"Out," Summerlea ordered. She went.

"This is a plea for my mercy." Kav Treadwell looked from Fenne to Lilz. His body seemed to deflate, as a pig's bladder blown up for a child's game might if pricked. "I never saw it before."

"Take her out of here," Summerlea said to the guard. Kicking and yelling, Fenne was borne away. Her father slammed the door. Her screams echoed in the hall.

"Oh, my friend," Northlands groaned. He seemed on the verge of weeping. "Oh, if only I'd known! If I'd had the slightest idea!"

It must be one of the later letters, Lilz thought, her hands tense in her lap. Her cheeks hurt. She'd bitten them.

"How could you keep these from me?" Northlands looked stunned. "Lilz, how could you?"

I was afraid. Her throat was too tight to say the words. *I was a coward.* Northlands went down on his knees beside the box and began opening the other letters, folding up the letters from her brothers and setting them aside with a gentleness that made tears spill down her cheeks. He cut another ribbon, one of Standfast green: the earlier letters. He opened one: it would be blustery, arrogant and insulting as only Makeready at his prime could be, Lilz knew. "This sounds more like Jen," Treadwell remarked, faintly smiling.

"Where did they come from, Lilz?" Summerlea asked.

"Lady Northlands gave them to me, your Grace." She couldn't look at either man. "I understood that his Grace her grandfather had ordered that all letters Sir Jen wrote should be intercepted. How she came by these, I don't know."

"She asked you to save them?"

"And hide them." She managed to glance at Kav Treadwell, who was sitting on his heels beside the box scanning the letters. He seemed to be putting them in chronological order.

"Does he mention poison, Kav?"

"I don't see that he suspected poisoning, at least, not in what I've read. He was surely very ill." Treadwell's voice was neutral enough, but the pain in his face was too much to bear. Lilz blinked away tears. She looked again at her hands and slowly unwound them from the thread. As she did, her mind finally clicked, leaving her feeling stupid: if Olen Hasten thought circumstances urgent enough to come barging into his daughter's house this way, the Presentation Day underdress might not need to be finished, after all. Lilz smoothed the lace in her lap.

When she looked up, Summerlea was standing at a window with his hands clasped behind him, gazing out at the rain. *Kav Treadwell, only a thegn with pretensions, Lilz, and you know it*— though he seemed to have forgotten that bitter insight—had finished sorting the letters and was now reading them, still on his knees.

"Your Grace?" Lilz said. Summerlea tilted his head without looking at her. "What's to happen now?"

"Can't you guess?" he asked of the weather. "Given Fenne, given Clock, given Stump, given Gudgeon?"

Lilz closed her eyes.

"She'll be arrested," Hasten said. "And tried. Whether she lives depends on you." He glanced at his son-in-law, who was still reading, now with tears standing on his freckled cheeks. "Both of you. Where's that ledger?"

Lilz leaned over and retrieved it from under her chair.

"We'd best get rid of it," Summerlea mused.

"I'll do that."

Treadwell spoke far too eagerly, far too quickly. Lilz watched the dych gaze at him. She could as good as hear his thoughts clack like the beads of her abacus: the letter, clearly from a lover, that Kav assumed had been sent to Fenne. The pleas from Makeready, diverted by Fenne. Fenne's tacit admission that she had planned to poison Treadwell's best friend. What if Kav should decide to rid himself of her? Perhaps by bringing the ledger to court as evidence?

"No," Summerlea said slowly. "No." He stared at her a moment. "Lilz can do it."

She wished she still had the lace in her hands to calm her. "Yes, your Grace. Of course."

"Make sure there's not a scrap of writing left. Fenne's future may hang on how thorough you are."

And mine, Lilz thought, as the dych crossed to the door. Please fate he won't have second thoughts for an hour or two.

"We ought to get back to the palace, Kav." Summerlea blew out his cheeks impatiently. "Bring the letters along if you can't wait to read them."

When they'd left, Lilz repacked her clothes box. She peeled the gummed paper label off the cover of the ledger and tossed it on the fire. The ledger itself she slipped in beside her clothes, up against the side of the box where she could grab it easily. No one was in the hall. She fetched a blank ledger from her office and put it on the fire in Fenne's sitting room with the pages fanned open. Her luck held. Even the cover was charred by the time her mistress came into the room. She picked up the poker.

Fenne watched Lilz poke at the smoldering leather for a moment. "Oh, I see," she said. "That record book. Good idea."

"I hope so," Lilz said. "I'm sorry about the letters."

Never mind." Fenne sighed. "I should have remembered. You did try to warn me."

"Not very cleverly, I'm afraid."

"I'm not very clever," the girl said with a shrug. "So if you'd been cleverer, I wouldn't have understood, anyway. Who's Beor?"

"I've no idea."

"Who gave you the letter?"

"A girl at one of the houses we visited from Summerlea, last summer. Somebody's younger sister. I don't know the name." Lilz turned the cover of the ledger with the poker. A little green flame ate along the edge of the board. "Blonde girl, darker hair than yours and duller. Blue eyes?"

"Can't place her."

Not at all surprised, Lilz said, "I suppose it doesn't matter."

Fenne went to the window and looked out. "Nothing matters, now. Oh, I wish papa could figure out what his father would have done!"

By late afternoon, a palace guard resplendent in crimson and ivory uniform sat in the front hall. Another had commandeered the houseman's stool and stationed himself in view of the back door. A third stood in the street, a fourth patrolled the watergate: Fenne was to be arrested that evening.

Arrest for Lady Northlands, wife of the king's favorite and daughter of a long line of peers, was not what Clock or Onma Stump or even

Makeready might have suffered. She would be confined, yes, but not before having time to pack whatever she wished to take with her. No tiny cell awaited her. She would have three rooms in the Old Palace, her own servants at her call, visitors, whatever amusements she might arrange. True, everything that entered the palace in her name would be searched for weapons: scant hardship.

The guards waited until Lady Northlands had eaten a leisurely dinner before ordering her own carriage and driver to convey her to the Old Palace. Two of them traveled with her, one on each side. Lilz, sitting on the opposite seat with Aster, watched the wet familiar streets pass by the coach window. Weariness, not physical but of the heart, settled into her despite her effort to shake it off. She couldn't give in. Not now. Above her head, the ropes securing her mistress's trunk and her own and Aster's boxes to the roof creaked as the carriage turned a corner.

How to get the ledger to Greencrags?

Chapter Twenty-Two

What to expect of Fenne's imprisonment, Lilz had only the meagerest of notions.

Their quarters, at least, weren't so bad: on the third floor, a steep climb tempered with a view over the inner courtyard through tall windows now shut against the rain. Though the rooms were small, each fireplace had an iron fireback to reflect heat, and the one in the room furnished as a sitting room was fitted with a crane for cooking. Bed chamber and dressing room rounded out the apartment. Fenne had a high, wide bed. Aster and Lilz had only pallets on the dressing room floor, but the straw fillings were fresh-scented and bug-free, and they were spread with clean sheets.

All far better than Lilz had feared—and all due to Summerlea, no doubt. What she had never even dreamt of wishing for, the rooms were patrolled by a cat, a fat tortoiseshell with white bib and boots who came to rub her head against their ankles and purr. Lilz hoped she would prove as a good a mouser as her sleek sides promised.

Fenne walked into the bed chamber and sat on the one chair. The cat jumped into her lap. She petted it absently, looking around the room. "It's so little," she said, in a small voice. "Isn't it?"

This room, the largest, was half the size of her Waterside dressing room, twice as big as the one Lilz and Aster shared in the attic. "Space aplenty," Aster said cheerily. "Shall I hang your dresses, milady?"

"Yes, of course." Fenne had stopped petting the cat, which now reminded her of her duties by pushing at her hand with its head. She looked down at it and smiled. "She likes me."

"A beauty, isn't she?" Lilz said. "What would you like me to do?"

Fenne shivered. "Light the fire. Then find some way to get us some tea before bedtime." She glanced at the bed, which had been turned down before they arrived. "I think I'll be cold without Kav."

Lilz spent a restless night. She rose early, poked up the fire in Fenne's bed chamber and put a new log on it, then took the kettle and went down the long stairs to the yard to pump water for breakfast tea and washing up. A few other servants already stood in line at the well. In the half-light of dawn the broad flagged courtyard seemed forbidding, though the rain had stopped before midnight and the paving was dry. No one talked. Waiting her turn at the pump, Lilz studied her surroundings. Other than the queue of servants and a lantern behind one window she saw little sign of life: one woman who crossed from one door to another with quick short steps, a man leaning against the wall near the gate whom she took to be a guard, another servant who came into the yard and joined the line, tapping a dull rhythm on his empty bucket with his fingers until shushed by the others. The clock in the tower struck six.

She returned to Fenne's quarters to find her mistress and Aster awake. The airy windows stood open. Aster had dressed and was laying out a breakfast of cold meats and bread brought from Waterside on the table in the sitting room.

"We'll have to think what to do about food," Fenne said. "We can't eat what they give us."

"Aster and I can go out," Lilz reminded her. "One of us can go to the market."

"Good idea." Fenne cast each of her servants a glance of such envy Lilz started. "You'll go, Lilz."

Later that morning Lilz got a gate pass—an engraved brass disc dulled by innumerable fingers—from the guard in the hall. She turned it in at the gate and set out on foot for the market, carrying the hamper that had held the food brought from home.

Before long she felt the creeping sensation of eyes on her back. Ridiculous, she told herself. The sun was high, the air balmy; a breeze diluted the normal stink of the city with sweet mountain air. Her errand was perfectly legitimate. Still, she couldn't shake the notion that someone was watching her: when a little later she heard a horse come up behind her at a fast trot she looked, not just to get out of the way, but at the people in the street. Sashlengths away, the man who had leaned against the courtyard wall that morning flattened himself into a doorway to escape the arrogant rider, throwing his cloak over his face as if the road were wet.

That's odd, Lilz thought, continuing.

A bread vendor leading a donkey hailed her as she neared the market. His wares were still warm, his sample sweet and his price fair. Lilz bought three wheaten loaves and tucked them under the cloth in her hamper. She passed a stand selling flowers, the woman hawking them already hoarse, the blossoms limp for lack of water. A pile of rosy apples caught her eye. The farmer spied her interest and called to her, "Fine white apples, mistress, so crisp you'll swoon with their savor!"

"Swoon, shall I?" she asked, grinning. "Now, landsman, do I look so delicate?" But she bought a dozen. He handed her an extra, "for your lovely bright smile." She rubbed the waxy bloom off on her pants and went on, eating the fruit. Crisp, white. Tart and juicy. Alone with no task to distract her, she just might swoon with its savor. Lilz glanced back at the stand.

The man from the Old Palace had stopped to talk with the farmer, who shook his head, his brow drawn down. The man left without buying. Lilz almost met his eyes. Instantly he turned away.

He's following me!

Now, that is absurd, Lilz told herself. Why would anyone follow an old sack of bones like you?

At a stall selling eggs she bought six, demanding to see that they sank in water before handing over her coppers. With the eggs cushioned in cloth, she went on.

Look back, she told herself.

Lilz, you are crazy.

It can't hurt to look.

Madwoman! She glanced over her shoulder and saw the stranger lean toward the old wife selling eggs, saw the woman's chin draw back and her head shake.

Summerlea's man? The dych must not trust me, Lilz thought. He's having me followed to see what I do. Yes. Much faster than culling my face from the reports of a thousand whizzers, when no one would know where to look first.

"Lilz!" someone shouted.

She turned to see who had called her, saw the man from the Old Palace scurry out of sight between two stalls, saw Reed waving and hurrying toward her. Of all people to meet, the houseman of Standfast House! What on earth was he doing at market?

"Lilz," Reed called again. "Wait up." He puffed toward her, rotund and beaming. "My lucky day," he said. "Haven't seen you in an eternity!"

"Not quite that," she said. "How are you, Reed?"

"Well, well." He patted his belly. "As you can see. And you?"

"Fairly well. What brings you to market?"

"Cook's taken ill."

"I'm sorry to hear it." Lilz started walking slowly, to lead Greencrags's houseman away from the man she was now certain had followed her. "Not in danger, I hope?"

"Who knows?" Reed shrugged. "He's not only taken ill, he's taken all his backgammon winnings to the south of Travaltia, so far as anyone knows."

"Oh, I *am* sorry!"

Reed grimaced. "So we're awaiting a new one, and the skivvies are cooking, and I'm stuck with the shopping. Seen any bargains?"

"Some wonderful apples near the corner of Market Street and Flax Alley." Now Lilz saw a space up ahead where she might say a word and not be overheard. She made for it as inconspicuously as she could, while Reed chattered beside her.

"Reed," she said urgently into his pleasantries, when they'd reached the space. "Can I rely on you?"

"Always, dear heart. Unless you want me to win at dice."

Lilz gave him a brief grin. "Nearly that chancy. Did you know my mistress is in residence at the Old Palace?"

"Yes, m'darling, the rumor's out." Reed rolled his eyes. "No better place for her, if you want my opinion, and not a bit soon."

Lilz shrugged. "I'm there, too, of course, though I can come and go. Reed, I've something to give your iarl, at the back of the stall, as it were. Could you let him know, as a favor to me?"

"He's in the country, as it happens. Why didn't you come over?"

"I would, but I'm being followed, I think by Summerlea's man—as much as my bond is worth to be seen going into your house if he is." She peered past Reed's thick shoulder. "Here he comes now. Look jolly."

Reed plastered a leer on his face. "Never mind," Lilz said. "It's been lovely to see you again," she added as the stranger neared, hiding her wink behind Reed's bulk.

"My pleasure," Reed said, with a bow. "And I thank you for the advice about apples."

The houseman turned back toward Flax Alley while Lilz moved on, glancing behind her as she went. Yes, the man stopped Reed to question him. Reed laughed and waved him away. Lilz drifted along the line of stalls and wagons in the opposite direction. Leaving the Old Palace, she had thought to stop at a stationer's for brown paper to wrap up the ledger, but now she didn't dare. Nothing to do but finish the provisioning.

She sniffed suspiciously at some roast pheasants. "Fresh cooked last evening, mistress, I swear," said the woman selling them.

"Not overly soured, perhaps. I'll have that one and that."

The woman exchanged the two fowl for two small silvers. "Do you know that fat man I just saw you talking to?" she asked.

"Oh, yes."

"He's been hanging about all morning, buying nothing. I did begin to wonder whether he might be a thief, fine clothes and all."

"He's a houseman I've met while serving my mistress," Lilz told her. "Quite harmless." She looked for Reed as she carried the pheasants away, but couldn't spot him. Was he waiting for me? she wondered. Sent by Greencrags, maybe, on the slim chance that Fenne would send her to market? Frowning over the notion, Lilz stopped to buy some violet-flavored hard candies to please Fenne's sweet tooth and turned back.

She returned to the prison to find Fenne in a rage.

"It can't be helped, Fenne," her father was saying. He turned at the sound of the door and glared as Lilz curtsied and crossed to the dressing room. "You'll just have to trust that Kav and I know what is best."

"What is it?" Lilz whispered to Aster, who sat tight-lipped on her pallet winding damp hair ribbons around a bottleneck.

"They've set the trial date." Aster glanced at the bag holding Lilz's hookwork. "It's for a week after Presentation Day, you may thank your fate. Milady is disappointed. She expected to be free for the gala."

Lilz set down the hamper.

"Also, that cat got into the ham."

That explained Aster's stiffness. "I bought some roast pheasant. Maybe that will appease her."

"May it have taken contagion from standing too long in the sun!" With a vicious hiss, Aster pressed her thumb against the end of the ribbon to stick it and set the bottle aside.

"Shh! Be careful."

Aster wiped away a tear with her wrist. "Oh, Lilz! Almost a whole month! How?" She looked up as the door opened. Fenne put her head in.

"Papa wants to see you, Lilz."

Lilz followed her mistress into the sitting room, where the dych stood in his characteristic pose, hands clasped behind him, staring out a window. Without turning his head, he said, "Did you destroy that ledger as I asked you to yesterday, Lilz?"

"She burned it, papa," Fenne said. "I could have told you that."

"You saw her do so?"

"Yes." Fenne sounded exasperated. "Right in my own fireplace."

Hasten sighed. "Very well, Lilz, you may go."

He's seen how the ledger could have been used to help Fenne at my expense, Lilz thought, returning to Aster. I have got to get it to Greencrags. But how? Can I trust Reed that far?

The question proved idle: though she went to the market every day or two, Lilz did not see Reed again. She did once encounter the Waterside cook, who advised her on the best way of pot roasting beef and sent a bundle of fresh herbs to the Old Palace for the purpose. Soberly following instructions, Lilz browned the meat in the kettle with a few small onions, added the thyme and rosemary to water and wine for braising, and was somewhat surprised to find she had produced a quite adequate supper, though her gravy was not the smooth brown liquor normally served at Fenne's table.

That small triumph was the first bright spot in two weeks. As she applied for her gate pass the day after, the hall guard told her Evin Clock had been assassinated on his way to a commoner's trial at the City House. "They took him out before dawn, of course," the man said. "All of a sudden out of the dark comes a horseman. Hu-u-uge fellow with hood drawn down." The guard's hands shaded his face. "The guards saw naught of him but a glimpse of beard. One says it was yellow, but the others dispute that the color may have been a trick of the lamplight." He leaned forward on his stool so suddenly Lilz stepped back. "And he shot the prisoner out of the grip of the guards. Straight through the heart, miss. No more ticky-tocky for old Clock, eh?"

The guard sat straight again. "Well you may look astonished, miss. 'Twas the finest of pistol work, they say, done all on the fly."

Raven? "Sky above," Lilz said weakly. The hand she had extended to take the pass went limp. *The lad will be paid with death.*

"A lucky twist of fate for your little iarlena, eh?" the guard remarked, winking. "What with the Stump woman 'cross the yard composing her memoirs in trade for her life. "

"I couldn't say." Lilz took the pass. "I think not."

Whatever the effect of Clock's murder on Fenne's fortunes or her own, Lilz could do nothing. She plugged on with her own problem. Sent one day to the Bank of Miense on her mistress's behalf, Lilz dared to stop at the stationer's. The next day Fenne was permitted to bathe in the cold downstairs room reserved for the purpose. Aster went to assist her. Lilz, left upstairs, wrote a letter to Greencrags on the brown paper she'd bought and wrapped up the incriminating ledger. Trusting to Aster's resentment and Fenne's laziness to give her charge of the hamper, she concealed the package under a cloth in the bottom of the basket. That she carried with her each time she left the Old Palace, on the off-chance that some opportunity might present itself, or that Greencrags would manufacture one.

When he did, only three days before Fenne was due to go to trial, Lilz had to stifle fits of laughter for the rest of the morning.

Two men had followed her by turns. This day the one on duty was the first Lilz had noticed. When she reached the market the spy was still with her, looking bored. Three loaves of bread lay in her basket. She had passed up some badly bruised pears and an insistent offer of spavined-looking turnips when she came upon a cartload of shriveled snap beans at the end of Flax Alley, in the spot where the apple farmer had once set up his business. A young man lounged against the side of the cart, chatting with another, while his unharnessed horse munched contentedly over the backboard.

Oddly enough, she recognized the man with his back to her first: Merrow Strengthen's youngest son, Lord Tessen, the youth who had attended Rovvo Standfast so faithfully during his near-fatal illness three years before. His long cloak was thrown carelessly over his arm. Beneath, he was dressed as one might expect of a goldsmith's apprentice, which he was. At the moment she noticed him he had thrown back his head to laugh loudly at some jest of his companion's.

The companion glanced at her. "Beans, mistress?" One eyebrow went up. "Fine flavored, I promise y', though not so fresh as yesterday." He was a tall youth, well-knit. Unkempt dark hair stuck out in greasy clumps under the brim of a soft farmer's cap. His rough brown wool shirt lay half unbuttoned over a bare chest—the day was warm—and three days' reddish beard colored his jaw.

Lilz stared.

"I'd gi' y'a good price, mistress." A thick country accent so altered his words she scarcely understood them. "Nay mind I ought to drive a hard bargain—y'do seem t'relish some'at y'see." The youth straightened, puffed out his chest, and patted a flat belly, his light brown eyes merry.

"*I'm* not in much want of snap beans," Lilz said, "but your nag may soon have them all if you don't attend." She swallowed her habitual *milord* just in time.

Greencrags slapped the horse's nose to drive it off. He took up all the beans he could gather in both grubby hands and turned to her. "So many? All for two coppers."

Lilz felt herself nod. Strengthens son lifted her hamper lid. As Greencrags started to drop the beans in, he glanced sharply at the ground. She let the basket fall. Beans scattered over the cobbles and one of the loaves rolled under the cart.

"Now look, Robin!" Lord Tessen guffawed. "You've unhinged the poor woman completely." Lilz, too, was laughing, incredulous. She squatted, gathering beans, while Greencrags wriggled under the cart to retrieve the errant loaf. Lord Tessen stepped closer. His cloak drooped to conceal her from most passersby.

"Poor Stone," she murmured as Greencrags crawled toward her clutching the bread. "After all his good care of you! Did he see you like this?"

"It's all Stone's work, as you ought to know. Ah, you have it! Excellent! I'd hoped only to make an arrangement." Standfast pushed the package she had handed him onto one shaft where it passed beneath the cart bed. "Remember, if you need me, come." He helped her to her feet. "My pardon I beg of y', good mistress," he said in a worried country voice, brushing at the filthy bread. "I fear I've gi'en your supper an unseemly seasoning."

"No matter," Lilz said. "I'll buy another."

"Let me give y' more beans." The iarl turned to grab some from the cart.

"No, no!" Lilz put her hand on the lid of the hamper. "I've no use for them, really. Ho, lad, will you listen? I can't use the things!" Beans showered on the cobbles as she stepped back. Beside her, Lord Tessen snickered.

"Let me gi' you a copper f' the loaf, then, good mistress. I've no wish to take food from your mouth." Greencrags reached into his pocket and pressed a coin into her palm. From the size, Lilz knew it was gold. She shook her head.

"Nay, I'll not take it back." The iarl shoved his hands into his pockets and grinned. "A landsman may play at lord if he like. Go and buy a new loaf before the vendor runs out."

What a good time he's having, Lilz thought. I hope that fool horse doesn't bloat. She went in search of the baker's donkey and replaced the casualty. Passing the cart again, she saw Standfast and young Strengthen bantering joyously with an exceptionally pretty young housewife. The horse was back at the beans.

* * *

The next three days were torture. Northlands had visited only five
or six times during the whole of Fenne's imprisonment. She had written
a letter pleading with him to come to her, which he had ignored.

"You never sent it," she now accused Lilz.

"My mistress, that's untrue. I gave it to the messenger at the gate.
You can see for yourself, if you like."

She did like. Fenne Hasten, Lady Northlands, caused her body-maid
Aster to array her in the most lavish clothing she had at hand and
went down to the gate to check the register of messages in person. Two
days before, the notation: "From Lady Northlands by the hand of her
bond-servant Lilz, a letter to Lord Northlands at the New Palace."

A runner was sent to the New Palace while Fenne waited, pacing
the length of the guardroom. Lord Northlands had been given the letter.
No reply had been sent. Fenne returned to her quarters humiliated,
in a black despair which soon took the form of berating her servants
for the slightest trifle. She emerged from conferences with her father
and counsel in vicious moods, also spent on Lilz and on Aster. The
cat slunk under her bed and would not come out.

The afternoon before the trial Lady Northlands came back from
a talk with Summerlea pale and silent. Lilz did not know what to say
to this new mood. Not long after Fenne entered her suite, the tower
clock struck. "Do you hear it, Lilz?" she asked. "It says *doom—doom—
doom—doom—*"

"No, my mistress. It's only ringing."

Fenne clutched her elbows as if she were cold. "Papa took me to
see the block," she said. "Where I'll have to lay my head if they find
me guilty."

"Dear heaven! Why?"

Fenne looked at her, shook her head, and went into the dressing
room calling to Aster to unbutton her.

The morning of the trial all three women woke before dawn. The dress
Fenne would wear had been made after her arrest from a design chosen
by her father: a dark brown taffeta with a collar that rose nearly to her
chin from a pin-tucked bodice. A narrow needle-lace ruche rimmed collar
and snug cuffs with a froth of cream. The entire effect was of sweetness
and innocence. Lilz saw the intent, but privately considered it dangerous:
most of the peers would merely be reminded that ordinarily a far greater
expanse of Fenne's skin was placed on view.

"I hate that dress," Fenne said. "You know what it reminds me of,
Lilz? It reminds me of that horror you and mother made me wear for
my presentation."

"It's the color."

"No, it's that it's meant for a little girl." Fenne held out her arms as
Aster began buttoning her drawers to her underdress. "What jewels
did papa say, again?"

"None, my mistress."

"None!" Fenne snorted. "I'll wear the amber and pearls grandpapa gave me. If I wore them for my presentation, surely papa can't object to my wearing them today."

"They won't show up very well," Aster remarked.

"No," Fenne said. "No," she repeated, more slowly. "But I feel I need them, somehow."

Lilz touched her shoulder. "Courage."

Fenne turned and threw her arms around her. "Oh, Lilz, whatever happens, I owe so much to you!" Her voice broke. "Please, please, don't ever forget all the wonderful parts of our lives."

"Never," Lilz promised, touched to tears.

Fenne's arms tightened. "You're almost my mother. Grandpapa understood that, but papa doesn't, somehow."

"It's all right," Lilz soothed. "It's all right," the age-old nonsense charm of a woman who knows too well that nothing is right.

"I wish I'd never *heard* of Kav Treadwell!" Fenne sobbed. "Everything's ruined, now."

"Chin up," Lilz said. "You've got a good chance. Your father has engaged the best counsel in Kinland and you're popular among the peers." The courtyard clock struck eight.

Fenne moaned. She stepped away from Lilz's embrace and sat down at the dressing table. "I guess we'd better get on with the hair, Aster," she said shakily. "Or, no, I want Lilz to do it. A plain woven braid, like papa said, only twirl the ends the way you used to?"

Lilz picked up the brush.

After breakfast, while Aster finished putting Fenne into her clothes, Lilz stood at one of the sitting room windows looking into the courtyard. Fenne, as a Peer of the Blood, would be tried in the Old Palace by any men of the peerage who wished to take part in her judgment. They had already begun to arrive. Lilz watched the bright cloaked figures ride into the yard, watched the servants lead the horses away and the men stand about in small groups waiting for the courtroom to open.

So the time had come. Even after all these months of expectation, of fear see-sawed with hope, Lilz couldn't quite believe it. A few ladies had come as spectators: the murmur of conversation below carried to her through the closed window. Almost as if a gala were on, as if these people would troop up to what had once been the throne room to dance as they'd danced in the new Hall on Presentation Day only a week before.

Two raps on the door: the dych. He strode into the room before Lilz could cross it and looked about. "Fenne?"

"Getting dressed, your Grace."

"Have you got a lunch packed for yourself?"

"No, sir."

"Pack one. This will be a long day and you'll surely be called to testify. Get yourself a good seat, as close to the front as you can." He plunked into one of the chairs and crossed his legs: in Court dress, with velvet trousers and a jacket stitched thickly with gold and blue silk, he was the picture of confidence. Lilz, heartened, went into the dressing room and opened the hamper.

"What are you doing?" Fenne asked, while Aster worked at her back with the buttonhook.

"His Grace your father has come. He bids me pack a lunch and get a good seat up front, in case I'm called to testify."

"No, stay with me."

"My mistress, your father—"

Fenne stamped a stockinged foot. "No. I want you with me right up till I have to go in. It's not as if they can't call you from wherever you happen to be!"

Lilz paused with a quarter loaf of bread in both hands. "Gladly, if you wish it, my mistress, but his Grace did say—"

"I'll take care of papa."

Lilz finished packing a lunch for Aster and herself. She left it in Aster's care and went to the bed chamber window. The courtroom had been opened. Some of the peers climbed the broad stone staircase she could just see at the end of the courtyard; others still stood about talking. Another half hour and Gudgeon—there he was now, riding into the yard at a trot with his nose in the air and a dozen men in his wake—Gudgeon would march into the courtroom, his secretary would sound the gong and the trial would begin. Lilz felt a thick excitement in her veins.

Behind her, a door opened.

She turned to see Summerlea staring at her. He had a blankness in his eyes like his father's. Frightening.

"Isn't she dressed yet?"

"Just coming, papa," Fenne called from the open dressing room.

"You were to hurry, Lilz."

"My mistress has asked me to stay with her."

"She's got me with her. Go."

In the old days, before King Lehrr the Prophet, the Peers of the Blood had taken as their personal servants others of their class, younger sons or unmatched daughters, sometimes merchants' children used to wealth. The servants' gallery in the old throne room occupied one side of the hall and reflected a different attitude toward those who served than did the secluded one of the New Palace. No screen divided this gallery from the nobility—only a low railing with several breaks in it. Rows of close-set chairs descended in tiers from the wall toward the festive-looking nobles, with the narrowest of aisles for access.

Lilz stood in one upper entrance. She'd come very late, after all. The gallery had been opened to spectators. It was packed: only one seat remained at the front, nigh under Gudgeon's eye. Getting to it would make a great disturbance. Indeed, in spots the way was blocked by people sitting on steps. Lilz stood against the wall beside the door, thinking that if she were called before the Lord Chief Justice she would make less stir if she didn't have to crawl across a dozen laps before gaining the aisle. The clock in the courtyard tower struck ten.

A flurry of motion near the dais seemed to herald the arrival of Gudgeon, but it was a false alarm: someone noticed that the sun shone through the high windows at the east end of the room right into the eyes of anyone sitting at the judge's table. Shades were drawn. The room became dim. A page ran up the steps of the dais and lit a lamp on the table. More lamps were lit and set at other small tables arranged at the foot of the dais. Lilz watched with interest. She had never before attended a trial. Would that be where Fenne was seated?

Now the gong sounded. Gudgeon ascended the dais, bowed to the peers, and sat behind the table. A small parade appeared from a side door: the prosecutor in his abbreviated red and cream cloak, Summerlea, the three counsel he'd hired, and Fenne, held between two large men who looked as if they felt rather foolish. Lilz started: Fenne was chained hand to foot. Everyone sat down.

The Lord Chief Justice nodded to his secretary, who came forward and began to read the charges against Fenne to a hushed audience. Lilz saw Greencrags near the front, his head tilted on knuckle and thumb. Clean-shaven, hair combed, clad in the rich fabrics of a Peer of the Blood, he could not have looked more different from the laughing young peasant of three days before. Lilz wondered what was going through his mind.

The secretary sat down.

"How do you plead, milady?" Gudgeon asked.

"Not guilty." Fenne's voice sounded like a child's. Well coached, Lilz thought.

The prosecutor stood and embarked upon a droning summary of the evidence he proposed to bring against Fenne Hasten, Lady Northlands, here accused of the willful murder of Sir Jen Makeready, and so forth and so on. And on. And on. Lilz caught her mind wandering. Even the accused yawned into her fist from time to time. At last the man came to a close and seated himself.

Fenne's counsel, all three of them, rose and conferred with old Gudgeon, who at first shook his head, then shrugged, then nodded. They returned to their seats. "Milady, you wish to address the peers on your own behalf?" Gudgeon inquired.

"Yes, your lordship."

"You may proceed."

Fenne stood. The chains rattled. She glanced at the peers, at the first few rows of servants, and at her father.

"Your lordship, I am unjustly accused," she said, in that high, clear voice. Small as she was, dressed as she was, in the dim light she looked scarcely old enough to have been presented. Lilz felt her mind snag on a thought—had Summerlea used his influence to schedule the trial at this time so the shades would be drawn, and Fenne have the benefit of the flattering light? She'd have believed it of his father without a second's reflection. Why not of the son? She glanced at him. He leaned back in his chair, in almost the same position as Greencrags two sashlengths away, a picture of attention.

"All the evidence brought against me can be read in two ways," Fenne continued, with perfect composure. "I wish to tell the peerage that I have in my household a bond-servant who has been with me all my life, whose affection for me has never wavered, and who would go to any length to secure my happiness."

Lilz felt for the wall behind her.

"The winter before his death, as you may remember, Sir Jen Makeready circulated a number of verses, caricatures"—Fenne stumbled over the word—"mm, car-i-ca-tures of members of the Court. Among them were several of me. My sole guilt in this matter is that I showed those verses to my servant, who became enraged on my behalf."

Don't panic, Lilz. She stepped softly sideways into the open door.

"I believe that my servant, out of misplaced loyalty, spoke to Onma Stump on one of the occasions when that woman had come to me in the course of her business, asking her to obtain some poison for the purpose of silencing Sir Jen. I am sure she made her request in my name in order to ensure the cooperation of Mistress Stump."

"Who is this servant?" Gudgeon interrupted. Lilz, from the corridor outside the gallery, heard Fenne say, "Her name is Lilz."

Don't panic. "Don't panic, don't panic," she felt herself mouthing as she moved along the deserted third-floor corridor hoping to look normal. Go get my clothes. Find a horse. No. *Don't panic.* Goldpiece in my pocket. Forget the clothes. Walk out normally.

No gate pass.

Footsteps behind her. *One of Summerlea's men.* Don't look. *Don't panic.* Stairs. Lilz started down. Which way out?

Footsteps still coming. How her heart hammered!

Lilz reached the second floor. Nobody here. *He'll think I've gone all the way down.* She scurried along the hallway. Hide. Where? *Don't panic.*

Running. *Too loud!* She forced herself to walk. Tried a door. Locked. Tried another. Locked. *This is a prison.* Sky above, couldn't they have left a warmth curtain on a single wall?

The man behind her started to run. *He's seen me.* Lilz darted forward. *No gate pass.* Catching up. She turned down a dark hallway to her right with not the slightest notion where she was going. A deep doorway beckoned to her. Door locked. Dark.

Maybe he'll run past. Head bowed against the heavy oak of the door, holding her breath, nearly choking on her pulse, she waited.

So quiet. Where is he?

He grabbed her.

Chapter Twenty-Three

His hand clamped over her mouth and pulled the back of her head to his shoulder. The scream she drew breath for became a shrill whine of protest.

"Lilz!" he whispered.

She pushed at his arms, struggling to twist out of his grasp.

"Lilz, stop! It's me."

Stone?

She stopped wriggling. He let go. She turned and burrowed her face into his shoulder. "Lilz, not now. We have to get out of here."

She released him instantly, gulping for breath, half sobbing. "Stone, I don't have a gate pass."

"I've got two. Come on."

He took her hand and led her quickly back to the main corridor, looked down its length, and pulled her away from the stairs. She ran with him past more doors, all closed, all surely locked. "Four, five," he gasped. "Here it is." This door opened onto a narrow staircase lit by a slit in the wall far above. She raced after him down worn limestone steps. At the bottom Stone turned, put a finger to his lower lip to caution her, and opened a second door.

Lilz squinted against bright sunlight. Stone strolled through the door. She followed. They were in the outer courtyard, a large grassy area where a few dozen servants stood about talking in small groups exactly as their masters had earlier. Some held the reins of still-saddled horses. Other mounts had been tethered to posts along the wall to her right. Stone pointed at them with his chin. She walked over to the row of horses, trying to look as relaxed as he did, trying not to look as if she might cry at any moment. Stone walked behind the line talking of nothing until he came to a fine bay with a saddlepad of Standfast green. He went past it and untied the same drab gelding he'd ridden to Waterside in the guise of a messenger, outfitted in the same anonymous tack. He reached into his pocket. "Here's your pass. You'll ride pillion. We'll leave by the postern gate."

"Yes," Lilz said breathlessly. She took the round metal pass in cold fingers and trailed Stone to the nearest mounting block. He swung into the saddle and smiled down at her.

"Up you come, now."

She fashioned a smile of her own and clambered onto the horse behind him, an arm around his waist for balance. "Pull your braid over your left shoulder," Stone told her. She did. "Sit close and slump a little." Stone guided the horse past the others at a leisurely walk and made for a small gate near the river side of the outer yard. He stopped at the lance held level across the break in the high yellow walls.

"Passes?" called the guard.

Stone held his upright in his fingers to display to the man. Lilz did the same. The guard nodded. Stone's pass landed in the collection bucket with a clink at almost the same moment as her own. Incredibly, the lance swung upright and the guard waved them on. The horse settled into the same kind of ground-eating walk with which her old favorite from Hasten House had carried her to House-Among-Oaks so long ago.

They rode along the riverside path at that unhurried pace for a hundred sashlengths or so, far enough for a bend to put them out of sight of the Old Palace gate. "Now we'd better move," Stone said over his shoulder. "Hang on." She felt his thigh muscles tighten. Their mount shifted into a smooth canter. "Left," Stone called a moment later, to warn her of a change of lead as they left the river path.

They clattered along an alley, the first of a maze even Lilz lost track of, now at a running walk that left no room for slips. The same reckless horsemanship as his master's, she thought, her face against Stone's sweating back. She circled Stone's ribs with both arms now, inhaling courage with the smell of him, afraid for him, for Greencrags, should anyone learn how he'd spirited her away from—

—From Fenne, that awful clear voice so quietly condemning the woman who had raised her to be hanged—

Lilz pressed her face into Stone's back.

He reached down and patted her knee. The horse slowed for a few sashlengths and stopped. "Here we are. Slide down and open the gate, can you?"

She dismounted jerkily, stumbling as she hit the ground, and opened the door into the yard of Standfast House. Stone walked the horse through. Lilz followed him in and shut the door.

"Bolt it."

Of course. The alley gate was always kept bolted. She remembered Stone's long fingers drawing the bolt back, the day they'd gone looking to see if someone had poisoned Greencrags. The same long fingers now caressed her cheek and lifted her chin. *Why does he look so sad?* "Go straight up to my master's rooms. Try not to let anyone see you. I'll be there in a few minutes."

Lilz nodded and went around by the walls to the servants' door as Stone called to the stable lad to come and cool down the horse. She put her head into the house, heard Reed talking in the kitchen, and closed the door behind her softly. A skivvy giggled.

Shoes in hand, Lilz went up the back stairs. At the second floor door she paused, listening. Downstairs, Reed's rolling laugh. She opened the door. No one in the hall. In twenty seconds she was standing in the middle of Standfast's sitting room, on the patterned green rug.

Blue draperies, whitewashed walls, the desk in the corner, all exactly as she had last seen them: unreal, something out of a dream she had just recalled having had many years ago.

She was still standing in the center of the room when Stone came in. He pulled her into an embrace and laid his cheek against her hair. "My poor Lilz," he said. "How horrible!"

"I'm all right." *Why is he so stiff?* She smiled one-sidedly. "Thanks to you. How did you rescue me so smoothly?"

"My master is most thorough." The corners of Stone's mouth twitched. "You taught him well, with that lesson of the Keeper of the Keys. He searched the library at Sweetdawn for information about the Old Palace as soon as Reed sent word about *her*. We found an old guide, from before the palace was a prison, accurate enough to show us where to look for a less-used exit. We thought something of this sort might happen, so we prepared to take whatever opportunity might arise."

"Those little stairs...the gate...."

"We did our exploring and rehearsed the route last Fairday, when we came up from Sweetdawn. We'd have come sooner, but Reed's message was delayed. I'll explain everything when there's more time." He smoothed a wisp of hair away from her face. "I have to go back. It's Rovvo's pass you used."

"Oh, of course. Stupid of me."

"You're just stunned. If you like, I'll fetch some tea before I go. The kettle's always on the boil, as you know."

"Thank you, yes."

Stone withdrew, as silently as if she were Greencrags himself. Lilz stood wondering what to do. To sit in one of the iarl's chairs without his direct invitation was an act of presumption she couldn't bring herself to. A fit of trembling came over her.

Stone returned with the tea. He'd brought buttered bread as well, but the sight of food sickened her. "Come into the bedroom," he said. He rested the tray on the end of the bed and pulled the iarl's breakfast table away from the window. "Sit down, Lilz," he told her, bringing the chair over. "You can't just stand there."

"No," she said distractedly. "No." Stone held the chair for her, something no one had done for twenty years, and set the tray on the table. Hot tears splashed down her cheeks. She wrung her hands in her lap and bowed her head.

"Lilz?"

"I've been telling myself—" A sob broke from deep in her chest. "I've—I've—" Stone put an arm across her shoulders; she leaned against his side and fought for control. "I've been telling myself for months, no, for years, that she might do this." She barely recognized her own voice. "I mean, I thought I believed she might, but I guess in my heart I didn't believe—"

"Shh." Stone went onto one knee beside her.

"Stone, I raised her from a baby. I was told I'd be her bond-servant when she was two days old."

"Take heart," Stone said. "My master will hear everything at the trial today. When he comes home we'll discuss what to do." She nodded. "He says, treat his rooms as your own. I'd add, don't light a lamp, don't show yourself at a window. Why don't you rest?"

Lilz glanced toward the bed.

"He won't be the least bit offended, don't you know that?" Stone smiled, a tight little smile. "Look at me—still here, despite the impurity of my vowels, one of *her* chief complaints." Lilz sighed. "Yes," Stone agreed. "I'm luckier than you." He gripped her chair to stand up. "Right now, though, I'd better get back to the Old Palace. I'm sure a furor broke out when you couldn't be found, and the lad can't leave without a pass *and* without a servant, not without attracting far too much attention."

"What will you do?"

"Make the best of the confusion as everyone leaves."

"Oh, Stone!"

"Don't worry." At the door, he paused. "If you can't bring yourself to rest on my master's bed, there's my cot in the dressing room. I"—he took a deep breath and looked away from her—"I won't mind your using that, either."

"What's wrong, Stone?"

"Later." He closed the door silently.

The tea was not the servants' tea: it was the fine tea imported from the Silk Countries reserved for the iarl and his guests, tea she scarcely ever tasted. Because Stone had learned who she was?

Worse yet, worse yet. To have Fenne betray her and Stone withdraw out of some misguided idea of respect, all in the same day? After all she had suffered in service to the Hastens?

By the time she had cried all the tears her heart insisted upon, Lilz was exhausted. The sun had stopped reflecting off the windows opposite and Greencrags had not yet come home. Was he still at the Old Palace, then, trying to explain why he and Stone had only one gate pass between them when a woman both knew was missing? She couldn't think about it. She wouldn't think about it. She sat for a few minutes staring at the shadowed facade across the street, her mind as blank as those windows. At last she got up and went into the next room.

Stone's cot smelled like Stone, solid and comforting. Eventually she fell asleep with his pillow hugged to her chest.

"Here she is."

Greencrags's voice. Lilz opened her eyes. A yellow light fell across the bed she rested on. Moving shadow blotted the light. Stone crouched beside her, his hand on her shoulder. "Lilz?"

"I'm awake."

"Is she dressed?" Greencrags.

"Yes."

Lilz turned onto her back, surprised. *Greencrags knows.* She reached for Stone's hand and pushed her own into it. After a moment he squeezed her fingers and sat on the edge of the cot. Was he remembering, too?

Fenne shrieking at Greencrags, Greencrags sitting his temper with obvious strain. Both slamming out of the house. As usual. Lilz was never quite sure how she had ended up here, whimpering with arousal and hope of sweet release, Stone's bare ass bucking under her spread hands, but she knew why: not out of love. Shared anguish, shared heartbreak had pushed her and Stone onto his cot. Afterwards, Stone had been contrite: he hadn't thought to ask how the moon lay with her. But they'd been lucky—in that respect at least. It wasn't lucky to discover themselves growing into real lovers. Not at all.

Greencrags wasn't nearly as dense as Fenne. He'd have noticed Stone's distress when Fenne took her bond-servant out of his house. Yes. Twice last winter he'd sent Stone to a meeting in his place, supposedly to discuss political strategy. The first time, Lilz had returned to Waterside almost at noon. Fenne had greeted her at the servants' door, grumbling about bandits coming down from the mountains and search parties nearly sent out. Lilz had claimed losing her way. She'd vowed never again to take an unmarked road, pointed out her mud-stained clothes and rushed upstairs to change, not only trousers but underwear, had washed herself quickly with the little water left in the pitcher before returning downstairs: Fenne, of all women, would recognize that odor. The second time, she and Stone had been more careful.

Now she sat up.

"How are you?" Stone sounded gentle.

"Still very tired. What happened?"

"The trial is continued until tomorrow." Greencrags brought the lamp into the room. "Do you mind?" he asked, gesturing at a chair.

"Mind, milord? The room is yours."

Greencrags sat down, his forehead wrinkled. "Exactly when did you leave?"

Oh, dear. Lilz leaned her head on her hands. "Gudgeon had just asked my name. I heard her say it when I was out in the hall."

"Ah. Well. Gudgeon asked a few more questions—your surname, which of course no one gave, who had bonded you, all that. By the time he was done I imagine you and Stone were on your way out the postern gate. It's more helpful than I'd have thought to have one of those nit-picking minds in charge, at times."

Lilz managed a smile.

"His last question, of course, was where you could be found. Summerlea got up and all but pointed to an empty seat in the front row. For some reason, he seemed to think you'd been in it. He began talking about how you'd made your escape when Fenne started her little speech, but Gudgeon himself had noticed the place was empty before the trial got under way."

Lilz sighed. "I was supposed to be there, milord. His Grace ordered me to take a lunch and get a good seat near the front, but when I got there the room was already crowded and I didn't want to climb over half the gallery. Oh!" She looked from the iarl to Stone. "I was too late because Fenne delayed me."

"The perils of chance," Greencrags said.

"No, she did it on purpose," Lilz said eagerly. "She knew what had been arranged. She was so sweet to me this morning, I almost cried. Did cry. Said she owed me...said I'd been almost her mother..."

"And stood before the Peers Assembled saying words she knew could cost you your life," Stone interrupted angrily.

Lilz turned to him. "Don't you see, Stone? She was scared. Summerlea showed Fenne the block yesterday. He must have done that to persuade her that she'd have to sacrifice me. But Fenne knew the plan. She kept me from sitting in that front seat on purpose. She gave me the only chance to escape she could devise."

"Some chance! Don't you think Milady Wicked's next step will be to say you've proven your guilt?"

"Stone, no."

"Open your eyes, Lilz. After hearing the prosecutor's summary and Milady Wicked's oh-it-must-have-been-my-servant even *I* wondered if I were rescuing a murderer!"

"Stone!"

"Please don't quarrel," Greencrags said softly. "I agree, Lady Northlands was extremely convincing, but if you recall, Stone, she is capable of being convincing about anything she chooses, including that the sky is green, the grass blue, and the husband she kept off at dagger's point either impotent or interested only in humping his faithful manservant."

Stone nodded, slumped. "Forgive me, Lilz," he whispered. She hitched around to sit beside him on the edge of the cot and leaned against him. "Go on," she told Greencrags, as Stone's hand cupped her shoulder blade.

"His Grace called to the gallery for you to come down. You didn't, of course. Gudgeon got a description and sent a couple of guards out to look for you. After awhile he ordered that the trial go on. We heard a deposition from Clock, so conveniently slaughtered and his shop so conveniently burned out, though not before Gudgeon had secured his records. The counsel Summerlea hired brought objections to every phrase of the King's case, all of them denied after due deliberation. An extraordinarily dreary day."

Greencrags blew out his cheeks. "At least Makeready died without sons, so if she's found guilty we'll be spared any hoopla over inheritance. That would take all winter."

"True." Lilz had focused so closely on Fenne and her own danger, the question of inheritance had never entered her head. "Tell me, milord, how did you get out of the prison with but one pass?"

Greencrags laughed. "Show her, Stone."

Stone stood up with a half-smile and took something out of his pocket. In his hand, in the lamplight, it looked like a gate pass, but when he gave it to Lilz she saw that it was only a piece of thin board cut to size and painted to roughly resemble a genuine pass.

She handed it back. "I don't understand."

Stone tossed the disc at the cot. Lilz looked to see where it had landed, but it was hidden. She raked the folds of the sheet with her fingers and found no disc.

"It's in your ear," Greencrags said.

"What?"

Stone reached toward her and drew the disc out of the air beside her left ear. She'd have sworn his hand had been empty. The iarl laughed. "Wonderful trick, isn't it? He used to entertain me whole rainy afternoons when I was little. The other day I did a rubbing of a real pass and we made this over the weekend."

"But—"

"If you ride through the gate in the company of a Peer of the Blood, showing something that looks like a pass to the man you've made sure noticed giving you one only hours before, motion as if you've thrown it into a bucket in which others are landing, and seem empty-handed afterward, the assumption—"

"I see," Lilz said, doubtful.

"And when the passes are counted, as some poor fool is surely doing at this very moment, no counterfeit is found and none is missing," Greencrags added. Lilz began shaking her head. "So many issued, so many returned."

"You two will kill yourselves with your cleverness someday!" Lilz protested. "What if the light had been brighter, or the guard more diligent? What if Stone had *dropped* it?"

"I couldn't have dropped it," Stone said. "It was on a thread, then."

"Tessen Strengthen was prepared to create a diversion, and you can imagine what a few hooves landing on the thing would have done to it," Greencrags added. "Don't be upset, Lilz. We're all here. We're all safe."

Still unhappy, Lilz abandoned the argument. "What happens tomorrow?"

"Tomorrow Onma Stump is to testify."

"She'll agree with Fenne, of course," Lilz said. "She has her own life to secure."

"If she keeps it through the night," Stone remarked.

"If she keeps it through the night," Greencrags agreed, starting to stroke the beard he no longer wore. "What's all this paper you've been sending me, Lilz?"

"It falls into two categories, milord. One is the material about the New Palace—Makeready's notes, Kav Treadwell's map, and the journal kept by the twelfth Summerlea. The other—"

I'm as bad as the Hastens, Lilz thought. Guarding my prospects as they do, with guile and treachery. She sighed. "The rest of it I thought would protect me from just the sort of thing that happened today. Did you look at the ledger I gave you?"

"I glanced through it, but it just looks like an ordinary daily record of expenses."

"That's exactly what it is."

Someone knocked on Greencrags's bedchamber door. Stone went out and came back carrying a tray with a teapot, three cups, and a pile of sandwiches on a plate.

"Why give the ledger to me?"

"For safekeeping. Did you look at entries for when Makeready was in prison?" The iarl, his mouth already around a sandwich, nodded. "You'll see twenty-two payments to Onma Stump for sundries. Each of them follows by a day or two one of Evin Clock's notations of poison sold to Mistress Stump for Fenne, and precedes by one day a notation of food sent to the Old Palace for Makeready."

"O.P.?" Greencrags asked.

Lilz nodded. The young iarl whistled and looked into his empty cup. "Why not just burn the thing? Stone, are you hatching that pot?"

Stone held the teapot by spout and handle. He looked as if he had been stabbed in the heart and hoped to stop the rush of blood by pressing the pot to his chest.

"It's not how it seems," Lilz said. Greencrags stood up and took the teapot from his servant. "Sit down," he said gently.

With Stone again beside her and the iarl pouring tea, Lilz said, "Summerlea himself told me to destroy the ledger. He had second thoughts the next day, but I'd burned a blank one and Fenne assured him it was this one, as I'd let her think." Greencrags nodded. "He believes I discarded the poison, you see."

"Ah," Greencrags said. "But?"

"In that tin box you have are twenty-two paper envelopes containing a white powder said to be a deadly toxin, sealed with Evin Clock's seal and dated in his hand, many with instructions from Fenne and one with a note from Onma Stump to Fenne. The seals of all but one are unbroken."

Greencrags put the teapot down carefully. "You wanted to see what it looked like."

Lilz smiled faintly. "Yes, milord."

"And the contents?"

"Still there, intact."

A knock sounded on the hall door. Stone and Greencrags exchanged a glance. Stone went to the door. "Your pardon, milord," Reed said in his most sonorous voice. "Meadowlands and his cousin, Lord Säen, are downstairs asking to speak to you."

Greencrags thrust a cup at Lilz and hurried her into his bed chamber. She set the cup down behind the partly open door and looked through the hinge-side crack.

"I told them I thought you'd retired early," Reed continued, from the hall. The iarl was stripping as fast as he could, flinging his clothes over the back of the chair. Stone moved to hang them up. "But they pressed most urgently," Reed said. "Shall I tell them to leave?"

"Not necessary, Reed," Lilz heard Ruppet say. "If he's awake, we'll talk to him."

Reed made a brief objection, stopped by Greencrags's saying, "Sky above, let them in," in a disgusted tone. "You might have waited until I got my nightshirt on," she heard him complain. "What's eating you, Ruppet?"

"We want to talk to Lilz. Where is she?"

"Fenne's too-zealous servant?" Greencrags laughed. "Go ask your sister. Or your father. Both far more likely to know where to find her than I."

Säen said, "How did you do it, Standfast? Not one gate pass is missing. But a boy in Hasten blue went out the postern gate riding pillion to someone whose description resembles your man here."

"The descriptions of half the men in Miense resemble my man. What's a boy wearing some shade of blue got to do with your sister's servant, Meadowlands?"

"Her hair could have been cut. Lilz's, that is." Lilz touched her braid. Pulled over her shoulder, it might look short, glanced at from behind. Did Greencrags think of everything? Or was that Stone? "She's certainly skinny enough to be taken for a boy."

"I haven't barbered anyone today." Greencrags sounded amused. "Have you, Stone?"

"No, milord. Except that I shaved you this morning."

Säen's voice came closer. "Maybe it wasn't cut, Ruppet. This could belong to Lilz." She squatted into shadow, to look up through the crack without showing her face. Säen plucked something invisible from Stone's cot and held it up.

"A hair? Stone's a man like any other," Standfast said lightly. "Did you come home while the trial was on, by any chance, Stone?"

"Yes, milord."

"For what purpose?"

"That which you have surmised." Stone sounded embarrassed.

"What color horse did you ride?" That was Ruppet, as always too self-absorbed to be aware of any double meaning. After a moment, Greencrags prompted, "Stone?"

"The gray, milord, as you know."

A short silence followed. "Here's a thought, Meadowlands," her host said. "Where's that guitar of Lilz's?" She winced. *Imprisoned.*

Ruppet said, "I don't know."

"If she hasn't got it, go sit by it. Now that I think back, I seem to recall that she values that thing next to her life. Use it as bait. Mouse to bacon, Lilz to sheepgut."

"There's an idea," Ruppet said slowly.

"Which I point out to you out of the bounty of my heart," Greencrags said. "Since you carry your nose too high to see it and your sister hasn't the wit. Now, will you gentlemen leave my house on your own feet, or shall I have Reed call my guards?"

"Well." Standfast ran his hand up the back of his head. "That was certainly unexpected."

"I told you long ago not to underestimate them, milord."

"It does present some problems." The iarl sat down and buttoned the cuffs of his nightshirt. "I'd intended to have you out of here tonight. Now I suppose that's not possible."

"They'll surely be watching the house," Lilz agreed.

"Stone, go arrange the lights to warn off Lealands, will you?" Standfast leaned his elbows on his knees as his body-man went into the hall. He looked up at Lilz. "There's your clothes, too. I hadn't anticipated that you'd be wearing their color. If you were fatter, I could dress you up in something of mine with the cuffs rolled, but as it is..."

"If you mean to hide me somewhere, I'll have another problem in two or three days, milord." The iarl raised his eyebrows. "I'll need some rags."

"Oh. I'd forgotten about that, too." He sighed. "Well, we'll find something. Heaven knows I have enough maids. Tonight you can wear one of my nightshirts. When Stone comes back we'll sort out the beds. Before we go to the Old Palace tomorrow I'll find you something to read.... Maybe you'll try making sense of all that stuff you've sent me. Then, after the trial...." He raised his hand as if to stroke the beard he'd once had, but leaned on it instead, his fingers over his mouth.

"Stone was right, milord," Lilz said, after gazing at him for several silent minutes. "That family bears a poison as lethal as any they ever bought from Evin Clock." Standfast glanced at her without moving. "What it kills is honor, self-respect, loyalty, affection. If Fenne Hasten had remained with you, you'd have been eaten into a shell from the heart out. Just as surely as I have been, despite my struggles."

He nodded twice. Sighed heavily. "I think you're far too hard on yourself, Lilz," he said, as Stone came into the room.

Chapter Twenty-Four

She heard Greencrags call something down the stairs to Reed. So Greencrags was home. With a glance at the papers she had scattered over his desk and the nearby floor that morning, Lilz stood to greet him as he entered the room. He looked weary and upset, although it was only early afternoon.

"What happened, milord?" she asked. "Is it over?"

He sighed and nodded. "Guilty."

"Was the margin great?"

Greencrags shoved his hands into his pants pockets and walked over to the windows. Light reflected from the house across the street made his velvet coat look dusty and the glow of his white lace jabot gave his face a fragile look. "More black tokens than red, but only a single white," he said after a moment. Lilz closed her eyes. "None of the Hastens could vote, of course, but Northlands did, though it's arguable whether he has the right."

"That accounts for the white token, then," Lilz remarked.

"No." Greencrags took a deep breath. "That one was mine."

"Yours, milord?"

He glanced at her. "I was one of the last to vote. None of the men who went to the box before me looked at Lady Northlands as they came down from the platform. Not one. Not even Kav Treadwell. I thought the balance might tip toward immediate execution, so—" The iarl rubbed his fingertips across his eyelids and looked at them with a frown. "It seemed a small gift."

"You are a generous man, Rovvo Standfast."

"Not really. Just not especially vengeful." Shrugging, he turned toward her. "With the black majority, though, who knows what Guyr will decide?" He sniffed. "He may even give her back to Northlands unharmed."

"Making your gift the more valuable."

"Possibly." Greencrags smiled briefly. "You haven't asked about your own interests, Lilz. Onma Stump testified that the whole plan was Fenne's, perhaps nudged by her grandfather, who seems to have used this solution to other problems. But she also said you carried out the actual poisoning on Fenne's orders. Gudgeon's put out a warrant for you. You'll have to stand for trial."

Lilz nodded, surprised only at the court costumer's daring.

"Lealands is coming over in a little while. We can talk strategy with him. I think with Clock's records, Lady Northlands's accounts and those envelopes, you may well get off. Unless milady decides to bring a charge of theft, but that's unlikely even for her, I'd think."

"I have never pretended to know what Fenne would do next," Lilz sighed. "Where's Stone?"

"Getting us something to eat."

Lilz closed her eyes, her head bowed to her tightly clasped hands. "I'm afraid I'm not very hungry, milord," she said.

The Dych of Lealands showed up alone in mid-afternoon. He was even balder and grayer than Lilz remembered him, with a spray of lines at the outside corner of each blue eye suggesting that his expression was not usually quite so somber.

"I talked to my counselor, who has a few ideas and some questions, but the fewer visitors on your doorstep, the better, I thought," he said to Greencrags, and to Lilz, "Ah, yes, I remember you, now. Rovvo's spoken of you, of course — your idea to search the histories for any granted rights and duties of a Keeper of the Keys let lapse, wasn't it?"

"Yes, your Grace, it was," Lilz acknowledged.

"I wish I'd seen old Summerlea's face when Rovvo applied for his place on the Privy Council!" Strengthen chuckled. "Nevan must have gone home and had kittens. Imagine him getting slapped with a fish two centuries old! Just shows the uses of history." He surveyed the room. "I assume you and Stone checked for whizzers, Rovvo? Good. Shall we start?"

Stone had set chairs for all of them near the desk, on which the things Lilz had sent Greencrags were now piled. "You'll think it odd to have Stone sitting in," Strengthen continued, taking a chair and picking up a paper at random. "But I've known him many years. He's a most insightful man."

"Yes, your Grace, I know." Greencrags gestured toward a chair. She sat down, as did he and Stone.

"Now." The dych cocked his head at her. "The first thing we have to know is who you are."

Lilz glanced at Stone, at Greencrags, back at Lealands, whose barely visible eyebrows now rose in a question. "I'm Lilz."

"Yes, yes," Strengthen said. "But you have a surname, or at least you did before Nevan Hasten got hold of you. What is it?"

She felt her eyes drawn to Stone.

"Come, Lilz, we can't go any farther without knowing. The whole plan for your defense may hinge on it," Lealands insisted.

All three men waited with expectant expressions for her to speak.

After a time Lilz cleared her throat. "It's Chantwell."

"Lilz *Chantwell*?" The dych goggled at her. "Sky above, not Darkforest's daughter! Oh, dear, yes, I see the resemblance now, though you've got your mother's coloring. My dear, dear girl! All these years I've thought you were dead!"

Stone hadn't known. Stone's eyes had shut. His face was turned slightly away. He looked pale. Lilz wanted to reach out and touch him, but Greencrags was in the way, Greencrags with his eyebrows high and his head shaking.

"You can't be a bond-servant," Strengthen declared. "Oerl wasn't Guyr by a long shot. He'd never have signed such papers for you, not even to favor Summerlea."

"In fact, your Grace, I'm not, but I learned that only a few months ago." *Oh, Stone! Look at me!* "For twenty years I thought I had bonded myself to the Hastens in a perfectly normal way."

"What are you to them? Did you find out?"

"I was a hostage for my father's word. I don't know any more about it than that. I've asked my brother Clâes, but he doesn't know, either."

"Hostage, mm? Why, I wonder?" Strengthen frowned: his forehead puckered, but his scalp remained smooth and shining. "Something not so important to the new dych as to the old, I suppose," he mused, "or they wouldn't have tried the line they did yesterday."

"I puzzled that out this morning, your Grace." Lilz put a hand to her face and paused, eyes again shut. Her temples throbbed. She had a sense of the earth shifting beneath her, of the serpent the old myths said was coiled at the base of the world waking, rising in smoke and darkness to hunt. The thought took her breath away.

"I think my father never went to the New Lands," she said, when she could go on. "I think he was held in the Old Palace. That's why I was made to lead the horse last winter, when Nevan Hasten died. So that my father could look down from the Old Palace and see that I was still in the Hastens' power, that the new dych knew why I had been placed there. Sometime between then and now, my father died." Greencrags reached over and grasped her hand. "Therefore they can now do with me as they please."

"No…no." Lealands looked puzzled. "What hold could your father have had on Olen Hasten, to make him agree to break the chain?"

"It was the old dych's idea, your Grace, not his son's."

"But you see what it means." Lilz shook her head. "My dear girl, with the chain broken, the Hastens are Dychs of Summerlea only at the pleasure of the king, not by ancestral right. The difference between the Iarl of Northlands and the Iarl of Greencrags, you see?"

"But—"

"That's exactly why the phrase was added to the investiture. Don't you recall the stir?"

"But I handed the reins—"

"To Olen Hasten at the entrance to the cemetery, yes, and he rode the horse away. I suppose they thought that might protect them. No. It's the full procession before the people that's necessary, their view of the new dych taking his father's place. I can't imagine any Hasten would agree to let you lead the horse simply as a signal."

"But it's the only idea that even begins to make sense." She looked at Greencrags, who patted her hand and withdrew his own. "Why my father should live so long, when the Hasten tribe is so quick with their poisons, I don't know, but what else is there?"

A short silence produced no other suggestions.

"Thirty years in prison." Lealands sighed. "I'd be sorry to learn that was so. Your father was a fine man."

"Not the whole thirty years, your Grace. At first he was free; it was only that he was forbidden any contact with the peerage. But he used to go away from time to time. One of those times he just didn't come back." Lilz shifted in her chair. "At first my mother thought he'd been caught talking with a friend and thrown into prison, but a month or so later she got a letter saying he'd decided to take his chances in the New Lands. But Clâes says the letter seemed fresh, as if it hadn't come far—not all bedraggled, like the one he had from our brother in Newton. So maybe Mother was right. Maybe Father was imprisoned. I was nearly fourteen, then, so that would be twenty-four years."

Strengthen considered this. "Unlikely, Lilz, I'm sorry to say. No, something else was going on in that procession. As you point out, murder of a man in prison isn't difficult. If Lady Northlands had a quarter the wiliness of her grandfather, no one would have thought twice about Sir Jen Makeready's death."

"And I wouldn't be caught in her net."

"True. *If* we can prove you were their hostage, though," Strengthen said, his eyes narrowing, "it would make a great difference to the conduct of your trial. They'd have to stay out of it, all of them, the cousins, too."

"I sent the proof to Stone."

"To me!" Stone whispered. The dych transferred his gaze to him.

"Well, Stone, let's have it."

"Your Grace, I don't know what she means."

"It's those pages cut from an old ledger that I sent you in early summer," Lilz told him. He shook his head. "A packet tied in blue flimsy?"

"Oh." Stone went into the dressing room without looking at her and returned with the still-tied packet. Strengthen opened it and glanced through the pages. "Trust Hasten not to invest any money for you," he remarked. "You don't happen still to be virgin, I suppose."

"No. The old man made sure of that at his first opportunity," Lilz said, with more rancor than she'd known she felt.

Strengthen nodded. "Just what I'd expect of him. How did this fall into your hands?"

"It didn't exactly fall." She explained: Greencrags's offer to buy her, her own curiosity about the exact terms of her bonding—"That should be in your papers," the dych interrupted—her exploration while Quern had gone to town.

"Is that when you stole the old journal?" Greencrags asked.

"No, that was later. And that led to something almost too strange to believe. I'll tell you someday, if you wish."

"Let's hear it now," Strengthen ordered. "It may be relevant."

"I doubt it." He made an impatient gesture, so she went on. "You must have noticed, milord, that old Ruppet spoke of something called an *antran*, as Makeready did in his notes?" Greencrags nodded. "I went looking for the one at Summerlea, along with a guard called Raven. We found it. Raven went through it somehow—at least, that's how I think of it, since *antran* is Travaltian for 'gate'—but all memory of the experience was gone when he came back."

"As with the dych's Wyllym?" Greencrags conjectured. Nothing would do now but the whole story, which Lilz told as briefly as she could, questioned by Strengthen and the iarl.

"Transposition request acknowledged," Strengthen repeated. "What do you suppose that could mean?"

"At the time, I wondered if it were some strange way to travel to the New Palace. Something that matches the whizzers and spies and the galloping stars and the Jewel of the King, but—"

"The Jewel of the King?"

"Kav Treadwell once told me it's really a device for making the voice loud. It doesn't have to be used by the king. He and Prince Jath got hold of it once and played with it, he said, and Guyr nearly skinned them alive with his tongue."

"Sky above," the dych murmured. "No wonder Treadwell's become so arrogant. But go on."

"The *antran*...I've thought about this a lot lately," Lilz said. "My mistress—that is, Lady Northlands—gave me some fine hookwork to do about a month ago. It's the same pattern, over and over, so to estimate my progress I counted the repetitions at the end of each day." Lilz found herself flexing her fingers and folded her hands in her lap. "Somehow one day I began thinking of a question Nevan Hasten asked me summer before last. He was very ill; he wasn't expected to live, but that time he rallied. Before that, though, he sent for me to come from Waterside, just to ask me one question: how many Kinlands are there?"

"How many *Kinlands*?" Greencrags exclaimed.

"My exact question, milord, in my exact tone." Lilz saw that she had Stone's attention. She smiled, but he looked away. "I'm not going to explain this very well, because I can't quite get it clear in my own mind. But suppose there are many Kinlands, next to one another somehow, like the scales of a lump of mica. You know how a dark stain can go through the lump, so if you peel the layers apart one doesn't look much different from the next, yet each is just a little different, and after ten or twenty layers the stain isn't at all the same shape.... Suppose there are also many worlds, each a little different from the next, lying nested together somehow, and men from one of those other layers, one of those other worlds, have learned how to travel to ours."

Lilz stopped talking. None of the men said anything. "I—it's just an idea. But do you remember that peculiar housemaid sent to Sweetdawn, milord?"

Greencrags rolled his eyes, as did Stone.

"Suppose she came from that other Kinland, or whatever it's called in that world. That would explain why she spoke so oddly, why she asked so many questions. They've come to study us, and she was one of their natural philosophers."

"Rather ineffective," the iarl commented.

"She might have been new at it. There are others I've seen and wondered about. A man at the palace who fled from me, twice. A vikent with a strange accent I thought at the time might be a country tongue."

"Then the whizzers are theirs." Stone sounded as if he had just resolved a life-long perplexity.

"Yes. I thought I saw the housemaid talk to one at Sweetdawn, then go downstairs and throw it into the air. Brook and I talked me out of the notion—or I did—but now I'm sure of it. And there's more."

Lealands squinted at her. "Go on."

"Last spring Meadowla—I mean, the new Summerlea—rode out to Summerlea Manor. Clock had just been arrested. The dych wanted to know exactly what Fenne had done to Jen Makeready. During the interview he got very drunk—"

"The man never could hold his liquor," Strengthen muttered.

"—Somehow the conversation came around to religion, to the old rumor that the Hastens cling to the Mothergod. Which is true, by the way. He said the worship of the Fathergod is an experiment, like the natural philosophers do. He said the royals know all about it. I tried to get him to explain, but he clammed up."

"I should think so," Lealands said, after another long silence. "What a petard!"

"I don't know..." Lilz stared unhappily at the rug, tracing the stems of the flowers with her eyes. "It's always so hard to tell if someone is talking about something he *knows*, or just about something he's surmised and come to believe...."

"That's true."

"On the other hand, the Hastens have always been closely connected with the Crown. The dych who kept the journal I sent you had a sister, milord. Her name was Fenne. She was the queen of Lehrr the Prophet."

Greencrags was leaning on the arm of his chair, chewing his left little fingernail. "Is there more?" he asked.

"You see the relation to the door Kav Treadwell found. The one he says bites."

"Yes, I saw that from the journal. And don't forget Makeready's notes—you saw them, Merrow. They tie into this, too." He flicked a glance at Stone and folded the bitten finger into his fist. "Well."

"You surely also see how these people, just by their presence, with their jewels that magnify speech and their whizzers and galloping stars and small spies, have twisted the paths of power in Kinland," Lilz went on. "We have been raised to believe all those things distinguish the monarch from the rest of us. That's exactly why the tradition of all the Peers of the Blood meeting to elect the best king of the royal line fell into disuse. But if they aren't royal powers granted by the Father? If some other-worlders came to King Lehrr and offered all the royal powers in exchange for a protected place in Kinland? If one of them, perhaps, proclaimed himself a god, or was so taken by Lehrr, who confused him with the Engenderer?"

Again, the three men were silent for some time. Again, Strengthen was first to speak. "Your father had something similar to say, long ago," he remarked, "but he didn't say it as clearly as you have. I didn't understand what he was getting at, and then I was off as envoy to Megetsa the following day. When I got home, a year later, he'd been banished. I wouldn't be surprised if he'd discovered what you have, and that was the cause of his banishment, given the Hasten involvement."

"Could that be the hold that gave me the reins of that horse?"

"In that case, your father was lucky not to be hanged by his bowels for treason. Never underestimate the Hastens."

"They couldn't try him before the Blood, don't you see?" Lilz said. "Too much might be revealed. I think that's what killed Prince Jath. Summerlea, the old Summerlea, swore he'd never accept Jath as king, because the prince had mistreated Fenne. I actually heard him say that the Peers Assembled could elect a monarch out of the strict succession. But I think his real reason was that when Fenne asked for her favor back, Prince Jath put on that atrocious display at open Court. Nevan Hasten must have seen how unreliable the prince might prove. So he was doubly determined that Jath not be elected king."

"But for that, he'd have had to convince three-fourths of the Blood that Jath didn't have some sort of extra-human capacities out of power of his father's loins," Strengthen pointed out.

"Yes, exactly. So he did the easier thing and poisoned him." Lilz half laughed. "Ironic, isn't it? My father discovered their secret, so to keep it close they brought me right into its center, and now I've found it out."

"I think we should keep it close a little longer," Strengthen said. "It's dangerous knowledge in a number of ways, if true, and cause for charges of treason if not. In any case I doubt it will be useful to your defense—which is what I came to discuss. Time's short. The longer we delay turning you over to Gudgeon, the guiltier you look.

I think now you should give yourself up at the City House tomorrow morning—Rovvo or I will go with you. When Gudgeon grants you a hearing, tell him who you are. That will cast your trial to the Blood. A delay, but your best chance, in my opinion. We'll have to hope the ledger pages will be proof enough satisfy his lordship."

"I have my birthnote and my orders of servitude, in the box with the envelopes of poison."

"Ah." Strengthen put his hands on his knees and nodded at her. "Good girl. Yes, bring those."

"And my father's signet. That should go to Clâes, really. No one has heard from my other brothers for years."

"You keep it for now. Rovvo, walk downstairs with me, will you? I want a quick word with you."

The iarl and his once-guardian left. Stone sat with his hands loosely folded in his lap. "Look at me, Stone, please?" Lilz begged.

He raised his eyes. They were wet. "If you so wish, milady."

"Don't milady me, Stone. I'm Lilz."

Stone's hands flopped helplessly. "You are Lilz Chantwell, the daughter of a iarl."

"I'm Lilz, plain and simple, twenty years a servant." She stood up. "Stone, please. I'm not a lady. I was never even presented."

Since she was on her feet, he also stood: the perfect servant. She put her arms around him. He turned his head away. "Stone? Please? I knew who I was last night. I thought you did, too."

"Ah, if only..." He disengaged himself. "But you're a Peer of the Blood, Lilz Chantwell. Someday you may reclaim your birthright. I'm only Beor Stone and that's all I'll ever be."

"May is a long way from will, Beor Stone," she protested. "And someday may not come before I'm dead. How many full moons do you think I've slept under, to value 'may someday' or anything 'may someday' might bring over the chance to love a man like you?"

Stone took a long breath. "And if someday comes tomorrow?"

"Then the day after tomorrow I'll be Lilz Chantwell, a Peer of the Blood, the crown of whose life would be to love and be loved by Beor Stone, a man of better heart, wit and honor than the sum of any dozen of those jackasses with frills on their shirts."

"Well said," said Greencrags. "If humbling."

Lilz turned. Greencrags stood just inside the door. He looked stricken. "I beg your pardon, milord. I didn't realize you'd come back."

The iarl shut the door behind him. He brushed at his perfectly starched jabot, a fine example of embroidery-in-air, and met her eyes. "I'd rip the lace off every shirt I own if it would give you a better opinion of me, Lilz."

"You're as crazy as Stone!" she burst out. "D'you think I'd be here if I thought *you* a jackass?"

The iarl grinned. "What a pair you are! Lilz, don't you see Stone wishes he'd heard your name from you without a couple of peers in the room? Stone, don't you see she thought you'd open that packet the minute you got it? Now apologize, both of you, and make up. This is no time to be at loggerheads."

No. Lilz suddenly saw the three of them as Merrow Strengthen might. "A pair we may be," she said, "but I think we're well matched by a young iarl I know." Stone, bless him, chuckled, and they were over the ridge, riding easy again.

The brick floor of the waiting room of the City House was barely visible under a layer of mud and broken straw dotted with spittle. Jammed between Lilz and a filthy young woman who sucked constantly at a crooked tooth, Standfast leaned forward, his brocade-clad elbows planted firmly on gray velvet trousers, his eyes on the people tramping past on their way to one kind of city business or other. Almost without exception, those people turned to look at him, an odd bird perched on the plain wooden bench, canary among sparrows. Lilz sat upright and watched the iarl.

She was wearing very dirty Hasten blue with a three-cornered tear in one knee—ever authentic, Stone had ridden down to the river to fetch a hawthorn twig to do the ripping. Carefully, Lilz reviewed the story she might need: where she had hidden in the Old Palace, how she had moved to escape the search before slipping out in the middle of last night, her long jog along the riverfront, which trees she had used for cover when others came by. How she had walked into the courtyard of Standfast House before dawn and asked for the iarl. How Reed had instantly called the guards. *Poor Reed!* How he had resented his role in that fiction, after all his loyalty!

Lilz bowed her head. If Stone could be with her! But Stone had been left at home: Lealands and Greencrags both thought it dangerous for him to be connected with her at all, considering what the postern gate guard had reported. Lilz concurred. But she was greedy for second-hand courage, even with Standfast's warm thigh pressed against hers. She'd feared even he wouldn't come back, she reminded herself. Earlier, in the disgusting little cell waiting for afternoon and Gudgeon, alone with six others, she had been afraid she had traded her life for nothing after all. But Rovvo Standfast had come ten minutes early, bringing her proofs with him.

"Lilz, bond-servant to Lady Northlands," the doorkeeper called.

"Here we go." Standfast put a hand under her elbow to steady her. "Chin up. Remember, he's a Ridehard."

Lord Chief Justice Gudgeon sat at a heavy oak table in the hearing room. Although dressed formally, he lacked the splendor he'd donned for Fenne Hasten: Lilz ranked with the common felons, and owed this quick audience only to becoming embroiled in a case involving the nobility.

Gudgeon peered at her. *He's short-sighted*, she realized. He hadn't let on in the Old Palace. "You are Lilz, bond-servant to Fenne Hasten, Lady Northlands?" He sounded bored.

"That is how I have been known, your lordship."

"What are you doing here, Greencrags?"

"Milady came to me with a strange tale and hope of protection." Greencrags bowed his head slightly. "Having heard her story I am convinced that she is innocent of the slander we both heard the day before yesterday, as is our good friend Merrow Strengthen." Gudgeon blinked. "We thought it best for her to come to Common Court and establish her identity before you as a first step toward clearing her name."

"Milady?" Gudgeon frowned at Lilz. "Does he mean you?"

"He does, your lordship, though he exaggerates somewhat. I was never presented."

"Should you have been?" Gudgeon's eyebrows climbed. "Who are you?"

Greencrags gave her an encouraging poke. "I am Lilz Chantwell, daughter of Dilyn Chantwell Peer of the Blood, the Iarl of Darkforest in banishment."

"Chantwell." *He's never heard of him*, Lilz thought, her heart sinking. "Ah, yes. What a long time ago! Have you proof of your claim to the Blood, miss?"

Lilz brought out her papers. "May I come to you, your lordship?" At his nod, she stepped up to the table and placed her birthnote before him.

"It's Lilz Chantwell's, all right, and you look about the right age, but how do I know that's you?"

"My orders of servitude." Her voice shook. Gudgeon took the papers and studied them. Frowning, he went back to the first page, then re-read the second.

"One moment." He beckoned to an elderly secretary. "Go sit down."

Lilz sank onto the front bench next to Greencrags, clutching each hand with the other. Gudgeon showed her orders to the secretary, who looked straight at her and murmured some reply. "I thought so," Gudgeon said. The secretary shuffled out of the room with her orders in his hand. The Lord Chief Justice picked up a stack of other papers and began reading.

"What's happening?" Lilz whispered to Standfast.

"I think he's looking up the record of your bond," he whispered back. "Courage." He covered her hands with his own. They were cold.

A long time later the secretary returned. Gudgeon leaned over to hear what he had to say, staring the while at Lilz. When the man was done reporting, Gudgeon beckoned. Lilz went back to the table.

"These papers are counterfeit," the Lord Chief Justice announced. "Not only are they not on the official printed form, the signature of King Oerl differs from its known appearance, although the signature of Nevan Hasten, sixteenth Dych of Summerlea looks genuine enough to me, and Father knows I've seen it often enough. No record of bondage of Lilz Chantwell, or any other Lilz, to the Hasten family can be found for that year or for two years either side of that date. You understand? You were duped. You were never a bond-servant."

"Yes, your lordship. I know that."

"But you spent twenty years with the family, as Lady Northlands pointed out at her trial."

"I discovered my situation only last spring. I have this..." Lilz, with a breath, set the ledger pages before the judge and pointed to the first entry of her name. "The hand is Nevan Hasten's."

"Hostage?" Gudgeon squinted at her. "What are these, old ledger pages? Where did you get them?"

"I stole them."

Gudgeon flashed her a severe look from under his thick eyebrows. He spread the pages beside the orders of servitude, glancing from one to the other, saying, "hmmm, hmmm," under his breath. "Well," he said at last. "Do you request trial by the Blood?"

"I do."

"I'll have to check the calendar, but you can probably expect to stand within a couple of weeks. You keep these." He handed the papers back. "They'll be part of your evidence, I have no doubt. Do you have counsel?"

"Yes, your lordship," Lilz said, weak with relief.

"Very well. You'll be notified. Guard? This prisoner will be transferred to the Old Palace to await trial."

Lilz went in chains through the streets where all her life she had lived freely, was signed in and led up to the second floor of the prison. A single tiny room looking out on a vent shaft would be her lot. All she could say for it was that it was almost clean.

Chapter Twenty-Five

Morning arrived with a head-splitting pounding at the door. Lilz jumped from the cot still half asleep, calling out, "What is it?"

"Porridge," said a gravelly voice. Greasy gray curls surrounding a woman's gray-pudding face appeared around the edge of the door. "Got a bowl?"

"No," Lilz said. Her stomach growled. "No, I don't."

"Ah, well, c'mere." The head vanished. Lilz went to the door in time to see the woman give a stir to a vast kettle of goo set in a barrow she had parked in the hall. She plopped a ladleful into a wooden bowl twitched from a pile in the barrow and handed it to Lilz. "Ain't got spoons," she said, forestalling the next question, and moved on.

Lilz crouched on the edge of the cot to eat, using three fingers to spoon up the tepid oat porridge. This should be safe enough—drawn from a common supply and served in a bowl chosen at random. She was not surprised to have the door left open: as on the floor above, guards posted at locked doors at the ends of the hall prevented escape. She wished she had thought to ask Greencrags to send her a spoon and some cloths. Now that she was awake, cramps in her belly announced the fast-approaching need for rags.

The porridge woman came back to collect the bowl fifteen minutes or so later. "Ain't you uneasy lyin' there?" she asked. "Where that poor man died what you're having your trial about?"

"Sir Jen Makeready? This was his cell?"

"Yes, poor thing, an' he did go down bad at the end. Made me look twice at my fambly, it did, to see what that fine gennelmun suffered." The woman lumbered out the door with the bowl.

"Miss?"

The bowl clattered into the barrow and the wheels creaked on. Lilz dashed to the door. "Miss, could you tell me—" But she wasn't going to be heard. She'd no money to pay for a rag, in any case. She went back to the cot and lay down, wrist on her forehead and knees drawn up, trying to suck the porridge from her teeth.

Lilz was not uneasy to lie where a man she knew had died. She thought of Sir Jen with sadness, wondering whether he had eaten anything she'd sent, and if so, whether it had heartened him. She hoped so. Her thoughts circled wearily, from her own troubles, to wondering what had become of Fenne, to the festering spot in which she'd tried to encyst her guilt over Jen Makeready—*Because you could have done something, Lilz, with only a little more risk and imagination surely you could have devised some way to save the man's life*—and each time lingered a little longer over that sore.

Tears were running down her temples when another knock sounded. "Lilz?" asked a cheerful rumble. "Are you awake?"

"Reed!" She sat up and wiped her eyes. "Oh, how wonderful!"

"I do believe it's me you're thrilling at, and not the basket." Reed grinned. "Shall I shut the door, then, love?"

"Oh, stop. No, of course I'm glad to see you. And the basket. What's in it?"

"Food, dearest, you won't want to eat anything that doesn't come from our loving hands, and a jug of sweet water and a bottle of wine, and I don't know what our iarl put in." Reed set the basket and a large stoneware jug under the window. "I've a few messages. It's Thornday, you know, so our iarl has a busy day. Privy Council now and open Court this afternoon. He'll be by this evening to see what else you may need. That's one. The law-boys will come to see you tomorrow. That's two. His Grace Merrow Strengthen has applied to his Grace Olen Hasten for the return of your bits and chattels. That's three. And let me see, weren't there four?" Reed pursed his mouth and squinted in a parody of concentrated thought. "Oh, yes." He snapped his fat fingers. "He who cannot visit loves you."

Lilz smiled. "Thank you, Reed. Please convey my thanks to our iarl and his Grace and express reciprocity to my non-visitor."

Reed assembled his leer. "He's no more that kind than I, but I'll give it a try."

"Oh, Reed!" Tears spurted. Lilz put her palms to her eyes and tried not to sob, without success. She felt a soft pat on her back. The cot groaned as Reed sat beside her.

"Lilz, I'm sorry. I know I shouldn't clown, but I don't know what else to do."

"It's all right." Lilz choked back a sob. "It's all right. Clown away, but I wish we were at Standfast House."

"Soon." Reed grunted to his feet. When she looked up, he was holding out a handkerchief. "I don't know if our iarl thought to send you a snotrag, but here's mine."

She took the square of linen and dabbed at her eyes. "Thanks."

"Keep it, my sweet. I'll have to be going—don't eat everything at one meal." Reed held up a hand in farewell and shut the door softly.

After a time, Lilz investigated the hamper. A stuffed roast fowl, several apples, a large rye loaf, a sweet cake, a bottle of wine, six flaky lard biscuits, carrots ready-scraped and wrapped in a damp cloth, some plums, a soft white cheese she could barely stretch her hand across, pickled snap beans—"No, Reed, I won't eat it all in one meal," Lilz said aloud.

She gnawed at a carrot to clean her teeth and dug deeper, to what Greencrags had sent. Two books of no significance she could see:

probably meant to pass her time. A deck of playing cards, for the same purpose. Pens, ink, paper, a tiny sharp knife. A plate, a bowl, a fork, a spoon, a spreader. A glass and a tin cup. Candles. Lucifers. Soap. Two golds' worth of silvers and coppers. Folded in the bottom of the basket, two big towels and half a dozen clean rags. Even a pin.

To her great relief, near midday a porter delivered her clothes box. Lilz set down the book she'd been reading, anxious to shed the blue pants and shirt and don some clean underwear. Her sewing kit lay on top of the clothes. Under it, a note: *Dearest Lilz—They say you are taken I hope this gets to you I am sure you need them. I pray you get off I would not like to see you hang—*Here Aster had vigorously scratched out a phrase. With much peering and tilting into the light from the vent shaft, Lilz made out, "unless you want me to come." Her brows twitched as she read on. *She is truly impossible I will not stay with her. I shall miss you I already do. All love and good luck, Aster.* As a postscript, *I was bid to say should I see you, Lord Ruppet has taken your guitar to Hasten House but it is still here.*

Caught between laughter and weeping, Lilz folded the paper and put it into her sewing kit. She went into the hall to talk to the guard. Five minutes and four silvers later she had arranged for a hot bath and a half cup of vinegar to help rinse the soap from her hair.

Greencrags's eyes were shadowed. He seemed weary to the point of looking shrunken, despite his still-crisp clothing and the smile he greeted her with.

"A long day, milord?"

"Eventful, Lilz. Let's put it that way." Greencrags looked around her small cell. "Didn't they even give you a chair?"

"No. But Reed brought the basket and the jug of water, which made everything much more comfortable. I thank you."

"A small favor. I see you got your clothes. At least they were prompt. Do you mind if I sit on your cot?"

Lilz shrugged. "A man died there, milord. After that, I don't suppose it makes much difference what anyone else does." He blinked at her. "This is Makeready's cell."

"Oh, poor Lilz!"

"I don't mind." She sat sideways on the cot and gestured for him to join her. "What made the day eventful?"

"It's Thornday, you know, so Privy Council met this morning. Guyr began by ranting at Kav Treadwell for being so heartless as to marry the woman who had murdered his friend. Treadwell protested that he had had no knowledge of it, but the king had the bit well in his teeth and no man on earth could've reined him. Certainly not Treadwell, who tried."

"Making things that much worse?" Lilz ventured.

Greencrags nodded, his smile tight. "As it happens. The king brought up the matter of the single white token, which Treadwell denied casting. I'd have owned up, but before I could be recognized Treadwell was bellowing at Guyr that Fenne should go to the block like any other murderer, he for one had no use for such a wife—"

"Oh, dear."

"—And if Guyr knew what was good for him, he'd sign the order of execution that minute, or Treadwell would take horse for north and home, and we'd all see how well the king liked that."

Lilz thought this over. "I take it, since you call him only Treadwell, that he's no longer Lord Northlands."

Greencrags sighed, shaking his head and half-smiling as men do when they can't quite believe what they've witnessed. "He is now officially Lord No-land. He's under house arrest at Waterside for the next ten years, with his wife."

"Sky above."

"A harsher sentence than poor Treadwell deserves, if you ask me." Greencrags again shook his head, with the same half-smile. "Ten years cooped with that woman, for piquing the king? You can imagine what his faction had to say."

"And you?"

"I kept my head well down, you may believe it. The grenades were flying a little too thick and fast for my taste." Greencrags cocked his head at her. "And you? A long day, too, for different reasons?"

"Not so bad, milord, thanks to some thoughtful person's having sent me a book or two. My clothes came around noon. My guitar, according to a note from Aster, is still wherever she is, although she was bid to tell me Meadowlands took it home with him."

"Before he heard you were in custody, no doubt."

"No doubt." They shared a smile.

"We'll get it back, don't worry." Greencrags sobered and leaned toward her. "Lilz, when this is over, I hope you will join my household." She frowned. "Please. Your political advice has always been sound. Also, I studied that ledger again last night, with the counsel Lealands hired. He was filled with admiration for the way your mistress handled her money. I know that was you; Fenne couldn't figure out how to trade a copper for a stick of candy. I'm nowhere near as wealthy as she is. If I'm to have the freedom to work at government, I need someone with a good head to manage my assets. You."

"I've made mistakes," she warned him.

"Who hasn't? But you're fundamentally sound and you're dead honest. Those are the practical reasons to ask you to come to me." Greencrags took her hands. "I have two others, both more important: I enjoy your company. Stone loves you."

Lilz felt herself redden. "The arrangement would be salaried, of course," Greencrags continued, withdrawing his hands. "I have no wish to exploit you as the Hastens did. You would have all the privileges the Blood provides you. I'm sure you could establish your own financial independence within a reasonable time."

"That's kind of you, milord."

"Kind? Simple self-interest, Lilz, as I've told you before." The tower clock began to strike. "That's eight. I have to go." Greencrags touched her shoulder and stood up. He glanced at each of the bleak stone walls. "I just wanted to see how you're doing. Before I leave I'll hunt up the warden and try to get you moved to another cell."

Lilz took a breath. "No matter. I—I belong here."

"I don't understand?"

Lilz, too, stood. Head bowed, she said, "To force me to meditate upon my life, milord. If I hadn't been such a coward, Makeready might still be alive."

"You did what you could."

"No. I—I could have told someone—"

"Whom?"

"I don't know. You, perhaps."

"Two years and more ago? I was far too raw then, you know that. I'd have charged straight in with a hullabaloo, the Hastens would have done what they thought necessary, Makeready would be just as dead and you and quite possibly me with him. Don't blame yourself, Lilz. Take heart." She didn't answer. "Lilz?"

"I'm scared."

"Of the trial?" She nodded. Greencrags took her head between his hands and pulled it toward his chest. She found herself looking at the tiniest of rust stains in the lace of his shirt, where the wax had flaked from one of Stone's pins. "You are not to be frightened," he said into her hair. "We'll keep you safe, Stone and I."

"Oh, Rovvo, please, no. Please, don't be clever. Be *careful*. No more back gates or sleight of hand or plain saddlepads or cartloads of beans—"

His arms were around her. "No more fancy stuff, I promise." He gave her a little squeeze. "Did you know you just called me by my first name?"

"I beg your pardon, mi— "

Greencrags put a finger to her mouth to stop her. "No, do. From now on. I hadn't thought about it before, but I want you to. Stone does—in private, anyway. " He brushed her cheek with dry lips and left.

As she had before going downstairs to bathe, before going to bed Lilz arranged the objects in the basket so that the least touch would dislodge one or two, and memorized the way they looked. She added the few silvers from her clothes box to the money Greencrags had sent and wrapped it all into a sash pulled snugly twice around her waist. Thin as she was, that left plenty of room for a knot. The heavy water jug she pushed under the cot, into the corner, as close to the wall as it would go, and put the chamber pot in front of it.

Morning proved the basket undisturbed. Well before the old woman with the porridge-cart pounded on her door, Lilz had eaten a good breakfast and cleaned her teeth with a rag. She could use a bucket, she thought, and wondered if any of her rescuers knew enough of needlework to buy thread for the project she had in mind, lace jabot and cuffs for a dress shirt for Greencrags. Something to keep her hands busy over the long days of waiting to come.

Reed had neglected to tell her what time the "law-boys" would arrive, and she'd forgotten to ask Greencrags. She dressed in her best shirt and skirt and spent half an hour putting up her hair: if she claimed to be of the Blood, she should do her best to look as if she belonged. Done, Lilz again arranged the basket. After a moment's hesitation she did the same with her clothes box. The money was still in her sash. Theft was as easy by day as by night: she wrapped the sash around her waist and tucked the ends under.

I must not be meek, she reminded herself. I must not be humble or servile. I must carry myself as I was taught. Head high. She walked several times the length of the cell with an imagined string fastened to the crown of her head to pull her into a noble line.

How the minutes dragged! Hour upon hour, not just one, between one strike of the tower clock and the next. Lilz finished the book describing the bizarre customs of the natives of the New Lands and opened the other, an essay on new theories of the planetary motions. She wished for her guitar and a book of tablature to improvise upon, and chided herself: she should be glad of her life! The planetary motions failed to hold her interest. Instead, she mulled over her memories of the man who had died where she sat. From there she fell into a brown study.

A rap on the door roused her.

"Counsel to see you, miss," the guard told her. "You're to come with me." Lilz had thought she'd feel relief. Instead, fear washed over her as she followed the guard down the stairs to a sitting room of an elegance suited to the conferences of peers with counsel. There she was put into chains and left to herself. She sank onto a red-cushioned gilt chair and looked at the windows. This must have been a formal reception room at one time; the windows were pieced glass in a design of colored birds positioned as if flitting through the trees outside. Ugly black bars marred the effect, harsher by far than bars over plain glass could ever have been.

A few minutes later the Dych of Lealands entered, accompanied by a man Lilz had often seen, but of course never formally met: a Breedwary, one of the lot disinherited from Riverside, forced to read law for a living. Younger son of a younger son, he'd probably have come to that even had his grandfather never raised maul in anger. He had an excellent reputation.

"Hello, Lilz, hello!" Strengthen, so overly-jovial he frightened her, introduced the lawyer, a pale man of about his own age with a gaunt face, stern dark eyes, and a gash of a mouth pressed shut over uneven teeth, his pallor accentuated by his lawyerly deep blue jacket. Lilz warmed to him immediately.

"I've reviewed the evidence, milady, and find it better than adequate," Breedwary said as the men sat down. "You did well to preserve it. We won't use the one private record, of course. The counterfeit bondage papers and the lack of registration will serve to show how you were used, without exposing your, er, explorations, which might be held against you." The man started to smile at her. His mouth instantly clamped over the unfortunate teeth. "I do foresee a problem, however."

Lilz tilted her head for the question, not trusting herself to speak.

"You were never presented to King Oerl, so far as I can tell?" She shook her head. "I fear the Hastens may seize upon that circumstance to argue that you are not entitled to trial by the Peers Assembled, in consideration of your father's, er, banishment."

Lilz swallowed. "I see."

"However, yesterday's Privy Council meeting has provided us with an opportunity I believe we should use." Lilz liked Breedwary's earnestness. "King Guyr broke publicly with the favorite, through whom some of the seventeenth Summerlea's influence has been exerted in the past," he explained. "At the moment the king is displeased with any and all of Treadwell's associates, leaving Summerlea in temporary disarray. Young Greencrags is a favored member of Crown Prince Oerl's hunt, a frequent companion. Through him we have arranged that you be transported to the New Palace under cover of darkness and be presented to Guyr. Late, yes, but better than nothing."

Her pulse began to pound in her throat. "I see."

The lawyer glanced from her feet to her face. "Have you anything, er, more formal to wear?"

"Only the dress provided by the Hastens for the sixteenth dych's funeral," Lilz said, her head shaking slightly at the thought.

"Oh, yes. That astonishing event." Breedwary's already narrow eyes nearly disappeared. "Did they tell you why it occurred?"

"No, milord."

"A great puzzlement to many, as you doubtless know. As I recall, that was a black dress, buttoning down the front?" She nodded. Breedwary pressed his mouth tight and sighed. "Not precisely suitable..."

And it doesn't even have all the buttonholes worked. Lilz opened her hands. "I have nothing else."

"Daughter of the Iarl of Darkforest, and she has nothing else." Breedwary clicked his tongue. "And he not nearly as hotheaded as my own immoderate ancestor. A most even-tempered man, highly intelligent. What a boon to Kinland he might have been. A shame."

"Why was he banished?" The words were out before Lilz had even realized she was thinking them.

The lawyer glanced at Lealands and back at Lilz. "That's another mystery, milady. Your father was said to have, er, maligned the king in the royal presence, but that seems so far out of character I have never understood it. All very quick, as you remember, Merrow."

"I was out of the country," Lealands reminded him.

'Ah, yes, I'd forgotten. Of course, your father couldn't speak for himself, not once the banishment took effect. Turned out in the middle of the night, weren't you?"

Lilz nodded slowly. She remembered her mother's horrified wail, the servants running about confused, her father's blank face. Herself helping her own weeping servant to push her clothing into trunks. Her eldest brother wanting to rip up a paper and her father preventing him. A smelly public carriage hired to take them to an inn, since while the horses belonged to the Chantwells the carriage belonged to the house that was no longer their home. It hadn't been the middle of the night, no. Late one winter morning.

"The black dress would be a good thing to wear to your trial," Breedwary was saying. "It can't hurt to remind the Blood of how, er, precarious its position can be. I suppose you'll have to wear it this evening as well. We will come for you at half past seven. You have a watch, of course?"

"No, I don't." Sold for dancing lessons, more than half her life ago.

"Dear, dear. Well, be ready as close to the time as you can."

"Milord, has the trial been scheduled?"

Breedwary looked shocked. "Has no one told you? It's set for Moonday, three days hence, at ten."

Lilz was returned to her cell, no longer in chains. Her clothes box had not been touched. She removed her everyday garments from the top layers and took out the black dress: not only were the buttonholes unfinished, the dress looked precisely as if it had lain folded under a weight for eight months, as it had. She had no way of correcting that. So tonight, twenty-five years late, she would be presented to the king of Kinland wearing crumpled black wool that buttoned down the front, three days before going on trial for her life. What on earth would her mother have thought?

A vision of Fenne sulking over the cut of her brown velvet presentation gown flashed across her inner eye. Lilz collapsed onto her cot, helpless with laughter.

By seven-thirty, Lilz had rebraided and repinned her hair twice. She wished intensely that she had a mirror, although she feared what it might show. Once recovered from her spate of hysterics, she had dampened the worst folds of the black dress and laid it flat on the bed to dry, hoping to restore its looks, but there was no denying that while she had effected some improvement, the garment was a disaster. It remained her only choice. To wear the skirt and shirt she had worn that morning would be the most grotesque of insults to the crown.

Greencrags looked her over, mouth compressed. "First thing after this trial is over, you'll send for a good dressmaker."

Lilz made a gesture of despair. "What can I do?"

"Nothing, I guess. At least your hair looks good."

"I don't want to damage your position," Lilz said unhappily.

"Don't worry. Prince Oerl knows your situation. He can explain to his father." *I hope*, she could almost hear him leave unsaid.

One of the prison guards who was to accompany them leaned through the door. "Are we going, milord? His Grace has arrived and the carriage is waiting."

They went down the stairs and into the yard, the guard with his hand around Lilz's upper arm. He handed her into the carriage, calling to a man on the other side to see that the door had been barred from the outside. Greencrags and Lealands got in. The second door was barred. The guard climbed on. A lurch, and they were on their way. Lilz sat straight and stared at Merrow Strengthen's knees across from her. At least she was not in chains.

Would the rag last out the evening? *Yes, Mother, I was presented,* at the age of thirty-eight in a dress that could scarcely have been less appropriate, with a bloodstain on the back. The hysterical laughter of the afternoon threatened again. Lilz tightened her mouth against it. "You'll be all right," Greencrags said softly.

They drew up at an entrance on the east side of the New Palace, one Lilz had never used before. "We're to pick up Prince Oerl," Lealands explained. The guard got down and unbarred the door.

"Elegant coach, Greencrags," said an amused tenor. The prince looked in. "Is this the lady? Come out, we'll walk through. It's shorter."

Lealands, then Greencrags, got out of the carriage. The guard reached up to steady Lilz on the steps. She got out feeling light-headed. Four palace guards waited nearby. The prince was casually but elegantly dressed, a youth of twenty-two who strongly resembled his late brother. He wrinkled his nose. "That's her only dress?"

"I explained about that, Oerl," Greencrags said.

"Oh, yes, that's right...but I hadn't quite realized...couldn't she have had her maid press it?"

"Your royal highness, she has no maid," Lealands put in. "And she is a prisoner."

"Oh, of course." Prince Oerl assessed Lilz. She wanted to creep back into the carriage and hide under the seat. *Hang from a string,* her mother's voice said in memory. She met the prince's gaze with the posture of a iarl's daughter. "You know," Oerl said, "she's almost exactly mother's size. Why don't I run in and see if she can borrow one of mother's old gowns? Father won't even notice if we're half an hour late."

"Your royal highness," Lilz began breathlessly, but the youth was already at the entrance, nodding to one of the palace guards to open the door. She glanced sideways at Greencrags, who had gone pale. "What now?" Her mouth was dry.

"We wait." The prison guards looked at each other. One stepped close and tucked his hand inside her arm. Lilz kept her back straight and her chin up, trying to breathe evenly.

Ten minutes later, a palace servant came to the door and called to them to come in. He glanced over her, head to toe and back, as they moved forward. Lilz saw his nostrils twitch. *String*, she told herself. The servant went before them through several twists of corridor, knocked on a door, and spoke to someone inside.

"You may enter," he said to Lilz. "Not you," to the guard clutching her arm.

"The woman is a prisoner."

"This is the queen's apartment. Only she is invited."

He opened the door wider and motioned Lilz through. She glanced at Lealands, who nodded. The guard began another protest, but sputtered into silence. Lilz went through the door. She found herself in a long dim room crowded with large white objects in rows. "Lilz Chantwell?" asked a quiet voice. Lilz turned toward it. An elderly woman in the crimson apron of a royal servant stood beckoning. Lilz walked after her, realizing that the white objects were dozens, no, hundreds of gowns hung under dustshields on wooden racks.

"Oh, now I know who you are," the woman said. "You're the one who walked in old Summerlea's funeral! I recognize the dress."

Lilz smiled briefly. "I imagine everyone in Miense would."

"My, it is a problem. It's really the only one you've got?"

Embarrassed, Lilz said, "Yes, I—"

"Oh, my dear, you needn't repeat your story." The woman's voice was amiable. "We've all had your situation explained. I'm Rose, the queen's wardrobe mistress. We'll find something suitable for you—something simple, I should think, don't you? The king's dinner is casual tonight. Come into the light so I can get a better look at your coloring."

Rose was quick and efficient. "Lovely hair, we don't want to spoil your do," she said, as she pulled the blue-gray gown she had chosen over Lilz's head. Watered silk, with a high neck bordered with a ruffle of lace. "There, we'll settle the shoulders so—yes, much better, don't you think?" Lilz looked into a full-length glass for the first time since leaving Waterside. I'm skinnier than ever, she thought, as Rose stepped behind her and attacked the buttons. "Brings out your gray eyes." Rose looked over her shoulder into the mirror. "Not a bad fit, really. Lucky that you're a little thinner than the queen, and not the other way around. Do you want to be painted?"

"I'm not accustomed—"

"Just a little rouge, then. There. My, the gentlemen won't recognize you! Come along, milady, the less we keep them waiting, the better. Men have no patience, have they?" Rose opened the door at the end of the room and propelled Lilz into the hall. "I'll be here when you're done, milady. Chin up."

"Ah, much better," Lealands exclaimed.

"Stone should see you," Greencrags murmured into her ear. They followed the same palace servant as before through more corridors, now so fast Lilz was forced to pick up her skirt. At the end of a hall Prince Oerl was waiting. "Here we go," Greencrags said. "This is the king's dining hall. A few peers should be with him."

Prince Oerl glanced over Lilz, nodded, smiled, touched a finger to his cheek to signal success in the Travaltian way. A servant opened a double door. The prince, Greencrags, Lealands, and Lilz went through. The prison guards were again barred.

A strong aroma of rich food and wine struck her nostrils. A dozen or more men sat at a long table, the king at the far side in front of a crimson curtain. Lilz slowly put names to the men: Riverside, instantly recognized by his flaming hair; the Ridehards, father and son. To her great surprise, Oakforest. Several others. Not Ruppet, nor his father, Summerlea. The prince went up to the king and said something.

"Ah," Guyr said loudly, but in a normal human voice. "Our belated lady. Come forward, come forward." Lilz started toward the other end of the room with the proud gait trained into her in childhood.

"Isn't that Fenne Hasten's servant?" she heard Oakforest say to Riverside as she passed.

"Well, Greencrags, you can be redvest tonight," the king said. "Announce the lady."

"Your majesty, I present Lilz Chantwell, daughter of Dilyn Chantwell Iarl of Darkforest, and his wife, Lady Merin Thrivewell."

"'Thrive*more*," Lilz corrected as she made the deep bow she had taught Fenne six years before.

"I beg your pardon, Lady Merin Thrivemore."

"Well, she's got a tongue in her head, at least, Greencrags, if you haven't an ear on yours," Guyr said cheerfully. "My men, a toast to the lady who arrived late for her Presentation."

Several of these men had not been born on the day she should have been presented, Lilz reflected. Prince Oerl, Greencrags, Oakforest. Some of the murmur that had greeted her name was doubtless explanation. She accepted the toast with a smile.

"Haven't I seen that dress before?" the king asked.

"Borrowed, your majesty," Lilz said.

"I knew I had a good eye. Well, young lady, good luck to you."

"Thank you, sir." Lilz backed away from the royal presence the required seven steps and left the room as she'd entered. Oerl stayed

behind, but Strengthen and Standfast came with her back to the
queen's apartment. Greencrags apologized for misspeaking her
mother's name, offered his congratulations and called her 'milady'
in jest. *And that's that,* Lilz thought. No gala or feasting, nor a single
figure danced. Not even a sip of the wine. She felt no loss.

The wardrobe mistress waited inside the queen's dressing room
to help her off with the blue-gray gown and on with her own hideous
black wool, still warm from a fresh pressing.

"How did it go, then, milady?" she asked, as Lilz buttoned the
black dress.

"Well," Lilz said. "There wasn't much to it, of course."

"No, milady, but it's official. I don't suppose you noticed, but the
secretaries attend upon the king everywhere but his bedchamber,
and sometimes there. Oh, let's not lose that hairpin."

A door opened quietly at the dark end of the dressing room. The
woman helping her looked up. Lilz turned.

"So you are Lilz Chantwell." The voice was soft, with traces of
Travaltian vowels. Queen Prenta stood in the lighted doorway, her
head on one side, as if judging an arrangement of flowers.

Lilz curtsied. "Good evening, your royal highness," she said, glad of
her mother's relentless drill so long ago. The queen came forward. Nothing
about this woman so like herself in shape, a woman dressed casually in
pants and shirt even Lilz might have worn, seemed at all intimidating.
"My deepest thanks for the honor of the use of your gown."

"A small matter. Sit down, Lilz Chantwell. I wish to speak with
you."

With me? Lilz perched on the edge of the chair the queen had
waved at. The queen seated herself a sashlength away and glanced
at the wardrobe mistress. "Leave us, Rose."

The servant bobbed a curtsy and picked up one of the candlesticks.
The queen watched her go to the far end of the room, where the door
she had entered by stood open. The door closed. Prenta looked back at
Lilz. She had placed herself just within the circle of light cast by the
candles on the dressing table, giving Lilz the impression she might
fade into shadow at any moment.

"I have so often wondered about you." Lilz had no idea what to
reply. Thank you? Why? Are you sure you know to whom you are
talking? The queen smiled slightly and went on. "It seemed a harsh
fate for you, not one I anticipated or I would have tried to prevent it.
To serve the sixteenth Summerlea, I mean."

Lilz responded to an overtone of gentle concern. "He was not a harsh
master to me, ma'am, nor his granddaughter a harsh mistress."

"I doubt *he* dared to be. But then, he held many surprises. He
may even have been kind out of remorse."

"Remorse?" Lilz echoed, wondering if the Travaltian-born queen
had found the right word.

"It was he who persuaded my father-in-law to banish your father."

"Nevan Hasten did that?" Lilz stared. "But why?" The queen made a small gesture, as if to say that affairs of state were beyond her. *This may be my one chance*, Lilz thought. *In three days I may be dead.* She gripped her courage and said, "Did it have anything to do with the *antranta*?"

"The *antranta*!" Prenta raised her brows. "Did your father tell you of them, so young? Or did you discover them on your own?"

"On my own, ma'am. Or rather, Sir Jen Makeready discovered them, and Kav Treadwell, snooping through his papers after his death, found the references and asked me to help him interpret them."

The queen shook her head. "Unlike Sir Jen, to be so careless. I thought that once I presented your father as an example he would destroy all his notes."

"My father did find out about the *antranta*, then?"

"Yes. And yes, that was why he was banished. Kinland was at war with Galtriva, yet again. The whole cause was the *antranta* and the use the Crown and the Hastens had made of their existence." Prenta sighed. "As always. Your father wished to announce all he had discovered to the Peers Assembled. What would the effect on the war have been?"

Lilz nodded slowly.

"Oerl, that Oerl, would never have borne seeing his power so eroded. The war would have been on our own soil, Kennish battling Kennish, with religion to spur them on." Yes. Even today, that was a danger.

"Oerl, my son Oerl, may close those gates. If so, it will do little. Those who use them can cross where they please. The *antranta* are merely conveniences, so that they will not find themselves standing in the midst of a panicking crowd when they arrive, or falling into a well that was not there the week before."

"Sir Jen wrote of *antranta* in the sky."

Prenta smiled and shrugged. "Those are not precisely the same. The *antranta* in the heavens admit the galloping stars. The Other-kin do something to the stars in their own world which they call 'launch.'" Lilz frowned. One launched a boat, or a spear. But a star? "Then in some way the star is guided to us, through those special *antranta*. The process has been explained to me, but I cannot explain it to you. I do not always entirely understand what they tell us."

"Who are the Other-kin?"

"May I have your silence? You are soon to go to trial."

Was the queen offering to use her influence with the Blood? *What does it matter?* Lilz nodded.

"They are men from another world similar to ours. We call them 'Other-kin,' as the men in the north of Kinland are called Far-kin. They call themselves by a name meaning 'students of mankind.' They value us because we have fewer inventions than they, and they hope that by observing us in our simplicity they will understand how to bring their own world into some kind of better adjustment. Again, it is not something I entirely understand, although they came to Travaltia first, as you may discern from the term *antranta,* meaning 'gates' to my people."

Prenta sighed and shifted in her chair. "They would be harmless if we paid no attention, as they are in the rest of the world and have been for two centuries. Their only purpose is to study. But Lehrr, as you call him the Prophet, was unprincipled and greedy and sought to make good use of them, as you no doubt learned from Sir Jen's papers. Therefore Kinland is burdened with his false religion, lives in fear of their whizzers—which do nothing more than show the Otherkin scenes of daily life that they may study at their leisure—and the monarchy steals power from the Peers Assembled with their toy, the Jewel of the King. It is possible, I suppose, that Kav Treadwell will speak of all this one day soon, goaded by his house arrest." She got to her feet, gracefully but seeming tired.

Lilz stood as the queen did. "And will he suffer the same fate as my father?"

Prenta shook her head. "Your father had King Oerl to deal with, as grasping a man as there ever was, with Nevan Hasten at his right hand. Darkforest was not a patient man. He went at once to Nevan Hasten with what he had learned, not suspecting that the dych shared the secret and used its power for his own purposes. As for Treadwell..." The queen sighed. "Guyr is but a shadow-king. Olen Hasten dulls his mind with drink. We are for now at peace, thanks greatly to that same Nevan Hasten. Treadwell will not be banished for his curiosity, not even should he find the courage to speak that your father had." The queen glanced at the door into the corridor. "Although Treadwell's courage has always seemed to me to be limited to the bedchamber," she added tartly. "We will converse again, Lilz Chantwell, if fortune favors us. Now, the hour flees. Your guards surely grow restless. You will soon be on trial. I hope you escape with your life, because in several ways I can use your help. We will speak of them later."

Nodding, the queen picked up a candle and went through the door she had entered by. A moment later Rose returned to show Lilz out.

"What on earth took you so long?" Greencrags demanded, the instant the door opened into the hall. "These two oafs were about to barge into the queen's private apartments to search for you."

"Forgive me." Lilz smiled at him. "I was talking with the queen. She knew my father, it turns out, and wanted me to know what sort of man he was."

"She must have known him extraordinarily well!"

The guards had Lilz by the elbows, hustling her toward the exit. Outside, the carriage waited, torches drove their flames into the night, the palace guards stood about with bland, bored faces. Handed into the carriage, Lilz sat back against the cushion. The queen had seemed ready to answer questions, she thought. But Prenta had raised more questions than she had answered.

Chapter Twenty-Six

Lilz wasn't sure about the basket.

She squatted beside her food supply. Hadn't she folded that striped cloth across the top a little more crookedly? She removed it with gentle care. That apple had been directly to the left of the half loaf of bread when she packed the basket before going to the New Palace. Now it lay more toward her, the stem turned to the other side. Under the bread, the cheese had taken on a pinkish hue overnight.

Oat porridge, she thought, not pleased at the idea. This was Satingday morning—whatever her luck, after this, only two mornings left in this wretched place with its wretched fare. Lilz changed her rag, put the bloodied one under the cot with the others, and sat down to await the gray woman's round. She wasn't even sure she should wipe the goo off her teeth once she'd eaten: the water jug was opaque, any undissolved powder invisible.

After breakfast she folded the lid of her clothes box back to use as a desk and sat on the floor to write some letters—to Stone, to Clâes, to Aster; a note of thanks to the queen's wardrobe mistress for her help and for making the black dress presentable. Reed could take her messages when he brought the books and the bucket Lilz had requested of Greencrags the night before.

The houseman arrived in mid-morning with a fresh jug of water and a loaf of bread as well. He wore his formal face and called her "milady."

"I'm Lilz, Reed, please," she said.

"I understood from Lord Greencrags that you were presented last evening, milady."

"In a manner of speaking." The houseman's professional mask did not change. "Reed, it's only because the counselor thinks I've got a better chance if I'm tried by the Peers Assembled than by the Common Court. It really makes no difference."

"If it makes no difference, milady, why do it?"

"To keep the Hastens from objecting to my trial."

Reed produced his servile nod. "Is there anything more Lord Greencrags can provide to make you comfortable, milady?"

"Reed!" Lilz plumped onto the cot, hands on her knees. "You know what my presentation was? Our iarl and Lealands hustled me over to the New Palace and we all went barging in on the king's dinner. Our iarl announced my name and parentage, only he got my mother's name wrong." Did a glint come into Reed's eye? "The king said something like ho-hum, better late than never, and our iarl and his Grace trotted me straight back here. Oh, yes, the king did tell his men to lift a glass to me, but they were all drinking anyhow and I don't s'pose half of them noticed." Did he hide a smirk? "As for me, I didn't even get a sip of the wine."

"Harsh treatment, indeed, milady."

Was he joking? Reed's face was so bland she wasn't sure. "Please, Reed. I've lived back of the door most of my life and I don't see any reason to move into the front hall now. If everybody I know starts miladying me, it wasn't worth it."

Reed considered this. "Out of curiosity, what is your name?"

"Lilz." He cocked his head at her. "Oh, all right. Chantwell. As in Godwit and Chantwell, Cabinetmakers."

"Your distant cousin?"

"My next-older brother."

"Ah." Reed relaxed, at last. "You didn't say if you wanted the bucket filled, Lilz my love, so I brought it up empty. If you like, I'll wheeze back down the stairs and pump you some water."

She smiled. "Please."

Before he took his leave, she told the houseman her suspicions about the basket. He examined the cheese, agreed, and tossed everything out the window with a promise of replacement—and his usual foolery. Nonetheless, Lilz was uneasy. How had she deformed her life last night? Assuming she still had one at sundown two days hence?

Afternoon brought a surprise. Lilz was fettered and chained and walked down to the reception room, wondering all the way whether some new difficulty had occurred to Breedwary or Strengthen. But the person waiting to see her was Fenne's mother.

"Lady Delle," Lilz exclaimed.

"Hello, Lilz." The dychessa turned from the window, where she had been tracing the lead outlines of the birds with one finger. "Oh, they've put you in chains!"

"Yes."

"Oh, my dear! I—" Lady Delle wandered across the room to the fireplace, empty on this warm afternoon. Three chairs stood nearby. She sat in one and motioned to Lilz to sit beside her. "I came to say goodbye."

"That's kind of you."

"Twenty years, Lilz. You gave your life to us."

Trust Lady Delle to put it that baldly, though, being Lady Delle, she probably had not the slightest notion just how bald it was. "Yes," Lilz said. "I suppose that's true."

"I—" Lady Delle frowned faintly. "You're a woman, too, Lilz. Have you ever loved a man from afar?" The words were rushed. "I mean, admired him and wanted him even though he scarcely knew you existed—" She glanced at her sideways, a furtive little glance Lilz couldn't interpret. "I guess not." She sighed. "But then if he notices you, when you thought all hope was gone forever...."

"I imagine that would be gratifying," Lilz said carefully. What now? Lady Delle's meanderings always had a point, if discernible only to her.

"Even when you're used to being noticed...." Lady Delle began smoothing flat her gloves, fine pale blue leather gloves matched to her fragile shoes. "Well. That was a long time ago. How are you, Lilz? You look so thin! Are they feeding you? Should I have something sent in?"

Sky above! "No, thank you. My meals are adequate."

"Oh! No, I didn't mean...I meant, should I send you something tasty? It'd be wholesome. Truly. You saved my life when Fenne was born, remember? And hers."

"I don't recall the situation as quite that serious," Lilz demurred.

"Yes. Yes, it was. I remember...you kept your head, but Coral didn't, and what was that old hall maid? Poppy? No, Pearl. Who'd have thought..." Lady Delle stared at Lilz. She looked puzzled. "I keep thinking I'm responsible for the mess we're in, somehow, but I can't think how that would be."

Lilz murmured something soothing.

"I never quite knew..." The dychessa jumped up and began pacing with a swish of taffeta. "I called on Lady Riverside just now. That's why...." She brushed at her ruffled skirt.

Why she's dressed up. "Oh?"

"She...her husband came home last night with a story...he dined with the king last night..." Fenne's mother rounded her eyes at her. "Did you see him there?"

Lilz nodded.

"Then it's true...Lilz, I swear, I had *no idea* you were a Chantwell. I mean, I knew you grew up in a good house—it's obvious the minute you open your mouth—but I just had *no* idea... Who'd think *his* daughter would be in the house? I mean, the same house with Nevan? You never said, did you? Or did you? ... I guess I didn't pay much attention, did I? Even when I noticed that you and Ruppet...." The dychessa broke off, her lip caught under her teeth, and slapped her gloves against her hand.

Ruppet and I? Lilz frowned. *What does she mean, Ruppet and I?*

"There must be some way...I can't just let...I'll have to talk with Ruppet. Yes, that's what I'll do. I'll talk with Ruppet, and he—oh!" Lady Delle stared past her. "Olen! Why are you here?"

"Come to collect you, Delle. You've done quite enough talking for today." Summerlea came into the room, took his wife by the arm, and steered her to the door.

"Goodbye, Lilz," she called over her shoulder. "I'll remember you, always."

Lilz, on her feet, stared after the dychessa. Her husband shot her a grim look and closed the door. She heard a stern mumble on a rising note from beyond the thick wood panel: the dych, but no words came through, either of his question or his wife's answering protest. The new Summerlea's spies must be as efficient as his father's, Lilz thought, to bring him here so quickly. What could Delle have to say that could be so important?

Something about me and Lord Ruppet? she wondered, as a breathless guard arrived to escort her back to her cell. But what? I never had care of him. I've scarcely even spoken to him since he grew up, or he to me.

She climbed the stairs, chains clanking, and walked into her cell. The guard turned his attention to her restraints. The irons fell from her right arm. Lilz looked at her left arm as the guard inserted his key into the other fetter. A key. The floor guard held her legs from behind as the one who had escorted her removed the ankle irons. Ruppet's the key. The guards left the cell, the chains over one's arm, and shut the door. Lilz sat down on the cot.

What about me and Ruppet?

Lilz stretched out on her bed, trying to review everything she could remember of Ruppet from the past twenty years...Ruppet and Säen, much of an age, Säen always a little in the lead because he was eight months older although Ruppet had been the taller even twenty years ago.... Though the nastiest tricks were usually Ruppet's idea... Ruppet will be twenty-six next spring. Wouldn't you think he'd grow up? ... Gangly Ruppet, with dark hair and those bright blue eyes. Like Clâes's eyes, set in Lady Delle's face made longer. In her mind's eye Lilz could see Ruppet standing beside his father at the old dych's funeral, half a head taller and...that's it. Ruppet and I look something alike. The same kind of build, allowing for sex. The same high forehead. The same long hands with squared-off fingernails—Ruppet had even remarked on that, as a boy of eight or nine. Like a family resemblance.

Ruppet is my father's son.

Lilz took the idea and looked at it, as if rotating an imagined object in her mind. In all these years she had never thought of her father as having any life apart from his family. But that was a child's view. Of course he had. All those times he'd gone away... And if, a few years into his banishment, her handsome father had encountered Lady Delle, a beautiful woman who had admired him "from afar" even before? Surely possible.

And I have broken the chain of his inheritance, Lilz thought.

The next day, the day before her trial, passed even more slowly than the wait for Strengthen and Breedwary to arrive for the conference two days earlier. Lilz had read every scrap of print in her cell well before midafternoon, and the thin book about the natives of the New Lands twice. She had written every letter of possible farewell she wanted to. Now she lay on her cot, idly thinking about the natives of the New Lands—*men, too, like us, for all they behave so differently*—and trying not to feel the occasional sick chill of fear that shook her from head to toe.

Lilz had seen a woodcut of the block.

The author of the book on the New Lands had lived a year in a native village. Lilz wondered if he had fit in as poorly as the housemaid at Sweetdawn. Such great confidence! Not a hint of doubt in any sentence he had written, no sign of uneasiness, never a suspicion that he hadn't shared fully in that so patently un-Kennish life....

The gout of blood from the severed neck had been colored red. All else was black and white.

Breedwary's grandfather, the man in the woodcut was supposed to have been. In the New Lands, he would simply have been driven away from the village, to survive in the dark fir-clogged forest as best he could until winter took him. Cold was an easy death, some said.

Black, red, white. The colors of the tokens each peer would be given as he entered the courtroom. One for the voting box. Two to return uncast. One, two, dropped audibly into the collection box to show that he had not voted twice.

Lilz shuddered.

The evening porridge cart came by, but she felt no appetite even for the food in her replenished basket, much less for that slimy paste.

The tower clock struck eight. This time tomorrow—

She was pacing, three steps each way, when Stone arrived with Greencrags.

"Take heart," the iarl said, after rehearsing her statement with her. "You've got a perfect case. You know that. Breedwary's been very busy, too, new ideas every other minute."

"Rovvo's so young," Lilz whispered, when Greencrags had announced that he felt the need of taking the air alone for half an hour or so and left, shutting the door. "How can he be so sanguine?"

Stone only shook his head. She leaned into his arms, feeling his warmth, his life, which this time tomorrow he would almost surely still have. His hand slowly caressed her back: comfort, not seduction. "I'm so afraid of the Hastens," she forced out.

"Lealands seems confident." Stone cleared his throat, as if his voice had broken only because of a little phlegm. She loved him for trying to deceive her.

"They've landed on their feet generation after generation. I have the feeling they always will win."

Stone's arms tightened. "Rovvo's gone the rounds of his faction. They'll all show up, and the Ridehards, too."

"Oakforest and Riverside were at dinner with the king Fairday night. Summerlea knows all about my presentation." She could feel a shock go through him. "His wife came yesterday afternoon to ask if it had really happened. The Hasten faction will be there in force."

"His Grace thinks that given your parentage—"

"Merrow Strengthen *knew* my father," Lilz interrupted. "He admired him. Breedwary, too. But no peer has spoken to my father for thirty years. Nobody has the faintest idea why he was banished. What will the younger men think and do? And the Hasten faction?"

"Some will surely vote their conscience." Stone sounded nearly as doubtful as he should feel. "Or the evidence."

"Will they?" Lilz freed herself from his embrace to pace again. "Why should they? Summerlea hasn't shown any weaknesses."

"Yet."

She sighed heavily. "I wish just once he'd show up at a Privy Council meeting drunk to incoherence! Not that it would do me any good tomorrow. No," she continued, shaking her head. "The best I can hope for is what Fenne got—more black tokens than red. And you know as well as I do that was only because she'd accused me. I'll have to pin my hopes on Guyr's mercy."

Stone sat on the cot. "Lie down with me, Lilz."

She gestured toward the bucket of soaking rags. "I'm bleeding."

"I know. I just want to hold you."

When Greencrags returned they were still lying fully dressed on the cot. Lilz had found the strength to cry, and Stone to urge hope.

From Fenne's trial, Lilz knew what was happening on the other side of the iron-bound oak door. Those peers interested in her trial had gathered; those spectators attracted by the prospect of watching a woman hear that she would die in an hour had found seats in the old servants' gallery. From the sound as the door opened and shut behind a page, the crowd was far smaller than the one the week before.

At the moment, she and her guards were alone. The Lord Chief Justice had looked in to see that she had arrived in the waiting room, as had Breedwary. Where Greencrags and Lealands were, Lilz had no idea.

The black wool dress proved to have an unexpected advantage: the full sleeves cushioned the irons around her wrists, leaving her far more comfortable than she had anticipated. The guard who chained her had left enough slack that she could move fairly freely and had used the lightest fetters he could find. "All a form, milady," he'd said. "I'd have them made of air if I could." Now she gave him a small smile as she clasped her hands in her lap.

The tower clock struck, dulled by the walls. Time. Where was everyone?

Breedwary arrived at the same moment as the prosecutor. He carried her tin box in the crook of his arm, on top of a leather folder filled with papers. The prosecutor grinned at her and opened the door a crack to peer through. "I think we're ready," he said. Lilz turned to Breedwary, startled. "Where?" she formed with her mouth, but he showed her a palm, shushing her. The prosecutor was arranging his cloak of office. "Me first, milady, then my learned friend, then you." He opened the door and strode forth, Breedwary at his heels.

The guards took Lilz between them as they entered the larger room. Like any gathering of the Blood, this smelled strongly of perfume and humanity; she stifled a sneeze. The shades had again been pulled. She was glad of her long skirt. It served to conceal the straddle the leg-irons forced upon her, leaving her able to give the effect of the tall, graceful gait she had reclaimed over the past three days. A murmur in the court died as she entered. Breedwary led Lilz to a seat, the same seat Fenne had occupied.

She looked toward the servants' gallery. Stone lifted his chin at her from the front row. She lifted her own to show that she had seen him and glanced at the other tiers. From here, they rose in overlapping frills of lacy carved wood chair backs to the stone back wall. Perhaps a third of the seats were filled. Aster waved at her from somewhere in the middle. Reed had positioned himself just behind Stone. A few of the Hasten House and Standfast House maids had come.

"The trial of Lilz Chantwell for murder and conspiracy to murder will now begin," intoned the secretary who had read the charges for Fenne to answer so few days ago. Lilz returned her attention to the judge's table.

"I protest, your lordship."

Most of the peers in the front rows turned around to see who had spoken. Lilz knew the voice. Säen Hasten.

"On what grounds?"

"The woman is a servant, not a peer."

"You identify her as a servant, Lord Säen?" Gudgeon inquired.

"Yes. I've known her since I was five years old. Her name is Lilz. She's bonded to the Hastens."

Whispers ran through the hall, as wordless to Lilz as rustling silk. She sat straight, her hands in her lap, without taking her eyes off Gudgeon.

"Ah, yes. Stand, please, milady, and face the Blood." Lilz got to her feet. The chains chinked as she turned. All those faces. Many she knew; most she did not, although she must know all their names by hearsay. At least a hundred and fifty had come. Surprising. "Does anyone else identify this woman as Lilz, the servant to the Hasten family? Oakforest, you? Anyone else? Meadowlands. Greencrags. Lealands." Lilz felt her heart flop. "Summerlea. Riverside. Coldsoil. Anyone else?" A few other men stood. "You may sit down, milady."

Lilz sat, with a side-glance at Breedwary. "All's well, murmured, almost inaudibly. She looked at Stone, who put a finger next to his eye to reassure her.

"You will recall," Gudgeon said, in one of his more pompous tones, "that at her own trial Lady Fenne Hasten accused Lady Lilz Chantwell, identified then only as her bond-servant, Lilz, of instigating and carrying out the murder of Sir Jen Makeready without her knowledge, in spite of which a number of you well exceeding the required three-fourths voted Fenne Hasten guilty." *But Greencrags cast a white token.* "Two mornings later, the defendant presented herself at Common Court." *At his insistence.* "In establishing her identity she produced two documents, a birthnote and orders of servitude. The birthnote was found to be genuine. Those orders of servitude, gentlemen, the orders that kept this woman of the Blood under Hasten orders for twenty years, were forged."

More than whispers at that: Gudgeon nodded to the page, who struck the gong. The room quieted. "No record of the bonding of Lilz Chantwell, or any other Lilz, to the Hasten family at any time within the lifetime of the defendant has been found. We have made the most painstaking of searches."

"May we see those papers, please?" Säen again. How honored he must feel to act for his uncle, Lilz thought.

Some time was spent in selecting a committee of peers to examine her evidence. While the argument about who should serve continued, Breedwary groped for her left hand in her lap and slipped something over her thumb. Lilz glanced down. Her father's signet.

"A clincher," he said. "If we need it."

The committee assembled itself near the judge's bench to look over her birthnote, the orders of servitude, an example of genuine orders signed by King Oerl, and the affidavit of some clerk in the City House. Säen had gotten himself appointed to the committee. Lilz heard him arguing in a low voice, his gestures short and sharp. Greencrags was not in the group. She looked at Stone, but Stone was watching Lord Säen. Eventually one of the Ridehards announced that the committee had accepted her as of the Blood, and everyone sat down.

"The trial will proceed."

"Reservation, your lordship." Säen again. "She has not been presented to the king."

Oakforest, of all people, said, "Yes, she has. I was there."

"Any other witnesses to the presentation of Lilz Chantwell, daughter of Dilyn Chantwell, Iarl of Darkforest, and Lady Merin Thrivemore?" Gudgeon asked. The Ridehards stood, and Oakforest, Greencrags, Lealands, and others. Another muttering began as older peers explained to younger men who the Iarl of Darkforest had been.

"The trial will proceed." Gudgeon nodded at the page. The gong sounded. "Any further protest? No? Read the charges, please."

Lilz pled not guilty. The prosecutor's summation of his case could not have been more than four sentences long. In essence, he simply repeated what Fenne had said. Lilz stared open-mouthed when he sat down. Gudgeon very nearly did the same. "Any more, good sir?" he asked.

"Nothing further."

Breedwary rose. "You have examined the evidence that the defendant is entitled to trial by the Peers Assembled and found it worthy," he began. "Nevertheless, you may think, until giving herself up to the Common Court the defendant fully believed herself to be a bond-servant bought from her future by Nevan Hasten, Dych of Summerlea, when she was but eighteen years old. More than half her life has been spent in the service of the Hasten family, you tell yourselves. Having heard the charges just read, and my learned friend's outline of the case for the Crown, you may well ask yourselves what difference it makes that the woman is of the Blood, given such a history?" He smiled and bowed. "Gentlemen, you are right to wonder. Until five days ago, the defendant believed herself to have become a servant despite a heritage as proud as any, although in truth she was the victim of a cruel hoax."

Lilz glanced at the Lord Chief Justice, who sat with his fingers interlaced and his head tilted, his attention fixed on Breedwary. Not the slightest sign that he had just heard a blatant lie crossed his face. Had Breedwary gone to him for advice?

The counsel went on, reminding the Peers Assembled of Fenne's marriage to Greencrags, of the annulment commission, of Makeready's protestations, of Fenne's often-expressed anger. He read the two verses of Makeready's that Lilz had seen circulated, and two others, rather more explicit, that she had not.

"Excuse me," Gudgeon interrupted. "I'd like to be quite sure of these assertions. Has anyone of the Blood seen these verses?" Half the hall stood. "I see."

Not advice, Lilz saw, as the Lord Chief Justice asked for dispute of the rest of the statement and got none. They had planned this out, as carefully as Jonquil had ever staged a masque, or Dolphin ornamented the tunes to his songs. Perhaps Greencrags wasn't as naive as she'd feared. He, too, must have deputies on the committee. She looked at the prosecutor. He was smiling, head on one side, the tips of his fingers matched, legs crossed and his foot jogging in air.

"Only last week we heard the evidence of Evin Clock, so recently deceased in so violent a manner," Breedwary went on. He caused a large slate to be brought into the room, on which he wrote the dates of Clock's sales of poisons to Fenne with a chunk of chalk, pointing out that the iarlena's was the only name of her household to appear in Clock's books.

"We've been over this," Gudgeon said. "If nobody objects, I count it as accepted, since everyone's seen it." Lilz braced herself, but if Säen had anything to say he kept quiet. "Shall we enter the dates Elm says food arrived at the Old Palace for Sir Jen into the record, too?"

"No, your lordship." Breedwary picked up the ledger. "Some of you testified last week that the so-called servant, Lilz, was highly trusted, even to keeping her mistress's accounts. More than that, she has for several years managed Lady Fenne Hasten's assets." He waited for a ripple of surprise to die down. "As well as her household accounts. This is a household daybook from the period covering the imprisonment of Sir Jen Makeready. It is, in fact, that very book alleged to have been destroyed by the defendant on the afternoon before Fenne Hasten's arrest, as we heard attested at the previous trial."

"Wasn't she supposed to have burned it to conceal her own guilt?" Gudgeon asked. He can't possibly be that ingenuous, Lilz thought.

"Indeed, your lordship, and if we examine it we can see why. For every date I have written large before you, we find two in the account that correspond: one recording a payment to Mistress Onma Stump for 'sundries,' and one a day later recording an item of food sent to 'O.P.', clearly an abbreviation for Old Palace. As we heard last week, Mistress Stump has testified that she delivered the packets of poison sent by Clock to Lilz Chantwell in person and at her request took the food to the Old Palace to be given to Sir Jen Makeready. We do not contest either assertion. I shall read out the items of food." Breedwary did so, pointing to each of the dates on the slate as he read the corresponding custard or sweetcake or soup from the ledger.

"What about that lethal veal pie we've heard so much about?" Gudgeon asked. "The one that arrived two weeks before the man died and put an end to that decrepit old hound of Elm's."

Two weeks! Lilz glanced at Breedwary, who had folded his arms and assumed his sternest expression. *But Sir Jen was desperately ill long before that!*

"Your lordship, Lady Lilz sent no veal pie."

The committee reassembled to examine this new evidence. Lilz watched them argue, weary. Sitting so straight with the chains dragging her down was becoming almost more than she could endure. Yet she felt she could not allow herself to slump. Her proud posture seemed something she owed to her parents, to all the Thrivemores and Chantwells before them. For a moment, she wondered whether Stone would comprehend the concept. Of course, he would. She glanced at him and was rewarded with a smile.

The evidence was accepted and the men returned to their places.

Now Breedwary brought out the tin box. This was the crux of her case. Lilz folded the signet on her thumb into her fist as the counselor lifted each envelope from the box, held it high before the assemblage, and read the date Clock had written on it. With each date, he crossed off the corresponding one on the slate. He came to the last envelope.

Only one date remained. With a flourish, he drew a line through it. "So you see, my lords, all the poison sold by Clock to Fenne Hasten is accounted for. Not one grain went into the foods sent to the Old Palace for Sir Jen Makeready's consumption. I ask you, is this the act of a woman whose loyalty to her mistress is such that she will kill unbidden? Or is it the act of a woman who believes her very life to be under that mistress's thumb, but who cannot bring herself to do cold murder when so ordered, and attempts to defend herself and the honor of her lineage as best she can?"

The committee reconvened amid more talk.

The younger Ridehard picked up an envelope. With a surprised gasp he turned to the man next to him and pointed something out. The man—a Clerkwell—nodded. Others crowded around the two.

"That's the envelope with Stump's note on it," Breedwary told Lilz in an undertone. "It's been resealed."

She glanced at him. "What if they notice?"

"They're supposed to. You didn't want it to leak."

"Question to the defendant, your lordship," Ridehard called out.

The Lord Chief Justice yawned. "Rise, please, milady." Lilz stood, her mind and pulse racing. "Go ahead."

Ridehard held the envelope toward her. Clock had sealed it in his usual orange, but a drop of Standfast green held the broken seal together. "Who opened this envelope?"

"I did, milord."

"Why?"

"I was curious to see what the poison looked like."

"Who resealed it?"

"I did, milord."

"Why?"

"I kept the poison with my own belongings. I did not wish to have it leak onto my clothing." Lilz heard an approving rumble from Breedwary.

"This wax is Standfast green," Ridehard pointed out.

"At that time, we had only recently moved to Hasten House. The end of a stick of the Standfast household wax was among the odds and ends we took. I used that." As she had done for other casual purposes, and might have for this if she'd thought of it.

Ridehard turned back to the committee. Lilz sat down at Gudgeon's nod and blotted her sweaty palms on her skirt. Breedwary might have given her more warning. Her heart slowed. The committee of peers went on examining envelopes.

The whole trial seemed tedious beyond belief. Lilz sat perspiring in the black dress, a fine garment for a march in bitter weather but much too heavy for a warm fall day. Logic notwithstanding, she could not connect this long-winded process with the idea that on the roof of the oldest part of this oldest of Kinland's buildings was a hacked and stained cube of ancient maple half a sashlength on a side, at which she might be required to kneel that afternoon, the better to present the nape of her neck to the headsman's axe.

The headsman had had scant practice of late. If he missed his first stroke? Perhaps better to have settled for a commoner's hanging, after all.

Suddenly the men examining the envelopes began nodding to one another. Lord Säen stood apart with his arms folded. "Your lordship," the elder Ridehard said, approaching Gudgeon. "We have other evidence we wish to offer to the Peers Assembled."

"Oh? Where did you get this?"

"From the envelopes. Details counsel did not mention." Breedwary made his faint rumbling purr. All according to plan, Lilz realized.

Gudgeon assented. Ridehard turned toward the assembly. "Except for the seal you heard my son ask about, all of these seals are intact. Many of us dealt with Evin Clock for necessary medications"—he frowned as a few of the younger peers tittered—"and we are familiar with his seal and his hand, by which these envelopes have been dated. In addition, there are notes on them, my friends, which you should know about." He looked from side to side to be sure he had everyone's attention and read, first, Onma Stump's note to Fenne hoping the powder would work to her good, then Fenne's instructions to Lilz. All of them. "Many of us are acquainted with the script of these two women and are satisfied that they are the ones who wrote," he added.

More whispering among the remaining peers. Säen reached out and snatched an envelope from Ridehard.

"I don't believe this is poison." He glared at Lilz. "She didn't have any envelopes a month ago. I think it's all a fake." He tore the envelope open and shook the white powder into his palm. "Talcum, that's what it is. You see? Perfectly harmless talcum." His hand rose toward his mouth.

"Lord Säen, no!" Lilz shouted, standing. "Stop him!"

Säen pivoted away from Ridehard, who snatched at his arm. Breedwary pulled her back into her seat. Lilz saw powder spill down Säen's dark trousers. "Oh, please!" Her hands were pressed to her face. "Please, don't be enough to harm him."

Lord Säen glanced at her and gingerly touched his tongue to his palm. A moment later he pulled a handkerchief from his pocket and spat into it.

"Is there any further evidence?" Gudgeon asked.

Breedwary stood and bowed. "None, your lordship." He sat down.

"Do you wish to speak for yourself, milady?"

Lilz rose. "I wish merely to say that, having no quarrel of my own with Sir Jen Makeready, I tried my best to preserve his life. I regret only that I was not able to do so."

The Lord Chief Justice nodded. "Remove the defendant."

* * *

The argument beyond the black oak door ebbed and increased, sometimes all but inaudible, sometimes shouted so loudly Lilz could almost make out the words. Breedwary sat opposite her in the little waiting room, elbows on his knees, clasping his narrow chin in one hand and drumming the fingers of the other. "What do you think?" Lilz had asked, when they'd first entered.

He'd shrugged. "Counting up the factions in attendance, acquittal seems possible," he'd said. "But given the number of Hastens, our most likely hope is for guilt to be punished at the pleasure of the king."

Now, twenty minutes later, another shift in the tone of the discussion seemed to signal something: the lawyer sat up and looked at the door. A few seconds later, it opened.

"The defendant may return," said the page.

Breedwary again led the way. The guards again walked beside Lilz, but neither bothered to hold her arms. When everyone was in place, the page struck the gong and they all sat down.

"We are ready to tally, milady," the Lord Chief Justice announced. She nodded. A big wooden box carved with the royal crest had been set on the judge's table. On its top was a box just large enough to admit a hand, open to the side. Under that, Lilz knew, was a slot, where the voting peer could drop his token without the color's being observed. To the side of the table, another box with a similar arrangement stood ready to collect the two extra tokens.

Gudgeon cleared his throat. "First row." He glanced at Lilz and at the peer sitting at the end of the first row of seats, a man she didn't know. He went to the table and dropped a token into the box, two into the second box, and returned to his seat. His glance and pleasant smile on his way back gave her hope the first token had been white. The rest of the men in that row had followed him forward and were shuffling past the two boxes. Lilz clutched her father's signet and listened to the tokens drop, glancing up whenever she could gather the courage.

After a time Breedwary began to purr. *Don't, don't!* Lilz wanted to plead. To tempt fate now? She looked at Stone, who was watching the peers file past the boxes with a somber face. Slowly, deeply, she made herself breathe.

Strengthen grinned at her on his way back to his seat. She looked away.

Halfway through the balloting, Lord Ruppet Hasten came past Lilz with a glare of such hatred she jerked backward. She followed him with her eyes: he turned as he started down the aisle toward his seat and gave her another baleful glance. That was a red token, she thought, and then, his mother must have spoken with him.

By the end of the hour-long balloting, she was able only to clasp one frozen hand with the other and stare straight ahead.

When the last peer had voted, the page carried the box of left-over tokens out of the hall. "One hundred sixty-three," Gudgeon told the prosecutor. He turned and repeated the number to Breedwary, who made a rapid invisible calculation with a finger on the tabletop.

"Forty-one would do it," he said to her. "It would be nicer to have forty-two."

Lilz, who had done the calculation in her head, nodded.

"If the dychs will come forward?"

Counting the Far-kin to the north, Kinland was divided into five dychdoms. Summerlea, Lealands, and two others came to the judge's table.

"Is his Grace the Dych of Mountainside present?" Gudgeon called.

"I don't think he's here," said a voice from the back, after a long moment.

"Can four certify the tally?" Lilz whispered to Breedwary.

"Oh, yes. Two would do."

She inhaled unevenly and turned her face forward. Gudgeon opened the box while the four dychs looked on. "I think it's obvious," he remarked, stirring the contents. "We'll have to count for the record." Summerlea looked at her with a tight smile. She couldn't tell if it was one of victory or concession.

Concession. Lilz began to feel faint as Gudgeon dug into the box and poured doubled handsful of tokens onto the table top. The white mountain was dotted here and there with black. Beside her, Breedwary began his odd purr. Someone reached out and slapped at a rolling white token to stop it from falling to the floor. Stone's face was in his hands. He looked up with such glad relief Lilz blinked away tears. Gudgeon was stacking the tokens by color in groups of ten; Summerlea leaning his hip on the table, arms folded; Lealands looking on with a grin, his thumbs hooked in the waistband of his trousers.

"One red, thirty-seven black, one hundred twenty-five white. Does that check?"

"Yes, your lordship," the secretary said.

"Free the lady."

A general babble broke out as the spectators in the gallery, some deeply disappointed, began climbing to the third-floor exits and the peers on the floor below collected their belongings. "A good case, milady," Breedwary said, thumping her back as if she were choking. "An excellent case."

"More important, well managed," Lilz told him. One of the guards asked her to turn her chair so he could remove her shackles. As he stood from that task, Breedwary slipped him a gratuity.

"Milord," the man murmured. He tucked the coins into his pocket before applying his key to the arm irons. Freed, Lilz resisted the urge to rub her wrists. Hands were coming at her to be grasped. Someone she had never seen before in her life was talking insistently into her ear about the wonderful man his close friend her father had been. An elderly iarl offered her a home. She saw Stone with his hand raised in a sign of victory. Meadowlands and his cousin stood near the door she would have to go through, Ruppet's dark head bent to Säen's Hasten blond. Slowly, Lilz was swept toward them as Breedwary accepted congratulations. Finally she and the lawyer went through the door, which shut. Someone behind her took a deep breath.

Breedwary turned. "Your Grace," he acknowledged.

Lilz, also turning, expected to see Lealands. Instead, Summerlea stood against the closed door. He wet his lips. "Thank you, Lilz," he said.

"For—?"

"For not testifying against Fenne. She would surely be dead if you had." A fist pounded at the door. Hasten glanced over his shoulder. He nodded slightly and drew himself up. "My father had many secrets, even from me," he said. "I am only now beginning to learn what I hope will be the worst of them. Please do remember." He opened the door and slipped through. Lilz heard Ruppet, very anxious, begin to speak as the door closed. What he'd said, she couldn't reconstruct.

"Meaningless," Breedwary commented. "Always a view to any possible future, Hastens. Come along. The queen commands your presence. There's a carriage waiting. We'll send a porter up for your things later."

Chapter Twenty-Seven

The carriage was the crimson, cream, and gold of the royal family, the attendants outfitted in the gold-trimmed New Palace uniform of crimson serge and cream velvet and haughty stares. His look of disdain hardened at the sight of Lilz's black dress, the footman barely brought himself to open the carriage door, let alone hand her in, despite Breedwary's assurance that this was indeed the woman the carriage had been ordered to convey to the New Palace.

The door slammed. This carriage did not lurch into motion. It glided through the narrow streets at what Lilz thought from the sound of the horses must be a good pace; the windows had been covered so that she could not see. Or be seen. Hugging herself, she sat half giddy with release and half pricked with apprehension, counting the turns to tell where she was. She wished Greencrags had come with her, or Strengthen, or even Breedwary, but she had not seen her two benefactors except at the trial and Breedwary had declined to come where he had not been invited, that was, into the queen's carriage.

A maid was waiting at the same palace entrance Greencrags had brought her to two nights before. The woman tried, but she couldn't quite conceal her surprise and distaste when Lilz descended from the carriage in her black dress, with no offer of an arm from the footman.

"Lady Lilz Chantwell?" the maid asked, as if she couldn't believe this was the person she had been sent to meet.

"I am she."

"Come with me, please." The maid nodded to a guard to open the door. She led Lilz past the closed door into the queen's dressing room and around a corner, down a long corridor fairly brightly lit with lamps in niches every three sashlengths or so, and finally into a large room flooded with sunlight. The queen, nearly as casually dressed as she had been two nights before, sat at a table near one of the windows. Three other women were with her. Lilz recognized all of them from various occasions at Hasten or Standfast House, or at Waterside.

"Your royal highness, Lady Lilz Chantwell." the maid said, although she should properly have given Lilz's name to the man at the door to be announced.

"Ah, Lady Lilz!" Queen Prenta jumped to her feet. "You bring the news of your acquittal in your person. Do you know my ladies-in-waiting?"

The ladies-in-waiting looked somewhat stunned as Prenta turned and introduced them. Lady Merrybrook, a woman Lilz had always thought ill-matched to her stuffy husband, was first to recover and say a good word to her. The others followed, the elderly Lady Blackwater remarking on her resemblance to her father and her sorrow at his banishment, "Thirty years ago if a day, my dear. I did so miss the society of your dear mother."

The skill with which Queen Prenta disentangled Lilz from the ladies-in-waiting was impressive. Each of the women must surely have believed that she had thought herself of the errand the queen had oh-so-obliquely suggested; within fifteen minutes all three of them, even Lady Blackwater, had left. "Come, Lilz Chantwell. We shall withdraw, for surely one or all of them will remember some omission requiring her to return," the queen said. She led Lilz into a small withdrawing room, also flooded with sunlight. The rich colors of Travaltia surrounded her; a faint perfume reminiscent of warmth and languor filled the air; the walls had been painted with lush garlands of fruits and flowers in no Kennish fashion.

"Sit here," the queen said. "And not on the edge of your seat as you did the night before last. We speak as equal women today."

"I thank you, ma'am."

The queen lowered herself gracefully into a chair beside a cold fireplace screened by a fan of peacock feathers. Lilz more awkwardly took the one across from her.

"I am not surprised by your acquittal," the queen said. "But I do confess curiosity. What was the final vote?"

"One red token, thirty-seven black, one hundred twenty-five white, ma'am."

"Ah." Prenta smiled. "Then I have not nattered myself at the extent of my influence. Kav Treadwell's outburst last Thornday has proven most useful; two-thirds of the Hasten faction was weaned from their bidden vote." She made an odd little motion. "A twitch of the finger, such as frees the lace from its pattern."

Lilz felt her jaw sag. "Contain your surprise, Lilz." The queen examined her for a moment with a smile. "You are clever and curious, or you would not be here," she said, the smile fading. "I am sure you would one day discover what I am about to tell you with no help from me. What you would then do, I do not know, but some of the possibilities frighten me, as queen of this country and mother of her next king." Prenta gazed at her soberly for several seconds. "I hope to speak is not a blunder. I do not think so. What you must bear always in mind is that I am a foreigner by birth and by upbringing."

Lilz nodded once.

"Therefore I must be most careful of my public life. Kinland is a nation in most delicate balance with its neighbors, a balance achieved at great cost in lives and in misery over the past century and more. I remember your mother well. I assume she taught you history?"

"Yes, ma'am. It's one of my pleasures in reading, as well."

"Then you will understand. May I have your word not to speak of any of what I tell you until you have thought it over well? Shall we say, for one year?"

"If making such a promise will not compromise my honor, yes, I give my word."

The queen laughed. "No one hearing that could doubt whose child you are! But you will see the importance. I must begin with some explanation, for which I ask your forbearance. From the moment I came to Miense thirty-five years ago I was locked in intrigue with Nevan Hasten, each of us circling the other like two cats with teeth bared and ears folded back, spitting and hissing and watching for an opening to pounce." Lilz must have shown her surprise at the image; the queen again smiled briefly. "Twenty-four years ago I thought I saw my opening. I pounced. Ah, you say to yourself, but Summerlea continued in all his power! Yes. My pounce cost me dearly...." The queen stopped and closed her eyes. Lilz waited. "Dearly. Still, I believe it was the right thing to do. For Kinland." The queen paused. "Is young Greencrags your lover?"

"My lover! No, ma'am."

"I asked only because of your gray eyes. But you do advise the young iarl on occasion?"

"From time to time, yes," Lilz agreed, startled.

Prenta nodded. "You have much of your father in you," she said. "But also your mother's patience. At least, so I infer from what I have heard." She chuckled. "The affair of the Keeper of the Keys was pure Darkforest. I laughed most heartily. It was your idea, of course?"

"Yes, ma'am."

"I commend you. I regret only that I did not see Nevan Hasten's face when he was told Greencrags would be made a member of the Privy Council." The queen was certainly taking her time to get to the point. Lilz wondered whether she'd had second thoughts about this conversation.

"What is your sense of your brother Clâes?" Prenta asked suddenly. "Will he make a good iarl?"

So the others are dead. Lilz caught her lower lip under her teeth.

"Oh, I am sorry. I see you did not know Clâes is the last one living." The queen leaned forward and touched her hand. "The New Lands are unsparing, Lilz Chantwell," she said, sitting back. "I believe it was Aust who died of winter cold and the ship bearing Dilyn and Milas which foundered before reaching shore."

"I see."

The queen waited a minute or more before speaking again. "And Lord Clâes? As Iarl of Darkforest?"

"He's bright and sensible." Lilz was puzzled. Would Clâes be granted their father's honors and title? Why now, after all these years? "He wasn't raised to be iarl, but of course he was tutored as a Peer would be. In time, he might fit into the role." She thought of Clâes cheerfully claiming the sunshine as his own in the stableyard at Summerlea. "He would find it difficult, I think."

"How would he perform other roles? Were he, say, Secretary to the Privy Council, or Royal Steward, or Lord Treasurer, or Prime Lord of the Peers Assembled, or King's Marshall? Or all of these, starting tomorrow?"

"Clâes?" Lilz stared. "Tomorrow? To be blunt, your royal highness, the nation might never recover. These positions require accurate knowledge and long training. They are best inherited."

"You are certain of that? Your brother could not step immediately into all of these roles and perform them as well as does Olen Hasten, who for all his efforts is not at all what his father was?"

"Never. My brother is an excellent cabinetmaker."

The queen nodded. "Now you will understand my need for secrecy. That gown you wore two nights past was made for me by Onma Stump."

Lilz blinked. Prenta chuckled. "Come, Lilz Chantwell, you must know my gowns do not appear from thin air! I am measured and the cloth cut to me as for anyone else. A queen frequently requires the services of the court costumer. Even a queen does not stand like carved marble to have the tape put around her waist, nor does she suffer the fittings of the muslin in utter silence. Not if she wishes to know what goes on at her court." She leaned forward.

"Onma Stump quickly understood that she would be well paid for information. A more profitable business than her gowns, exquisite as they are. She need pay no one to stitch one fact to another, as she must pay to have pearls stitched to silk, not so? She understands also the necessity for discretion. Twenty-four years ago—a little longer, yes—she came to me in great distress. She had been pressed to give aid in concealing a murder."

No, Lilz thought. No.

"She is but five years older than me, Lilz Chantwell. Twenty-four years ago her position at Court was new, her business still insecure. A good customer, an important man who could hold the means to her future, imposed upon her to lend him a trunk, which he returned very heavy, asking her to accompany it to the estate his family has occupied for many generations. It is a distance of two days. In the inn that night, Stump could not contain her curiosity. She had an extra key. She opened the trunk."

Pure Darkforest. *Banish me, will you, Summerlea? My son will inherit your titles and influence.* Lilz put her face into her hands.

"I see you have guessed what she found. Your father's body. He had been shot."

So that was the favor Onma Stump did that got her enmeshed with the Hastens. Lilz wanted to jump up and run.

"I am sorry." When Lilz looked up, she saw the queen wiping away a tear. "I have paid as much. I now believe, having seen the evidence of Evin Clock, that it was Nevan Hasten who poisoned my son Jath, through the offices of the servant later found drowned. Why, I do not know."

That, Lilz could tell her. "Prince Jath was Fenne Hasten's lover," she said. "She wished to end the affair. He did not."

"Thank you." The queen took a deep breath. "Yes. I thought perhaps Summerlea had found that spectacle at open Court too embarrassing to tolerate. He was a man of boundless vanity, which he confused with pride." Let her believe, Lilz thought, remembering the crusted wounds Jath's teeth had left in Fenne's skin, the silvery scars when they healed. She only nodded. "I wonder how young Greencrags escaped?" Prenta mused. "He was taken sick, I remember, at a time Clock's records show Hasten House to have had a severe infestation of rats."

So it *had* been the old man. Duplicity beyond duplicity. "I was sent to see how sick the boy was," Lilz told her. "While I was there, his body-man came to him with soup said to have been prepared by his wife. I knew Fenne could not cook. I advised the body-man not to feed his master anything that came as a gift, and the boy recovered."

"How fortunate." The queen sighed. "Ironic, as well, since it was I who deprived myself of the possibility that you, with your quick mind, might be in my household at the time my son was taken ill—as, perhaps, a lady-in-waiting as your mother had been. That is what I am trying to explain to you."

Lilz waited.

Prenta again drew a long breath. "Onma Stump continued her journey as requested by Nevan Hasten. On arriving at Summerlea, she found the dych and his youngest son before her."

Säen's father, Lilz thought. Who died of jaundice.

"She was given a night's lodging," the queen continued. "On looking from her window she saw what was to be done. A hole had been dug beside a wall behind the house. The next day her trunk was returned to her. The inside was damp with scrubbing, but brown stains remained. The hole had been filled overnight and the gardener was planting, I believe, clove pinks in the earth."

Lilz put her hand to her mouth. Clove pinks. Only against the wall of the kitchen garden. How often she had enjoyed their scent, suspecting nothing!

"You know the place?" Lilz nodded. "I am sorry. I hope it had no great sentiment for you." Prenta smiled sadly. "Perhaps I should not have mentioned the pinks." She sighed. "I am so concerned to be accurate…. When Mistress Stump came to me I saw that I could break the power the Hasten family holds over the throne. I gathered my evidence. Summerlea had been careless. The crime had been observed—by a whizzer." The queen smiled. "Or so I told him. In fact, the whizzers report only to those we discussed two nights past, the Other-kin. They recover few of them, in comparison to the number sent out. Useless for spying. "

"But I have my human spies as Nevan Hasten had his. I knew of the murder, but my spy was young and did not know your father's face. When I learned it was he, I called Summerlea to me and told him I had proof he had murdered the Iarl of Darkforest. I pointed out that the iarl was a iarl even in banishment. I reminded him of the inheritance laws of Kinland. I suggested that should he desire to remain free of investigation, he could insure his continued prestige by seeing that one of the Chantwell children led the black horse in his funeral procession. I had no idea I would wait so long to see my plan fulfilled. I...I was young, and so much less experienced than I believed." The queen opened her hands toward Lilz, as if asking forgiveness. "After some bluster, the dych agreed. As insurance for that occasion, I caused him to sign a confession and agreement."

"I was available," Lilz said. "That's why me." She was talking to herself, not Prenta. "He couldn't ask Clâes, but there I was, right in his household."

"Believing yourself bond-servant to his family. You see how carefully he provided."

Lilz felt sick to her stomach. "In his records he refers to me as a hostage for my father's word. But you say my father had been dead four years."

Queen Prenta narrowed her eyes. "A nasty man, with a nasty sense of humor, Summerlea. I am sure he snickered as he wrote the words. Words designed to protect him, should I die without revealing what I knew, as I am sure you see."

"Yes." Lilz could imagine the flourish of Nevan Hasten's pen. "But I've interrupted your story, ma'am."

"Summerlea." The queen sighed deeply. "You see the choice I offered him. Immediate exposure, with your brother Dilyn to inherit all the positions and titles the Hastens had held for so many generations, or a formal break in the chain, with the chance that his son Olen could repair his own position. I frankly intended that he take the second. Your oldest brother was a man of twenty-two, yes, but not educated to govern. Peace with Galtriva was uneasy, without treaty. Despicable as he was, Kin-land needed Nevan Hasten. "

"Although my father-in-law was still alive, as I expected Hasten began to cultivate Guyr assiduously. On the one hand, that presented problems: Guyr is easily led. I would have preferred to do all the leading. On the other hand, Summerlea could be depended upon to yield when pressed. I looked to the future. Jath was two months old. I determined to raise him in enmity to the Hastens, but then came little Fenne. I had not planned on little Fenne."

"No one ever has," Lilz said bitterly.

The queen sighed. "True. So Oerl has taken Jath's place," she continued. "In some ways, that is best. Oerl is more humane, more diligent and more intelligent than was Jath. He will be a better king." The queen stopped speaking. After a moment, she sighed. "That is a difficult conclusion for a mother, but it is so.

"My plan, of course, did not end with the funeral of Nevan Hasten. But the man I had marked to replace his son most unfortunately died only a few months before he would have been named. So I kept silence, and the present dych was installed at Guyr's pleasure. I suspect that is also for the best. The people should be prepared for the transfer of the dychdom, not possible while old Hasten lived. But the chain *is* broken. People will long remember your cold march, Lady Lilz.

"Therefore I have looked about for an able substitute for Ruppet Hasten when the time comes. I think Greencrags is the man. You see what I ask of you. To take revenge on the Hastens in silence, difficult as that may be. Help me groom Rovvo Standfast to become Dych of Summerlea, in exchange for which your brother will be restored to his natural inheritance. For that, Lord Clâes need only petition the Lord Chief Justice. Certain difficulties have already been eliminated."

Jath was two months old. That meant Ruppet had been about eight months old. Had her father met the dych and taunted him? Was that what got him killed? Or had Summerlea learned that he'd fathered Ruppet—some unguarded remark of Delle's?—and hunted him out to silence him? Had the uncreased letter been written at the end of a pistol? ... Or perhaps not even written by her father, perhaps written by Nevan Hasten....

Her mother was a Thrivemore, an only daughter, last of that line, raised to put her country first. What would she have thought of replacing the wily, seasoned Dych of Summerlea with an untried youth, even her own son?

Exactly what Lilz had thought, not ten minutes before. In exchange for her silence and cooperation in the ruse, perhaps help for her children: passage to the New Lands for the three oldest, apprenticeship for Clâes, a life-long haven for her no-longer-marriageable daughter after her death? And the knowledge that her silence was best for a country not yet sure it was not at war.... Perhaps with the hope that in a few years Milas, by then more versed in the needs of the Court, might make his claim?

I know what honor is, the old dych had told her. And that she would thank him one day. Lilz shivered.

"My father's bones are at Summerlea Manor," she said.

"I believe that can be remedied at no cost to the plan."

Lilz tilted her head at the woman across from her. She had almost forgotten this was the queen. "My brother has sons."

"But their mother is a Godwit, a commoner. They are not fully of the Blood, or I would have taken careful interest years ago. The iarldom dies with Clâes, barring a second marriage with issue. You see that."

No, Lilz thought. *There's Ruppet.* Ruppet, who, learning that he was her half-brother, had just voted for her immediate execution. If Clâes should die before Ruppet...*Ruppet can prove nothing.*

What would Father want? *Father put a cuckoo in Summerlea's nest to take his revenge.* But Father's dead. He never knew Ruppet. Ruppet was only a kind of joke. Or perhaps her father hadn't even known Ruppet was his son, perhaps he'd simply enjoyed Lady Delle's favors with the extra spice of knowing she was newly-married to a Hasten.... Banished, he might not have known there was a son until Nevan Hasten pulled the trigger. Or even then.

"Why was my father killed?" she asked.

"I have no idea. Perhaps he had threatened anew to speak about the *antrata.*"

"Did your spy say whether Nevan Hasten acted in anger?"

"Anger! Hasten? So controlled a man? No, he caught your father unaware when he visited the privy at an alehouse. He didn't even say a word of warning."

No word of warning. He was only eliminating a danger, quick and clean, as he'd slaughtered the injured horse...to spare his oldest son? Who had married a famed beauty, the prize of the kingdom, not two years before? But surely he wouldn't have agreed to his son's marrying a woman with a reputation like Delle Makeright's! Unless that came later.... Why hadn't Ruppet succumbed to some infant's disease? Because of redheaded Cals, so soon after? Lilz closed her eyes. Round and round about. This led nowhere.

What would Clâes want? *To be free as a bird.* He might not even want to claim his title.

In fact, Lilz told herself sternly, the question was far simpler, as her mother would have seen instantly, as she herself would have seen sooner on a calmer day: which was the better man, Ruppet Hasten or Rovvo Standfast?

Scarcely a question at all. "I will help you," she said.

"Ah." The queen sat back with a broad smile. "Among the four of us, then—you and I and Standfast and my son—we can formulate a plan to deal with the Other-kin. The openness with which they were once treated in Travaltia might serve as a model." She smiled again. "My people are no longer troubled with them, as I told them you the other night."

Yes, Lilz thought. That might help. If everyone knew, for instance, that the Jewel of the King is just a machine to magnify his voice, it would no longer appear that he must be chosen by the Fathergod... yes. But they would have to go slowly. She hoped she would live long enough.

* * *

The carriage waiting for Lilz after her talk with the queen belonged to Standfast House. Its bright green and ivory paint was waxed and buffed, the gilt trim gleaming. Greencrags's finest horses, a white pair with rosebuds braided into their manes and their tails plaited into something resembling hearth whisks, stood patiently in polished black harness. All very impressive. Surely intended for a triumphal ride home from her trial: she was sorry Greencrags had been denied that.

Best, as Lilz discovered when the footman lowered the steps, Greencrags had sent Stone to escort her.

Stone, too, pulled the carriage shades, but they had time only for one long embrace and a few extra kisses before halting at the front door of Standfast House. Reed met them halfway down the steps, his professional gloom shattered by a grin. He tried to control his mouth, failed, and ended by hugging Lilz and pounding Stone on the back as they entered the house.

Greencrags had arrived ahead of her, with Lealands and Breedwary. A huge cold meal had been set out on the dining room buffet. Reed rushed to carve the roast mutton while Lealands and Greencrags pelted Lilz with questions and congratulations. Breedwary stood to the side smiling, his haggish teeth forgotten.

"Oh, I'm famished! May I?" Lilz gestured at the buffet. "Last night I could barely eat an apple and I had no appetite at all this morning."

"We can't let you starve, not after all that!" Greencrags stepped forward to serve her himself. "Did you see Summerlea! I thought the man would faint."

He handed her a plate that might have satisfied any two of her brother's sons on a hungry morning. "You were wonderful, Lilz! I don't see how anyone could bring himself to vote against that evidence, let alone cast that red token."

Lilz stuffed half a hard-boiled egg into her mouth.

"I wonder whose it was? Probably Säen Hasten," Lealands remarked.

"No, that was Lord Ruppet," Lilz said thickly, chewing.

"Meadowlands!" Strengthen frowned. "I thought he looked angry."

Cold chicken. Delicious. "Never mind. It'll blow over."

Lilz put her plate on the table and slid onto a chair. She accepted a glass of chilled white wine from Reed. Stone sat down on one side of her, Greencrags on the other, while across from her Breedwary solemnly dug into a generous mound of a delectable-looking aspic salad. Had—? Yes, Rovvo had helped her to that, too. Every bit as savory as it looked.

A few toasts followed, rowdy with joy.

"What did the queen want of you?" Lealands asked, at last.

"It's almost amusing." Reed was pouring thirds of wine; Lilz stopped to sip. "Someone told her I'd managed Fenne Hasten's money. She wants me to persuade Lord Greencrags to accept my financial advice, to free his time to serve the Crown. In other words, just what he's been trying to persuade me to do for the past year."

"Mmm." Strengthen's eyebrows, what there was of them, climbed. "Once in a while I wonder about Prenta. Just as you think she has no more interest in Kennish affairs than a carthorse, she'll very quietly do something so shrewd it takes your breath away."

"Yes." Lilz glanced at Greencrags. "I remember thinking once that were she a man, Queen Prenta might almost be a match for Nevan Hasten."

"What do you think now that you've talked to her twice?" Merrow Strengthen pointed at something on the buffet for Reed to serve. Out in the hall, excited voices announced the first congratulatory visitors; Greencrags jumped up to go welcome them.

"I think we have all significantly underestimated our queen," Lilz murmured. So far as she could tell, only Stone heard her.

Chapter Twenty-Eight

Autumn settled in, with its cold rains. Lilz sat at her desk one Satingday afternoon with her chin on her hand, looking out at the heavy
slanting drops that spattered against her window. A fire crackled in
the hearth of her sitting room at Standfast House. The black wool
dress had long since been given to charity: she wore new silk-lined
wool trousers of the dark green emblematic of the Chantwell family,
a white linen shirt tucked down the front and finishing in a ruffled
collar and cuffs, and over the shirt a knit wool sweater of Chantwell
green that allowed the ruffles to show. She felt both elegant and comfortable as she watched the rain, and she reveled in the feeling.

Lilz stretched and brought her attention back to the papers spread
on her desk. She'd carried some of Greencrags's records into the dower
suite, which she now occupied, but on this chilly afternoon they
needed little immediate attention. Lilz was simply planning, as she
had once for Fenne, and did now for Rovvo Standfast. A half-share
in a merchant vessel under construction looked appealing. A reliable
shipwright and an experienced captain boded well; the percentage of
each cargo's profit that would go to Greencrags could provide a good
income for years, with luck.

She opened a drawer for a pen. Pushed to the back of the drawer
was a single folded sheet of heavy, cream-colored paper, a letter from
the Iarl of Oakforest that had arrived for her ten days before. She
knew it almost by heart.

Oakforest had started by congratulating her on the outcome of her
trial, which she thought a bit tactless at first. Reading on, she had
realized that he simply had not known how to begin: *I have struggled
with my conscience for so long...*poor man. *You, having once been
a servant, must know what it is to stand powerless before another.*
That she did. And so did Oakforest with respect to Nevan Hasten, it
appeared. *Do you recall that his granddaughter took refuge at House-
Among-Oaks, when question of her virginity arose and a substitute for
the examination was being sought?* he'd asked. *You broke the news that
Sir Jen had died. How shaken I was, you cannot imagine: two weeks
before, I had stopped at Hasten House for some things Fenne wished
to have...* Yes. Lilz remembered the list the houseman had handed her.
She'd bundled everything up, and while he waited Oakforest had gone
in to see Summerlea. *I'd bought a large veal pie to give Makeready, as
I told the dych. He laughed, saying he doubted the man would eat any
gift from a member of the Hasten faction. On my way back to House-
Among-Oaks I handed in the pie at the Old Palace gate, but thinking*

*of Summerlea's comment and wishing Sir Jen to have the pleasure of
the pie did not give my name.*

Oakforest never had cared whether anyone credited his generosity,
Lilz thought now. *Poor man.* He hadn't thought twice about the pie
until Makeready died, and then thought Summerlea had somehow
poisoned his gift. Elm's talk had only served to confirm the idea. Lilz
dipped her pen, beginning to list questions about the ship proposal.
Moonday morning, Greencrags would meet with the builder; depending
on the final construction estimate she might advise finding another
investor to spread the risk.

A tap on her door disrupted her thoughts.

"Yes?" she called.

Reed put his head in. "Lord Säen Hasten to see you, Lilz. I've
seated him in the small reception room. Shall I murder him right
away, or will you see him first?"

"Thanks, Reed. We'll let him live a few minutes longer. I'll be right
down."

She blotted the pen she had been using so the ink wouldn't dry
and clog the nib before she came back, marked her place among
the papers by turning the ones she'd attended to sideways, slipped
her feet back into her black leather house shoes, and got up. Before
going down to find out what Lord Säen could possibly want of her
she made sure her shirt was tucked in smoothly and patted her hair
to see that it was still in place. Her mind turned again to Oakforest's
letter. How frightened he must have been! And how relieved to find it
was only Elm's dog who had died "of my ignorant hand." Or old age.
Or gluttony.

In his last sentence the iarl had begged, *I pray of you, burn this.*
Lilz hadn't decided yet whether she would. Probably yes, she thought,
going down the front stairs to the small reception room.

Säen huddled close to the fire. He turned as she came into the
room and started to rise, only to sink back into the chair as she
motioned him down. To her surprise, he was formally dressed. Above
the white lace of his shirt his face was gaunt and tinged with yellow,
his blond hair lifeless.

"You're looking very well, Lilz," he said.

"Thank you, Säen. I wish I could say the same for you. We heard
you were ill. I take it you're better?"

"Much." Säen made stilted conversation for a few minutes— the
foul weather, the good harvest, a few inconsequential rumors, to which
Lilz responded politely. At last he stopped and tilted his head at her.
"You never have liked me, have you, Lilz?"

"Not especially."

"I don't know why."

Pleased with the freedom to be blunt, Lilz said, "You were an
appalling child, Säen. I got quite tired of your tricks—like having a cat

bring daily offerings of mice with their heads chewed off and entrails dragging, only without the cat's benign intentions." Säen shrugged and looked at the floor. "Also, as you surely must realize, the world has seldom seen so thoroughly obnoxious an adolescent as you were. So, while your manners have improved immeasurably, you can scarcely fault me if I suspect that your heart is much the same as ever."

"I guess I deserve that, though I'd argue it," Lord Säen acknowledged. Säen "But if that's how you feel, why did you save my life?"

"I've often wished you distant, Säen. Never dead."

"I honestly believed that powder was talcum." Lord Säen stretched out his still-jaundiced hands and looked at them. "Uncle Olen had me convinced you'd counterfeited that evidence. If you hadn't yelled, I'd have eaten the whole envelope's worth." He met her eyes. The whites of his own were still dull. "Considering how sick I was with the little I tasted, no power on earth could have kept me alive."

"True."

"I came to thank you, Lilz."

"What I would do for any human being." Lilz, her arms folded, studied Lord Säen, who now clasped his hands between his knees and looked into the fire.

"Makeready was lucky you were where you were," he said.

"Was he? He died a long, harsh death. He might have been glad of Fenne's poison."

"No, Lilz. I've just been as sick as he ever was. I never wanted to die, though when I was lucid I feared I might." Lord Säen looked again at his hands. "I've heard the king's physician thought Sir Jen had been crabbed of the gut. No one cut him afterward to find the growths, however, so I suppose we can't say for certain."

Lilz nodded slowly. Cancer was certainly possible: the man had wasted so badly and been in such pain. But so young! More likely, the intrigue he had lived by had claimed him as its victim. But why so slowly, and by whose agency? Even the king was not an unlikely suspect. Too late now ever to know for sure.

She stood up and held out her hand to be touched in farewell. After a moment, Lord Säen also stood. He took her hand in both of his.

"Lilz ... if there's ever anything you want that I can give you, you have only to ask and it will be yours on the instant. I promise."

"Thank you, Säen. I'll remember that."

"You don't believe me, do you?"

"No."

"I've promised," Säen said earnestly. "On my honor. Try me, whenever you want. You'll see." Lilz smiled, a wintry little smile that made Säen drop her hand, and rang for Reed. She said a polite farewell to Fenne's cousin—who had not mentioned her once—as Reed helped him into his cloak. She was already on her way up the stairs when Reed closed the door.

Back at her desk, Lilz found her earlier pleasant mood broken. *I must warn you of Lord Ruppet,* Oakforest had written. *And, truth be told, as I am so timorous you must also be wary of me.*

What *did* Säen want? He might honestly be grateful...but he was Lord Ruppet's friend as well as cousin, and Ruppet...Lilz looked out at the darkening sky. She'd met Ruppet by chance only a few days ago, and been glared at with every bit as much enmity as on the day he'd voted for her immediate execution. Not an encounter to fill her with unquestioning trust of Säen!

She sighed and returned her gaze to the papers spread over her desk. So many problems to see to: easing into the society of Thornday open Court in order to hear all the gossip, finding an appropriate wife for the Iarl of Greencrags, managing the day-to-day details of a iarl's household, seeing that his investments prospered. Consulting with the queen on Rovvo's political education. Exactly what to do about the *antranta.*

Queen Prenta was right: Kinland would never be rid of the people who had caused a palace to be built for their convenience if their presence were kept secret. Even were the *antranta* closed, the Other-kin would be here, like the man who had gone to the New Lands and lived in that native village, confident of his welcome although the savages surely must have resented his eating their hard-won food with no return but his relentless curiosity.

Rumors of Other-kin presence were already gaining life, thanks, Lilz suspected, to Kav Treadwell. Perhaps they would be forced into the open before she and Prenta and Greencrags could prepare the way.

What then? A resurgence of the old religion? More wars, fate forbid? The headiness of knowing that a toad or a rabbit or a bird was exactly that, and nothing more, that the legend that they were spies had grown out of ignorance—what would that release? Would the students from the place beside find their whizzers dunked and ruined at so great a rate they must be abandoned? Then what?

Lilz thought of the false housemaid, and of Nevan Hasten, who in his last illness had remarked to Fenne that while he did not fear death itself, he resented not being able to see how events continued. How the story ended, he'd said. But the story never does end, Lilz thought. Only the single minds that have watched a small piece unfold come at last to death. *Something for Rovvo to put in a poem.*

Dusk had invaded her room, lightened only by the flicker from the fireplace. Lilz took a spill from the vase on the mantle to touch fire to a lamp. At any moment Greencrags would be home from an entertainment staged for Prince Oerl and his friends, Stone with him. Stone would come to her as he always did, to share a few minutes' conversation before his master needed him. Lilz smiled, imagining Stone's kiss of greeting, Stone's report of the servants' tales of their masters, as she placed the lamp on the desk. How she missed that easy chatter!

She sat down to look again at the ship proposal, but found her thoughts circling back to the *antranta*. Somewhere in the palace Stone and Greencrags had just left, a blue carpet covered a granite floor. Beyond a door that stung any unwary hand, the strangers talked in their other-worldy speech. They are men like ourselves, Lilz thought, as she had of the natives of the New Lands. They'll want to see how the story goes on. Whizzers or no whizzers, they will watch us somehow. A thought she'd had often: but this time it about-faced. *We are men like them.* One day we may travel as they travel, go, if not to their world, to some other. We will be the strangers; Kinland, the Place Beside.

Lilz shuddered. Let's hope we aren't so much more warlike than they seem to be because the shape of the stain in our layer of mica is different, she thought. Let's hope we've developed their good will by then. Otherwise—

Vague visions of unimaginable conflicts shook her, people hounded to their deaths out of mere suspicion, greedy monarchs finding subtler means of exploitation than any dreamed of yet.

But that would take years, lifetimes. She, at least, would not be here to see.

I will live my life as best I can, she decided. I'll do my best to point us toward peace. It's all I can do.

Stone drummed his fingers on the open door and came in, hands outstretched. Smiling, Lilz laid her pen aside and went to greet him.

"You'll never guess who came to call," she said.

The End

www.ingramcontent.com/pod-product-compliance
Lightning Source LLC
Chambersburg PA
CBHW070834280626
47161CB00015B/591